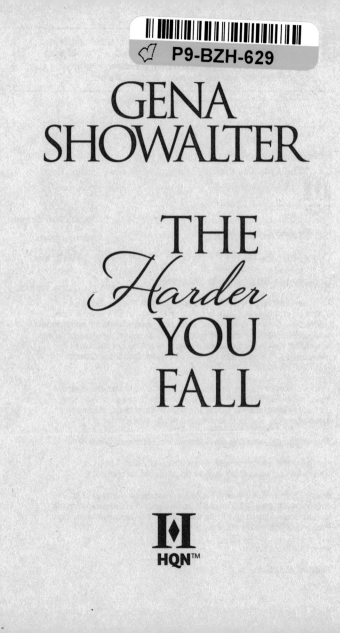

P9-BZH-629

GENA SHOWALTER

THE *Harder* YOU FALL

HQN™

ISBN-13: 978-0-373-78892-7

The Harder You Fall

Recycling programs
for this product may
not exist in your area.

This edition published by arrangement with Harlequin Books S.A.

For questions and comments about the quality of this book,
please contact us at CustomerService@Harlequin.com.

® and TM are trademarks of Harlequin Enterprises Limited or its
corporate affiliates. Trademarks indicated with ® are registered in the
United States Patent and Trademark Office, the Canadian Intellectual
Property Office and in other countries.

www.HQNBooks.com

Printed in U.S.A.

To Allison Carroll for your invaluable feedback. And for taking me on despite my warnings about "the process."

To Craig Swinwood, Margaret Marbury, Loriana Sacilotto, Dianne Moggy, Susan Swinwood, Michelle Renaud, Stacy Widdrington and Fritz Servatius—and so many others at Harlequin—for all you do on my behalf.

And to Lisa Wray for going above and beyond as we prepare for the launch of each new book.

And to one of the most awesome ladies I know, Liz Berry. I owe you a bear hug!

You guys rock so hard!

To Kresley Cole and Beth Kendrick, the Chef Boyardee gang!

CHAPTER ONE

~~Sister dearest,~~
~~My darling Brook Lynn,~~
Yo!

So, check it. I've totally invaded your old bedroom to watch snow fall in the backyard. (Insert a couple minutes—or an hour!—of whining because your window alcove is better than mine.) BUT. Despite such a heinous injustice, I'm smiling so wide my jaw hurts. I remember the first time we built a snowman. I *still* think he looked like a puffer fish. Anyway. You cried "He's dying" when the sun came out, and I collected snowman-blood (water) in a jar to host a proper bathroom funeral. We were pretty cool kids, huh? Now, though, we're (technically) adults. Boo! You're my best friend—yay! congrats!—but you're also Jase's fiancée. You're part of his family, beloved by his friends, and that means I have to share you. I'm afraid, so very afraid, of losing you.

But then, I deserve to lose you. For years you took care of me like a mother takes care of her child. You sacrificed for me. You loved me when I was unlovable and helped me when I scorned you. Saying thank you a thousand times wouldn't be enough. Saying I'm sorry a million times might be

a start. You, sister, are a treasure. A gift. And I'm
going to prove it. But not by giving you this letter.

No, this letter will self-destruct as soon as I'm
done writing it because I don't want to tell you
everything you mean to me—I want to show you.
And I will.

Yours forever,

Jessie Kay

On a frigid December morning, the greatest snowpoca-
lypse Strawberry Valley, Oklahoma, had ever experienced
claimed its first victim. Jessica Kay Dillon's pride. With a
moan, the former beauty queen picked up her now-aching
butt off the icy sidewalk, balanced her basket in her hands
and, as bitter gusts of wind nipped at her, scanned nearby
shop windows. No prying eyes watched her. Thank God!

If no one witnessed your epic fall, had it ever really
happened?

Jessie Kay inched forward—*careful, steady*—but
as she turned the corner her feet slipped and her arms
flailed to no avail. Down she tumbled, landing with a
hard smack. Dang it! She banged her fist into the ice-
glazed concrete. She was going to die out here, and it was
totally his fault. Lincoln West. One of the three owners
of WOH Industries.

Stupid West and his stupid sandwich order!

She wouldn't say she hated him, but she would maybe
probably definitely unplug his life support to charge her
phone. In only six months, he'd become the bane of her
existence.

She should have listened to her sister and canceled
today's deliveries. Brook Lynn, the owner of You've Got
It Coming—*Busy life? Let us feed you!*—believed safety

came before commerce. But nooo, oh, no, Jessie Kay had insisted she could do the job, even though jumping from an airplane without a parachute would have been smarter. And yeah, okay, there was a perk to venturing out: the awe-inspiring winter wonderland. The hodge-podge design of shops—plantation-style buildings, metal warehouses and whitewashed bungalows—looked as if they'd been painted with diamond dust. But honestly? Awe-inspiring sucked buckets of ass right now.

Teeth chattering, she lumbered to her feet and carried on like a good little frozen soldier. At this point, giving up and returning to her car would be a blemish on YGIC's sterling rep. *Great start, deplorable finish.* No, thanks. What it wouldn't do? Melt the ice in Jessie Kay's veins. The heater had been busted for years, the window scraper a necessary tool for survival. And it wasn't like going home would do any good, either. The heater there basically operated on fumes and prayers.

In a perfect world, she'd fix both today. But this was a crap world and she needed more than the usual TLC—tears, lamentations and cursing. She needed cold, hard cash. Another reason she'd opted to brave the storm.

Brook Lynn, the sweetheart, paid her a hundred dollars a week to help prepare orders and make deliveries. Money she felt guilty for taking. *I owe her, not the other way around.* But take it she did. She had to. Pride, the whore, never made even a token offer to pay for *anything.*

The funds were just enough to cover utilities and the mortgage she acquired soon after Mom died. Tips covered essentials, like three squares a day. And to be quite blunt about the matter, she'd expected people to fork over more than the usual buck or two for today's troubles. But had they? No! She'd gotten the usual, plus a few propositions from the sleazier men.

Wanna take a break, Jessie Kay? My wife's stuck at her sister's and my couch is real comfy...

Come on in and have a beer, Jessie Kay. I'll warm you up with a little body heat...

Once a bad girl, always a bad girl.

If her parents still lived—God bless their precious souls—they would have wept fat tears of disappointment over her jezebel rep. They'd loved her and had only wanted the best for her even though they'd both had legit reasons to hate her before they died.

She would be the first to admit she sometimes tried to forget those reasons in not-so-healthy ways.

Well, *used to* try to forget in not-so-healthy ways.

A few months ago, Brook Lynn—the world's greatest *everything*—had almost died, and Jessie Kay—the world's worst—had been too busy partying like a rock star to help. Talk about a wake-up call! From that day forward, she'd sworn to walk the straight and narrow. If ever her sister needed her again, she'd be there. No ifs, ands or buts about it. Amen.

Every storm begins with a single drop of rain, Momma once said. *Don't despise small beginnings.*

The good-girl thing, well, no one anywhere ever had *ever* had such a small beginning.

She slowly snaked around the next corner, relieved when she remained on her feet, and finally she reached the WOH offices. Despite the cold, she paused at the front window to prepare for the battle to come. And there would be a battle. There always was.

In the foyer, elementary-school-teacher-turned-receptionist Cora Higal manned her desk with military precision. There was no sign of West. Gorgeous, successful, too-smart-for-his-own-good West.

He possessed a charming wit and kind smile. For everyone but Jessie Kay.

In July, he and his two best buds slash business partners had left the big, bad city to move to her hometown. She'd drooled over the magnetic West at first sight, but when he'd shown no interest in her, she'd moved on to the suave Beck Ockley, who *had*.

What she hadn't known at the time? Beck was the king of the hit and run. Well, he used to be, until he met Harlow Glass. Now he was the king of commitment. Anyway. His majesty's "relationship" with Jessie Kay had ended after a single night.

That was fun, honey. I'll see you around.

The rejection had stung, and she'd thrown a good old-fashioned pity party, getting drunk off her booty and sleeping with Jase, the trio's designated hulk. But their "relationship" hadn't gone anywhere, either. In fact, Jase hadn't even waited until morning to get rid of her. He'd jumped ship an hour after the deed was done.

He later ended up engaged to Brook Lynn.

Apparently, all a guy had to do to find his soul mate was screw Jessie Kay.

West had to consider her sloppy thirds. A man-eater. A good-time girl. Fruit from the poisonous tree.

Well, he could suck it! Had she always made the smartest choices? No. She'd chased a sense of happiness with men rather than finding it within herself—and just how the heck was she supposed to be happy with herself? She'd also made mistakes so abysmal they belonged in record books. Just ask her dead parents! But what right did West have to judge her?

According to Brook Lynn, who had the inside scoop, West used to dabble with self-medication, too, drinking and getting high. And his track record with women? Deplorable. He only dated one gal a year for two months, no more, no less, then dumped her for some made-up reason when the clock zeroed out…and crap, it was too cold to stall any longer.

A bell tinkled as Jessie Kay entered the building, and much-needed warmth enveloped her.

Cora glanced up from the papers she was stacking, her black bob swaying at her shoulders. "Miss Dillon."

"Ms. Higal." She stomped her boots to dislodge clumps of snow as she studied an eclectic mix of boring and spectacular. The standard beige walls were decorated with stunningly detailed pictures of the video game characters West had designed. Tables she could have picked up at a local garage sale for less than five bucks were littered with shiny computer parts and what looked to be robotic limbs.

How cool was that? Her inner child, probably the most mature part of her, suddenly longed to play.

Cora said, "Mr. West is—"

"Not surprised you're late." The rugged male voice came from the back of the room, where West leaned a shoulder against the entrance to his office. "Tell me, Miss Dillon. Is making people worry a sport to you?"

Their eyes locked, and hated tingles spilled over her. For a moment, a single heartbeat, tension so intractable she couldn't breathe thrummed between them. He was the sun she orbited, the vortex she couldn't escape. Then he turned, revealing his back, and she was able to suck in a mouthful of air, but his image remained burned in her mind.

He stood well over six feet tall and had the lean, sexy

muscle mass of a man who'd spent quality time in a gym. A fact perfectly complemented by the pin-striped suit he wore. He had dark hair and even darker eyes, the depths fathomless, mysterious and so sublimely sensual she sometimes forgot her new resolve to avoid ABBs. Adorable bad boys.

She wanted what her parents had. What Brook Lynn and Jase, Harlow and Beck had. She wanted *more*. And for the first time in her life, she was willing to wait for it. No more settling for scraps.

Sometimes people forget that falling in love isn't enough. Momma, always so wise. *You have to fall in like, too. Your dad...he thinks I hung the moon.*

Jessie Kay had no doubts about that. When she'd helped her sister pack up to move-in with Jase, they'd found a secret panel in the closet. Stored inside were letters their dad had written their mom while the two were dating.

When you smile, my sweet Anna Grace, I see my future in your eyes.

No one had ever experienced that kind of reaction to Jessie Kay's smile, and there was no way West would be the first. Which was one of the many reasons he wasn't dateable, despite her crush on him. Well, not on him, but on his looks. Yes, there was a big difference. While she would love to give his face and body a tongue bath, she only wanted to give his brain the finger.

"Well, don't just stand there drooling, Miss Dillon, go on back," Cora said, pulling Jessie Kay from her musings.

"Thanks." For nothing. She clutched the wicker basket closer to her chest and trudged forward.

The moment she crossed the threshold into West's

office, the temperature seemed to rise another twenty degrees, the air saturated with the heady scent of caramel. Her tingles returned and redoubled.

He'd removed his jacket and now sat at his desk, rolling the sleeves of his white button-down to his elbows, revealing strong forearms with mouthwatering sinew and a dusting of dark hair.

"Don't pretend you were worried about me, *Mr. West.*"

He reclined in his chair and folded his hands over his middle, peering at her the way a snake must peer at a mouse—intent, ready to strike, hungry.

A ball of thorns grew in her throat, and she gulped. Maybe he wanted to devour her in a sexual way. A few times she'd wondered if he liked the look of her the way she liked the look of him. Or maybe he just got off on taking down an opponent.

Yeah. That one.

"Are you here to feed me or to stare at me?" His tone mocked her.

Jerk. "I'm here to correct you. You said I was late, but you couldn't be more wrong. Breakfast orders are due to arrive between seven and nine."

"It's ten thirty-six."

Oops. Was it really? "You didn't let me finish. Breakfast orders are due to arrive between seven and nine *except* on ice days. I'm allowed an hour or so of leeway."

"Again, it's ten thirty-six."

"I said *or so.*" When his expression failed to soften, she added, "Could I have picked up the pace to reach you sooner? Yes. However, falling and breaking my neck is *your* dream come true, not mine."

He showed no mercy. "Since news stations have talked about nothing but this winter storm for the past week, I knew it was headed our way and did something revolutionary. I planned ahead."

She offered him a brittle smile. *The customer is always right*, Brook Lynn often said. And Jessie Kay agreed...unless the customer was a douche bag, and then he was just a douche bag. "Had I planned ahead, I would have canceled your order."

"But you didn't. So. I'm assuming your tardiness means the food is free."

She breathed in and out and remembered another bit of sage advice her mother had given her. *You can't control when a bird flies over your head, but you* can *control whether or not you let one build a nest in your hair.*

In other words, she couldn't stop certain emotions from rising up inside her, but she *could* stop herself from reacting to them.

And she had to, had to, *had to* stop herself. Brook Lynn recently challenged her to a bet. First girl to yell or throw things in a fit of temper had to let the supposedly composed sister pick her wardrobe for a week.

Knowing Brook Lynn, Jessie Kay would be wearing a nun's habit. Shudder! She'd much rather see her sister in a bikini constructed with two pasties and a curl of ribbon.

Over the years, tormenting each other had become a very fun game.

"You're wrong, as usual," she told West with a sugar sweet smile. "Also, you're too limited in your thinking. Time isn't linear, it's circular."

That grabbed his attention. Intrigue brightened his eyes as he straightened, propped his elbows on the desk and linked his fingers just below his chin. "Explain."

With pleasure. "Time has no beginning and no end. It always has been, always will be, and it never stops, which means time is an ever-continuing circle of new beginnings and new ends."

The intrigue intensified and mixed with...admiration? "You're implying the concept of being late is—"

"Bullcrap."

"—erroneous because what is present will become what is past and what is past will become what is future. Therefore, no matter the lateness of the hour, you're always on time."

"I liked my description better, but yeah. And being on time in this weather means I've earned a bonus. Today, your sandwich is fifty dollars more than usual."

He studied her for a long while, silent. "In terms of excuses, yours is the best I've ever heard. I'll give you the extra fifty."

She fought the urge to preen. "Should we make it an even hundred?"

"Why? Did you sprinkle the sandwich with crack?"

"No. But I *did* finally factor in my mental anguish."

One corner of his mouth twitched as if—no way, just no way—he might smile. But of course, his frown deepened, and he turned his attention to his keyboard. "Leave the food. Get your money from Cora and go. I'm busy."

Hot and cold. Sweet and sour.

He was soooo lucky Jessie Kay abandoned the dark side, or he'd be receiving *special* toppings on tomorrow's order.

"I hope you—" *choke* "—enjoy." She placed the bacon-and-marshmallow sandwich at the edge of his desk, in his periphery without actually broadcasting how precariously it teetered. Yes, the sandwich was protected by paper, but the floor was the floor and to a man of West's fastidious nature, it would be utterly tainted the moment the two made contact.

Maybe she still dipped a toe in the dark side every now and then.

Just to be contrary, she said, "There's a life outside of computers, you know." He wanted her to go, so she would stay a little longer. "You should check it out."

He never glanced her way. "Send me a link, and I will."

Har har.

As she watched him *click clack* at the keyboard, she thought that maybe…wow, this was hard to admit but… being his friend would have been kind of awesome. Except for his weird dating quirk, he'd clearly managed to get his life together. A feat she only dreamed of achieving. He could have shared his secrets for success.

"You should be nicer to me, you know. I'm Brook Lynn's maid of honor, and you are Jase's best man. I can make your walk down the aisle easy, or I can make you wish you were dead."

"I'll take my chances."

Frustrating man! Why did he hate her so much?

She vividly recalled their first meeting at the town's annual Fourth of July barbecue. She'd noticed the trio of new man-meat standing beside a booth selling strawberry ice cream cones. West had been the first to snag her interest, and when he'd looked over at her, she'd experienced an instant, full-body sizzle. Then he'd raked his dark gaze over her and his lips had twisted in disgust. Disgust! An emotion she'd easily recognized because she saw it reflected back at her every morning when she looked in the mirror.

Big girl that she was, she'd tried to talk with him

about it. Problem? Let's find a solution. But he'd turned to Beck and muttered, *I can't be here*, as if her presence ruined his good time.

Her already fragile self-esteem had plummeted, and she'd eagerly accepted Beck's offer of comfort. A man who'd made her feel like the center of his world.

Until the sun had risen the next morning.

Great. Now she wanted out of this office, like, yesterday. "The lottery is up to one hundred and thirty-eight million. I should probably buy my ticket." She tried for a breezy tone, but just sounded desperate. "See ya around, West."

"Lotteries are a tax on people who suck at math. You know that, right?"

"Someone's gotta win, and I'm good at getting lucky."

A muscle jumped beneath his eye, a testament to growing anger—why anger? "Which guy are you after now?"

Was that a slut reference? "I'll tell you which guy I'm after," she snapped—only to remember her bet with Brook Lynn.

Right. *Hide the hurt.*

"Ben and Jerry, that's who. Hope you enjoy your sandwich," she repeated. "Or not. Yeah, probably not." With another sugar-sweet smile, she bumped her hip into the edge of his desk. The computer parts and papers scattered along the surface rattled and shifted, and as she glided toward the door, she heard a telltale *thump*.

A very black curse echoed off the walls.

Without turning around, she lifted a hand and waved her fingers at him.

"I expect a new sandwich, Jessie Kay."

"Let's see what that expectation gets you…"

She really needed to get out of the food-service industry. But first, she needed to figure out what she wanted to do with the rest of her life. Besides gut-punching West at some point, of course.

Only one slight problem. So slight it probably wasn't even worth mentioning. She'd barely graduated high school, had been too busy having fun to study, and she had no real skills other than tying a cherry stem with her tongue. *Go me!* As an aspiring millionaire, that little talent might not get her very far.

Cora clucked as she handed over a twenty and a fifty. Ten for the sandwich and five for the delivery, plus the five he usually gave her for a tip, on top of today's *time management* tip.

"Listened to our conversation through the speakerphone, did you?" Jessie Kay asked drily.

"A good assistant must anticipate her boss's needs. Speaking of, you should give him a break, Miss Dillon. He's had a rough go of it lately."

"Excuse me? Did you just say *he's* had a rough go of it?" Please! "I'm an orphan schlepping a sandwich to an ungrateful bazillionaire during the new ice age. *I* deserve a break."

A roll of the older woman's eyes. "Both of his friends are now engaged."

"So? My sister and best friend are now engaged. That's a cause for celebration." Except, she sometimes wanted to sob like a baby. She loved Brook Lynn and Harlow with all her heart, but sooner or later things were going to change. The girls would direct their full attention to their new families, and rightly so, while Jessie Kay, the only single gal, would become nothing but background noise.

Part of her wanted to pull away now, slowly, so it would hurt less, but the rest of her was determined to enjoy their time together while it lasted. To finally prove her love. "Just—" *mind your own business* "—have a nice day, Miz Higal."

She soared through the door, cold air delivering a thousand bitch-slaps of shock. How she longed for the arrival of the next season—tornado—which would lead to her favorite season—hotter than hell.

Maybe she'd text her club buddy Sunny Day and go somewhere to blow off a little steam…and what the heck was she doing, reverting to old habits? No, no, a thousand times no.

Daniel Porter stepped from the shadows, stopping her in her tracks.

"Jessie Kay."

"Move. Now." She wasn't putting up with insults from another man. And this one *would* insult her. They used to date, and they hadn't parted on friendly terms.

"Sorry, but I'm right where I want to be."

Stubborn to his core. But then, he was an Army Ranger, so he had to be.

He'd returned from an overseas tour a few months ago, and one of the first things he'd done was ask her out. She'd said yes so fast her tongue had practically caught fire. He was a beautiful man with dark hair and emerald eyes, the body of a warrior, and the aloof attitude that made (crazy) women dream of taming him.

It wasn't long before she'd realized he expected to jump straight into bed, no dinner, no movie, and she'd gotten the impression he'd climb out the window the moment they finished. So, night after night she'd *insisted* on dinner and a movie, doing nothing more than kissing him goodbye every time they parted. Finally he'd moved on. But instead of being honest about his reasons for dumping her, he'd blamed her continued association with Jase and Beck, the men she'd once slept with. As if she'd ever go for round two with Brook Lynn and Harlow's leftovers.

"Fine. I'll move." She sidestepped him, but he was used to dealing with hostiles and just sidestepped with her.

"I want to apologize for the way I treated you," he said, and she stilled from shock alone. "For the way I ended things."

An actual apology? That was a first. And after her interaction with West, it was also a soothing balm. Unless… "Is this a ploy to get into my pants?"

"Only partly."

The corner of her mouth quirked up, and some of the starch faded from her shoulders. "Your honesty deserves a reward. You're partly forgiven."

"Good. Will you have dinner with me?"

"What!"

"Dinner. With me. Afterward, I'll walk you to your door where we will part with a handshake."

He'd just…asked her out? On a proper date? And he wasn't going to push her for anything more than a meal? "I don't… I can't…"

"I miss you. I had fun with you, and fun isn't something I've had in a long, long time. Walking away from you was a terrible mistake."

Words every girl longed to hear. And part of her really, really wanted to say yes to his invitation. Any interaction with West tended to bruise her feminine pride, leaving her feeling battered and just a little unworthy of a happily-ever-after. A feeling she'd struggled with since her father's death. A feeling that had only grown worse when her mother died…and as Jessie Kay made mistake after mistake. Now she had so many faults, her name should be San Andreas.

"I'm going to be *fully* honest with you, Daniel. I'm not interested in you romantically." Once upon a time, she'd said yes to every guy who asked her out. She'd thought, *He wants me. To him, I'm worth something.* And what a high it had been. But the high had never lasted, and she'd always ended up having to chase a new one.

Better decisions, better life.

"But," she added, "I could be convinced to become your friend."

"I've never had a female friend. Especially one as hot as you."

"Well, I've never had a guy friend as hot as you. We can break each other in nice and easy."

A grin stretched from ear to ear. "All right. For you, Jessie Kay Dillon, I'm willing to give it a shot."

For her. As if she was something special.

Ugh. Earlier she'd thought about clubbing and now she was flying high because a guy had given her a compliment. *My self-worth is not dependent on others.*

She raised her chin. "Great. But do us both a favor and remember we're doing this on a trial basis. You screw it up, you get cut. In more ways than one."

CHAPTER TWO

LINCOLN WEST NEARLY put his fist through the front door of the WOH building. Fury was a prowling, fire-breathing dragon in his chest as he peered through the window, watching Jessie Kay interact with Daniel Porter, a man she used to date. A man younger than West, and even younger than Jessie Kay. What the hell were they discussing? Daniel's need for a diaper change? The latest in pacifier technology?

Had the two started dating again? The way Daniel was grinning at her...

An animal-like growl split West's lips, surprising him. He didn't give two shits who Jessie Kay dated. Yes, she was temptation wrapped in seduction, a Southern beauty with a viper's tongue, a rapier wit and a bone-deep grit that rivaled his own. Yes, she'd basically blown his mind with her brilliant concept of time. But it didn't matter; she was completely off-limits, which made his behavior today a complete non sequitur.

Knowing she would insist on making sandwich deliveries despite the weather, he'd waited outside her house this morning, his car hidden by a mound of snow. He'd followed her into town to make sure she arrived in one piece, and as she'd distributed the goodies in her basket, he'd sat in his nice, warm office staring at the clock, bordering on panic when she failed to arrive at a reasonable time.

He'd planned to follow her home as soon as she left the office. Now Daniel could have the honor.

"I've known that girl since she upended my third-grade class." Cora stapled a bundle of papers together. "Always in trouble for talking, always tardy, but always kindhearted. If anyone was having a bad day, she'd be the first to offer comfort and whatever dessert her mother had packed in her lunch box."

He wished he'd known Jessie Kay back then. He would have been the kid she comforted, the one who received her dessert. Maybe they would have grown up to be friends. He'd had very few of those over the years. Hell, besides Jase and Beck, both of whom he'd met in foster care, he'd been alone.

Boo hoo. Poor baby.

He snapped, "Not another word about her," and stalked to his office.

He couldn't afford to like Jessie Kay. He just... couldn't. There was too much feeling there. Some of it good—too good—and a lot of it bad.

The day he'd met her, he'd flashed back to Tessa, the only girl he'd ever loved. The girl he'd lost. He'd promised to throw her an elaborate party, a "congrats for passing your GED exam" only to forget. When she'd shown up expecting an adoring crowd, flowers and balloons, she'd gotten a coked-out West, cold beer and leftover pizza.

She'd burst into tears and driven away...and he'd found out a few hours later she crashed her car and died instantly.

The flashback had unnerved him. There'd been no reason for it.

Jessie Kay looked nothing like Tessa. The two were as different as night and day, in fact. While Tessa had been short and slender with dark hair and dark, almond-shaped eyes that hinted at a multicultural heritage, Jessie Kay was tall and curvy with pale hair and navy blue eyes that were always simmering with enough heat to blister.

The only thing they had in common? Both were beautiful. And, honestly, they were the only two women in the world capable of jacking up his blood pressure with only a glance.

When he'd been sober, he'd treated Tessa like a queen. Now he was always sober, but he only ever treated Jessie Kay like a portal to hell. Not on purpose. Or maybe it *was* on purpose. The first time he'd seen her, he'd wanted her with an intensity that had scared him stupid, but she'd ended up sleeping with Beck, and later on, Jase.

It's my turn now.

The thought—one he'd had many times before—pissed him off. There was no reason good enough to risk bad blood between him and his friends. Not that either guy would care if he and Jessie Kay hooked up. They encouraged him to go for it at least once a day. They liked her. The problem was West. If he had her—this woman who sometimes haunted his dreams—would he grow to resent his friends for beating him to the finish line?

The mere possibility always stopped him from making a move. Always pissed him off more than the "my turn" nonsense. He would let *nothing* come between him and his boys.

West tossed the contaminated sandwich in the garbage, fell into his chair with a grunt and loosened the knot in his tie, which was currently choking the life out of him. If food touched the floor, it never touched his lips. In one of the foster homes he'd lived, the father found it hilarious to watch the kids in his care eat off dirty linoleum, their hands tied behind their backs.

Get used to it, boy. Some people aren't meant for better.

Not all of the homes had been hellholes. Most had been pretty decent, granting him a better life than he ever would have had with his mom. Della West had never mistreated him and might have even loved him, but she'd loved her heroin more.

A knock sounded at his door. He glanced up to find Beck standing in the open doorway.

The six-foot self-proclaimed sex god strode into the office and plopped into the chair across from the desk. Flakes of snow dotted the guy's hair, giving the gold and brown strands a deeper depth of color.

He unwound a cashmere scarf and shrugged out of his coat. "Saw Jessie Kay and Daniel Porter on my way in. You all right?"

He wished his friends had never clued in to his struggle—wanting her, but not wanting to want her. "I'm fine."

"Well, could you do me a favor and inform your face? You look like you're constipated."

"Haven't you heard? Constipation is the new black. All the cool kids are doing it. Or *not* doing it."

Beck snorted, his amber eyes twinkling. Unfortunately, the amusement didn't last long. "Seriously, my man. You good?"

The guy worried about him. That wasn't new. To be honest, West worried about himself.

As a kid, he vowed he wouldn't end up like his mother. And for most of his teenage years, he'd succeeded, treating drugs and alcohol like the enemy. Then Jase was sent to prison for a crime West and Beck helped him commit, and West had wanted to escape reality, just for a little while. *Coke isn't heroin*, he'd rationalized. The same rationalization he'd used the next time...and the next...

When Tessa died, it wasn't long before the highlight of his day was cutting blow and snorting from any flat surface he could find—before he woke up nearly every morning covered in his own vomit.

Eventually he lost his scholarship to MIT, which was just another reason to get high. He'd failed himself, but more important, he'd failed his friends. Jase had taken full responsibility for their crime so West could go to school, get a degree and make something of his life. Beck wasted years trying to get him clean.

Even now, guilt was too strong to shake.

He'd failed Tessa worst of all. He'd even failed his mom. When he'd finally sobered up, putting himself in a place to help her with her own problem, it was too late. She was already dead. One overdose too many.

"Don't worry. I'm not going to relapse. I'm attracted to Jessie Kay, but I'm not in love with her." He would never allow himself to fall so deeply again.

"Why not? She's the total package. A lady in the kitchen and a wildcat—"

"Stop talking," he said through suddenly gritted teeth.

"Everywhere else." Beck had always dealt with tense situations in one of two ways: teasing or taunting. "Why? What'd you think I was going to say?"

Refuse to resent. "If she's so world-class amazing, why didn't *you* fall for her?"

"One of the hazards of jumping into bed too fast."
Beck shrugged. "You find out later you're better off as
friends. Besides, she's not Harlow."

She wasn't Tessa, either. And now this conversation
was over. "All right. If I've passed today's sobriety test,
I've got work to do."

"Happy to say you passed the sobriety test. Sad to say
you failed the asshole test."

"Not that. Anything but that." He shook a fist toward
the ceiling. "Why? Why me?"

"And now you've failed the shithead test. Where's my
thanks for showing up just because my best friend is a
workaholic and he'd throw a he-hissy if I suggested we
take an ice break?"

"Here." West flipped him off. "This is your thanks."

Grinning, Beck stood and gathered his discarded garments. "Heartwarming. I'll be in my office if you need
me."

Alone, West admitted that, despite his levity, he wasn't
actually in a good place. Could he pass a true sobriety
test?

Let's find out.

He unlocked and opened the bottom drawer of his
desk. A bottle of Lagavulin stared up at him. He traced
a finger over the cold glass.

Drink me, the whiskey said. *Just a sip. I'll help you
relax.*

Truer words had never not been spoken. But West
knew the sense of relaxation would only last for a little
while. Later he would fall back into his foul mood and he
would need another drink…and then he'd turn to coke.
The bane of his existence. The demon on his shoulder.

There'd been many mornings when, in the prime of

his addiction, he'd frantically raced through his apartment on a hunt for money. He'd checked for loose bills under couch cushions and inside the washer and dryer, and when he'd found nothing, he'd snuck into Beck's bedroom to rifle through dresser drawers. His desperation had been greater than his shame.

He'd needed a fix, and he'd needed it bad, but without cash, he wouldn't get anything but grief from his dealer. He'd even contemplated doing what his mother used to do to get *her* fix...

He scrubbed a hand down his face, tried to forget... *Can't ever forget.* His mother allowed her addict "friends" to do whatever they wanted to her body as long as they shared their supply. Sometimes she even sold herself to strangers. Anyone with a few dollars to spare.

One guy—

Call me Uncle Sam.

West shuddered. Whenever Sam had finished with Della he'd come looking for West. Not knowing what else to do, West had hidden in cabinets, under his bed and even inside the trash can. Sometimes he'd stayed hidden. A few times, he'd been found.

The fact that he'd *ever* considered selling himself...

He gave his head a violent shake to dislodge the claws of the past. His self-disgust remained.

"Drinking isn't on my schedule." He slammed the drawer shut, turned the lock and breathed in and out with purpose. He always stuck to his schedule. A habit he'd developed in rehab. Structure kept chaos—a trigger—at bay, every task a baby step that required time and attention to ultimately walk him to the end of his day as clean as a man like him could be.

Too many stains on my soul.

Speaking of his schedule… Four little words stared up at him from the screen of his phone. *Follow Jessie Kay home.*

Why had he penciled in such a thankless task?

Because he liked the way her sun-kissed skin flushed to a deep rose whenever she got angry? Because he liked the snarky things that came out of her mouth? A mouth he longed to taste. Because he liked the burn in his blood every time she stepped into a room? Liked the rush of matching wits with her?

Because he didn't want the madness to end?

Idiot! Fool! A man could become addicted to a woman like her. Especially a man like him. And yet he still picked up the phone and pressed the button to connect him to Beck.

"I'm heading out for a little while."

SATURDAY MORNING, WEST dressed in running shorts and a T-shirt that read "Goal Scouts." During soccer season— March through October—he coached a team of under-privileged kids. Off-season, he played indoors with the big boys. A great source of therapy.

He anchored his shin guards in place, tied his shoes and glanced at the clock—8:59 a.m. Right on time. He smoothed the wrinkles in his comforter, ensured the lid to his dirty clothes hamper was closed and sailed into the kitchen to mix three protein shakes.

"Hey, man." Jase strode around the corner, dressed and ready for the game.

Both Jase and Beck opted to join the indoor team rather than watching the action from the bleachers.

Jase played goalie. He had the body of a tank, and nothing got past him. Also, other teams tended to soil their pants with a single look at him. Everything from the spikes in his dark hair to the feral glaze in his green eyes said *screw with me and pay the ultimate price*.

Not exactly an idle threat. Having spent nearly a decade behind bars, he had a few issues and a whole lot of pent-up rage.

Aaand just like that, guilt burned through West like acid. "Hey." He couldn't meet his friend's gaze as he slid one of the shakes across the counter. "Drink up."

"Seriously?" Jase got in his face, forcing eye contact. "This is how you're going to start the morning?"

"Since when do you have such a beef with protein?"

"I don't care about the protein, and you know it. I care about the way you're looking at me right now. Or trying *not* to look at me."

Right. Jase actually expected West to forgive himself for the part he'd played in the prison sentence. And for a while, he'd tried. But guilt was the monster in the back of his mental closet, always there, always lurking, waiting for the perfect opportunity to strike. His friend had suffered unimaginable horrors, and for what? So West could throw his life away?

So, no, West wouldn't be forgiving himself anytime soon.

"You're the reason I'm what Brook Lynn refers to as a romance novel lover's dream. Reformed and rich," Jase said. "I'm grateful."

West started WOH simply to keep himself busy during his recovery, but the hobby quickly became a cash cow. "You wouldn't have gone to prison *at all* if I'd reacted differently to Tessa's—"

He couldn't say the word.

The night it happened, he'd been a newly minted

eighteen-year-old kid fresh out of the foster system. He'd lived with his boys and had his eye on the prize: a happily-ever-after. Tessa had invited him to a party, but at the last minute he'd opted to stay home and tinker with a new motherboard. He could sell it, make money and buy his girl the world. She'd gone with her cousin, instead. Beck had gone on a date with a girl he'd met earlier that day, and Jase, a carpenter, had still been at work.

A sobbing Tessa had returned in the middle of the night. She'd always been an emotional girl, so he hadn't reacted at first. Then she'd thrown herself into his arms and gasped out, "He…he… West, he *forced* me," and everything had changed.

Dark rage swallowed West whole. He'd gotten the rest of the details out of her, picked up Jase and Beck, and hunted down the piece of shit responsible. The guy had been sleeping peacefully in his bed.

Yeah. They'd broken into his apartment.

West threw the first punch. When he felt cartilage shatter and saw drops of blood leak onto lips that had assaulted Tessa, he smiled without humor. He only wanted more blood, more destruction—wanted to deliver more pain.

The guy fell to the floor and cried, "She begged me for it!"

As he tried to crawl away, West kicked him in the ribs. A starting bell. Jase and Beck joined the boot party, and it was a brutal, savage thing. Wrath unleashed. Violence without equal. The three of them continued until the bastard stopped moving…stopped grunting…stopped breathing.

"West." Jase's voice drew him back into the present.

"You shouldn't have asked us to hide our involve-
ment." Back then, they'd lived by a strict code. What
one requests, the others do. The end. But West had soon
found himself trapped in a prison of a different sort, one
built from guilt and shame. "Especially me. You expected me to move to Massachusetts, to finish school and
start a family with Tessa." He released a sharp breath.
"I never even set foot out of Oklahoma. And you know
what happened to my girl."

"I don't regret my decision. I never have."

No. Not true. "You must." Emotion clogged his throat.
"Beck and I used to visit you every week. I saw your
bruises…know what happens to young, scrawny boys
behind bars…" At eighteen, Jase had been *extremely*
scrawny.

A muscle jumped in his friend's jaw. "That's the past.
Over. Done."

"Is it?" Sometimes West woke up to Jase's screams.
*Shouldn't have brought this up. Too painful for us
both.*

I can do this. He pasted on a happy face and rolled
with the punches. "You're right. Of course. Over and
done. Now drink your breakfast like a good boy."

Jase peered at him for a long while, silent, before finally sighing. He tasted the shake and grimaced. "What'd
you put in this thing? Arsenic?"

"Can't be that bad." West took a swig and shuddered.
Yeah. It was that bad. "Arsenic would taste better. Brook
Lynn awake?" The girl was magic in the kitchen. She
could throw together—

"She left earlier this morning for a dress fitting. Something about gaining a pound and seams busting."

Women and their weight. When would they realize

skin-and-bones only impressed other women? Men preferred soft and lush…like Jessie Kay, rounded in all the
right places.

Down boy. "Maybe Harlow—"

"Nope." Jase shook his head. "She's helping Jessie
Kay with breakfast deliveries."

First he'd thought the name. Now he'd heard the name.
Can't escape her.

"Oh, and before I forget," Jase said, mercifully changing the subject, "I selected a construction company."

"Good." A few weeks ago, they'd decided to build
two additional homes on the acreage. One for Jase and
Brook Lynn, one for West and his misery. Beck and Harlow would keep the farmhouse since she'd grown up here
and loved the place almost as much as she loved her fiancé. "What do you need me to do?"

"Call the owner on Monday and tell him what you
want. I'll text you his number."

Beck stumbled into the kitchen. He was dressed
and ready to go, but his hair was unkempt and his eyes
rimmed with red. "What are you two yakking about?"

"Your bachelor party," Jase deadpanned. "You want
one stripper or four?"

"Dude." Beck scratched his chest. "*My life* was a bachelor party. I don't need another one."

Jase snickered. "Afraid the little woman will protest?"

Like he wasn't just as whipped.

"Actually, I'm afraid the little woman will ask the
strippers for tips and I'll die of a heart attack before I
have the privilege of saying my vows."

West handed him a shake. "Stop bragging about your
love life and drink your breakfast, Becky. You need it."
The guy was an attacking midfielder, his skill with a ball

unsurpassed. He remained calm under pressure, dishing out all kinds of abuse. "You step into the arena half-asleep and you'll have your ass handed to you."

"I should be so lucky." Beck drained half the glass without reacting to the bitter taste. "It's a nice ass."

"Your modesty humbles me." West was fast and agile, so he played center forward, stealing the ball—his ball—whenever it needed stealing. And it *was* his ball. Always. When he stepped onto the field, a sense of possession overtook him. *Mine.* Which was probably why he ended up the top scorer of every game.

That, and his skill, tenacity and strength. He spent a good portion of every day in the gym. He would never be weak again. He despised helplessness almost as much as he despised chaos.

"My modesty is just one of the many amazing things about me." Beck finished off the rest of the shake. "Good stuff. Thanks."

West glanced at his wristwatch. 9:28 a.m. All right. "Time to go."

He grabbed the duffel containing a change of clothes and climbed behind the wheel of his Mercedes. Jase had called eternal dibs on the front passenger seat, so he claimed his prize and Beck settled in back, all without protest or complaint. The two respected West and his schedules.

My soul mates.

He drove through the town square, where different families meandered along the sidewalks. Everyone was bundled up for warmth, and *everyone* paused to smile and wave as he passed.

To West, it was a scene straight of out a movie, too

picture-perfect to be real, but he smiled and waved right back.

"Who we playing today?" Jase asked as they crawled along the highway. Ice had been sanded and salted, but there were still slick spots. At this rate, they'd reach the downtown Oklahoma City arena in fifty years.

"The Ball Busters."

"Last year's league champions." Beck grinned, the baring of teeth a little evil. "That'll make our win today a thousand times sweeter."

"Exactly. Show no mercy." West adjusted the air vents, ensuring blasts of heat reached the backseat. "After we wipe the field with their faces, they'll be knocked out of this year's play-offs."

"Trash talk already." Jase nodded his approval. "I raised you boys right." A beep from his phone. He checked the screen and cursed.

"What?" West and Beck demanded in unison.

Jase rubbed the back of his neck. "Brook Lynn will be late to the game."

Such an extreme reaction over so little? As if the guy couldn't go half a day without seeing his girl?

If West ever dated Jessie Kay—

Are you kidding me? Could he not go one day, one hour, without thinking about her? Without hating her and craving her, practically foaming-at-the-mouth eager to get his hands on her. To shake her and learn her... And anything else that came to mind.

"Jase, my man, I love you. I really do." West turned on his blinker before changing lanes. "But codependency is an ugly bitch."

Beck reached out to pat Jase on the shoulder. "What he said is true, but it doesn't matter. Bitches adore us."

Very true. Young, old, single or married, females simply couldn't get enough, bad boys like Beck and Jase their kryptonite. West attracted his fair share of attention, but never in droves. The multitude must suspect he wasn't just a bad boy; he was damaged beyond repair.

When he reached the arena, he parked in back, grabbed his duffel and beat feet inside, the frigid air like needles against his skin, smelling of car exhaust and burning wood rather than wild strawberries, a scent that somehow pervaded Strawberry Valley even in winter. A scent that had somehow come to represent home.

When Jase had voiced a desire for a fresh start in a small town with wide-open spaces and the sense of community he'd never gotten in foster care, West had panicked. Leave his penthouse apartment? His routine? Never! Except at the behest of his friends. Then he'd do both in an instant. He owed Jase and Beck his life, and by all that was holy, he would pay his debt.

Always better to be the lender rather than the borrower.

At first, he'd hated Strawberry Valley. Residents considered his personal life a reasonable topic of conversation, and his bank balance open to public scrutiny. And yet, those same residents had had Jase's back at a time when anyone else would have chased him off with pitchforks and torches.

Now there was nowhere else West would rather live.

A few feet past the door, he drew up short, feeling as if he'd just been punched in the chest.

No. Please, no.

Jessie Kay was here.

She and Harlow stood in line at the concession stand, completely unaware of the crowd of drooling men staring at them, some of those men basically pawing at the ground like bulls about to charge.

Little wonder. Harlow had hair so black it gleamed blue and eyes the color of a morning sky. She was a Disney princess come to life. And considering her love of romance novels, the description couldn't have been more perfect. Meanwhile, Jessie Kay was the villain of the tale. The merciless evil queen so beautiful, so utterly flawless, her every movement and word so touched with black magic, she entranced everyone around her.

It wasn't just the skin that looked as soft as silk, or the waterfall of pale hair that begged for a man's hands, or the eyes so deep and blue you drowned a thousand times with only a glance. It wasn't even the lush, red lips made for sucking—and being sucked. It was the essence of her: pure, luscious seduction.

Her hands danced through the air as she spoke to Harlow, her chest heaving. A succulent chest covered by a too-tight T-shirt that read "Goal Scout Deliveries Free Today Only." Her jeans appeared painted on, and the cowgirl boots she wore had enough rhinestones to outshine the sun.

She stole his breath.

Jase came up beside him and hammered his shoulder with enough strength to crush an ordinary man. "Now you know. Brook Lynn sent Jessie Kay in her place. I'd hoped we'd beat her here, and you'd never know she'd come. Sorry."

Well. The guy's he-fit after reading Brook Lynn's text suddenly made more sense.

Beck stalked past them, an arrow with a target. As always, he devolved into an intense, possessive mani-mal whenever his fianceé was near, casting a warning glare at every man in her vicinity, all *mine, I'll kill before I'll share.*

Harlow squealed, happy to see him. Jessie Kay stiffened and *slooowly* turned toward the door, as if she needed a moment to prepare herself for a coming blow. Her gaze linked with West's and...just like that, the rest of the world ceased to exist. Desire burned through him, even vibrated in his bones. The air between them thickened, suddenly supercharged with enough electricity to bring down a rhino. Breathing was far more difficult— when the ability at last returned.

How did she do this to him? How did she ensnare him so easily? And with only a look?

A drug. She's a drug.

She had to be. Only cocaine had the same effect on him.

At the moment, he didn't exactly care what she was. *Devolving...*

Mine. Want.

A group of people spilled through the entrance, and someone knocked into him. As West stumbled, managing to catch himself before a fall, the...whatever he had going with Jessie Kay ended, broken abruptly.

Anger replaced his fascination, and he growled a curse at the person responsible. A curse he then turned on himself.

"Sorry, sorry," the guy called as he continued forward.

West returned his attention to Jessie Kay, unable to stop himself, hating himself, but she'd reached the front of the line and now worked her black magic on the pimply-faced teenager behind the counter.

Grinding his molars, West strode to the locker room to store his bag.

"—see the blonde?" some guy was saying. The guy

who'd plowed into him, in fact. Without a coat to block the view, West was able to see the black-and-crimson shirt proudly boasting "Ball Buster" on back.

"The one in the cowboy boots? Dude. How could I miss her?" another member of BBs responded. "Those tits were spectacular."

A command to move never registered, but suddenly West was across the room, the guy's neck in his hand. He seethed with fury and aggression, his words lashing like a whip. "You're an asshole." He slammed the guy into the bank of lockers. "You don't talk about her like that. Ever."

Hazel eyes bugged out and air wheezed from a throat close to closing up shop.

"He's sorry, man. *We're* sorry," the friend rushed out. "We didn't know she was yours. Let him go, okay?"

"Let him go," Jase echoed, now at West's side. "Ending the life of a fool isn't on your schedule."

He was panting, West realized, as if he'd just run a ball up and down the field for several hours. Any second, he would snap, and there would be no stopping him until it was too late.

Can't let that happen. Not around Jase.

West gave a final squeeze before unlocking his fingers and stepping back. The offenders raced out the door, practically leaving skid marks in their wake. Predatory instincts surfaced, the urge to give chase almost too strong to ignore.

"I know you want Jessie Kay," Jase said softly. "I know you wish you didn't. You need to go out with her or forget her, because you can't go on like this. I see that now."

He saw it, too, but he couldn't go out with her and there was no way he could forget her.

Still he said, "I'll clean up, dry out." Recovery terms.

One hundred percent accurate in this case. "You have my word."

This behavior wasn't good for him, and it certainly wasn't like him. He was the one who thought everything through, who planned the beginning from the end before ever acting. But it was her, Jessie Kay; she was to blame for his uncustomary outburst. Months of looking at her, sparring with her and fantasizing about her without ever actually touching her had finally destroyed the calm outer shell he'd cultivated while living with his mom.

He remembered the day he'd learned it was better to hide his emotions than share them. He'd made the egregious mistake of telling his mom about Sam, and she'd cried for days, shooting up more than usual until finally overdosing. At five years old, he'd tried to give her CPR. He'd seen people on TV do it—the wrong way, it turned out. When he'd failed to revive her, he'd banged on his neighbor's door, begging for help.

He'd helped all right. By calling 911 and social services. West was taken away for the very first time.

"We can't afford trouble with the law," Jase reminded him. "Especially this kind of trouble."

"I know. Don't worry about me. Seriously." West's hands curled into fists. "I'm just jacked on adrenaline because of the game."

Disbelief shadowed Jase's features, but he said, "Maybe you should take a breather and sit out the first half."

"I'd rather eat nails. The field is the only place I can legally kick ass."

"Just make sure the asses you kick don't have to be carried away on stretchers."

Those tits were spectacular.

West laughed without humor. "I can't make any promises."

CHAPTER THREE

JESSIE KAY SAT in the bleachers, embarrassingly awed. West was a warrior of old and the arena was his battle-field, his body his weapon. And what a weapon it was.

He *owned* the ball. When someone else had it, he took it. When he had it and someone tried to steal it, he knocked that someone into a wall with a full-on slam. He threw insults, elbows and knees like they were confetti.

Tomorrow, the members of Team Ball Buster would feel as if they'd tangled with an F5 tornado and lost, guaran-dang-teed.

It—was—hawt. *West* was hawt.

Jessie Kay's gaze remained glued to him. Sweat glistened on his bronzed skin, and blood trickled from several cuts he'd sustained. The injuries only made him sexier. She wanted to kiss him all better. With tongue.

Dang. The future of her new good-girl status looked pretty bleak right about now.

He shoved someone else into the wall, a loud thud echoing, and she sighed dreamily.

Harlow gasped with concern. "Butter my butt and call me a biscuit. This sport is *brutal*. It's making my stomach churn."

"Churn with happiness, right?" Brutal equaled awesome.

"Would I need a vomit bag for happiness?"

"Not likely."

"Then no, not happiness. Beck has such a violent past. I'm nervous this kind of aggression will lead to flash-backs and nightmares."

Jessie Kay knew the guy had grown up in foster care, same as West and Jase, and that not all the homes had been safe havens. "Beck doesn't look traumatized out there, honey. He looks as thrilled as a bull with teats."

Harlow rolled her eyes. "A bull would *not* be thrilled with teats."

"How do you know? A guy with boobs would be over the moon. Anyway. You mentioned Beck's past. What do you know about West's?" *Subtle, Jessie Kay, subtle.*

"About as much as you do, I'm thinking. Which means not a whole lot."

Well, crap.

Her phone buzzed, and she checked the screen. Sunny Effing Day.

Got a line on party of the century 2nite. U in??

She didn't have to think about her response.

No thanks, but tell me all about it in the morning ☺ ☺

Sunny: Girl, U know there's a big chance I won't even remember the deets, right??

Yeah. And that was one of the bigger problems for Jes-sie Kay. She hated remembering the things she'd done, but she hated *not* remembering the things she'd done even more.

"So, uh, what do you think of him?" she asked Harlow. "West, I mean."

Harlow's gaze sharpened on her. "Well, he's certainly a charming devil, isn't he? Why?"

She ignored the question, saying, "Of course you'd think he's charming. He's nice to you."

"He is, which is probably why I think he's smart, driven and witty. And handsome. And strong. I love his dedication to Beck and Jase."

"But?"

"But…sometimes he can stand in a full beam of light and I still think he's surrounded by darkness."

Yes! That! "I thought I was the only one who'd noticed." She'd often wondered if something bad had happened to him as a kid. Something more than the bits and pieces she'd gleaned over the months. Orphaned at a young age. The death of a girlfriend. A lost scholarship. "I bet this kind of aggression is cathartic for him. And Beck. Because this conversation does *not* revolve around West. I bet brutal field play would be cathartic for *me*. Hey! Maybe we should start a team of our own."

"No way, no how."

Excitement filled her, and she clapped her hands. "We'll call ourselves Victorious Secret and our motto will be 'We Live to Spank You.' Duuude. Yes! I'm basically the smartest person in the world. Ever. You in? Of course you're in. Practice begins tomorrow."

"I'm *out*." Harlow shuddered with horror. "I have zero desire to be tossed around like some kind of meat bag just because I have possession of a ball anyone can buy at any sporting-goods store for less than twenty dollars."

"Puss! You were the town bully for years. Where is your predator spirit?"

"In my pants," she deadpanned, "where Beck likes to visit."

Yeah. Okay. The fact that Jessie Kay hadn't gotten any since the Jase/Beck debacle could maybe possibly definitely for sure begin to explain her desire to attack strangers and bask in their misery, perhaps even dance in their blood. That and the fear that she not only sucked as a person, she sucked as a lover. Why else would so many guys ditch her so fast?

Throughout her life, she'd had too many hookups and too few relationships, nothing ever lasting more than a few weeks. And more often than not—or, you know, *every* time—it had been the guy who'd left her, not the other way around.

Why was she such a failure? What made her so unworthy of more?

Her winning personality should only ever seal a deal.

Like Daniel said, he'd had the time of his life during their dates, laughing with her—not at her—until he pulled a muscle. And yet, he'd still let her go. And after him, she'd gone out with Dorian Oliver, a childhood friend of Beck's who lost his wife to cancer years before. He hoped to find love again, and honestly, he'd seemed really into her, always making excuses to get his hands on her.

You cold?

But after only three dates, all of which had ended with a passionate kiss at her door, he'd pulled the plug.

A good thing, actually.

According to Momma, a girl shouldn't give her pearls to pigs. Dorian was as far from pig-like as possible—a sweetheart who treated her with nothing but respect and kindness—but the message fit all the same. If she didn't have a future with a guy, why waste her precious time? Especially considering she'd wasted so much already.

She was twenty-seven years old and the dreaded thirty was creeping up on her like an insidious disease. Or the worst thing on the planet—a spider. Did she have a single prospect? No! Because the only guy capable of eliciting a lasting response in her was a bastard of the highest order some days, most days, and a charmer without equal the others. Again, a charmer to everyone but her for reasons he'd never had the courtesy to share with her. Not that it mattered…even though he could melt her panties with only a glance.

The next piece of beefcake she welcomed into her bed would like the crap out of her, figuratively speaking, and that was that.

You outshine the sun, Anna Grace. There's nothing about you I would change.

Her father's words to her mother only solidified her vow. Jessie Kay's next man wouldn't set a timer on their relationship, like *some* people she knew. He would fight tooth and nail to stay with her, no matter what.

Basically, the relationship equivalent of West and his soccer ball.

Her phone buzzed again, and when she checked the screen, a smile bloomed. Since her run-in with Daniel earlier in the week, they'd stayed in constant contact.

Daniel: Come over tonight. We'll eat SpaghettiOs, my fave. Just for the privilege of your company, I'm willing to watch *The Big Bang Theory, How I Met Your Mother* or *New Girl*

Her: You know what would be cool??? If those 3 shows were combined. *How I Banged the New Girl Before I Met Your Mother* ☺ ☺ ☺

Daniel: OK. You owe me a new phone. I just spit coffee all over this one

Her: Consider it the price you pay for being friends w/ such a "sass mouth" (as Mom used to say) and too bad for you, I'm hanging w/ my girls 2night

Daniel: Pencil me in soon. Pleeease (look at me, willing to beg)

Her: We'll see!

Daniel: Since I'm not getting sex from you, I'm only in this friendship for the fun, remember?

Her: Fine. I'll consider giving you a few minutes of JK time tomorrow—but I'll hear your thanks NOW

Daniel: Someone needs to spank your ass…but thank you

She so did not want to be buoyed by his eagerness to spend time with her, but dang it, she was. Maybe she *should* try dating him again—

No. No! No second chances in the romance department. Ever.

Build a house on sand, and the first storm that comes along will topple it. Build on a firm foundation, and the house will withstand anything.

She would give anything for just one more conversation with her mom. Just one more hug.

The crowd erupted into bloodthirsty cheers, jolting her from her thoughts, and she glanced up in time to watch another member of Ball Busters hit the wall, impact so strong it even shook the bleachers. As the guy slipped to the floor, he left a smear of crimson behind. Through it, Jessie Kay met West's stare.

She saw hunger...such gnawing hunger...

He gave her a look so raw and carnal, she felt stripped of every piece of clothing in less than a second. That look said he couldn't go a minute more without having her in his bed. That he would suffocate without her. That she'd become the center of his world—his gravity.

It was a lie. A nasty, nasty lie.

Or she was only seeing what she wanted to see. A problem of hers.

Even still, goose bumps broke out over her skin and fire blazed in her veins. *Savage, sexy beast. Gimme.*

Before she did something stupid—like throw what was left of her panties at him—she buffed her nails.

"Hey, Jessie Kay, Harlow. I finally made it."

She turned to see Brook Lynn climbing the bleachers and sighed with relief. Her sister had always been her saving grace.

The blonde, blue-eyed beauty had rescued Jessie Kay from certain disaster so many times over the years, she'd earned a JK life-preserver badge. If the little darling hadn't become the mother they'd lost, despite being two years younger, Jessie Kay would have ended up on the streets...and oh, crap. Guilt gnawed on her soul. Guilt like she hadn't felt in years—because she hadn't let herself feel it, numbed by keggers and "romance."

She was the worst sister ever. She'd destroyed Brook Lynn's entire world. She was the worst *daughter* ever. She'd escorted her mother to death's door, rung the bell and ran away. She'd insulted her father hours before he died and, and, and—

She focused on that, the least horrendous of her crimes, hoping to stop the panic attack in its tracks. And for a moment it worked, the arena disappearing, replaced by the kitchen walls of her childhood home— the home she still lived in—morning sunlight shining through the large bay window.

"Go change out of those shorts and into something appropriate," her father demanded.

"But Daddy—"

"You're still a child, Jessie Kay. My baby girl. You shouldn't wear skintight pants with the word *naughty* scripted over your backside."

"I'm not a child! I'm—"

"No argument. Just action."

She stomped her foot. "Sunny has a pair just like them, and her dad thinks they're cool."

"He isn't your dad. Go change."

"Well, I wish he *was* my dad!" she shouted. "I like him better."

She raced to her room, and a short while later Daddy left for work…but he'd never come home.

A manager at Dairyland, he'd been speaking to one of his engineers about a broken machine. A machine that exploded, killing them along with half the workforce.

He'd died thinking she wanted a different father.

"Hey, hey. You okay?" Soft hands cupped her cheeks.

Jessie Kay blinked and found her sister sitting beside her, familiar features darkened with concern. "I'm fine."

She gave her sister a big ol' bear hug, and she probably held on far too long, probably clung far too tight, but dang it, she loved the girl. "Just thinking about Daddy," she said when she pulled away, careful to articulate her words.

Brook Lynn was born with a severe case of hyper-acusis—a condition that caused her to hear even the quietest everyday noises at a screaming volume—forcing her to wear bulky devices in both ears to muffle and even mute sounds.

"We've talked about this." Brook Lynn gave her cheeks a firm pat. "Do I really need to give you another lecture?"

Parents and children fight. That's part of life. You and Dad exchanged heated words, get over it. You both walked away knowing you were loved.

Brook Lynn hadn't witnessed the fight, and Jessie Kay hadn't wanted to spill the details, but she'd done it anyway. Panic attacks had been a way of life for her back then, and her sister deserved to know one of the many reasons why.

"No. I remember the last twenty thousand."

"Good." Brook Lynn nodded. "Now tell me what I missed game-wise."

The soccer game. A life raft. "West has tried to murder everyone on the field, and Jase has guarded the goal as if it's your virtue.

"In other words," Brook Lynn said with a grin, "we're winning."

Exactly. "So how'd the fitting go?"

"You mean the modern-day torture session I willingly signed up for? Well, if you ever decide you'd like to acquire a few body-image issues, just gain a few pounds before trying to zip your wedding gown and watch the seamstress's horrified expression in the mirror."

No one insults my sis—but me. "So you've gained a few pounds. So what? You've done Jase a favor. You've given him more of you to love."

Harlow snorted. "While your logic is impeccable—"

"I know, right? You're welcome, Jase," Jessie Kay shouted to the field.

He didn't hear her over the cheers and boos rising from the crowd, but somehow West did and he frowned over at her. The distraction cost him. He'd been waiting for the ball to cross the centerline, and when it did, he missed it, for the first time allowing a member of the other team to soar past him, heading for the goal.

Oops.

"—going to have a pity party, invitation one, if yesterday's brownies…and this morning's cupcakes…ruin *my* wedding gown," Harlow finished.

Jessie Kay barely paid attention to her friend, mumbling, "You're getting married this freaking weekend. The only thing you need to worry about is the death of your dating life."

"Before Beck, I had no dating life. My scars—"

"Are hideous. We know, you've told us." She watched as West jumped back into the fray, slamming his big, delicious body into the guy who had his ball. "We love you, anyway."

When the final buzzer sounded, the Goal Scouts won four to zero.

Her takeaway? Mercy didn't exist in soccer.

Knowing the boys had to shower and change, she and the girls made their way to the lobby to wait. The

Ball Busters emerged first, each man making an obvious point to avoid her gaze as he passed her.

Had she become total dog food since the game kicked off?

"Jase," Brook Lynn squealed, rushing over when her fiancé stepped into the room, his hair damp and his skin scrubbed clean. "You were freaking awesome."

He winked at her. "You know I can't help that."

"Hey. That's my line." Beck shouldered his way past his friend to get to Harlow. "We're going out to celebrate our victory. Tell me you're coming with us, love, or you'll break the heart you resurrected."

Harlow smiled sweetly at him. "Are you paying?"

Sweat beaded on Jessie Kay's palms as West moved into view, his gaze hard and steady on the exit, as if he couldn't wait to leave. He wore a black cashmere sweater and an old pair of jeans tucked into well-used combat boots. He was casual sophistication with a mule kick of dominant alpha, and he outshone every other man present.

"I'm not paying," Beck said, and Harlow pouted. "But West is."

Harlow—Jessie Kay's ride—fist pumped.

West arched a dark brow. "I am?"

"Well, then, we're definitely going." Harlow nudged Jessie Kay with an elbow. "Right?"

A free meal? "Sure. Count me in."

West motioned to the door with a clipped wave and she thought—hoped—he would put his hand on the small of her back to usher her forward. But as they walked to the parking lot, he maintained a steady distance between them. Of course, Jase decided to drive Brook Lynn's car and Beck decided to drive Harlow's, the two couples entering their respective vehicles and leaving Jessie Kay and West standing outside. Alone.

Wasn't awkward *at all*.

He opened the passenger door for her. "Get in."

Shocked by the gentlemanly gesture but not the bossy command, she slid inside the vehicle. And instantly regretted it. The air smelled like him, pure seduction and sweet caramel. Trembling, she buckled up and peered out the window, refusing to give in to the urge to watch his big hands molest the steering wheel.

"By the way," he muttered, "you still owe me a sandwich."

"It's your word against mine." Going for casual, she said, "So where are we headed?"

"A hamburger dive I've loved since I was a kid."

"Wait. Hold everything. You were once a kid?" She gave a mock gasp, hand fluttering over her heart. "I'm sorry, but I demand proof."

"Too bad. There's none available."

Please. "Surely there are pictures."

"No."

"Well, why the heck not? Did you destroy them? I bet you destroyed them. Didn't think you looked handsome enough?"

Without any inflection of emotion, he said, "Actually, no one cared enough to take any."

No. No, she refused to believe it. If he was potent now despite the shadows haunting his eyes and the tension that always radiated from him, he must have melted hearts as a child.

When she glanced over at him, however, her confidence withered. He kept his attention on the road, his posture stiff and his knuckles bleached of color. Just then, he was a man who'd revealed more than he liked.

He'd just told the truth, hadn't he?

Wow. His own parents, however long he'd been with them—not to mention all those foster parents—hadn't spared a few seconds out of their busy days to immortalize a moment of his childhood? How gut-wrenching. Wrong on every level.

Sadness for the little boy he'd been washed over her. "I'm sorry," she said softly. "Even if you'd looked like you were born downwind of an outhouse, I would have snapped a thousand photos of you. And then used those photos to blackmail you later, but my reasons are inconsequential."

"Thank you?" He changed lanes to pass a minivan. "But it's not like I have a monopoly on crappy childhoods."

"In this car you do. I had a great one."

"You sure about that? You were what, around thirteen when your dad died in an explosion at work? You were only seventeen when your mom drowned and your uncle showed up to save the day only to leave with the insurance money."

She blinked over at him. The entire town knew her history—well, they thought they knew—so it wasn't a big surprise West had the basic info. He was just the first person to ever state the facts so plainly. "I was a teenager in both instances, not a child. Big difference."

"Not really. Pain is pain."

"And don't go thinking you know everything about me, either," she added as if he hadn't spoken. "There's more to both stories. A lot more."

"Do tell."

And share her deepest, darkest secrets with the man who thought she'd been scraped off the bottom of a shoe? "No, thanks." She had enough trouble with her past without adding his commentary.

Even now, she thought of her mom falling...*because of me*...her mom screaming, begging for help...*because of me*...and she wanted to bawl like a baby who'd lost her favorite blankie, hug Brook Lynn, apologize forever and, and, and—

As the panic attack knocked at the door of her mind, she forced her thoughts to fast-forward to her mother's funeral, when she'd basically self-imploded. She'd gotten drunk for the very first time and given her virginity to the skeevy boy who lived down the street. The one who'd thought he was God's gift to the entire town. The one who'd told all his friends she was easy.

From that point on, she had been.

She'd given no consideration to Brook Lynn's care because she'd counted on Uncle Kurt to take care of everything. He'd promised. Only, like West had said, Kurt fled soon after collecting the insurance check. By then, Jessie Kay had been such a hot mess, the fifteen-year-old Brook Lynn had to pick up the slack, getting a job delivering papers, collecting donations from Strawberry Valley Community Church and doing everything within her power to keep two teenage girls together, fed, clothed and sheltered and, and, and—

Can't breathe. Need to breathe.

A warm hand squeezed her knee, giving her the jolt necessary to focus on something other than the past.

"Jessie Kay?" The gentleness of West's voice shocked her more than his touch.

Inhale, good. Exhale, better. "I'm fine. Really." Or

she would be. As soon as she reached her sister. Brook Lynn had a way of making everything A-okay.

"You sure about that?"

Convince, move on. She offered the brightest smile she could manage. "Are *you* okay? You actually seem concerned about my well-being."

He yanked his hand away from her. "I don't know if you've heard the rumors, but my heart is made of stone. Of course I'm not concerned."

She remembered the look he'd given her during the soccer game and decided his heart wasn't made of stone but of fire.

Not that she'd share her observation. But maybe she could get him to admit it.

"You were right. About my childhood. It was absolutely tragic." Offering an exaggerated frown, she traced a fingertip down both of her checks to mimic tears. "You should feel sorry for me and be super nice to me from now on."

He suddenly looked as if he was fighting a smile. "You know, upon further reflection, I'm certain my childhood was far worse than yours. *You* should feel sorry for *me* and do everything I tell you."

Well, well. "Color me intrigued. What's the first thing you'd tell me to do?"

He glanced at her, proving her theory: he *burned*.

"I'd want you—"

She shivered and—

"—to tell me more about your childhood."

Withered in her seat. "What do you want to know?"

"What did you want to be when you grew up?"

Polite interest? Or was he actually curious? "You'll laugh."

"Maybe. Probably."

Had to respect his honesty. "Mostly I wanted to be *that crazy cat lady*."

He choked on a breath. "An old woman who wears rollers and a robe, and has a hundred cats prowling through her house?"

"Exactly. I wanted a cat but Dad was allergic. Once a month Mom drove me to the shelter where I got to pet a roomful of strays. The employees used to joke about *that crazy cat lady* who came in every few weeks to adopt a new one. I was so jealous of her."

"That is…" He frowned. "Ridiculously adorable."

He sounded surprised. "What about you? What did you want to be?"

"Sorry, but we're not done with you. When you realized crazy cat lady wouldn't pay the bills, what'd you want to do?"

"Become a high school teacher."

"Subject?"

"English."

He wiggled his brows. "How do you come on to a high school English teacher?"

Her brow furrowed. "Uh…how?"

"Over? Under? To? Around? Outside?"

She snickered. "You preposition her." Silly man. *Sexy* man.

"Now I *have* to know your childhood dream," she said. "Tell me!"

"I had big plans, was going to be the youngest, hottest cop on the force."

A puzzle piece clicked into place. "Had fantasies about taking down bad guys, did you?" Made sense, considering some of the hellholes he must have lived in.

"Something like that."

"Now you create video games that allow you to defeat every kind of bad guy imaginable, so in a way, you've achieved your dream."

"That's true." A sizzling pause. "You've played my games?"

Caught! "Once or twice," she admitted. For years she'd fought—and lost—an addiction to "Donkey Kong." Barrels! The lady! Her dad taught her how to play, their special time together, and, well, winning became an obsession.

As soon as she'd learned of West's accomplishments, she'd maybe kinda sorta rushed out to buy his greatest hits. "Alice in Zombieland." "Lords of the Underworld." "Angels of the Dark." "Everlife." Used, of course, because she couldn't afford new.

"Evil is always afoot," she added, "but the good guys always save the day."

His frown returned, deepened. "Let's listen to the radio." He jacked up the volume.

Didn't like her observations? "Giving you the silent treatment won't be a problem," she called over the music.

"Really? Because you're still talking."

"Oh, that wasn't talking. This is." For the rest of the drive, she chatted about nothing. Loudly. The weather, her love of donuts, the price of thongs—so little material should cost less!—and finally, her last gynecological exam.

They reached the diner just as she got to the part about the cold speculum. He parked in back and sighed with relief when she quieted.

Rather than waiting for him to open her door—would he? wouldn't he?—she jumped out.

"Do you have to move like that?" West called as he emerged.

"Like what?"

"Like you're in heat."

Her eyes narrowed. "Don't like, don't watch."

"Impossible," he might or might not have muttered.

What the heck!

The other couples were already inside, seated at a rickety table in back, next to a Christmas tree. Ugh. Christmas. Her least favorite holiday was only three and a half weeks away. She and Brook Lynn would have to celebrate—again—without their parents.

Hate the holidays!

Despite the holly-jolly decorations, Jessie Kay fell in love with the diner at first glance. The red vinyl booths and black-and-white-tiled floor charmed her. Though the mint-green walls were cracked and crumbling, and there were water stains on the ceiling, the flaws only added character. Life had happened here. And really, how could you complain about anything when the smell of hamburgers, bacon and chili dogs saturated the air?

Only two chairs were free at the table, and of course, they were right next to each other.

West pulled one out for her, his gentlemanly ways shocking her all over again.

"Thank you," she muttered as she sat.

"You're welcome," he muttered back, sliding in beside her.

Things had always been strained between them, but now she knew the sweetness of his concern as she'd fought a panic attack, knew the feel of his hand pressed against hers, the kindness he showed to even a woman he didn't exactly like, and the strain reached a whole new level. *I want!*

Danger! Headed to a hot zone.

"So...you guys been waiting long?" she asked, hoping for a distraction.

No one paid her a bit of attention. With Harlow marrying Beck—this freaking weekend—and Brook Lynn marrying Jase—in less than five freaking months—the girls were caught up in a conversation about the weddings while the guys reminisced fondly about Ball Busters they'd injured.

Dude. I think you broke his femur. Congrats!

The waitress arrived and, to Jessie Kay's irritation, placed her hand on West's shoulder, as if it had every right to be there. "Y'all know what you want to drink?"

Overfriendly much?

The group snapped to attention, Jase kicking things off. When it was West's turn, the waitress stripped him with her predatory eyes and said, "Don't worry, sweetie. I remember what you like. I'll take real good care of you, promise."

With a wink and a grin, she sashayed off, and dang it, even Jessie Kay had to admit her milkshake would bring all the boys to the yard. Short and slender, she had the kind of curves most women spent years in a gym—or thousands on surgery—trying to achieve. Her dark hair was pulled back in a ponytail and swished from side to side, acting like a summoning finger, demanding anything with a penis follow fast.

"Looks like you have a groupie." The venom in Jessie Kay's voice baffled her.

I'm not jealous. I can't be jealous.

West meant nothing to her.

She tried for sweet. "How nice that must be for you." And how nice for Ponytail. The fact that she hadn't made the horrendous gaffe of sleeping with both West's friends, well, she might actually have a chance to score him.

"*A* groupie?" He shook his head, the picture of masculine confidence. "How cute."

"You should have seen the one who showed up at the office a few days ago." Beck draped his arm over Harlow's chair, something Jessie Kay's dad used to do whenever he was seated next to her mom. Daddy could never go more than a few minutes without touching Momma.

When we're not together, Anna Grace, I think of you. And when I think of you, I smile.

"She and West shook hands," Beck continued, "and I swear they made a baby."

"Twins." West rubbed two fingers against the dark stubble on his jaw. "Maybe triplets."

"You are *such* a romantic." Jessie Kay clutched her napkin to her chest. "How does anyone resist you?"

"That's a very good question." He met her gaze, and it shocked her—thrilled her—to watch his pupils expand, black spilling over all that gold. A forest fire wafting smoke. "Why don't you provide the answer?"

All eyes landed on her, and she shifted uncomfortably. "My opinion doesn't count. To me you're like a third cousin twice removed."

"So...kissing cousins?" Jase asked her.

As she sputtered with indignation, Ponytail returned with their drinks, making sure to shove her cleavage in West's face. Did she have no shame?

"Y'all ready to order?"

"Sure." West petted the woman's hand, which had

once again migrated to his shoulder. "I'll have the special, whatever it is."

After everyone else had placed their orders—requesting the special as well—Ponytail skipped off to give their ticket to the cook.

"I take it back." Jessie Kay frowned at West. "You don't have a groupie. You *are* a groupie. *Her* twins had you completely entranced."

"Hardly." He peered at Jessie Kay for a while longer, the wheels clearly turning in his head. Finally he nodded, as if he'd just made a decision. He leaned toward her, coming closer and closer. His voice a rasp of heat, ensuring only she could hear him, he said, "I happen to be a fan of someone else's twins."

Her jaw dropped, and her mouth went dry. Had he just—no, no, impossible…but…maybe. Had he just come on to her?

Wide-eyed, she turned her attention to Jase. "Did West sustain a massive brain injury during the game?" First he'd been nice to her. Then he'd complimented her movements—in heat? Yes! Now he flirted with her.

Actually he might be more than injured. He might be dying.

"Why?" Brook Lynn and Harlow asked in unison, instantly concerned.

"What's wrong?" Brook Lynn demanded.

The guys merely smiled slyly at her, as if they were privy to a secret.

"Maybe he finally had some sense knocked into him," Beck said.

"Maybe someone else wanted what he wants, and he decided to take it. At long last," Jase said.

Meaning…someone else had wanted her and West had decided to make a move?

No way. Absolutely no way. No one but Daniel wanted her, and he didn't count.

Reeling, needing a moment to regroup, she tossed her napkin on the table. And, just to be tactless, she added, "I'm headed to the lady's crapper. Alone," she added for the girls' benefit. "If I take a while, don't come looking for me."

Brook Lynn dropped her head in her upraised hands and moaned. "My sister did *not* just say those words at such a loud volume. I'm in a happy place. With butterflies and roses."

West continued to stare at her, the forest fire growing hotter…so hot all that smoke reached her, twined around her. Barely able to breathe, she backed away from him. Whatever this was, whatever had changed between them, whatever he was doing, she wanted no part of it—because deep down she wanted *all* of it.

CHAPTER FOUR

WHAT IN SAM HILL was wrong with him? *Had* he suffered a brain injury? West wondered.

He'd teased Jessie Kay. He'd flirted with her, had actually come on to her, and he hadn't been subtle about it. Before that, he'd even shared little tidbits about his past, something he'd only ever done with Jase and Beck. He'd even asked about *her* childhood, and he'd sincerely wanted to know!

And in the car, when she'd paled, gasping for breath, he'd felt an instinctive need to help her, whatever the cause of her distress. To make things better for her. To *be* better for her. The beautiful girl with the keen mind, sharp wit and vengeful nature. Who else would tell him about a pap smear?

She charmed him, and the madness had to stop. For every reason he'd already considered, and a thousand more.

If they ended up together, the relationship would fail in two months. No more, no less. Because yes, he scheduled his relationships like everything else. He never deviated, never would, for reasons he would never share.

He could handle Jessie Kay's upset over the situation, but not everyone else's. Brook Lynn and Harlow would side with her and hate him, and though Jase and Beck would side with West, they'd also have to side with their girls. Eventually, West would find himself cut from the family.

He needed his boys like his needed his lungs. Couldn't live without one, couldn't live without the other.

Brook Lynn threw her straw wrapper at him. "You better start being nice to my sister, Lincoln West."

"I wasn't mean. Not today," he added with a grumble.

"She has a tough outer shell, but inside, she's actually a marshmallow."

Was she? He only knew a little about her past.

There's more to both stories...a lot more.

If he knew everything about her, would he want her less? Or even more?

Could he want her more? He already ached for her every minute of every day.

Neither of his friends realized the attraction had flared at meeting one, and he would never tell them, didn't want them dealing with guilt for taking something—someone— he wanted. The predicament was his fault, anyway.

He'd met Jessie Kay at a Fourth of July BBQ and a few hours after he'd walked away from her, he'd returned, thinking he'd reintroduce himself to the woman he hadn't been able to get out of his mind. But by then, Beck had set his sights on her. And when either of his boys expressed an interest in something, *anything*, West moved heaven and earth to ensure they got it. Period. Such deprived childhoods deserved extravagant adulthoods. *Owe them everything.*

He'd walked away again. And he didn't regret his failure to step up and stake a claim on Jessie Kay. Nope. Not even a little.

Jase kissed his fiancée's knuckles. "You just made a

huge tactical error, angel. Never tell a man a woman is a marshmallow."

"Why not?" she asked, truly confused.

Beck arched a brow. "Why else? Because he'll want to eat her."

Harlow slapped his chest. "Oh, my gosh! You are *such* a pig."

But the guy wasn't deterred. "Tell her, Westlina."

He smiled without humor. "It's true. If the guy has a sweet tooth."

"The way you were looking at my sister…you better not have a sweet tooth." Brook Lynn wagged a finger in his direction. "I worry about her enough, thank you very much. She lives alone in a crumbling house. She's struggling to make ends meet, and she's determined to trek the straight and narrow. There's no reason to tempt her onto the winding and wide."

Do I tempt her?

Every muscle in his body hardened like a rock. Every—single—one. "Don't worry. I prefer savory to sweet." At least, he always had before.

The stiffening got worse as Jessie Kay strolled around a corner. Her navy gaze avoided him. Probably a good thing. The scent of her—pecans dipped in cream and sprinkled with cinnamon—invaded his senses, more potent than any drug, heating him to the point of sweltering, intoxicating him until his head spun. A warmth and high he'd missed with every fiber of his being. A warmth and high he couldn't allow himself to enjoy. The more he liked it, the more he'd crave it…the more difficult it would be to let go.

Clearly, he needed to select his next relationship. He usually had someone hooked and reeled by August and thrown back into the sea by October, avoiding the holidays. The move to Strawberry Valley had screwed with his schedule.

And even though sexual relief wouldn't be a cure-all, it would be a bandage, and that was good enough. Anything was better than nothing right now.

"Y'all are suspiciously quiet." With a frown, Jessie Kay eased into her chair. "I don't like it. Makes me want to slap you to sleep, then slap you for sleeping. Someone say something before I go into detail about my last period."

"*Please* say something," West said, almost desperate.

Brook Lynn moaned. "Happy place, happy place."

"Jessie Kay, why don't you tell everyone about the indoor soccer team you'd like to start," Harlow suggested.

Beck set his beer on the table with a clink. "You want to start a team? Have you ever played?"

"No, but I have plenty of experience knocking people around." Jessie Kay threw a one-two punch at air. "I just need a coach...someone like West. His skill is—"

"Oh, no, no, no." West shook his head for emphasis.

She ran her tongue over her teeth but still didn't face him. "Why not?"

"We'd kill each other." And, more important, he'd be on her before the end of session one.

"For all you know, I'm the next David Beckham," she said, lifting her chin.

"Ball handling is not a skill you pick up like this." He snapped his fingers.

Her gaze narrowed. Through a haze of fire and heat, a storm brewed, lightning flashing. "Well, good news. I'm already quite good at *ball handling*. Just ask your friends."

He pressed his tongue to the roof of his mouth.

Brook Lynn moaned, once again hiding her face in her hands. "Happy place. Happy place."

Beck choked on the drink he'd just taken.

Harlow rubbed him between the shoulders, saying, "Jessie Kay Dillon, you lock that snark up tight right this second. You know my he-slut likes to pretend I'm the only woman he's ever been with. Reminders of past escapades only confuse him."

Jessie Kay wilted, looking like the very picture of remorse and shame. "Sorry. My temper…"

Maybe she *was* a marshmallow.

"Wait. Did I just win our bet?" Brook Lynn vibrated with excitement. "Huh, huh, did I?"

"No! Are you kidding me?" Jessie Kay pointed her fork at her sister. "You wipe that smile off your face. The parameters of our bet say something has to be thrown. A fist, an elbow, even a handbag."

"Insults can be thrown," Brook Lynn insisted.

"They sure can, but I just *complimented* myself. Everyone heard it." She flipped her silken hair over her shoulder, the feminine action making his gut clench. "Since West is being ridiculous, I'll just hire Beck—"

"No way." Beck shook his head. "I love you like a sister, but no."

She tried again. "Jase will—"

"No, Jase will not." Jase gave a more insistent shake of his head. "I love you like a sister as well, but it ain't gonna happen."

Jessie Kay released a heavy sigh. "Fine. I'll hire a stranger. If he falls in love with me, stalks me and murders me when I refuse to return his affection, it's on you guys. It's just… I *neeeeed* an outlet for my…temper."

The most adorable blush spread all the way to the collar of her shirt. "Yes. My temper. You heard Brook Lynn doing her best to provoke me, right? She's a dirty, dirty cheater, and I can't allow her to beat me."

How much farther did that blush go? How hot did it burn?

Need for her, now sharper than razors, scraped at West's chest. He gripped the arms of his chair in an effort to fight the desire to reach for her.

Just one touch…

The waitress arrived a second later, handing out plates piled high with a chicken-fried-steak burger, smothered with cheese and gravy, tater tots on the side. She was a new hire, and he'd interacted with her a grand total of four times, but she smiled at him as if they were the best of friends. Something she hadn't done during his last three visits. He wondered if she'd looked him up and found out how much he was worth.

Wouldn't be the first time.

"Thank you," he muttered.

"You are so welcome, honey."

"Get a room," Jessie Kay said under her breath.

The waitress pretended not to hear and bent down to whisper into his ear, "You want to put in an order for dessert? We're about to sell out of our world-famous brownie pie, but I'll put one aside if you'd like…"

"Yes." His gaze returned to Jessie Kay. "I suddenly have a craving for something sweet."

"Well, then, maybe you'd like a side of me instead?" With a wink, the waitress sauntered away to help another table.

Jessie Kay took a bite of her burger. Her eyes closed, and she groaned the most rapturous sound of satisfaction. "Is this the best thing I've ever eaten? No." She scooped up a dollop of gravy with the tip of her finger and sucked it into her mouth. "But try to take it away from me, and I will cold-bloodedly murder you."

West had to fight a sudden grin, oddly charmed by her brashness. Unlike the waitress, he'd never had to wonder about her motives. She enjoyed what she enjoyed, disliked what she disliked, and wanted what she wanted. Very little else ever factored into her decisions.

"Try to take it away from her," Brook Lynn whispered to Jase. "Help me win the bet. Please, please, please."

Jase's brows winged into the locks of hair hanging over his forehead. "Victory is more important than my life?"

"At this precise moment? Yes!"

The way they were together, leaning into each other, totally at ease, playful, flirty, assured of the other's affections, made West envious. Made him miss Tessa more than usual—her laugh, the way she broke into song at random times and danced around the room. He more easily forgot the hard times, when she'd sunk into a deep depression and refused to eat or leave their bed.

Jessie Kay bumped her shoulder against his. "Hey. You never spoke up at the arena. You *are* paying for everything, right?"

"Right."

She raised her arm, signaling the waitress. "I'm gonna need one of these to go." She gave her sandwich a little wave. "Oh, and a dessert of my own. The brownie pie, to be exact. And don't try to tell me you're sold out. Bad things will happen."

"But—"

She hiked her thumb in West's direction. "Everything goes on his tab. He *insisted*."

"Sure thing." The waitress pursed her lips and hurried off.

"Happy place," Brook Lynn muttered.

"What?" Jessie Kay gazed around the table. "What'd I do this time?"

Brook Lynn heaved a sigh. "Just because someone else is paying doesn't mean you should order the lobster."

Those bedroom blues brightened. "They have lobster?"

"Happy place. Happy place."

Jessie Kay threw a tot at her sister. "Hey! I love you, and my lifelong goal is to show you just how much, but that's not going to stop me from shaking your brain out of your ear if you don't tell me whether or not they have lobster."

"They do not."

Jessie Kay's shoulders hunched with disappointment, and West had to fight another grin. She might not like him for his money, but she sure wasn't afraid to spend it. Strangely enough, he liked her more for it. She didn't give a shit about his opinion of her. A singular experience.

The waitress reappeared, pouting at him. "Bad news. Because your sister demanded the last brownie pie, the only dessert we have left is the s'mores trifle. It's really good though. That okay with you, gorgeous?"

"Sister?" Jessie Kay scowled. "Do I really look like his sister? I clearly come from grade-A stock while his ancestors made a few poor choices along the way."

Singular creature. "Yes," he told the waitress. "I'll take the s'mores trifle, but make sure you add extra marshmallows."

THE NEXT WEEK flew by, with only a few necessary adjustments to West's schedule. Adjustments he made only because he'd found his next relationship. Monica Gentry, owner of Bodies by Monica.

She'd shown up at WOH Industries on Wednesday, hoping to hire him to film her first workout video, not realizing he only created computer programs, video games and animated commercials. They'd had lunch instead.

He'd found something familiar about her, but when he'd looked her up later that night, he'd realized he knew nothing about her. What he learned: A handful of her former employees hated her. They'd posted scathing reviews about her leadership style, calling her intense and neurotic. But who wasn't neurotic?

And really, she'd had to be fierce to build her gym franchise from the ground up. A feat he admired. He and Beck had had to claw their way over, under and through wall after wall of rejection; but all the while West had continued creating games and programs and Beck had continued making calls and pitches, going door-to-door until Dane Michaelson of MG&E paid millions for exclusive rights to his flow software, a program tracking oil and natural gas from the ground to its buyer. Not only had the deal put WOH Industries in the crosshairs of other business, but Dane had become a close friend, even introducing West to Strawberry Valley, his hometown, which had led West to introduce Jase to the town when the desire to move struck.

West glanced at the clock on his nightstand. 7:59 a.m. Beck's wedding was set to take place in three hours, one minute.

He stood, made his bed, then showered for ten minutes, towel-dried for two, shaved for another ten and when he dressed, he ditched the usual Saturday-morning soccer gear in favor of a tux.

He'd never thought this day would come and once upon a time he would have bet the bulk of his fortune Beck would remain forever single. Enter Harlow. The black-haired beauty had obsessed the guy from moment one, and in the end, he'd stepped up to be a better man for her.

Would I have stepped up for Tessa if she'd survived the crash?

The real question: Would he have gotten clean?

During her depressions, nothing he'd said or done had helped her. Guilt and frustration had eaten at him and more often than not, he'd ended up doubling his hit. And his hangover. And his bad mood. His bad mood had only fed hers. A poisoned cycle.

He glanced at the clock. 8:40 a.m. Right on time. Yesterday he'd called and asked Monica to accompany him to the wedding. She was an attractive woman in her late twenties, and she fit his usual criteria. Uncomplicated, eager, and he could take her or leave her. He didn't crave her more than air to breathe and when they were apart, he didn't wish they were together.

He stalked into the kitchen where Beck stood at the stove, flipping pancakes with a surprisingly steady hand, the features many had referred to as "half angelic, half demonic" utterly relaxed and—joyous?

West took a seat at the table. "This is weird. You should be freaking out, demanding I help you sneak out of the country. Instead you're making breakfast."

His friend smiled, a peek at the angelic side. "I'm giving Harlow my name, legally binding her to my side. Why would I freak out?"

West could think of several reasons. "Your life will be forever altered. You'll be set on a new, uncharted path and your happiness will be inexorably tied to someone else's."

"I mentioned Harlow will be legally bound to me, right? My life will be forever altered in the best way. I'll traverse that new, uncharted path with her rather than alone, and my happiness is already inexorably tied to her. She's my other half."

He envied his friend. He couldn't imagine being so optimistic. Not by marrying Tessa. Not by sleeping with Monica. Not even by sleeping with Jessie Kay.

Something low in his gut curled with heat. Maybe he'd feel a *little* optimism if he had the blonde in his bed.

He'd purposely avoided her all week, hadn't so much as ordered a sandwich. Anytime she'd come up in conversation, he'd left the room. If he'd thought about her, he'd quickly distracted himself with work or exercise.

He'd worked and exercised *a lot*.

To his consternation, she'd remained at the forefront of his mind, a fascination he couldn't shake. He'd even considered detouring from his usual MO—a feat in and of itself—and sleeping with her once, just once. No harm, no foul.

Problem was "just once" had never worked out for him in the past.

Beck slid a stack of pancakes in front of him, saying, "You've been spacing out a lot lately, thinking about Jessie Kay." A statement rather than a question. "Don't try to deny it. I recognize the signs. A glaze of hunger in the eyes. Tightness around the mouth. A muscle jumping in the jaw. Jase had the same look when he met Brook

Lynn. I'm made of stronger stuff, of course, and managed to keep my cool with Harlow."

"No, I—"

"Even now your hands are clenched."

West studied his hands—yep, they were clenched. He eased the pressure on his fingers, saying, "Don't kid yourself. You were practically foaming at the mouth with Harlow."

"You do realize you're describing yourself right now, yes?" Beck didn't give him time to reply. "Why are you resisting your smart-ass Southern belle anyway? If you think Jase and I care—"

"I don't." He leaned back in his chair, crossed his arms. "Would you resent me if you found out I'd slept with Harlow before you fell for her?"

A light sprang to life in Beck's eyes. "Ah. I get it. You're afraid you'll get possessive of your girl and pissy with your bros."

West adjusted his cuff links, gave a clipped nod.

"As Jessie Kay would say, you're letting the horse out of the stall before the race has even started." Beck tossed back a bite of pancake. "Let's say you spent years with Harlow, banging the hell out of her. Today, this moment, it wouldn't affect how I feel about either of you. You were her past, and I'll always be her future. I love you both. I need you both. I'll take you both however I can get you."

An ache razed his chest. Were things really that simple?

"What's doing?" Jase padded into the kitchen. His dark hair stuck out in spikes. He was shirtless, wearing only a pair of faded sweatpants.

"West is deciding whether or not to make a move on Jessie Kay," Beck replied.

"I change my vote to no. Unless you're going to give her a real shot." Jase scratched his chest. "She's better for you than she ever was for us, but there will be serious aftermath when you dump her."

When, not if. The end was never in question.

West pursed his lips. "You handled the aftermath of your one-night stand just fine."

"And who says she'd want more than two months with him, anyway?" Beck asked. "Who says *she* won't dump *him*?"

Yes. Who said.

He scrubbed a hand down his face. "If I *did* date her, and I *did* dump her, and there *was* aftermath, your girls would hate me."

Jase poured a glass of orange juice. "Agreed. Brook Lynn can forgive anything—except an insult to her sister."

"But the girls love us and wouldn't try to block you from our lives," Beck said.

"Is that what's had your panties in such a twist?" Jase asked.

"Maybe." Agitated, West glanced at his wristwatch. Nine-sixteen. Shit. He'd planned to leave the house by nine-ten. "I've got to pick up Monica. I'll meet you guys at the church."

He made up the lost minutes on the road. He'd taken defensive driving classes a few years ago as research for a video game, and the skills he'd learned had come in handy ever since.

As he parked in Monica's driveway, his phone beeped. He glanced at the screen, his gut tightening when he saw Jessie Kay's name.

Which pair do you prefer?

Two photos accompanied the text. The first, a glittery heel with silk flowers sewn over the ankle strap. The second, a plain white flat.

He wrote back: Why does my preference matter?

Because your best friend is getting married & the woman he loves wants every detail to be perfect. You know him better than anyone else so… ☺ ☺ ☺

Your shoes are part of those perfect details?

Oh, those are Harlow's shoes. She can't decide between fashion & comfort, even though no one but Beck will see her feet—& he won't see them till he strips her down & gives her the business. I should know, right!

His grip flexed on the phone. She loved reminding him of her past, didn't she?

Then her next text came in and he forgot why he was irritated with her.

THESE are mine. ☺ ☺

The accompanying photo revealed black hooker heels with a fat red bow perched on the ankle. A present ready to be unwrapped. With his teeth. After he stripped her and tossed her on the bed.

Sex fantasy about Jessie Kay? Now? *Really?* He punched the wheel, the horn releasing a short but thunderous blast.

A few seconds later, Monica strode out the door, and

he felt like a total douche for not greeting her properly. Despite the frigid temperature, she wore a little black dress with spaghetti straps and a hem that ended a few inches below her pantyline. No hat, coat or gloves to keep her warm, proving she placed fashion before comfort. She didn't race to the car but held up her index finger to demand he wait.

Having already budgeted for the standard fifteen-minute time suck all women required despite knowing when he would arrive, he gave her a curt nod. He could have followed her inside the house, a beautiful Craftsman-style bungalow with three stories and a wraparound porch, but he popped a caramel candy in his mouth and stayed put. Even though he'd expected the wait, the lack of respect always annoyed him.

He and Monica would be discussing it—and his expectations—tonight. If she proved amenable to his two-month time limit, the countdown on their relationship would begin. He would gift her with a wristwatch, and expect her to use it. They would go to bed, and by morning, he would forget he'd ever desired Jessie Kay.

His friends might approve of her, of them, but the risks were still too great, the rewards not great enough.

He sent her another text: Tell Harlow to go w/ out a bra & Beck won't ever even glance at her feet.

Like a puss, he waited for a response. One that never came. He wanted to call her, and would have given in to temptation if Monica hadn't bounded outside at long last. He checked his watch. Seventeen minutes. His sense of annoyance only intensified as he entered the cold to open her door for her.

Though her teeth were chattering, she paused to kiss

his cheek before sliding inside. "Will I do?" she asked after he settled behind the wheel.

"You are flawless." And she was. Nothing out of place, her makeup red-carpet worthy. Her dress every man's wet dream.

So why am I not reacting to her?

"Oh, I wish." She smoothed a hand along the hem of the dress. "I'd hoped to wow you, but my hair wouldn't cooperate, and no matter how many hours I worked out, I couldn't lose the extra pound I packed on."

False modesty? Or straight-up female crazy?

Jessie Kay would have said something like, *I know! You don't deserve me.* And he would have smiled, charmed. Always freaking charmed. But he didn't pick his girlfriends for companionship, so he remained silent.

Monica's gaze swept over him, and he thought he glimpsed a hint of the intensity some of her former employees had mentioned. "Look at you. Sex on a stick and absolutely delicious."

"Thank you."

She frowned at him. Waiting for him to protest?

"Seriously." Her voice lowered, a whisper that drifted through the vehicle. "I'm not sure I'll be able to keep my hands to myself."

How would Jessie Kay react if Monica petted him during the ceremony? With jealousy? Or indifference?

Jealousy, pretty please. He wanted to see jealousy on her so badly he shook, even though he had no right to the desire. No right to keep thinking about her. They weren't together. In fact, he'd done everything in his power to push her away. He'd snapped at her, baited her. Insulted her time and time again.

I suck.

He'd been a total ass to her, and right then, right at that moment, it absolutely shamed him. His momma hadn't raised him better, but only an idiot wouldn't learn on his own.

Observe. Understand. Act.

Observe: He owed her an apology.

Understand: So he craved her. So what? So he wouldn't let himself have her. So the hell what? That wasn't her problem; it was his. He had no right to treat her like an archnemesis.

Act: He would offer that apology, and he'd do it with a smile. Afterward, there would be no more picking fights with her. No more snide remarks about *anything*. He would keep his distance, and he would be polite. He would wrap himself in Monica, literally and figuratively.

For the first time since moving to Strawberry Valley, his life would go back to normal.

CHAPTER FIVE

WEST HAD BROUGHT a date.

The realization hit Jessie Kay like a bolt of lightning in a freak storm. Great! Wonderful! While she'd opted not to bring Daniel, and thus make West the only single person present—and embarrassingly alone—he'd chosen his next two-month "relationship" and hung Jessie Kay out to dry.

And she knew the girl was a two-monther. West didn't date outside the parameters of his crazy.

Jessie Kay stood in a hidden doorway in back of the sanctuary, one usually only used by church personnel. Harlow had asked for—cough, banshee-screeched, cough—a status report, so Jessie Kay had abandoned her precious curling iron in order to sneak a peek at the guys.

Scowling, she pulled her phone from the pocket of her dress with every intention of texting Daniel. Oops. She'd missed a text.

Sunny: Party 2nite?????

She made a mental note to respond to Sunny later and drafted her note to Daniel.

I'm at the church. How fast can you get here? I need a friend/date for Harlow's wedding

A response didn't come right away. Maybe he was still in bed. He'd gone on a hot date last night and the girl had stayed the night with him. She knew because he'd texted Jessie Kay to ask how early he could give "the snore queen" the boot.

Sooo glad I never hooked up with him.

Finally, a vibration.

Any other time I'd race to your rescue, even though weddings are snooze-fests. Today I'm in the city on a job

He'd started some kind of high-risk security firm with a few of his Army buddies.

Her: Fine. You suck. I clearly need to rethink our friendship

Daniel: I'll make it up to you, swear. Want to have dinner later???

She stored her phone without responding, adding his name to her mental note. If he wasn't going to ignore his responsibilities whenever she had a minor need, he deserved to suffer for a little while.

Of its own accord, her gaze returned to West. The past week, she'd seen him only twice. Both times, she'd gone to the farmhouse to help her sister with sandwiches and casseroles, and he'd taken one look at her, grabbed his keys and driven off.

Would it have killed him to acknowledge her presence by calling her by some hateful name, per usual? After all, he'd had the nerve to flirt with her at the diner, to look at her as if she'd stripped naked and begged him to have *her* for dessert. And now he ignored her?

Men! This one in particular.

Her irritation grew as he introduced his date to Kenna Starr and her fiancé, Dane Michaelson. Kenna was a stunning redhead who'd always been Brook Lynn's partner in crime. The girl who'd done what Jessie Kay hadn't, saving her sister every time she'd gotten into trouble.

Next, he made the introduction to Daphne Roberts, the mother of Jase's nine-year-old daughter, Hope, then Brad Lintz, Daphne's boyfriend.

Jase and Beck joined the happy group, but the brunette never looked away from West, as if he was speaking the good Lord's gospel. Her adoration was palpable.

A sharp pang had Jessie Kay clutching her chest. *Too young for a heart attack*.

Indigestion?

Yeah. Had to be.

The couple should have looked odd together. West was too tall and the brunette was far too short for him. A skyscraper next to a one-story house. But somehow, despite their height difference, they actually complemented each other.

And really, the girl's adoration had to be good for him, buoying him the way Daniel's praise often buoyed Jessie Kay. Only on a much higher level, considering the girl was more than a friend to West.

Crap! Jessie Kay was actually kind of…happy for West. As horribly terribly insanely awful as his childhood had been, he deserved a nice slice of contentment.

Look at me, acting like a big girl.

West wrapped his arm around the brunette's waist,

drawing her closer, and Jessie Kay's nails dug into her palms.

I'm happy for him, remember? Besides, big girls didn't want to push other women in front of a speeding bus. Well, they might want to, but they never followed through.

Jessie Kay's phone buzzed. She checked the screen.

Brook Lynn: Hurry! Bridezilla is on a rampage!!!

Her: Tell the soon-to-be Mrs. Ockley the guys look amazing in their tuxes—no stains or tears yet—& the room is gorgeous. Or just tell her NOTHING HAS FREAKING CHANGED

The foster bros had gone all out even though the ceremony was to be a small and intimate affair. There were red and white roses at the corner of every pew, and in front of the pulpit was an ivory arch with wispy jewel-encrusted lace.

With a sigh, she added an adorable smiley face to her message, because it was cute and it said *I'm not yelling at you. My temper is not engaged.*

Send.

Brook Lynn: Harlow wants a play-by-play of the action

Fine.

Her: Beck is now speaking w/ Pastor Washington. Jase, Dane, Kenna, Daphne & Brad are engaged in conversation, while Hope is playing w/ her doll on the floor. Happy?

She didn't add that West was focused on the stunning brunette, who was still clinging to his side.

The girl...she had a familiar face—*where have I seen her?*—and a body so finely honed Jessie Kay wanted to stuff a few thousand Twinkies down her throat just to make it fair for the rest of the female population. Her designer dress was made of ebony silk and hugged her curves like a besotted lover.

Like West would be doing tonight?

Grinding her teeth, Jessie Kay slid her gaze over her own gown, one she'd sewn in her spare time. Not bad—actually kind of awesome—but compared to Great Bod's delicious apple it was a rotten orange.

Jealousy struck her again, and struck harder. Dang it! Jealousy was stupid. Jessie Kay was no can of dog food in the looks department. In fact, she was well able to hold her own against anyone, anywhere, anytime. But...but...

A lot of baggage came with her.

West suddenly stiffened, as if he sensed he was being watched. He turned in Jessie Kay's direction. Her heart slamming against her ribs with enough force to break free and escape, she darted into Harlow's bridal chamber—the choir room.

Harlow finished curling her thick mass of hair as Brook Lynn gave her lips a final swipe of gloss.

"Welcome to my nightmare," Jessie Kay announced. "I might as well put in rollers, pull on a pair of mom jeans and buy ten thousand cats." Cats! Love! "I'm officially an old maid without any decent prospects."

Brook Lynn wrinkled her brow. "What are you talking about?"

"Everyone is here, including West and his date. I'm the only single person in our group, which means you guys have to set me up with your favorite guy friends. Obviously I'm looking for a nine or ten. Make it happen. Please and thank you."

Harlow went still. "West brought a date? Who is she?"

Had a coil of steam just risen from her nostrils? "Just some girl."

Harlow pressed her hands against a stomach that had to be dancing with nerves. "I don't want *just some girl* at my first wedding."

"You planning your divorce to Beck already?"

Harlow scowled at her. "Not funny. You know we're planning a larger ceremony next year."

Jessie Kay raised her hands, palms out. "You're right, you're right. And you totally convinced me. I'll kick the bitch out pronto." *And I'll love every second of it—on Harlow's behalf.*

"No. No. I don't want a scene." Stomping her foot, Harlow added, "What was West thinking? He's ruined *everything.*"

Ooo-kay. A wee bit dramatic, maybe. "I doubt he was thinking at all. If that boy ever had an idea, it died of loneliness." Too much? "Anyway. I'm sure you could use a glass or six of champagne. I'll open the bottle for us—for you. You're welcome."

A wrist corsage hit her square in the chest.

"This is *my* day, Jessica Dillon." Harlow thumped her chest. "Mine! You will remain stone-cold sober, or I will remove your head, place it on a stick and wave it around while your sister sobs over your bleeding corpse."

Wow. "That's pretty specific, but I feel you. No alcohol for me, ma'am." She gave a jaunty salute. "I mean, no alcohol for me, Miss Bridezilla, sir."

"Ha-ha." Harlow morphed from fire-breathing dragon

to fairytale princess in an instant, twirling in a circle. "Now, stop messing around and tell me how amazing I look. And don't hesitate to use words like *exquisite* and *magical*."

The hair at her temples had been pulled back, the rest hanging to her elbows in waves so dark they glimmered blue in the light. The gown had capped sleeves and a straight bustline with cinched-in waist and pleats that flowed all the way to the floor, covering the sensible flats she'd chosen based on West's advice. "You look... exquisitely magical."

"Magically exquisite," Brook Lynn said with a nod.

"My scars aren't hideous?" Self-conscious, Harlow smoothed a hand over the multitude of jagged pink lines running between her breasts, courtesy of an attack she'd miraculously survived as a teenage girl.

"Are you kidding? Those scars make you look badass." Jessie Kay curled a few more pieces of hair, adding, "I'm bummed my skin is so flawless."

Harlow snorted. "Yes, let's shed a tear for you."

Jessie Kay gave her sister the stink eye. "You better not be like this for your wedding. I won't survive two of you."

Brook Lynn held up her well-manicured hands, all innocence.

"Well." She glanced at a wristwatch she wasn't wearing, doing her best impression of West. "We've got twenty minutes before the festivities kick off. Need anything?"

Harlow's hands returned to her stomach, the color draining from her cheeks in a hurry. "Yes. Beck."

Blinking, certain she'd misheard, she fired off a quick

"Excuse me?" Heck. Deck. Neck. Certainly not Beck. "Grooms aren't supposed to see—"

"I need Beck." Harlow stomped her foot. *"Now."*

"Have you changed your mind?" Brook Lynn asked. "If so, we'll—"

"No, no. Nothing like that." Harlow launched into a quick pace, marching back and forth through the room. "I just… I need to see him. He hates change, and this is the biggest one of all, and I need to talk to him before I totally—flip—out. Okay? All right?"

"This isn't that big a change, honey. Not really." Who would have guessed Jessie Kay would be a voice of reason in a situation like this? Or *any* situation. "You guys live together already."

"Beck!" she insisted. "Beck, Beck, Beck."

"Temper tantrums are not attractive." Jessie Kay shared a concerned look with her sister, who nodded. "All right. One Beck coming up." As fast as her heels would allow, she made her way back to the sanctuary.

She purposely avoided West's general direction, focusing only on the groom. "Harlow has decided to throw millions of years' worth of tradition out the window. She wants to see you without delay. Are you wearing a cup? I'd wear a cup. Good luck."

He'd been in the middle of a conversation with Jase, and like Harlow, he quickly paled. "Is something wrong?" He didn't stick around for an answer, rushing past Jessie Kay without actually judging the distance between them, almost knocking her over.

As she stumbled, West flew over and latched on to her wrist to help steady her. The contact nearly buckled her knees. His hands were calloused, his fingers firm. His strength was unparalleled and his skin hot enough to burn. Electric tingles rushed through her, the world around her fading until they were the only two people in existence.

Fighting for every breath, she stared up at him. His gaze dropped to her lips and narrowed, his focus savagely carnal and primal in its possessiveness, as if he saw nothing else, either—wanted nothing and no one else ever. But as he slowly lowered his arm and stepped away from her, the world snapped back into focus.

The bastard brought a date.

Right. She cleared her throat, embarrassed by the force of her reaction to him. "Thanks."

A muscle jumped in his jaw. A sign of anger? "May I speak with you privately?"

Uh… "Why?"

"Please."

What the what now? Had Lincoln West actually said the word *please* to her? *Her?* "Whatever you have to say to me—" an insult, no doubt "—can wait. You should return to your flavor of the year." Opting for honesty, she grudgingly added, "You guys look good together."

The muscle jumped again, harder, faster. "You think we look good together?"

"Very much so." Two perfect people. "I'm not being sarcastic, if that's what you're getting at. Who is she?"

"Monica Gentry. Fitness guru based in the city."

Well. That explained the sense of familiarity. And the body. Jessie Kay had once briefly considered thinking about exercising along with Monica's video. Then she'd found a bag of Kit Kat Minis and the insane idea went back to hell where it belonged. "She's a good choice for you. Beautiful. Successful. Driven. And despite what you think about me, despite the animosity between us, I want you happy. I know! I'm as shocked as you are."

And she didn't want him happy just because he'd had a crappy childhood, she realized. He was a part of her family, for better or worse. A girl made exceptions for family. Even the douche bags.

His eyes narrowed to tiny slits. "We're going to speak privately, Jessie Kay, whether you agree or not. The only decision you need to make is whether or not you'll walk out of this room. I'm more than willing to carry you."

A girl also had the right to smack family. "You're just going to tell me to change my hideous dress, and I'm going to tell you I'm fixing to cancel your birth certificate."

When Harlow had told her to wear whatever she wanted, Jessie Kay had done just that, creating a blood red, off-the-shoulder, pencil-skirt dress that molded to her curves like a second skin…made from leftover material for drapes.

Scarlett O'Hara has nothing on me!

Jessie Kay was proud of her work, but she wasn't blind to its flaws. Years had passed since she'd sewn anything, and her skills were rusty.

West gave her another once—twice—over as fire smoldered in his eyes. "Why would I tell you to change?" His voice dipped, nothing but smoke and gravel as he added, "You and that dress are a fantasy come true."

Uh, what the what now? Had Lincoln West just called her *a fantasy*?

Almost can't process…

"Maybe you should take me to the ER. I'm pretty sure I just had a brain aneurism." She rubbed her temples. "I'm hallucinating."

"Hallucinating isn't a symptom, funny girl." He ran his tongue over his teeth, snatched her hand and while Monica called his name, dragged Jessie Kay to a small room in back. A cleaning closet, the air sharp with antiseptic. What little space was available was consumed by overstuffed shelves.

"When did you decide to switch careers and become a caveman?" she asked.

"When you decided to switch careers and become a femme fatale."

Have mercy on my soul.

He released her to run his fingers through his hair, leaving the strands in sexy spikes around his head. "Listen. I owe you an apology for the way I've treated you in the past. Even the way I've acted today. I shouldn't have manhandled you, and I'm very sorry."

Her eyes widened. Seriously, what the heck had happened to this man? In five minutes, he'd upended everything she'd come to expect from him.

And he wasn't done! "I'm sorry for every hurtful thing I've ever said to you. I'm sorry for making you feel bad about who you are and what you've done. I'm sorry—"

"Stop. Just stop." She placed her hands over her ears in case he failed to heed her order. "I don't understand what's happening."

He gently removed her hands and held on tight to her wrists. "What's happening? I'm owning my mistakes and hoping you're in a forgiving mood."

"You want to be my friend?" The words squeaked from her.

"Yes, I think I do."

He *thinks*? "Here's the problem. You're a dog and I'm a cat, and we're never going to get along."

One corner of his mouth quirked with lazy amusement, causing a flutter in her pulse. "I think you're wrong…kitten."

Kitten. A freakishly adorable nickname, and absolutely perfect for her while also absolutely unexpected.

Oh, she'd known he'd give her one sooner or later. He and his friends were old school and enjoyed renaming the women in their lives. Jase always called Brook Lynn "angel" and Beck called Harlow everything from "beauty" to "hag," her initials. Well, HAG prewedding. But Jessie Kay had prepared herself for "demoness" or the always classic "bitch."

"Dogs and cats can be friends," he said, "especially when the dog minds his manners. I promise you, things will be different from now on."

"Well." Reeling, she could come up with no witty reply. "We could try, I guess."

"Good." His gaze dropped to her lips, heated a few more degrees. "Now all we have to do is decide what kind of friends we should be."

Her heart started kicking up a fuss again, breath abandoning her lungs. "What do you mean?"

"Text frequently? Call each other occasionally? Only speak when we're with our other friends?" He backed her into a shelf and cans rattled, threatening to fall. "Or should we be friends with benefits?"

Aaand the tingles returned, sweeping over her skin and sinking deep, deep into bone. Her entire body ached with need so powerful it nearly felled her. How long since a man had focused the full scope of his masculinity on her? Too long and never like this. West took everything to the next level. Somehow he reduced her to a quivering mess of femininity and whoremones.

"I vote…we only speak when we're with our other friends," she said, embarrassed by the breathless tremor in her voice.

"What if I want all of it?" He placed his hands at her temples and several of the cans rolled to the floor. "The texts, the calls…and the benefits."

"No?" A question? Really? "No to the last." Better. "You have a date."

He scowled at her as if *she'd* done something wrong. "See, that's the real problem, kitten. I don't want her. I want you."

WEST CALLED HIMSELF a thousand kinds of fool. He'd planned to apologize, return to the sanctuary, witness his friend's wedding and start the countdown with Monica. The moment he'd gotten Jessie Kay inside the closet, her pecans-and-cinnamon scent in his nose, those plans burned to ash. Only one thing mattered.

Getting his hands on her.

From day one, she'd been a vertical g-force too strong to deny, pulling, pulling, *pulling* him into a bottomless vortex. He'd fought it every minute of every day since meeting her, and he'd gotten nowhere fast. Why not give in? Stop the madness?

Just once…

"We've been dancing around this for months," he said. "I'm scum for picking here and now to hash this out with you, and I'll care tomorrow. Right now, I think it's time we did something about our feelings."

"I don't…" She began to soften against him, only to snap to attention. "No. Absolutely not. I can't."

"You *won't*." *But I can change your mind...*

She nibbled on her bottom lip.

Something he would kill to do. So he did it. He leaned into her, caught her bottom lip between his teeth and ran the plump morsel through. "Do you want me, Jessie Kay?"

Her eyes closed for a moment, a shiver rocking her. "You say you'll care tomorrow, so I'll give you an answer then. As for today, I... I... I'm leaving." But she made no effort to move away, and he knew. She did want him. As badly as he wanted her. "Yes. Leaving. Any moment now..."

Acting without thought—purely on instinct—he placed his hands on her waist and pressed her against the hard line of his body. "I want you to stay. I want you, period."

"West." The new tremor in her voice injected his every masculine instinct with adrenaline, jacking him up. "You said it yourself. You're scum. This is wrong."

Anticipation raced denial to the tip of his tongue, and won by a photo finish. "Do you care?" He caressed his way to her ass and cupped the perfect globes, then urged her forward to rub her against the long length of his erection. The woman who'd tormented his days and invaded his dreams moaned a decadent sound of satisfaction, and it did something to him. Made his need for her *worse*.

She wasn't what he should want, but somehow she'd become everything he could not resist, and he was tired, so damn tired, of walking, hell, running away from her.

"Do you?" he insisted. "Say yes, and *I'll* be the one to leave. I don't want you to regret this." He wanted her desperate for more.

She looked away from him, licked her lips. "Right at this moment? No. I don't care." As soft as a whisper.

Triumph filled him, his clasp on her tightening.

"But tomorrow…" she added.

Yes. Tomorrow. He wasn't the only one who'd been running from the sizzle between them, but today, with her admission ringing in his ears, he wasn't letting her get away. One look at her, that's all it had taken to ruin his plans. Now she would pay the price. Now she would make everything better.

"I *will* regret it," she said. "This is a mistake I've made too many times in the past." Different emotions played over her features. Features so delicate he was consumed by the need to protect her from anything and anyone… but himself.

He saw misery, desire, fear, regret, hope and anger. The anger concerned him. This Southern belle could knock a man's testicles into his throat with a single swipe of her knee. Even still, West didn't walk away.

"For all we know, the world will end tomorrow. Let's focus on today. You tell me what you want me to do," he said, nuzzling his nose against her cheek, "and I'll do it."

More tremors rocked her. She traced her delicate hands up his tie and gave the knot a little shake, an action that was sexy, sweet and wicked all at once. "I want you…to go back to your date. You and I, we'll be friends as agreed, and we'll pretend this never happened." She pushed him, but he didn't budge.

His date. Yeah, he'd forgotten about Monica before Jessie Kay had mentioned her a few minutes ago. But then, he'd gotten used to forgetting everything whenever the luscious blonde entered a room. Everything about her consumed every part of him, and it was more than irritating, it was a sickness to be cured, an obstacle to be overcome and an addiction to be avoided. If they did this, he would suffer from his own regrets, but there was no question he would love the ride.

He bunched up the hem of her skirt, his fingers brushing the silken heat of her bare thigh. Her breath hitched, driving him wild. "You've told me what you *think* you should want me to do." He rasped the words against her mouth, hovering over her, not touching her but teasing with what could be. "Now tell me what you really want me to do."

Navy blues peered up at him, beseeching; the fight drained out of her, leaving only need and raw vulnerability. "I'm only using you for sex—said no guy ever. But that's what you're going to do. Isn't it? You're going to use me and lose me, just like the others."

Her features were utterly *ravaged*, and in that moment, he hated himself. Because she was right. Whether he took her for a single night or every night for two months, the end result would be the same. No matter how much it hurt her—no matter how much it hurt *him*—he would walk away.

CHAPTER SIX

DANGER SIGNS FLASHED inside Jessie Kay's mind. Before, she'd wondered about West's feelings for her. Why he was so rude to her and why he'd tried to charm her at the diner. Now she had a pretty good idea. He wanted her, but he didn't want to want her. The same way she wanted him but didn't want to want him.

He couldn't have been clearer about his desire to go all the way if he'd pressed a massive erection between her legs—which he had. Even now she gasped with need, attempting to cut all ties with logic, common sense and self-preservation.

I know your parents don't want us to be together, Anna Grace. I'm from the wrong side of the tracks and you're...you. The one every girl wants to be, the one every boy wants to date. But when it comes to the man you marry, only one thing should matter. Who is willing to do anything to make you happy? That's me. I'm that man.

"Are you wanting a one-night stand?" Jessie Kay asked, hoping...praying for a denial.

"Yes." West's voice was nothing but a rasp.

Well. His affirmation wasn't exactly a surprise, but it sure was disappointing. He would take her here and now, then return to his date, acting as if nothing had happened. Because it hadn't—not really. Not for him. Jessie Kay meant nothing to him. A moment of pleasure, easily forgotten.

I'm an appetizer, she's a meal.

I'm the drive-through, she's the five-star restaurant.

I'm the slut a man can bang, never the girl he'll take home to momma.

The knowledge hurt Jessie Kay deep inside, pouring salt on old wounds that festered. West hadn't asked her to be his date—and he never would.

"Do you have many of those?" she asked, trying to control her temper. "One-night stands, I mean."

"No." The grip he had on the hem of her dress tightened, pulling the material down, revealing the upper edge of her bra. "You would be the first."

The firmness of his tone said she would also be the last. "Why make an exception for me? Because I'm *special*?"

He frowned at her sneering tone. "Because we'll be good together. Because I can't stop thinking about you." Pretty words, but not really an answer. "I'll take care of you, Jessie Kay."

Oh, he would, she had no doubt about that. But he would only take care of her until he finished with her and zipped up his pants. "Then what? We pretend it never happened?"

His eyes narrowed, flashes of fire under his lids. "Yes," he hissed. "We pretend. We become the friends we were meant to be."

Something inside her snapped, and she pounded her fists into his shoulders. "You think I'm easy to get and easy to walk away from. Well, I think you're a bastard. How about that?"

"I think you're a woman with needs. I know I'm a man with needs, and I know we can help each other out."

Help each other out. The phrase echoed inside her mind, again and again, more insulting each time. "I don't need your help, West. I take care of myself *very well.*"

"But you'll have more fun with me."

"Don't be so sure. You haven't seen the things these fingers can do."

His fury switched direction, now projecting a take-off-your-panties heat that singed her to the bone.

"I'm not looking for a one-night stand, or even a two-month affair," she said. Not that he'd offered the latter. She swatted his shoulders again, just for good measure, and this time, he stepped back, putting distance between them. "I'm especially not interested in becoming your side slice."

"You wouldn't be a side slice." His lids lowered, looking heavy, and his lips softened. "You'd be the full meal."

Dang him! She shivered. "Your girlfriend is waiting outside this room. You plan to screw me and return to her. You'll sleep with her tonight."

"Monica isn't yet my girlfriend."

Jessie Kay had begun to melt—*the brunette isn't his girlfriend; there's a chance I can win him*—only to stiffen. *Isn't yet*, he'd said. Yet. He intended to move forward with the girl. More than that, he hadn't disputed the rest of Jessie Kay's claims. He *would* return to Monica. He *would* sleep with her tonight.

Scratch an itch with me now, return to regular programming later. Maybe, like Jase and Beck, he'd even decide to marry the girl who came after Jessie Kay.

Dark emotion flooded her, choking her until she almost couldn't breathe past the gloom. "The next man I'm with will value me. I will mean something to him."

A flare of his nostrils. "You mean something to me."

"Don't kid yourself. If I meant anything at all, you never would have put me in this position."

He ran his hand down his face and backed away another step.

"Do you have any idea how bad it hurt when your friends discarded me, as if I'd dared to overstay my welcome? No," she said with a shake of her head. "You don't, because you don't know me. You can't. Otherwise you wouldn't be trying to do the same thing."

He shoved his hands in his pockets, glaring down at his feet. "You're wrong," he said, and for once, there was no emotion in his voice. "I do know what it's like to be discarded. But it doesn't stop the ache I have for you, the constant hunger nothing else has been able to satisfy."

She couldn't allow herself to focus on those words. *Doesn't stop the ache I have for you...* She'd cave—could already feel her resistance melting again. "You're telling me a woman actually cut you loose?"

"Many women, but not the way you think." He met her gaze dead-on, his features more ravaged by the second. "Not romantically."

"Then how—" Ohhh. Emotionally. His foster moms, probably. Used for a monthly check, only to be given up when the money stopped flowing? Dang it, the ache returned and she would have sold her soul for a chance to comfort the boy he'd been...the man he was. "You know being with me right now would be wrong. You said so."

"More and more, I don't care what's right. I just care about having you in my arms."

The raggedness of his tone was a hot caress that left

fire in its wake, burning her from the inside out. "Pretty words don't mean squat. Actions do."

Want to enjoy your future? Momma once asked. *Then treat your present with respect. Soon it will be your past.*

West reached out, traced a finger over the seam of her lips before cupping the back of her neck. "What if I offered you two months rather than a single night?"

Her mouth went dry. "Have you ever dated a woman longer?"

"Yes. Tessa."

"How long were you with her?"

"Three years."

"You remained faithful?" she asked.

"Of course."

"And since her, you've never dated a woman for more than two months?"

"That's right."

She latched on to his wrist with every intention of pushing him away, but she ended up clinging to him, desperate for an anchor as she drifted away in an endless sea of temptation. "You would still be with Tessa if she'd lived?"

A slight hesitation before he gave a clipped nod.

The hesitation intrigued her. "Why the time limit now?"

He closed his eyes as he drew in a long, drawn-out breath. "Others have asked the same thing, but I don't talk about it. Not with anyone."

"Too bad. Sharing your past and your secrets is something you do with friends—and the woman you claim to desire."

He stared at her, silent. Despite the overhead light illuminating him, darkness still managed to cling to him.

It was there in his eyes, ravaged and ravaging, shredding everything her desire for him had managed to revive, leaving her a hollowed-out, empty shell. The same feeling her parent's death had elicited. The same feeling she'd tried for years to fill and mask with parties and men, and oh, how easy it would be to slip back into old habits, to find solace in the familiar, if only for a little while.

"If you ever want to reconsider your answer," she whispered, "we can revisit the terms of our friendship. Right now, if you ask me for two months, I'll say no. I deserve more. I deserve better."

He nodded without hesitation. "You're right. You do." With lightning speed, he threw a hammer-like fist into the row of cans beside her, sending several flying into the wall behind the shelf, leaving cracks and holes in the plaster.

Despite the action, she knew he hadn't lost control of his temper. Control radiated from his every pore, pulled at the angle of his jaw and shoulders and held him in a rigid clasp, granting no quarter. He'd known what he was doing and had hoped…to what? Scare her? Send her fleeing?

Please. She'd angered this man time and time again, dishing as many insults as she'd received. Heck, she'd probably dished more. But he'd never threatened her physically. Not in word, and not in deed. He had his faults—a whole lot of faults—but violence against women wasn't one of them. If anything, he treated women with deference, opening car doors, pulling out chairs, even for his enemies.

"Feel better?" she asked.

"No." He pushed out a weighted breath. "But I do owe you yet another apology, kitten."

Shivers, tingles. Heat. "Stop calling me by that ridiculous nickname."

"You have claws. You're soft. And for just a second, I made you purr. You're a kitten, plain and simple. Now be a good kitty and allow me to offer that apology. I acted quixotically today—"

"Ugh. Big fancy words are stupid. They are *not* a turn-on." They were. They so were. "Talk to me like I'm five and failing your class."

His eyes narrowed. "Your nipples just hardened."

Lord save me. "First, you wouldn't talk to a five-year-old like that. Second, why the heck are you looking at my nipples? Stop."

"I'm a man, and they just sat up and said hello. What was I supposed to do? Ignore them?"

"Yes!"

"Why are big words such a turn-on to you?"

"Why is the sky blue?"

"Molecules in the air scatter blue light from the sun."

Aaand her nipples hardened further. Apparently, smart, smart-ass answers were also a turn-on.

"And now I need a drink," he muttered, scrubbing a hand down his face. "I'm not going to live through the day."

The way he'd said those words—*I need a drink*—pricked a land mine inside her head, the different emotions in his voice like shrapnel. Longing. Regret. Shame. Hatred.

"I know the score. You're a recovering drug addict, and alcohol is your gateway." He'd once stated her past so plainly; she saw nothing wrong with stating his in the same manner. Besides, she'd seen him drink once before, at a party he'd thrown in Tessa's honor. He'd not been a happy drunk. "You don't need a drink," she said, "you need a good, firm spanking."

Wary now, he rubbed at the back of his neck. "How did you know about the drugs?"

"I overheard Brook Lynn and Jase talking—when I pressed my ear to their door."

"Is that why you won't be with me? I'm a bad bet?"

"I won't be with you because you're an asshole with a mysterious time limit. And a girlfriend! I've decided to be angry on her behalf."

"She's not my—"

"But I don't believe for one second you're a man who will one day succumb to the dark allure of drugs. The strength you needed to get clean...sugar bear, *that* is a major turn-on."

He snorted, some of the tension leaving him. "You said friends share their pasts. I'll think about sharing mine with you, which is more than I've ever done for another."

Her heart skipped a beat. More than he'd done for another...more than she'd ever expected him to do for her.

"Just remember. Your past isn't as tragic as mine," she said, "so I can't possibly feel sorry for you."

"Mine is far worse than yours. You should bawl like a baby."

His hands settled on her hips and squeezed as if the foundation at his feet was crumbling and she was the only lifeline. A hold of possession, one that made her body liquefy even as her breasts swelled with a need she could no longer fight. Her spine softened and tilted forward, putting the most needy parts of her in contact with the most needy parts of him.

"Tell me…would you be the executor of the spanking?" He brushed the tip of his nose against hers, his warm breath fanning over her lips.

"If you were my man, trust me, I'd see to your discipline on a daily basis. I'm sweet like that." She ran her hands up the lapels of his jacket, hoping to mask her trembling. "And now, I'm leaving. This conversation can't go anywhere but the danger zone." She straightened his tie before heading for the door.

"Kitten," he called as she placed her hand on the knob.

She paused, part of her hoping he would close the distance, yank her against him and claim her lips, steal her breath, put his big, beautiful hands on her, all over her…finally ending the torment she'd lived with since the moment they'd met. The other part of her, the part that hoped he'd want her today, tomorrow and every day after refused to budge.

"What?" she asked with a tremor.

"You still owe me a sandwich."

THE WEDDING KICKED OFF forty-seven minutes late, screwing up more of West's schedule. The lack of order bothered him, a thorn in his side, but he kept his mouth shut. His friends were more important than anything else. And he had a distraction, his mind continually returning to the cleaning closet.

He'd offered Jessie Kay a one-night stand, and she'd responded with bitterness. Now he cursed the men who'd come before him. Yeah, even his friends. He then cursed himself. He hadn't slept with her, but he'd hurt her just the same when he'd suggested a hit-and-run. A

one-and-done. A bang-and-bail. No wonder she'd re-
buffed him so fervently.

Jase had been leaning against a wall when West
emerged, had looked him up and down and arched a
brow. "Is that for me? Dude, I'm flattered. I had no idea
you felt that way. All right, you caught me. I had an in-
kling. You know I'm engaged to Brook Lynn, right?"

West had punched him in the shoulder. "You *wish*
this was for you."

"Only in your dreams. Listen. Your date is causing
a scene, asking everyone where you are, searching the
entire building for you. You're lucky I'm such a good
friend or she would have burst in on you. Calm her down
before I'm forced to kick her out. I don't want Beck or
Harlow upset."

He'd nodded his thanks and gone in search of Monica.
She'd attempted to draw him into a conversation—*We
have so much in common. A love of schedules, caramels
and Mercedes*—but his taciturn demeanor had upset
her. And how did she know about the schedules and
candies? Google?

When he'd merely grunted one-word responses, she'd
snapped, "Who's the blonde you dragged away?"

As if she had a right to be jealous. Angry, yes. She
was his date, and he'd paid more attention to someone
else. But not jealous. Not yet.

"She's the bride's best friend." He'd offered no more.

Monica had taken it upon herself to approach Jessie Kay.

He'd almost called her back to his side, not wanting
the woman he found cloying conversing with the woman
he found fascinating—the woman he still wanted—but
he'd pressed his lips together in a mulish line.

When he'd first gotten Jessie Kay inside that closet, he'd almost gone up in flames, and it hadn't been long before the last of his restraint had burned away. He'd pressed her against those shelves, kissing her more than a want—it had been a need. But he'd resisted. For the rest of her life, she would have regretted the timing, and he would have regretted her regret.

Might have been worth it.

The soft curves of her body had conformed to the hard planes of his, and now he only ached worse. For release. For her.

No one else would do.

Having her was an obsession. A sickness no drugs or therapy could cure.

She was *already* an addiction, wasn't she.

He couldn't walk away, not this time; he needed more of a specific woman, would do almost anything for a single taste.

His hands curled into fists. He hated feeling helpless, of free-falling into the unknown. With no parachute, he would crash.

Sometimes, you couldn't walk away from a crash. You could only crawl.

Panic hit him, but he fought it, counting the seconds on his watch. *One, two...ten...twenty...forty...* He almost had himself under control when Beck and Harlow emerged from the choir room, both smiling jaw-cracking smiles. It was clear they'd done more than talk. A lot more. Once pristine, they now sported flushed skin, mussed hair and wrinkled clothes.

Harlow noticed the stares and knowing grins and lost a little of her glow. "Oh...uh."

"Harlow Adrienne Glass, Hag for short," Jessie Kay

exclaimed. "You sly little hussy. Seducing your groom while the pastor was waiting? Your lady balls are obviously bigger than mine. But let's compare just to be safe."

The flush returned to Harlow's skin, and she sputtered, but hardly anyone else noticed her reaction. They were too busy wagging fingers at Jessie Kay.

West marveled, suddenly seeing Jessie Kay in a new light. She'd taken center stage to cut through tension and draw attention away from her friend, hadn't she?

This girl...she definitely had a gooey marshmallow center.

And West definitely had a sweet tooth.

Harlow focused on the pastor, who was doing his best not to laugh. "We didn't...we wouldn't... I mean, we came close, but..." She buried her face in the hollow of Beck's neck. "Help me."

Beck rushed to the rescue, saying, "She attacked me, and I almost couldn't stop her from having her wicked way with me. We need to make an honest woman out of her as soon as possible, Pastor Washington. To preserve her tattered soul."

Harlow gasped and slapped his chest. "You wretch!"

Beck caught her hand, winked and kissed the center of her palm. "You wouldn't have me any other way, dumpling."

"I would. I so would."

Everyone took their proper place, Beck and Harlow moving under the arch, the pastor stepping in front of them. Jessie Kay and Brook Lynn lined up at Harlow's left while Jase and West lined up at Beck's right. Dane, Kenna, Daphne, Brad and Hope claimed the front pew, with Monica sitting on the second, her gaze resting on

West adoringly. Too adoringly for such a short acquaintance. He wished he'd resisted the urge to bring her.

Beck vowed to love, honor and cherish his woman, adding teasingly, "But I expect you to always obey me. I can't be budged on that. It's tradition."

Harlow laughed gaily, now utterly unburdened by the weight of worry. "I'll obey you in…never."

"Challenge accepted." Beck kissed her as if he couldn't go without her taste a second longer.

"Not yet, young man." Pastor Washington released a sigh of amusement and exasperation.

Beck didn't stop, and Harlow didn't try to make him. The joy the two projected thrilled West, even as it taunted him. What would he feel when he actually kissed Jessie Kay?

When. Not if. A mistake—or a truth?

He watched Jessie Kay as she watched the ceremony. Tears gleamed in her eyes, a few even streaking her cheeks. Not only did she have the marshmallow heart, she had romantic delusions. She was the kind of woman he usually avoided. But staying away was no longer an option.

Pastor Washington shook his head and muttered, "I now pronounce you husband and wife. You may kiss your bride."

Jessie Kay must have sensed West's scrutiny. She glanced over at him. A moment of pure, electric heat arced between them, and the urge to stalk to her, grab her and carry her out vibrated in his bones. His mind flashed to a fantasy he hadn't known he had. Jessie Kay sitting beside him on a couch, his arm draped over her shoulders while they chatted, her hands moving with dramatic flair, making him laugh. Peace and happiness surrounded them. So much happiness.

Whatever expression he wore here and now affected her. She stepped toward him. He stepped toward her. They would meet in the middle and—

Beck and Harlow broke away at long last. Jase cheered, and Jessie Kay jolted. She returned to her spot in the bridesmaid's line. West cursed. Monica jumped to her feet and clapped, smiling at him as if *he'd* done something remarkable. Dane, Kenna, Daphne, Hope and Brad whooped.

Jessie Kay continued to stare at West and he continued to stare at her.

For a moment, one precious slice of life, West remembered what it was like to be whole again. To be a man with a future and a hope for something better. To want and to dream and to *expect* something better.

That. That was the true danger of being with Jessie Kay. He would have better, but he would be unable to keep better.

Two months. No more, no less.

CHAPTER SEVEN

ON MONDAY, JESSIE KAY finished her lunchtime deliveries for You've Got It Coming and drove home with a lead foot. A nap awaited. If someone interrupted her snooze, well, they'd soon wish they were dead. Unless they offered her a box of chocolates and ten million dollars. Her forgiveness could be bought.

What a crap day this turned out to be. A mechanic she'd dated last year had placed an order. She'd dropped off the sandwich at Lintz Automotive—*Dr. Carburetor will see you now!* As she'd walked away, the guy had patted her butt as if he had every right. His friends had whistled and laughed.

Men sucked. *I'm done with all of them.*

Well, except for Daniel. He was so awesome he could almost pass for a woman.

Speaking of her new bestie, he'd confirmed for dinner tonight. Afterward, they would be watching the DVD of her choice.

Mental note: *ask him to bring those chocolates and all that money.*

Half the money?

Whatever he could afford?

Fine. No money.

At home, she settled on the couch with a pillow and fuzzy blanket. With a sigh, she closed her eyes and—

The doorbell rang. Of course.

Grumbling, she marched to the door with every intention of committing cold-blooded murder...only to gasp when she saw what waited on her porch. The most beautiful bouquet of yellow and white flowers in the world, ever.

"For you." Pearl Harris from Secret Garden was a strawberry-blonde with alabaster skin and the most adorable smattering of freckles across her nose. She handed over the bouquet, the scent of chocolate and vanilla wafting from the petals. "Girl, you've got yourself a *serious* admirer. He came in and designed the arrangement himself."

"And *he* is...?" No one had *ever* sent her flowers.

"Like I'm really going to spoil the surprise. You'll have to open the card to find out. *If* he signed it. I tried to talk him into dictating to me, but he refused. Wrote every word himself, then sealed the envelope and added tape." Pearl plucked out the card.

Jessie Kay balanced the vase against her hip and hurriedly claimed the card. Her hand was trembling.

Pearl leaned in closer. "Well? What does it say?"

"I'll be finding out on my own, thank you very much." She stepped inside, the glass door closing behind her.

Pearl pouted.

Too bad. Jessie Kay closed the wooden door with a kick.

Her heart hammered as she set the vase on the kitchen table and ripped open the envelope.

Kitten,
I know I should apologize for my behavior—
again—but I can't bring myself to regret putting

my hands on you. I've never held anything quite so fine. Consider the flowers a token of my appreciation.

Yours,

Lincoln West

Oh, sweet heaven. Was he trying to kill her? Death by spontaneous combustion?

Beams of light filtered in from the bay window, lovingly caressing the flower petals. She couldn't stop smiling as she smelled the roses once, twice, three times, even as she grabbed her phone to send Mr. Lincoln West a text.

Your non-apology ACCEPTED. The flowers are gorgeous. Thank you ☺ ☺

His response came a few seconds later.

I chose the flowers that smelled like candy. They reminded me of you—edible.

Her heart beat harder.

Her, a little shocked: Are you flirting w/ me??

West: Maybe a little. You're irresistible. You need to work on that.

Her: And mess w/ perfection??? Nah

West: Excellent point. The male species is doomed (and happy for it)

She clutched her phone close to her chest and twirled. Never, not in a million years, would she have guessed her relationship with West would evolve into near kisses in closets and flirting via text. An actual friendship was developing. And like West, she was having a little trouble regretting it...

ON WEDNESDAY, THE good mood West had going evaporated in a puff of smoke. Just boom, gone, leaving a frothing-at-the-mouth he-beast. It happened the moment the gossip train rolled through his office—Edna Mills, owner of Rhinestone Cowgirl, a jewelry store located around the corner of WOH Industries. Edna prattled on and on about spotting Jessie Kay and Daniel Porter at the Great Escape Café an hour before. The two had looked cozy while eating breakfast. The morning-after meal.

Had they spent the night together?

West wasn't sure why he cared. It wasn't like *he* was dating the girl. They'd almost kissed. They'd flirted. No more, no less. Big deal. He'd had more intimate contact with his pillow.

The problem—*had* to be the problem—was that he was sick and tired of dealing with happy couples. Beck and Harlow had opted not to travel for their honeymoon, instead holing up in their bedroom at the farmhouse. If West overheard one more role play of Thor and his mighty hammer...

Jase and Brook Lynn were no better. Plus, Brook Lynn had a furmance going on with her pet, Sparkles the World's Worst Dog. *Who's a good boy? You're a good boy, yes, yes, you are. Oh, Mommy loves you.*

Hope had stayed the night once, bringing Steve, the

world's other worst dog, and she'd talked nonstop about Bobby Yates, the cutest boy in her class.

Since the wedding, Monica had called once a day, despite the fact that he'd sidestepped when she'd tried to kiss him, and they'd ended up parting with an awkward hug at the door. He'd told himself, why settle for a substitute? Why not wait for Jessie Kay, the one he really wanted?

The one who might have spent the night with Daniel.

West rubbed the burn in his chest. He should call Monica, set up another date. Being with her would be easy. Two months of sex and fun and pretending he was a normal guy with a normal past—a reprieve before he returned to his misery. Could be just what he needed to clear his head.

The headboard of his bed suddenly *thump, thump, thumped* against the wall. With Beck's bedroom right next to his, West didn't have to wonder what was going on. Any minute now, the moans and groans would—

"Oh, Beck. Yes. Yes!"

Yeah. That. At least she hadn't called out, "Thor!"

He strode to the kitchen, only to grind to a halt when he spotted Jase and Brook Lynn making out on the table. The table he would now have to burn, along with his corneas.

Can't stay here.

He returned to his bedroom, swiped a bag from the closet. Cursing under his breath, he began to stuff clothes and toiletries inside.

Bang, bang, bang.

He stuffed faster, blindly grabbing anything he thought he might need. He'd spoken to the contractor on Monday, and plans for his home were being drafted.

The only problem? The five-thousand-square-foot beauty would take a year to build—maybe longer.

He wouldn't survive.

At his desk, he swiped up the flash drive with details about the upcoming WOH Christmas party. Brook Lynn had become the company party planner, but she was so busy with her business and her wedding, Jase hadn't wanted any other burdens heaped on her "delicate" shoulders.

West scribbled a note—"Staying somewhere else for a while. You guys sicken me. Will let you know where I end up. W." He taped the note to his bedroom door and beat feet to the Mercedes.

The night was dark and gloomy, the moon full and shrouded by wispy gray clouds. If he were living in a video game, he'd call it a werewolf moon and expect to be bitten by midnight. The ice had melted at least.

Where should he go? Harlow had lived in a trailer right here on the acreage for a while, but Beck had recently hidden it to stop her from spending the night in it every time he pissed her off.

He could go to the office, West supposed. This wouldn't be the first time he'd slept on the couch. But he had no desire to face Cora's inquisition. The woman could be relentless.

There was the Strawberry Inn, the only motel in town.

And by morning, everyone would know his business.

He could always go to Monica's.

His hands tightened on the wheel. Yeah. He'd go to Monica's and finally do what needed doing. Meaningless conversation, emotionless sex, uncomplicated relationship—in that order—but he didn't end up parked in Monica's driveway.

I'm in trouble.

He popped a caramel candy in his mouth, the sweet flavor centering him, reminding him of times his mom had held him close, cooing her love while they'd eaten the treats together.

I'm where I want to be. I'll deal with the consequences.

He clasped the handle of his duffel and headed to Jessie Kay's front door.

The poor side of Strawberry Valley was like the poor side of any other town, with small, run-down homes on small lots. A few yards were a hoarder's paradise, junk piled high. Others were filled with dead weeds, nothing manicured, nothing landscaped. Someone had made an attempt to clean up Jessie Kay's yard, but nothing short of a total reboot would help.

Same deal with the porch. At his feet, the cement was severely cracked and in front of him, rotted wood planks looked ready to collapse.

He had more money than he could ever spend, while Jessie Kay lived like this?

His too-hard knock boomed louder than he'd intended. A minute passed, then another. If she was out on a date with Daniel—or worse, *inside* with Daniel and simply distracted...

West knocked again, nearly taking the door off its hinges.

He remembered when Jessie Kay had dated Dorian Oliver, one of Beck's closest friends. The two hadn't lasted more than a few weeks and he'd always wondered if he was the cause. If Dorian had gotten tired of West's daily call, when he'd asked how things were going, his voice all snarl, zero polite.

Perhaps he should acquire Daniel's number.

Observe. Understand. Act.

He tested the knob, discovered it turned easily, and wanted to smile and curse at the same time. "Jessie Kay," he called, stepping into the living room. There wasn't really a foyer. He expected warmth, but a chill pervaded, as if she hadn't turned on the heater. "You here?"

As he waited for her to stomp around the corner—maybe he'd interrupted a bubble bath, and she wore only a towel and drops of water—he studied her natural habitat. Well-worn furniture from early-era Goodwill, if he had to guess. Threadbare patches in the shag carpet. Yellowed wallpaper peeled at the corners. A pile of laundry consumed the end of the couch, and empty candy-bar wrappers and coke cans spilled over the coffee table.

A noise suddenly screeched from the back of the house. A cat being murdered?

He dropped his bag and surged forward. At the entrance of the kitchen, however, he stopped and choked back a laugh. There she was, alone, with earbuds in her ears. She sang along to…a song he couldn't identify.

"Gonna love you foreverrr…something something something…give it to you so goood." As she dried a plate, she gyrated her hips in a dirty bump-and-grind.

Suddenly the desire to laugh abandoned him. Desire hit and hit hard.

Pale hair free of pins cascaded down her back, gleaming like melted honey as they swayed. The long-sleeve shirt she wore hung off one shoulder, baring skin so luscious his mouth watered for a taste. Her legs were covered by skintight pants that were tucked into a pair of calf-high boots with faux fur trim.

Those legs…he wanted them wrapped around his face and later, his waist.

She was every fantasy he'd never known he had, and his blood burned for her. His hands itched for contact.

As she belted out a high note, charming him even while making him cringe, she spun in a circle, intending to dance the plate to the rack. Spotting him, she released a scream sharp enough to burst his eardrums, jolted back, tripped and fell. As she gasped for breath, she held out the plate as if it were a deadly weapon.

"It's just me, kitten."

"West? What the heck!" Glaring at him, she lowered the plate and yanked out the buds. "What are you doing here?"

"Would you believe me if I said I'm enjoying the show?"

She scowled at him. "If your goal was to give me a heart attack, congrats, mission accomplished." Grimacing, she rubbed her lower back. "I think I bruised my pancreas."

"It'll heal." He offered her a hand up.

She ignored it, standing under her own steam. "If you're here for your sandwich, feel free to make a peanut butter and jelly. Pay no attention to the expiration dates. They're meaningless. Don't let the door hit you on the way out. Or do. Whatever."

"We'll deal with the sandwich another day." He noted the bouquet of flowers resting in the center of the table, and satisfaction urged him to pound on his chest like a gorilla. "Tonight our business revolves around a different topic."

"All right. Enlighten me." She crossed her arms over her chest.

In due time. "First, explain why your door was un-locked."

"Because I like it that way."

"Anyone could have walked in."

Lips pursed, she waved the plate up and down his body. "Obviously."

"You're not understanding me, kitten." He claimed the dish and set it on the counter while staring down at her with enough menace to scare her to the bone. "Any-one could have walked in. They could have done *any-thing* to you."

"Are you threatening me?" She raised her chin, un-afraid, stubborn and beautiful, so damn beautiful. She was everything right in a world gone wrong.

A deception. All of his problems currently started and ended with Jessie Kay Dillon.

"If ever I threaten you, kitten, you won't have to ask. I'm simply pointing out an obvious security fail."

"Well." Some of the starch left her. "I assure you, I have nothing worth stealing."

"You sure about that?" He stroked his gaze over her, this woman who was so finely honed she had no equal. "I can name a few things I'd like to take."

A hitch in breath that came faster and faster. "You're flirting."

"You're welcome."

She shook a fist at him. "Don't you know the very moment you start flirting with temptation, you've lost the entire war?"

"We're at war?"

"Yes! Your body clearly wants to invade mine."

He snorted, then looked down and said, "At ease, men. We've entered hostile territory."

For a moment, she looked ready to burst into laughter. But the moment passed and the sparkle of amusement faded. She sighed, toying with the ends of her hair, utterly feminine and sweeter than sugar. "Today was a really bad day."

On instant alert, he demanded, "What happened?"

"What usually happens when I walk through a bone yard."

He flipped through mental files, came up empty. "A bone yard?"

"A sea of boners. Horny dudes. Basically, a room full of guys I used to date."

"Got it. What happens?"

Her face scrunched up with the most adorable disdain. "My butt got smacked. A lot more than usual. I think I'm bruised."

A bomb of anger detonated inside him, sharp bits of shrapnel cutting through any sort of composure he managed to gain. "Who? Give me names, and I'll make sure it never happens again."

"That's kind of you to offer," she said, brightening. "Unfortunately, I'm going to decline. I already slapped the offenders."

"Did you draw blood?"

She fluffed her hair. "A few specks."

"Then I'm satisfied vengeance was achieved." For now. "Just tell me one thing…" He shouldn't ask. He knew better. But he did it anyway. "Is Daniel Porter a former boyfriend…or a current one?"

"What! Gross. He's like a little sister to me."

Some of the tension West had carried since his encounter with Edna suddenly evaporated. He had to fight a smile. "Start locking your door. Better yet, I'll start locking it for you."

Navy blues flared with a mix of surprise and confusion. "Okay, I admit it. You've lost me. You're planning to come over every night just to lock my front door?" She arched a brow. "Are you going to tuck me into bed, too?"

"I'm willing to do both, yes, but I won't be leaving afterward." *Keep it light, easy.* "Good news, kitten. I'm moving in." At the diner, Brook Lynn had mentioned her worry about Jessie Kay being on her own, always struggling to pay the bills. Well, he could help out. He was altruistic like that.

Frowning, she cocked her hip to the side. "I think I just had a stroke. I *couldn't* have heard you say—"

"I'm moving in. Yes. We're going to be roomies. Starting tonight."

One clipped shake of her head. One succinct denial. "No."

"The farmhouse is overrun with happy couples and—"

"No. And there are only two happy couples. The place is hardly overrun."

"Romance is a contagious disease. My insides need a shower before they become infected."

"I bleed for you, I really do, but my answer is still no, no, a thousand times no. There are a bazillion other places you can stay. Your office. Or the inn. Hey, I know. What about your new girlfriend's place? I'm sure she'll be *thrilled* to have you."

"First, I don't want to question your math, but three doesn't actually equal a bazillion. Second, I considered each of those places already, and yet here I am. Third, I don't have a girlfriend."

Another shake of her head. "No. Just… I don't know… buy another house or something."

"That'll take too much time."

"Rent a house."

"In this market?" He prayed she knew *nothing* about the market. Now that he was here, he didn't want to leave.

"What about our mutual lust?"

He liked that she didn't shy away from the issue or try to deny what they felt for each other. *Keep things casual.* "Can you not resist me? It's okay if you can't, but—"

She threw a dishrag at him.

"How about this?" He rubbed the wet spot just over his heart. "Let me stay and I'll pay rent." He kept his starting offer low, giving her room to bargain.

No woman could resist a good bargain.

"No way—" She chewed on her plump bottom lip, reminding him of their time in the cleaning closet, when *he* was the one to torment that lip. "You'll pay rent *and* utilities. You'll even kick in a little extra for—"

"Let me guess." He fought another smile. "Your mental anguish."

"Such a smart boy." She patted his cheek. "Oh, and just so you know, I'll be putting booby traps in my bedroom."

"Just so *you* know, disabling booby traps is a specialty of mine."

"Shooting a .22 is a specialty of mine."

Was it really? "That's kind of hot."

"That's not my problem. Now. I'll show you to your bedroom, since it's where you'll spend the bulk of your time. Did I forget to mention the living room and kitchen are off-limits?"

"Unless I pay extra, right?"

"A plus plus, Mr. West. Someone's in jeopardy of becoming teacher's pet already!"

He withdrew his wallet, presented her with a hundred-dollar bill. "This should cover all the extras."

"For one night, yes." She stuffed the cash in her bra before waving for him to follow.

He trailed her down the hall, and it was a special kind of hell. The sway of her hips mesmerized him. The curl at the end of her hair beckoned him. *Grab me. Fist me.* The shape of her ass dazzled him. Perfect twin globes with just the right amount of bounce. Toned and bitable.

This might not have been his brightest idea.

My favorite mistake.

"Well," she said, stopping in the second doorway on the right. "This is it."

He came up behind her, wanting to be closer, *needing* to be closer. At five-eight, she was tall, but at six-three, he was a lot taller. She stiffened...at first. As one second ticked into another, she softened. The heat that emanated from her intensified, wrapping around him until he felt embraced.

"What do you think?" she asked, breathless now. Just the way he liked her.

The room was small and furnished for a princess. The queen-size canopy boasted pink sheets and a ruffled skirt, the perfect complement to the white vanity with a beveled mirror. "Can't wait to do my hair and makeup," he said drily.

"I'd stay in the rose family, if I had your skin tone."

A subtle fruity fragrance danced through the air. A perfume he knew he'd soon find infused in his clothing. Glitter shimmered in the carpet threads—they were mini land mines, and it was only a matter of time before they exploded all over him and he would look like a stripper named Wild Wild West.

"Still want to stay?" Jessie Kay asked with a gleeful grin.

That grin nailed him in place, reminded him of the peace he'd felt at the wedding. The *rightness*. He wanted to stay *more than anything*. "You're stuck with me, kitten."

"Your masculine sensibilities aren't highly offended by the décor?"

"Flash me a few times a day and my masculine sensibilities will be too drunk on testosterone to care."

"Flash you? Sure thing." She extended both her middle fingers. As he chuckled, she added, "Since I've been the only human living here—do *not* ask about the raccoons—I haven't had the toilet in the bathroom connected to your room fixed...or the one down the hall. So unless you want to cough up an extra thousand every time you use mine, you'll need to hire a plumber. On your dime, of course. Also, this is Brook Lynn's old room so don't go changing things around. If she and Jase break up, she'll move back, and I want the place to be perfect for her."

"Are you serious? Those two will never split."

"You telling me *you* believe in happily-ever-after?"

"Yes. With the right person." He moved around her to enter the room. His only other option? Grab her and kiss the breath right out of her.

"So...you actually think everyone has a one true love? Do you also believe in unicorns and fairy dust?"

"And dragons and trolls."

"Zombies?"

"Don't be ridiculous."

She snorted.

"You doubt because you've never fallen." And, he realized as fury poked at him, he didn't like the thought of her falling in the future.

"I've seen true love. I don't doubt that it's real…for others." A pause as deep as an ocean, as turbulent as a storm, all hints of playfulness leaving her. "Was Tessa yours?"

He gave a single incline of his head.

Wistful, she said, "How did you know she was the one you'd be with forever?"

"I looked at her and couldn't imagine a future without her."

Longing softened already delicate features as she toyed with the hem of her shirt. "My dad said something similar about my mom." A pause. "What do you see when you look at *me*?"

He could have sidestepped the issue, but he met her earlier bluntness with bluntness of his own. "I look at you and I get stuck on an image of you naked in my bed. I wonder if you'll taste sweeter than caramel, if you'll whisper my name or scream it. If you'll crave a soft and gentle ride or a hard one."

Her hand fluttered to her heart as she backed a step away from him. "West." A husky rasp.

He held her stare. "What do you see when you look at me?"

Her mouth opened and closed, but no sound emerged.

"What do you see?" he insisted. He had to know.

"West…don't ask me… I don't think you'll like the answer."

"Tell me, anyway."

"I see…heartbreak waiting to happen. I'm sorry." With that, she turned and fled into her bedroom, slamming the door behind her.

CHAPTER EIGHT

SHOCKINGLY WARM AND toasty for the first time since the arrival of winter, Jessie Kay stretched with lazy abandon. She blinked open heavy-lidded eyes, brilliant morning light streaming through the crack in curtains she'd made from her childhood comforter. She still loved the elegant ballerinas and colorful butterflies. What would West think of—

West!

She jolted to her feet, her heart racing at warp speed. He'd moved in. He was here, tucked away in the bedroom across from hers.

I look at you and I get stuck on an image of you naked in my bed. I wonder if you'll taste sweeter than caramel, if you'll whisper my name or scream it. If you'll demand I give you a soft and gentle ride or a hard one.

A whimper escaped her. Those words had floored her. They'd thrilled her. They'd scared the crap out of her. And really, they'd angered her. He'd looked at Tessa and seen his future. He looked at Jessie Kay and thought of sex. Because he equated her with lust and only lust. Not companionship. Not partnership. Not even happiness. Just garden variety lust, what any man could feel for any woman.

A girl can get a rise out of biscuits. Doesn't mean a darn thing.

I wish I'd listened to you a long time ago, Momma.

Sighing, Jessie Kay swiped up her phone, intending to send a message to Daniel. They were supposed to meet for breakfast, which was her favorite time to hang out with him. The perfect start to her day. She paused when she noticed two texts from Sunny.

What's this I hear about U getting flowers? Is some1 romancing my girl?

Hey, if I say "Party tonight" please tell me you'll B in. Pleeeeease! I miss the old days when U were fun!

Jessie Kay typed: Sorry, chica, but this gal hung up her party hat for good. If you ever decide to knit sweaters or play bingo, I'm your girl! ☺

She ignored the question about the flowers. What happened with West was private.

Sunny: THIS IS CRAZINESS! U blow chunks!

No, for the first time in her life, she didn't.

She typed the message to Daniel, still amazed he'd become one of her most treasured friends so quickly. But then, he never made a pass at her, and he genuinely seemed to enjoy her company.

I'm too tired for breakfast. You free for dinner instead?

Lunch wasn't an option. Jessie Kay planned to meet her sister, Kenna and Harlow at Two Farms for a little girl bonding.

Daniel texted back.

I am now. I'll pick you up at 7

Her: Pick me up at 5.

Daniel: Only people over 60 eat at 5

Her: We have plans after we eat (I'm taking up soccer & you're taking up watching soccer)

Daniel: Any hot girls gonna be there???

Her: You mean besides ME?

Daniel: That's so obvious I didn't think it needed to be stated

Her: Don't know about other hot girls (sorry) BTW you're driving

Daniel: Fine. I'll suffer through the silver-fox special & your practice but you'll owe me

Her: Buck up. You're getting the better end of the deal—my company

Already feeling peppier, she showered. She hoped the hot water would wash away the lingering effects of West's confession—the goose bumps, tingles, aches and the low-grade passion-fever—and for a while, it actually worked. But as she dressed in clothes too sexy for delivering sandwiches, the sensations returned and redoubled, tormenting her.

If she survived the day, it would be a miracle.

Hinges creaked as she opened her bedroom door and peeked into the hall. No sign of West. She released a breath she hadn't known she was holding. Maybe he'd decided to break free of his workaholic shackles and sleep in this fine Thursday morning. Maybe she would go the entire day without seeing him. He hadn't yet placed an order.

As she tiptoed through the living room, confusion overwhelmed her. She felt as though she'd been transported into someone else's home. Empty wrappers and cans had been thrown away. Her blankets had been folded. A new—and bigger—TV sat in place of her old one. Three remote controls were perfectly aligned on the freshly polished coffee table.

In the kitchen—crap. West. And oh, wow. He was shirtless and pantsless. The only thing between her hungry gaze and his deepest secrets was the towel wrapped around his waist. Like her, he'd just taken a shower. His damp hair was several shades darker than usual.

Want to run my fingers through those strands.

He stood at the stove, his back to her. The strength she saw in those wide shoulders shocked and amazed her. She'd known he would pack a powerful punch underneath his suits and soccer gear, but she'd had no idea he would knock her into next week. The delicious ripple of muscle and sinew appeared carved from stone. The dimples on his lower back begged, *Kiss me here. Lick...*

Computer nerds and desk jockeys should not look like this.

He dropped a piece of bacon, and rather than bending down to pick it up, he stared at it as if it had just threatened to castrate him. He even backed away from it, not stopping until he hit the counter, the fork in his hand dripping grease down his arm. The pieces of bacon still cooking in the pan began to smoke and burn, but he didn't seem to notice.

How odd. "I'll get it." She raced over to remove the pan from the fire and turn off the gas. She picked up the manna from heaven—RIP, sweet morsel—tossed it in the trash and cleaned the grease from the floor.

As she straightened, she took in rope after rope of West's muscled chest. He had a tattoo of a human heart resting over, well, his heart with the name *Tessa* arched above it. A wave of longing swept through Jessie Kay. Oh, to have such a powerful man so devoted to her that he inked her name into his flesh. A brand marking him forever.

He continued to stare at the floor, where the bacon had gone to die.

Some kind of daydream? A space-out? Or, like with her and her panic attacks, a flashback of sorts?

Yeah. That, she thought, and her heart actually ached for him. She recognized the signs. The skin around his eyes and mouth had pulled tight, and his breaths were uneven.

The urge—the bone-deep *need*—to help him bombarded her. Brook Lynn had always brought her around with a touch or a joke.

Jessie Kay placed her hands on West's knotted shoulders, got all up in his personal space, and when he finally blinked at her, she said the most shocking thing possible to a long term commitmentphobe. "I'm pregnant with your triplets. Congrats, baby daddy!"

The blinking stopped, and he stared at her as if she'd just morphed into that discarded piece of bacon. "*Daddy* will never receive my nickname seal of approval."

"Like that matters." Relief was a soft brush of wind against her skin. "But what would you suggest I call you?"

"Sexy. Lover. My sun and stars."

She laughed and he began to laugh with her. But they sobered all too soon. He circled her wrists with his fingers, sending her pulse into overdrive.

"Thank you," he rasped.

"What happened?" she asked, hesitant.

At first, she thought he would refuse to tell her. Their friendship was new and tentative, not even close to tried-and-true. But he surprised her, saying, "One of the foster homes…we were only allowed to eat off the floor."

"Oh, my gosh. West! That's terrible!" And it made her wonder how many other horrors he'd endured as a child. Made her hate herself for knocking his sandwich to the floor that day in his office.

Realization struck. West hadn't shed his baggage after all. Getting clean was only one piece of the puzzle.

There had to be a way she could help him. A way to replace bad memories with good ones.

"By the way, you're late." He was all business now. Wishing he'd kept his mouth shut about the foster home?

She allowed the subject change because she wanted him relaxed and happy here. Because he was her tenant, and she was a kickass landlord.

"Late for what?" she asked. "My morning drool? From now on, you have to wear a shirt."

A slow smile bloomed, and oh, it was a wicked, wicked sight. "Late for breakfast. Also, I took the liberty of planning the rest of your day. You'll find your schedule on the table."

"A schedule? For me?" She swiped up the sheet of paper in question. "Seriously?"

THURSDAY
5:30—Breakfast with West
6:00—Leave for Brook Lynn's
6:15—Help prepare sandwiches
7:00—Leave for sandwich deliveries

Blah blah blah... He'd even scheduled bathroom breaks.

12:00—Lunch at WOH offices (You still owe me a sandwich, kitten.)

Blah blah blah...
Finally the list ended with West tucking her into bed at 10:00 p.m., a side note mentioning the importance of beauty Zs.

He held up the coffeepot. "How do you take your life's blood?"

"Cream. Ten sugars."

"I have no idea if you're kidding or not."

"Of course I'm kidding. Twenty sugars." She waved the paper in the air. "Are all your roommates this lucky?"

"Yes."

"And your girlfriends?"

"Yes." Said with a little more bite. He poured the coffee, but only added a splash of cream and two measly spoonfuls of sugar.

Amateur hour. She confiscated the saucer, poured in as much cream as her cup could hold and tipped over the container of sugar until her sweet tooth said *I guess that'll do—for now*.

"About that schedule. You can't just plan my day, West. That's *my* job."

"A job you're not doing." He took her cup, tasted the contents and grimaced. "If we're going to live together without killing each other, there has to be order. The early bird makes the schedules."

Frustrating man. She reclaimed her cup and drained half the contents. Feeling a little more human she said, "I'm sorry, but your schedule—while totally *not* appreciated—won't work for me. I'm having lunch with my girls, dinner with Daniel and afterward, I'm going to my first soccer lesson, which starts at eight. In the city! A ten-o'clock bedtime is impossible."

He went still, the muscles in his back knotting. "Dinner. With Daniel."

"Yay. Your ears are working."

"Why are you seeing him?"

"I told you. We're friends."

"Friends who used to date."

"Key words, 'used to.'"

"I don't like the two of you spending time together," he said very quietly, very firmly.

"Why? Because you're jealous?"

The moment the words registered, she gasped.

He growled.

She studied him anew. The stiffness of his stance. The to-the-death madness in his eyes. The flare of his nostrils each time he exhaled. The stark color in his cheeks. The hard line of his mouth. The stubborn set of his jaw.

Someone save me. He *was*.

"I want the best for you, Jessie Kay. He isn't the best."

Can't smile. "Sure, sure. Whatever you say. But I was serious when I told you there's nothing romantic between us. I'm not attracted to him, and he's not attracted to me."

"He's a guy. Trust me, kitten, he's attracted to you."

Shivers, tingles, heat. "Let's be honest, *puppy.* You don't really have a right to—"

"I don't like it," he interjected.

"Well, I don't like your association with Monica, but you and I aren't a couple. What we like and don't like doesn't matter. And don't go throwing a hissy he-fit. I'm not trying to manipulate you into asking me to be your forever girl or anything like that. I'm just stating facts."

His motions jerky, he scraped the burned bacon into the trash. "Who agreed to coach you?"

Another subject change. Fine. "Some guy named Mark Polo. And yes, that's his name." She'd called the indoor arena where the Goal Scouts practiced and played, and Mr. Polo had been the only person willing to take her on for the little cash she had to spare.

"He couldn't find a goal with a flashlight and a map." West carried a different pan to the table, scooped an omelet onto a plate for her and another omelet onto a plate for himself. "Cancel the lesson."

"Thank you for the food and the advice. I eagerly accept the first, but regretfully decline the second."

"Too bad." He sat across from her. "*I'm* going to teach you how to play soccer."

What! "But you said—"

"I'll only charge you the use of the living room and kitchen whenever I want."

It was a bargain she couldn't resist. The drive to and from the arena would be hell on her beater of a car and all her grocery money would have to be used on gas.

"You've got yourself a deal...my sun and stars."

He smiled at her. "That's better."

"Except I kinda feel like I should bleach my tongue to kill nasty germs."

He took a bite of omelet, swallowed. "Your practice starts at six. Don't be late."

"I'm meeting Daniel at five. That's not enough time to eat and—"

"Six. Do *not* be late. I mean it, Jessie Kay. Being on time is important to me. Every minute counts."

"Why?"

A flash of panic—a flash she didn't understand. "It just does."

"Fine." She pushed out a sigh. "Before I forget, you should know Daniel is going to watch the practice. I told him—"

"No. He's not allowed to watch."

"But I *promised* him—"

"Un-promise him. And don't be late," West repeated, his gaze locked on her, smoldering with so much heat she actually felt burned. A common occurrence in his presence. "If you don't respect my rules, kitten, I won't respect yours."

Rules? "I've never given you any rules."

"I can think of three offhand." He held up an index finger. "Always wear a shirt." A second finger lifted. "Stay out of your bedroom." Another finger. "Keep my hands to myself."

Oh...crap. If he touched her...just one touch...what remained of her resistance might finally crumble.

BY THE TIME Jessie Kay finished her morning deliveries, she was thirty-seven minutes off West's stupid schedule and stressed to the max. She'd constantly glanced at the clock on her phone, sweating bullets despite the frigid temperature as one minute bled into another. How did West live this way? *Why* did he live this way?

She finally caved and texted Beck for answers. He would be an easier nut to crack than Jase.

I need your help. West moved in w/ me & I just received my 1st schedule. (shakes fist at sky) WHY ME????

Beck: My boy called this morning, told us about the move-in. We're still in shock. You tell me what's going on w/ you two & I'll tell you about the schedule

Her: You're gonna break bro code just for deets? You suck as West's friend but you rock as mine (good choice!) ☺

Beck: Bro code will remain intact. As soon as we learned where West had gone, we decided to help you out for his benefit (& yours)

Here went nothing.

Her: What's going on between us: we've admitted we lust for each other, but we've decided to be friends, nothing more. Happy now? Talk!

Beck: Ignoring lust only causes the fire to burn hotter. Just ask Harlow. But at least you and West are finally on the right path

A flutter in her heart.

Her: The schedule, please

Beck: It's something he learned in rehab. Keeps his mind busy so he won't relapse

Fear of a relapse. Ding, ding, ding. Of course!

The people who said "a little fear is good for you" only lied to themselves. They claimed fear kept them from doing stupid things. Wrong! Common sense did that. Hello! Fear of any kind was a prison, keeping you shackled—she should know. So as much as West's schedules helped him, they also chained him. He allowed himself to do this but not that and vice versa, never leaving room for spontaneity.

What would it hurt to show him there was a different way to live? If he liked it, he liked it; if he didn't, he didn't. But at least he'd be better informed.

Excitement blooming, she texted West:

On my way to lunch w/ the girls. You remembered I can't bring you a sandwich today right? ☺ ☺ ☺

West: You have an emoticon addiction

That was it? That was all she got? Oops. Spoke too soon.

West: I remembered

Well. Not the best response, but not the worst, either. Whatever. She had to kick off her plan now or never…

Her: OH! Before I forget—I need a copy of YOUR schedule. You don't want me to accidentally screw it up, do you??? ☺ ☺ ☺ ☺ ☺ ☺ (admit it, smiley faces make you happy)

Casual enough?

An email came in next. A freaking email.

Lincoln_West@WOH.com
Subject: Read it, love it, live it
See attached. You're welcome.

Smartass. She opened the document and read the intricately detailed plans for his day. Shower, cook a green pepper and mushroom omelet with bacon on the side for Jessie Kay, dress—he'd even written down what he planned to wear—drive to work. He'd logged the length of time he would be in the car, along with a sidebar in case there was a traffic jam. For work, he'd listed everything he needed to get done and every phone call he was to make and the minutes he would allow for each. He'd already scratched out lunch with her and penciled in a protein shake at his desk. He also planned to work out.

Had to keep those muscles in top form.

He'd scratched out, rewritten, scratched out and rewritten a call to Monica.

A text arrived just as Jessie Kay finished reading.

West: Naked pictures also make me happy

She smiled with evil delight. The only way to show him what life was like without a schedule was to trash today's schedule. And he'd just given her the perfect way to do it…

She looked the document over one more time, making note of the events she could liven up. The conference call with the star beside it. The meeting with Beck about upcoming projects. The call—not going to call—call to Monica. Excitement building, Jessie Kay set reminders on her phone before making her way to Two Farms, the only fine-dining experience in town. Said no one. Ever. Well, except for Mr. Calbert, the owner. He said it all the freaking time.

"Hey, Jessie Kay. Wait up."

As she meandered along the sidewalk, Billy Johnson raced across the street to keep pace beside her. They were roughly the same age, and he was kinda cute… she thought she remembered making out with him at a party one night.

"I just left Style Me Tender." He raked a hand through his newly shorn hair. "Daniel Porter and his dad were there."

"That's not exactly headline news, Billy." Mr. Porter and Mr. Rodriguez, the owner of the salon, were best friends and always together.

"Yeah, but Mr. Porter asked Daniel if you guys were dating, and he said you were just friends."

"He didn't lie."

"Glad to hear it…because I just bought a new truck and would love to take you for a ride."

"Take you for a ride" had always been code for "have sex at Make Out Hill." *He really thinks I'm* that *easy.*

I'll wait forever for you, Anna Grace.

"Do me a favor and spread the word," she said through gritted teeth. "Jessie Kay Dillon has closed the candy store. And now, good day, sir."

"But—"

"I said good day, sir."

As he sputtered for a response, she marched the rest of the way to the restaurant. A bell tinkled as she entered. The girls had beaten her there and snagged a booth in back. As she made her way over, she took in the wood paneling, the hand-carved tables and the cement floor painted to resemble marble.

She and Brook Lynn had worked here for years—and yeah, okay, her sister had worked a lot harder than she ever had, and guilt still burned inside her for it. But… Jessie Kay had despised this place with every fiber of her being. Not because she'd disdained the work but because different guys had come in at different times, requesting her as a waitress. They'd heard she gave a little something extra to her customers, aka a good time. Her butt had received multiple pats a day and once or twice her breasts had been squeezed.

Now, at least, she didn't feel as if she were choking on disappointment every time she entered.

She hugged her sister, saying, "Fess up. You recently lost your temper, didn't you?" before plopping in her seat.

"I most certainly did not. And stop trying to distract me." Brook Lynn planted her elbows on the tabletop, letting her know the seriousness of the subject trumped proper etiquette. "What's this we hear about West moving in with you?"

Oh. That.

In unison, Kenna and Harlow said, "Yeah. Tell."

"He showed up last night, desperate to escape the inconsiderate, horribly disgusting couples who can't keep their hands off each other. How could I say no?"

Brook Lynn buffed her nails. "Haters gonna hate."

Harlow leaned forward, expression a little too feral. "Are you guys sharing a room?"

"No," she said, then sighed. "Not yet." After seeing him in nothing but a towel and a sardonic smile…

My resistance is basically toast. Hot, buttered toast.

A chorus of "ohhhs" erupted.

"Oh, my gosh." Brook Lynn pressed her hands together and placed the steeple over her mouth. "You guys are going to get married and have a million babies, I just know it."

Jessie Kay rolled her eyes. "We were bitter enemies and now we're friends who have admitted to a mutual attraction. That's as far as we've gone."

A warm, buttered corn-bread muffin hit her in the chest, crumbs landing in her hair.

"Hey!" she said, scanning the table for the culprit.

"What about your ban on sex?" Kenna picked up another muffin, ready to launch it. "Last time we had lunch, you told us you'd decided to wait for a man who would love you the way your dad loved your mom. You told us to hit you with a crowbar if you started crushing on anyone inappropriate."

"I even brought one." Harlow lifted a freaking crowbar. "I love West, but unless you get him to break the two-month date-and-dump cycle, I can't let you mess around with him."

These girls were kneecap-breaking serious about protecting her heart.

She might not have found the romantic love her parents had shared, but she had something just as good, if not better. The love of her friends.

"No need to worry. West asked me to sleep with him, a onetime thing, and I said no." Her phone beeped, and she held up a finger, requesting a moment as she checked the screen. She smiled. Time to send Mr. West his first schedule-crushing picture.

"Why are you smiling that like?" Kenna demanded. "I don't like it."

She opened the camera app on her phone. "Why? Smiles represent happiness."

"Except you look like an evil overlord who finally destroyed the world."

"Because I'm destroying *West's* carefully constructed world. Trust me. It's for his own good." She took a cleavage selfie and texted the photo to his phone.

Better than a smiley face???

Harlow gaped at her. "Did you just send him a picture of your chest?"

"My *very ample* chest, yes." If he responded as she hoped, he would be extremely uncomfortable during his conference call, but he'd also look forward to something that wasn't on his precious schedule—seeing her again.

Aaand sixty-three seconds later, a beep sounded.

YOU'RE NOT WEARING A BRA???

She laughed with pure glee.
Another text came in.

Come to my office. Now. In-person showings are better than pictures

She typed: Can't. I'm busy. But maybe I'll send another pic later...

Maybe he'd be so eager to see it that he'd pencil in a spontaneous call to her, just to beg that she hurry.

"Uh-oh. She's got it bad," Kenna said.

"I know! Isn't it great?" Brook Lynn beamed.

"Know what you want to eat, ladies?" Melba Redus, an older waitress Jessie Kay had worked with in the past, arrived with notebook and pen in hand.

"We sure do," Jessie Kay said, hopefully ending the conversation about West.

The moment Melba marched off, Brook Lynn got them back on track. "We need to be sure you don't sabotage your own happiness. Or rush into something you shouldn't. So, we're going to make some lists."

No. Please, no. Not Brook Lynn's infamous lists. Jessie Kay remembered the last one. A fun list consisting of gems like:

Drink blue Gatorade out of a Windex bottle in front of strangers.

Become Cinderella for a day.

Solve a mystery.

Her sister hadn't realized those strangers would call 911, thinking death was imminent. Or that being Cinderella would mean toiling in summer heat all day long rather than attending a glamorous ball. Or that the mystery would involve a missing orgasm.

Wait. Maybe a few lists wouldn't be so bad.

No. Bad Jessie Kay! "Here's a list," she said. "'Things I need. Number one. New friends.'" She tapped her chin. "Yeah, that covers it. I don't need to add anything else."

Kenna wagged a finger at her. "Zip it, Dillon. This is happening."

"Since you're so resistant to help," Brook Lynn said, "we'll only make one list. It will detail all the things West has to do for you before you can even consider sleeping with him. You'll thank us later."

Save me. "Guys, lists are as bad as schedules."

As the girls ignored her and bounced ideas off each other—*he can't glance at other women while he's speaking with Jessie Kay, he must introduce her to work associates with pride, and he has to hold her close all night long without making a move on her*—her phone rang. The screen displayed a number she didn't recognize.

Grateful for the distraction, she answered. "Hello."

"I'm calling for Jessica Dillon."

A woman's voice, unfamiliar. "This is she." Right? That sounded weird. "This is her." And that sounded even worse. Whatever. "This is me. Jessie Kay."

Her dreams of being an English teacher had long since crashed and burned. With good reason!

"Hello, Miss Dillon. I'm Hilary Dumas, executive assistant to Monica Gentry."

Monica Gentry. The woman West had brought to Harlow's wedding. Jessie Kay's fingers tightened around the cell, nearly cracking the plastic case.

"Who is it?" Brook Lynn whispered.

Monica, she mouthed. She and Monica—Monica and her?—had spoken for a few minutes before the ceremony, and they hadn't parted on the friendliest of terms.

He asked me *out. He's here with* me. *I don't appreciate the way you're looking at him.*

Maybe you should talk to him *about the way he's looking at* me, Jessie Kay had replied.

Maybe I will, but right now I'm talking to you. Back off, or I'll make you regret it.

A threat she'd accepted as her due after what had transpired in the cleaning closet.

"We'd like to hire You've Got It Coming to cater our first company Christmas party," Hilary continued. A pause crackled over the line. "This Saturday."

What! "I'm not the one in charge of bookings. And please tell me I misunderstood and your party is *not* a mere two days away."

Around her, the girls went quiet and peered at her questioningly.

"I was given your number and told to call you specifically. I'm sorry for the last-minute notice," Hilary said, "but we are willing to compensate you for the rush. And if you're interested, I can email or fax the details within the hour."

Why Monica wanted to hire Jessie Kay specifically, well, she could guess, and the reason had nothing to do with You've Got It Coming's sterling reputation and starred reviews. Perhaps West had told her about his new living arrangement, and she hoped to threaten Jessie Kay again. Perhaps the brunette wanted to make another play for him. Either way, money was money, and Jessie Kay said, "If by compensating us for the rush you mean paying You've Got It Coming triple the usual fee, we're on board." Surely Brook Lynn would agree.

Hilary accepted the price increase without hesitation, and the call ended soon after. Reeling, Jessie Kay explained the situation to the girls.

"Oh, my gosh. We've got a thousand things to do." Brook Lynn bounced in her seat. "Man, I wish Mom and Dad were here to see what we've made of the business."

Jessie Kay withered. *Mom isn't here to see what you've made of the business because of me.*

For all the days of her life, Brook Lynn would be deprived of the woman's presence, support and guidance, and it was clear, so very clear, there'd never been a worse sister than Jessie Kay, never been a person more deserving of being severed from the root of what she loved most, the very person she'd hurt more than—

"You stop that right now, Jessie Kay." Arms wrapped around her, drawing her in for a bear hug. "I mean it."

Her face pressed against her sister's neck, her accelerated breathing gradually calming.

"What happened to Mom was an accident. You have to stop carrying the blame."

Brook Lynn had been there, but she hadn't seen everything go down. She knew the worst of the details only because Jessie Kay had told her one night while drinking, desperate for her sister to understand all the reasons she should hate her. But even then, Brook Lynn had supported her, only increasing her sense of guilt.

She drew in a deep breath and straightened. Unable to meet the gazes of the other girls, she said, "All right. We have a lot of planning to do and only a short amount of time to do it. Let's get to work."

JESSIE KAY RAN errands the rest of the day, gathering everything she and Brook Lynn would need for Monica's party. She paused when necessary to send West texts of different parts of her body—her feet strapped in the high heels she'd tried on but hadn't bought at Vintage Rules, where You've Got It Coming purchased all their tablecloths, then the curve of her hip with the barest peek at her red lace undies, then her lips, puckered and ready for a kiss. The photos were a welcome distraction from her troubles.

So was West. All three times, he responded with texts begging for more. Texts she ignored. Well, pretended to ignore. She thought of nothing else, and couldn't stop smiling.

How could she have known teasing him would be so much fun—for her?

She texted Daniel.

Hate to do it but I'm canceling dinner & practice. 1) new catering job 2) West is now my soccer coach so practice has been upped to 6. 3) Practice will take place at my house & there's no room for spectators

Daniel: No prob. Got word your "candy store" is closed so I was thinking about canceling on you anyway

Like he really wanted her treats. As their friendship had grown, they'd developed a brother-sister vibe. Well, stepbrother and stepsister.

Her phone vibrated. Daniel again.

Hey, did I ever tell you West came to my house soon after we broke things off?

Her: WHAT! He did? Why? TELL ME!

Daniel: Oh, oh, oh. What's this? Is someone a little too curious?

Her: I'm currently at Strawberries & More. If you don't start spilling, I'll buy yeast infection cream & tell everyone it's for you but you're too embarrassed to buy it for yourself.

Daniel: You play too rough. And so does he. He told

me he'd kill me if I hurt you again & no one would ever find my savaged body

But…but…that had happened back when she and West were on unfriendly terms, always snipping and snapping at each other.

He'd been looking out for her, even then?

Daniel: The guy can be nice one minute & cold-blooded the next. If you're into him, be careful

Jessie Kay stuffed her phone in her coat pocket and snatched a cart to push down the aisles of the grocery store—she wasn't really at Strawberries & More but some health food store in the city. Brook Lynn had made another of her infamous lists, this one detailing all the items needed for the health-conscious hors d'oeuvres Monica insisted on serving. Some things Jessie Kay had never heard of. Oca? Romanesco? Tiger nut?

Not even gonna look that last one up.

Despite her unfamiliarity with the ingredients, she'd volunteered to do the shopping. There had been a time not so long ago when Brook Lynn wouldn't—shouldn't— have trusted her with such an important task, but those days were behind them, and it thrilled her. Plus, she'd come up with a way to shake up West's dinner plans, at the same time replacing his memory of floor-eating. And she couldn't wait to begin.

CHAPTER NINE

WEST READ OVER his schedule, frowned, then read over it again. How was this possible? He hadn't done half the things he'd planned to do. Not that anything had been pressing. He'd gotten off course sometime during lunch and never recovered. Never even realized it until now. He'd been too busy watching the clock.

Speaking of, he glanced at the clock on his office wall. 5:16 p.m. Forty-four minutes until Jessie Kay's soccer lesson was set to begin. He'd expected to feel nothing but dread, but right now he hummed with sizzling anticipation.

"What's this I hear about Jessie Kay closing a candy store?" Beck asked.

West forced his focus on his friend, who plopped into the chair across from his desk. "I heard the same thing." Several guys had visited the office to ask him if he'd heard the bad news. Several women had visited, too, demanding to know if he was engaged to Jessie Kay.

His reply? "We're in talks." Let them stew on *that*.

He'd added, "Since Daniel is gay, he'd make a great bridesmaid, don't you think."

Jase, who'd driven Brook Lynn to her lunch with the girls, perched in the chair next to Beck. "By the way, you were staring at the clock as if you wanted to hump it."

"It's a sexy clock. A twelve on a scale of ten."

"Please. That clock is a hard five, and you know it," Beck said.

"I was going to say soft six," Jase said.

"That's because you spent a decade behind bars. You're desperate."

Jase barked out a laugh.

How could the two joke so easily about Jase's incarceration?

West scrubbed a hand down his face. "Today has been...different." He and Jessie Kay had flirted non-stop via text, ensuring he maintained a low-level arousal even while going about his business. He'd loved every second, even as he'd *hated* every second.

His curiosity about her was now off the charts. What had shaped her into the woman she was? What had driven her to parties and men she'd known were bad for her? What had changed her?

Bottom line. The girl had flat-out enchanted him.

He did not use such a puss word like *enchanted* lightly.

If they continued at this pace, they'd end up in bed sooner rather than later. And yeah, *hell yeah*, he wanted her there. He wanted her there more than he'd ever wanted anything. He wanted her naked, wet and willing. But the obstacles in their way hadn't miraculously vanished. His reasons for avoiding an entanglement with her hadn't changed.

In fact, he now had another reason to add to the list. He would hurt her, and he would rather die than hurt her.

So why hadn't he stopped flirting with her?

Observe. Understand. Act.

He couldn't understand and didn't want to act.

"Wait. That's all we get?" Beck spread his arms, all *dude, you mean Santa isn't real?* "Today was different?"

"That's right—that's all you get." His phone buzzed. Thanks to Jessie Kay's illicit photos, the sound now caused a Pavlovian response, his blood heating in an instant.

Jessie Kay: Are you done w/ work? Can you come home now? I've got something to show you… ☺ ☺ ☺

"I've got to go." He jumped to his feet. As his friends sputtered a response, he swiped up his briefcase and coat and strode out the door.

He drove so fast he set speed records. He also *broke* speed limits.

Sheriff Lintz pulled him over.

The lawman braced his arms in West's open window, the brim of his Stetson pushed back, revealing a kind but weathered face. "What's got you in such an all-fired hurry, son?"

"Just eager to get home." The truth, but not the whole truth. No need to start more rumors.

"Heard you'd moved in with our Jessie Kay."

"Yes, sir."

Dark eyes crinkled at the corners as Sheriff Lintz smiled. "Well, then, I can't rightly blame you for speeding, she's a mighty fine woman, but do me a favor and set your cruise to fifty. That way I won't have to give you a ticket and Jessie Kay won't show up at the courthouse pretending to be a lawyer, raving about the injustice on our roadways—again."

West tried not to smile. "Did she really?"

"Only every time one of her friends got a ticket." Sheriff Lintz straightened and tapped the hood of the car. "Go on now. Get home to your girl."

Your girl.

The words felt so...right.

West obeyed the limits the rest of the way home, but flew up the porch steps as if his feet were on fire. Unfortunately, the front door was locked, and he had yet to get a key. No matter. With a couple of paper clips he removed from the documents in his briefcase, he let himself inside, warm air greeting him. He'd paid an obscene amount of money for an electrician from the city to drive out here and fix the heater in the middle of the night, while Jessie Kay had slept peacefully.

"Jessie Kay?"

"In the kitchen," she called.

He schooled his features to reveal only mild curiosity as he strode through the living room. In the kitchen...

He stopped short. She kneeled on a blanket that had been spread across the floor, and she was smiling up at him, bowls of food surrounding her.

"Surprise! We're having a picnic. Oh, and I made this just for you. A gift to celebrate our new friendship." She held out a single cupcake with checkered black-and-white frosting. An edible soccer ball. "It's cookies and cream, soon to be your new favorite thing in the world."

She looked so eager, so uncertain, but even with a blanket, the floor was the floor and he shook his head. "I'm sorry, Jessie Kay, but I can't—"

"Don't say no," she rushed out. "We're roommates now. We need to take time to get to know each other."

"We can take time at the table. Tomorrow." No way he'd eat tonight's offering.

Pouting, she set the cupcake on a plate. "Why put it off? Tomorrow you'll probably do something dumb—it's time to face facts, you're a guy so it's inevitable that you'll screw up—and then I'll refuse to speak to you ever again."

"That's a risk I'm willing to take." It wasn't. It so wasn't.

"Are you sure?" She reached up to trace her fingers over the collar of her shirt. A new one with buttons—the top three were unfastened, drawing his gaze to the most succulent cleavage he'd ever seen. Cleavage he hadn't been able to get out of his mind all day. "I'm amusing and charming and you'd miss me terribly."

"This is true."

"So, save us from an argument and sit down. Talk with me, *eat* with me, and I'll give you a reward."

Every muscle in his body clenched. "What kind of reward?"

"You tell me. What do you crave?"

You. To finish what they'd started at the wedding. Finally. Blessedly. His body *hungered* for hers.

Too many obstacles...

There was only one thing he wanted as much as he wanted this woman in his bed.

"Your secrets," he said.

She frowned. "I have no secrets worth sharing."

"You do. I want to know everything about you."

The color drained from her cheeks. "But...we've only just agreed to be friends."

"And what better way to cement our friendship?"

"I can think of several. But if it's secrets you want—"

"It is."

"—why don't I tell you about the time a goat chased me down Main Street?"

"That's not a secret. I've heard the goat story from at least six people in town. Tell me the bad stuff. The things no one else knows."

"But…"

"Consider this a trust exercise. You'll fall, and I'll catch. Or I can go to my room and starve…" He took a step back.

"Wait." Her eyes narrowed to tiny slits. "Will you be sharing *your* secrets?"

Would he? "If you insist."

"I do."

He nodded reluctantly. "Then so be it."

"But I get to eat the cupcake and—"

"*My* cupcake." He sat on the blanket before he could talk himself out of it, clasping the cupcake in a kung fu grip. "My gift."

Gift. The word echoed through his mind. It *was* a gift. A gift she'd made just for him. In all the years of his life, he'd received only two others. A bike from one of the better foster families—not that he was allowed to keep it when he moved—and a pair of shoes from Jase and Beck when his old ones fell apart, his feet far too big for them.

"Thank you," he grumbled. He had no idea how to moderate his voice as different emotions flooded him… drowned him.

"You're welcome. Now. Let's get started, shall we?" She picked up a plate and began to stack different ingredients in the center. "Guess who's finally getting his sandwich. Hint: he thinks I'm the most beautiful woman in the world."

No reason to deny it. "He does." West loosened his tie, kicked off his shoes and tried to act nonchalant as sweat broke out on the back of his neck. "Why a picnic?" As if he couldn't guess.

This morning, he'd told her how he'd once been forced

to eat off the floor. This was her way of easing the sting of the memory. A sweet gesture, but not one he really appreciated.

"Here's a better question. Why *not* a picnic?" She handed him the plate of food and put together much smaller portions for herself. "We're not just roommates, we're friends. You said so. I picnic with my friends."

"Have you picnicked with Daniel?" he couldn't help but ask.

"No. Why?" She smirked at him. "Would you like to call and invite him?"

"If he invades my picnic, I'll gut him and feast on his remains."

She snorted. "That's not disturbing *at all*."

West got as comfortable as he could, leaning against the wall, stretching out his long legs. His stomach twisted into so many knots he could only pick at the double-stacked club as he asked, "Did you have picnics with your family when you were young?"

Her smile was morose. "Every summer my dad would take us camping. We'd spend a week at the lake and have a picnic every night."

West had clearly delved into sensitive territory already— one of her secrets? "Did you have fun?"

"While he was alive, yes."

"You still went camping after he died?"

Now chalk white, she toyed with a piece of bacon. "My mom thought it would be good for us. A way to re-member him, to feel close to him."

"You didn't feel close to him?" He popped a bite of ham into his mouth before he realized what he'd done. The flavor...wasn't bad.

Fidgeting, she said, "Enough about me. Tell me one of *your* secrets."

"What would you like to know?" He braced, preparing for the worst.

She met his gaze straight on. "How did you feel when Jase killed the man who'd hurt Tessa?"

Not the worst, but close. How would she react to the truth? "I was glad—because I helped him deliver the beating. In fact, I threw the first punch."

She didn't recoil, as part of him expected. She merely tilted her head, confused. "You were there? But... Brook Lynn never mentioned... I don't understand..."

"Why wasn't I sentenced?" The muscles in his jaw ached from being clenched so tightly. "Jase took full responsibility and asked me to stay quiet." He made no mention of Beck. His friend's secrets were his own to share—or not. "I did, and I've had to live with guilt every day since."

She stared at him for a long while. Disappointed in him? Disgusted? Angered on Jase's behalf? "Guilt is like flypaper, isn't it. As the years go by, everything from shame to dread sticks to it."

He nodded, couldn't yet speak.

"But why do you feel guilty? You gave your friend what he wanted."

"What we want isn't always what we need."

"Yeah. That's true," she replied softly. "He needed you."

No placations? *You were only a kid...*

"Sometimes I wonder," he said in a voice just as soft, "if I stayed quiet because Jase asked...or because I was too afraid to come forward." The admission burned his throat, his mouth—his soul.

She reached out and patted his hand. "Does it really matter? You're not the boy you used to be, and you'd do things differently now. You've grown and learned, and like my momma used to say, you shouldn't carry your mistakes, you should set them down and use them as stepping stones to a better future."

The strangest thing happened. The burn of guilt faded. Not a lot, but enough to notice. He *was* a different man. "I would have liked your momma."

"She was a good woman. I'm trying to heed her advice myself."

Intrigue. Curiosity. "Tell me your biggest secret, Jessie Kay. The one that haunts you. The one I can see swimming in your eyes."

She shifted, visibly nervous. "I'll tell you tomorrow."

"So I'm the only brave one at this picnic? Got it."

"Hey!" Glaring daggers, she pointed her fork at him. "I'm brave, too."

"Prove it."

A minute passed in silence, then another.

"I'm waiting," he said. "You promised, after all."

"Fine. I always sometimes make good on my promises." She lifted her chin. "But are you sure you want to know?"

"Positive."

"Then get comfortable. This will take a while."

He motioned for her to continue.

She opened her mouth, snapped it closed.

"Jessie Kay—"

"Fine." She sighed. "The summer my momma died was such a rainy one, the river flooded. She told us not to do more than dip our feet in, but I ignored her. I wanted to swim, and I thought she worried for nothing. Everything looked calm, but it wasn't long before the current swept me away. I screamed for help, and she dove in after me. After a big-time struggle, she got me back to shore, but as she tried to crawl up behind me, the current pulled her away. She called my name, screamed it over and over, but I couldn't reach her. And then she was gone, swept under and whisked away."

She plucked at the fabric of her shirt, adding, "I left Brook Lynn at camp and ran downstream for what seemed like hours and finally I found our momma. Her body had washed ashore, but she was already dead. Rocks and stumps had slashed her up pretty good. Let's just say there was no saving her, and leave it at that."

And just like West, she'd had to live with guilt every day for the rest of her life.

"I'm sorry, kitten." He was the one to reach out this time. He clasped her hand and held on tight. "For years after Tessa died, I woke up expecting her to be in bed beside me. Then I would roll over and remember what had happened."

Tears welled in Jessie Kay's eyes. "And your heart and soul would be shredded all over again."

He gave a clipped nod. She got it, all of it, because her pain was a mirror of his.

"I would think about never again making a new memory with Mom—think about *Brook Lynn* never making a new memory with her—and sob into my pillow until my tear ducts swelled shut. And anytime something good happened, I wanted to share the details with her. Anytime something bad happened, I wanted to be enfolded in her arms. But more than anything, I wanted Brook Lynn to share the good times and bad with her, because even though she tried to hide it, I knew she wished for it and…and—"

She was breathing fast, too fast. Panicking? He leaned over, picked her up by the waist and settled her in his lap to enfold her in *his* arms. "I've got you. You're safe now." He gently petted her hair.

She went still and quiet before sagging against him. "I'm sorry. That was…yeah. Kinda embarrassing."

Treading lightly, he said, "Thank you for sharing with me."

"You already thought so little about me. Now you know the worst."

"I've never thought *so little* about you. And knowing the worst isn't a bad thing."

"Liar," she said without heat.

He kissed her temple. "The men in your past, they didn't know you. They liked the look of you—how could they not—but they never saw below the surface. I do. I see, and it only makes me want you more."

She stirred against him, sitting up. Her eyes went wide. "How do you know what they saw?"

A well of tenderness he'd never experienced. "If they'd seen what I see, they'd still be with you."

She gasped, licked her lips. "Pretty words, nothing more. You've only ever offered me a single night."

"That's my damage and has nothing to do with you. And I would happily offer you two months, but you've already told me your answer." He set her away from him—before he pressed her to her back and demonstrated all the things he'd dreamed of doing to her. "Just so you know, I need at least twenty-four hours' notice if you want to add a freak-out to your schedule." He tried for a light, easy tone while his palms itched for contact and his blood scalded his veins.

A little laugh escaped her. "Consider this your notice. Lately I seem to have one a day."

"Do you know the triggers?"

"Yeah. I start thinking about my sister and everything she's been deprived of because of me, and the ability to breathe abandons me. I just feel so...worthless."

"You are *not* worthless. In fact, I don't ever want to hear you use that foul nine-letter word again."

She stared at him, her mouth hanging open. "You're angry. You're actually angry on my behalf."

"Of course I am. You're so far from the *W* word it's comical."

"But—"

"You amuse the hell out of me. Do you know how hard that is to do? You do everything in your power to make the people around you comfortable and happy, even when they won't appreciate your efforts. You threaten big, hulking brutes when they start dating your sister, and you mean what you say. 'Hurt her and die.'"

"Anyone would do those things."

"No. They wouldn't." He toyed with the ends of her hair. "You need to start liking yourself, Jessie Kay. Only a crazy person would dislike you." He tweaked her nose. "I have something for you."

"A present? For me?"

"No." He didn't give gifts to anyone, ever. "It's a necessary accessory—for me." He stood, pulling her to her feet. "Stay here." He wasn't gone long, but she was practically jumping up and down with excitement by the time he returned.

"Gimme!"

He fought a grin as he held up the wristwatch he'd told himself he'd bought for Monica. An out-and-out lie, he now knew. He'd never spent more money on a watch, or picked one so delicate, with diamonds sparkling around the face. "I'd like you to wear this," he said as he anchored the piece around her wrist. A perfect fit. Not too big, not too small.

"West." She traced the center with trembling fingers. "It's absolutely gorgeous."

"Are you going to tell me it's too much and you can't accept it?"

"Don't be ridiculous. It's not enough and you should have spent more. I just… I've never worn a watch because *I* decide what time it is."

"A habit I will break. You're welcome."

She didn't even glance up at him, just continued to pet the watch. "Pretty."

He rubbed at his aching chest. "You'll wear it?"

"Always. If you expect me to give it back when you move out, well, sorry not sorry, but that's not happening."

"I won't want it back. It's yours. To help you keep track of your schedule…to help me stay sane."

"Okay. You convinced me. I'll do better with my time management. Promise. Well, half promise. I need wiggle room."

She accepted that easily? No argument like so many others had given? He could have kissed her.

He wanted to kiss her. Hard, then soft. With tongue, then with teeth.

"Now when you make me mad I can threaten to pawn it." She held the watch to the light, still petting the thing as the diamonds glittered more brightly in the light. "But

I never will, will I, baby? Because we're best friends forever."

"You're talking to the watch, aren't you?"

"Duh. I'd never coo at you like this."

He fought another grin.

"Oh, guess what," she added. "I came home while you were at work and remembered to lock the door on my way out."

"I noticed."

"So how did you get in?" Aaand still she petted the watch. "I didn't give you a key."

"Kitten, locks aren't a problem for me."

"Breaking and entering isn't a skill most people possess."

"Most people didn't grow up with a junkie mom who sometimes—most times—spent their grocery money on drugs. If I wanted to eat, I had to steal from the neighbors."

Her hand fluttered to her heart, her eyes filling with heartbreak. "You're never going to win our who-had-it-worse contest, so stop trying."

Not the words he'd expected, and he barked out a laugh.

"If you'd lived in Strawberry Valley" she continued, "I would have shared my lunch with you."

"I believe it. Word is, you were the sweetheart of the elementary."

"Who told you— Oh, Cora." She smiled ruefully. "I had my moments, but mostly I was a holy terror, repeating everything I heard adults say."

"Such as?"

"Well, in third grade, I got every kid in the cafeteria to chant 'I want an ice-cold beer.' In the fourth grade, I used show-and-tell to regale my class with a most unsuitable joke. I didn't even know what it meant. I just remembered the way my uncle Kurt laughed when he told it."

West waved a hand. "I'm listening."

"What comes after sixty-nine?"

"Seventy."

"No. Mouthwash."

He rubbed his fingers over his smiling mouth. "Naughty, naughty Jessie Kay. Did you earn yourself a spanking? Never mind. Don't answer that." Too dangerous. "It's time for your first soccer practice."

He grabbed the cupcake—for her benefit. She'd gone to so much trouble baking it, there was simply no way he could allow it go to waste.

He placed his free hand on her lower back to urge her forward and felt a quiver of awareness dance through her. A quiver that ignited his own.

Ignore it. Now, more than ever, he had to resist her. If the thought of hurting her had bothered him before, it utterly ravaged him now.

In the living room, he set the cupcake on the coffee table, but kept his eye on it as he moved furniture around, creating a small area free of obstacles.

"Shouldn't we go outside?" she asked.

"No need. Not for the basics. Stand beside the TV," he instructed. "No, more to the right. Good." He plopped onto the couch, tossed her the soccer ball that had been resting on a pillow and reclaimed his cupcake before resting his feet on the coffee table. "Now. Tap the top of the ball with your left foot, then repeat with the right. Do it over and over as quickly as you can."

Frowning, she hopped once, twice. "Like this?"

"Exactly. Pause as little as possible. Go until I tell you to stop."

She glared at him, hands on her luscious hips. "That's it? That's how you're going to teach me to be the best player in the history of ever? Why don't I just wax on, wax off while I'm at it?"

Funny. "Go."

"You're just going to sit there?"

"No. I'm going to enjoy my cupcake and watch a movie. *Go*."

"I hope you catch a stomach bug and vomit out your guts," she said, at last jumping into motion.

As he flipped through the channels, pretending to watch the screen, he ate the cupcake and swore he'd entered the gates of heaven. As Jessie Kay tapped the top, the ball rolled forward. After she replaced the ball and gave another tap, she lost her balance and stumbled forward. The exercise was designed to help her feet get to know the ball, something she desperately needed to learn.

By the ten-minute mark, sweat beaded on her forehead. She was panting. To his consternation, *he* was sweating and panting. After a while, he focused fully on Jessie Kay—the screen he'd never really seen completely forgotten. Her breasts bounced, and her skin flushed to a delicate rose.

Why was he supposed to resist her again?

"You were wrong, you know," she said through wheezing breaths.

"About?"

"I'm wearing a bra today. I just moved the lace aside for the picture."

Lace...nice.

She's trying to kill me.

"Bra talk is forbidden during practice."

"My legs—"

"Leg talk is forbidden as well," he told her.

She rolled her eyes. "When did you start playing soccer anyway?"

"The foster home where I met Jase and Beck. The dad played, and he used to spend hours with us in the backyard, teaching us how to kick and steal and block. I've played ever since." No, that wasn't exactly true. He'd taken a few years off in favor of getting high.

When he'd gotten clean, he'd needed a distraction—other than his schedule—and the game had provided one.

"All right," he said when she looked ready to collapse. "Let's try something new."

"Thank God," she huffed as she threw herself on the couch.

"Grab your coat and a pair of gloves."

"You mean we're actually going outside, where you're going to teach me more than basics?"

"Only if you stop talking and do as you're told." He went to his bedroom, dug out the cones he'd asked Brook Lynn to drop off after lunch, donned his own coat and returned to the living room. He led Jessie Kay to the backyard and just like he did for his elementary school players, he set the cones in a square. "You're going to dribble a figure eight around every cone, without letting the ball get away from you." Mist wafted in front of his face. "After you make it around the square, you're going to do what's called an inside hook and head back the other way."

He demonstrated the inside hook, planting his right foot behind the ball and his left foot to the right of the ball. With his left foot, he lifted to his toes and pivoted. With his right, he kicked, using the inside of his foot, all while his body turned the opposite direction, forcing the ball to roll in front of him.

"Fancy," she said, sounding impressed and excited.

"Sometimes necessary to retain possession of the ball. Sometimes a simple way of slowing things down."

"Right." She got into position and launched into action. Dribbling wasn't her strong suit. Not yet. Every few seconds she lost control of the ball, kicking it too far, forcing her to chase it around the yard, but she never gave up, never complained, and she wasn't too self-conscious to make mistakes in front of him, all of which he admired greatly.

"So…Monica Gentry called me," she said, fighting for breath. "Well, her assistant did."

He frowned. "Why?"

"She asked You've Got It Coming to cater her company Christmas party. On Saturday."

"That's only two days away."

"Which is why we asked for triple our normal fee. Anyway. I have to spend all day tomorrow cooking with Brook Lynn, so make sure that goes on my schedule."

Earlier Monica called to invite him to the very same Christmas party. In a moment of desperation, he agreed. He had to do whatever proved necessary to get Jessie Kay out of his head and his life back on track. But he'd regretted the decision ever since. Canceling now would make him an ungentlemanly ass.

"I'll be there," he admitted, the words leaving him like a curse. "At the party."

Jessie Kay stumbled but quickly righted herself. "You'll be there…as Monica's date?"

He ran his tongue over his teeth. "A friendly date, not a romantic one."

"But you're still seeing her?"

No emotion in her tone or in expression. She was suddenly a blank slate, and he couldn't stand it. "As a friend, like you and Daniel. She asked me to attend. I said yes."

"Well. Good for you." Up went her chin. "I hope you two have the *best* time. And now I'm going to shower up and go to bed. Got to get an early start tomorrow."

"Practice isn't over."

"I beg to differ," she said as she walked away.

Every cell in his body rebelled. *Get her back.* "Jessica," he called.

She paused in the doorway. "What?"

His mind overruled his libido. "If you want to practice with me, buy a sports bra. Nothing with lace."

"Well, then, you'll have to buy me one." She cupped her breasts. "Make sure you get the right size."

The back door slammed shut, but he rushed forward, unwilling to part from her, entering the house right on her heels. "I asked you to be with me. You said no. I'm trying not to hurt you."

"You're failing." She stomped down the hall. In her doorway, she whipped around to scowl at him. "You shouldn't settle for a woman you don't even like."

"There's a reason I do what I do."

"Tell me."

"No."

Fury blazed in those navy eyes, simmered beneath the flush in her skin, pulled tight at those lush red lips. "You're worth more than a perfunctory relationship with no future. You and Miss Gentry aren't right for each other and you know it. In two months, you'll be even more miserable than you are now."

He wanted to deny her prediction. He couldn't. "You once told me I looked good with her."

"There's a big difference between looking good together and being good together."

He should hole up in his own room. He shouldn't push this.

Observe. Understand. Act.

Sometimes the best course of action was to walk away. But something dark and dangerous lived deep inside him, a beast with an unquenchable appetite for this woman alone, and it wanted to push and push and push until she ceded everything she had to give.

Screw it.

"I'll call Monica tonight…if you'll tell me why you don't want me to see her." The low rasp of his tone whispered in the air between them. "If you'll tell me what you want from me."

"I don't want you to see her because…because…I want you to fall in love again," she said almost desperately. "I want you to find happiness."

Not even close to good enough. "You're speaking too abstractly, avoiding what makes you uncomfortable. You're speaking of things I can't control. Get personal," he all but snarled.

"Why should I? *You* are putting the burden of responsibility on my shoulders, leaving none for yourself."

She wasn't wrong. He scrubbed a hand down his face.

"But let's take you out of the equation for a moment. *I* want to fall in love." She ran her tongue over her lips, those full, pink lips, and he watched, helpless to do otherwise, wanting, craving, wishing, and maybe she sensed it, sensed his desire, because in a snap, her body language changed from stiff and straight as a board to soft and supple. "I want to find happiness, and there's nothing abstract about it." Her voice had even softened.

"Jessie Kay—"

"And I *can* control my actions," she continued, "by choosing the company I keep and cutting the people who *impede* that happiness."

With those few words, she utterly eviscerated him. "I would love a chance to make you happy. And I could do it. I know I could. *You* know I could," he said. "But…"

"Only for two months."

He nodded.

Gaze hot on his, she flattened her hands on his shoulders and walked him backward until he hit the wall. He could have spun her, could have caged her, but he remained in place, letting her have her way.

She rubbed her cheek against his. "What makes you think you'll be done with me in two months?"

He was rock hard and throbbing, and he didn't think he'd *ever* be done with her. "Done or not, I'd leave."

"Well, I'm sorry, sugar bear, but I want more."

"I can't give more."

"Be real. You *won't*." She rolled her hips once, twice, rubbing against his erection. Pure. Seduction. Raw and carnal. He loved it, suddenly lit up from the inside out, burning for her—for more. For everything. "Tell me why."

"Kiss me." He gripped her by the waist, ready to yank her closer for good, to strip her, to take her—and he had to take her, all the reasons to resist suddenly insignificant—but she latched on to his wrists and pinned his arms at his sides.

Another show of power and control. Yet again, he could resist, and if he did, there was no way she could hold him in place. But he would rather die than scare her away.

"Kiss me," he repeated.

"No," she said but nipped at his lips.

"Jessie Kay," he rasped, her name a curse or a prayer, he wasn't sure which.

"Tell me." She angled her head and grazed her teeth over his earlobe, her warm breath caressing his skin. "Please."

The whispered "please" pushed him over. If he scared her away, he scared her away, but he had to try for more. He just had to. "I'll give you five seconds to make a decision about me. Take me up on my offer and strip, or walk away. If your hands are on me when I get to zero, I'll make the decision for you. One."

She gasped but remained with him.

"Two. Three."

"West." Still she remained with him…and he began to hope, to pray.

"Four."

Just as he opened his mouth for the final count, his body primed and ready, her arms dropped to her sides and she stepped back.

He swallowed a curse.

"One day you're going to want a woman more than you want your reason, Lincoln West. You're going to crave her with every fiber of your being, but *she'll* be the one to walk away from *you*. And then, some other guy will come around and sweep her off her feet." With that, she marched into her room and slammed the door.

He reeled. He stewed. He would kill any man who tried to sweep Jessie Kay off her feet.

My job. My privilege.

He took a moment to breathe, willing the wild inferno inside him to calm. She was right to walk away. But he couldn't leave things like this. He had to—

The door wrenched open and she screamed, "Spider! Kill it! Kill it dead!" She rushed behind him and fisted his shirt to hold him in place, as her shield. "Why aren't you doing anything?"

Having her so close once again was a torment as much as a pleasure. "You want me to go inside your room, kitten, you have to let go of me." *Good luck getting rid of me once I'm there.*

One by one, her fingers lifted from his shirt. He stepped forward, his first glimpse inside her inner sanctum surprising him. The bedsheets had rainbows and unicorns, and the curtains were decorated with ballerinas and butterflies. The nightstand looked like it stood on human legs with feet encased in actual tennis shoes. The dresser looked like something out of *Alice in Wonderland*, tall and skinny, tilting to one side while scrawny arms reached out.

"Have you killed it yet?" She came up behind him to peek over his shoulder, only to release an ear-piercing scream. "The bastard just looked at me and licked its lips. Grab the .22 in the top drawer of the nightstand and shoot it!" She tried to push him forward while also pulling him backward. "We'll tape its remains outside my window as a warning to other spiders."

Adorable, aggravating girl. "Where is it?"

"How can you not see the fist-sized abomination

sharpening a mental fork and knife? It's there." She pointed, hastily jerking back her arm.

He spotted the dime-size arachnid and rolled his eyes. "What do I get if I save you from such a ferocious beast?"

"My eternal gratitude?"

He'd take it...even though he wanted more.

CHAPTER TEN

J ESSIE K AY SPENT the next day with Brook Lynn, as planned, doing her darnedest to resist the temptation to text West. After he'd disposed of the spider without killing it—a heinous crime against humanity—she'd wanted to just go ahead and hand over rights to her soul or her body, whichever he preferred. Or hey, why not both? He affected her in ways no one else ever had.

Rubbing against him had basically blown a gasket in her brain.

Matching wits with him had set her mind aflame.

Why not give him more than she'd ever given another? A chance for more.

Earlier she'd called Beck, seeking more advice.

"How can he not see how good we are together?" she'd asked.

"I'm sure he does. Just as I'm sure it terrifies him. His schedule is fighting for its life."

Made sense to think of the schedule as a person. The bastard! To it—him—Jessie Kay was the enemy and Monica the ally.

"Right now he's like a drowning man flailing for a life raft," Beck had added. "As soon as he goes under, the old West will die and a new West will rise."

Patience is a virtue. Patience is a freaking virtue. Got to have him. Soon!

Ugh. The urgency made zero sense. To her, sex had always been sex. Some encounters had been good, really good, and some had been bad, really bad, but either way, the act itself had always been secondary, something she could live without, what came before and after it far more important. First, the anticipation and seeming adoration. Then, for just a little while, a sense of belonging to someone else. Of course, after *that* she'd always experienced crushing disappointment.

Never good enough to keep.

Would things be different with West?

Silly question. He wanted a one-night stand or a two-month affair. Things would be the exact same. Wham, bam. Hello and goodbye.

"I love the way your watch glitters." At the stove, Brook Lynn stirred a pot of sweet-smelling liquid.

"I know." Her gaze constantly gravitated to it. "The only thing prettier is the bracelet you made from a twine of daisies in the third grade."

"You still have that thing?"

As if she'd ever part with it. "Of course. A few of the stems still have petals."

"I had no idea you were so sentimental." Brook Lynn smiled at her.

"Only with you."

"Maybe with West, too? He sure knows how to give good gift."

"He says it's not a gift but an insurance plan for his schedule." Clearly, he just had a problem with the thought of giving her—anyone?—a present. Another foster-kid problem? Or just a man thing?

The wedding march suddenly burst from speakers somewhere in the room, and Jessie Kay frowned.

"Stir the jaboticaba sauce, would you?" Brook Lynn abandoned her post to grab her cell phone.

Ah. A personalized ringtone.

As Jessie Kay did as requested, her sister adjusted the devices in her ears and spoke with…had to be the seamstress.

"No. No! I told you I don't want sapphire bridesmaid dresses, I want cerulean." Brook Lynn paced through the kitchen. "Don't you dare tell me it's too late. We have five months… No, no. Are you even listening to me? I'm going to—"

"Lose your temper?" Jessie Kay offered helpfully.

"Hang up and think about everything you've told me." Brook Lynn very carefully placed the phone on the table.

"I'll go out on a limb and guess…there's trouble with the bridesmaid dresses?"

Her sister stomped her foot. "Dang it! This makes me wish the zombie apocalypse would go ahead and kick off already. I could use my sword to rectify the situation without getting arrested."

Brook Lynn believed with all her heart that zombies were a sure thing, and it was freaking adorable.

Jessie Kay hated the stress the dress thing was causing her sister, but at long last saw an opportunity to help the girl and prove her everlasting love. "Don't you give it another worry. You pick the material you want and I'll sew the dresses. And for the first time in history, the bridesmaids will completely outshine the bride."

Brook Lynn gave a little laugh, a mix of relief and amusement. "Really? You don't mind?"

"Mind? I'm willing to beg for the privilege. More than anything, I want to help you the way you've always helped me."

"You don't have to—"

"Let me do this. Please."

Brook Lynn gave her a bear hug. "Thank you."

"Absolutely my pleasure."

The doorbell rang, causing her sister to frown. "I wasn't expecting company."

"I was." Jessie Kay set the spoon next to the pan. "I hope you don't mind, but I invited Daniel to help us out."

From the corner of her eye, she noticed Jase standing up. He'd spent the past hour on the couch, drawing designs for his new house. Jessie Kay raced past him, pushing him back onto the cushions.

"I've got this."

She opened the door and Daniel smiled his patented shit-eater grin before kissing her on the cheek.

She kissed him back—a peck on the mouth. *He* never made her feel like girls named Monica were more important.

"Something smells good." He sniffed the air.

"Stop flirting."

"I was talking about the food."

"Lying is beneath you. Now, come on. We've got work to do." She dragged him past a now-scowling Jase, saying, "You guys know each other, right? Right. No need for intros." In the kitchen, she urged Daniel toward the table. "Sit and chop the rest of the vegetables."

"Sir, yes, sir. FYI, it already looks like a vegan slaughterhouse in here."

"Those vegetables deserved to die," Jessie Kay said. "They tried to impersonate human food."

"Hey, Daniel," Brook Lynn said with a little wave.

"Hey." He grimaced as he looked over the pile awaiting his attention. "These things are edible?"

"I know, right?" Jessie Kay took the chair at his right. "This looks like a hairy nut sac and this looks like a demon foot. Taste it."

"No way—"

She placed the demon foot at his lips.

He flinched. "That has to be the foulest thing I've ever had in my mouth."

"Good to know." She made a notation on the list Brook Lynn asked her to make.

"You mean you didn't know?"

"Why would I? *You* are the official taste-tester."

Jase stomped into the kitchen, looking mad and bad to the bone. He took a seat at the table, directly across from Daniel. He didn't say anything, just stared.

Any other man would have peed his pants, but Daniel— Army Ranger, yo—was braver than most. He remained relaxed and at ease as Jessie Kay fed him bite after bite of mystery ingredients.

"Jase Hollister," Brook Lynn finally said. "Contribute or leave."

"Oh, I contributed."

A second later, hinges on the front door creaked. Footsteps sounded.

"What did you do?" Brook Lynn demanded.

For the first time, Jase smiled—and it was scarier than his scowl.

West sailed into the kitchen, draped his jacket over the back of the only remaining chair and sat. "Hello, everyone." His gaze locked on Jessie Kay and narrowed. "Thought I'd take my lunch break here."

Her heart slammed against her ribs. He'd come for her. Oh, sweet heavens...

What if he staked a claim?

"Your schedule must be crying," she said.

"Sobbing," he replied, surprising her.

"Well." She cleared her throat. "I don't need to make introductions. I hear you and Daniel have already met."

West appeared far from abashed. "We have. I'd love a chance to continue our previous conversation in private."

And make good on his threat? "He's busy."

In a loud stage whisper, she told Daniel, "Whatever you do, don't go into a supply closet with him. He gets handsy."

"I'm not the only one." West smirked at her. "Nowadays I prefer hallways."

Her cheeks pinkened as her mind flashed with images of pressing him against the wall, rubbing against him—being rubbed on by him.

"Oh, my gosh." Brook Lynn came over and leaned against Jase. "You made my sister blush, West. I don't think I've *ever* seen her blush. What happened in the hallway? I must know every detail."

Jessie Kay raised her chin. "He gave me a good old-fashioned bump and grind, that's what."

"Before that," West said, still utterly unabashed, "she sat on my lap."

"I did not—oh, yeah. I did." And she'd loved every second.

Jase smiled his I'm-going-to-murder-you smile. "In case you didn't know, Danny boy, West and Jessie Kay live together."

"Temporarily," she interjected. "And yeah, he knew. I don't keep secrets from him." Except for everything she'd shared with West.

West stiffened. His eyes narrowed to tiny slits.

"Look." Daniel focused on him. "I'm her friend, and you're not going to scare me away. You want to be with her, great, but you need to get used to having me around. I'm not going anywhere. You also need to get your shit together and treat her right, or *I'll* be the one making threats."

Her heart swelled with pride as she peered at him. He'd just *fought* for the privilege of hanging out with her—without the bonus of sex or any kind of making out.

"Daniel," she said as a lump grew in her throat. "You are officially my hero."

"Mine, too." Brook Lynn beamed at him.

Jase crossed his arms over his chest. "You are officially my target."

West placed a hand on his friend's shoulder, which visibly calmed him, then looked to Daniel. "You're a prick and you're annoying as hell...but you're also right."

What the what now? Daniel had just said one of the sweetest things ever, and West lost his jealousy, just like that?

But West wasn't done. "She's the kindest, silliest, most complicated person I've ever met, and she deserves friends who see the treasure she is. Friends who will stand up for her, love her and make her happy. She deserves the best."

Scratch that. *West* had just said the sweetest thing ever.

He thought she was a treasure? Didn't he realize that honor belonged to Brook Lynn?

"Thank you," Jessie Kay whispered.

He didn't stick around to bask in her surprised glow. He stood and strode out of the kitchen...out of the house, leaving her reeling.

THE NEXT DAY was a buzz of activity, distracting Jessie Kay from the mess West had made of her mind, and maybe kinda sorta her heart. He thought she was a treasure!

This morning, he'd left her a note beside the coffeepot.

"Your acumen is as radiant as your smile."

And by the canister of sugar, there'd been another.

"Your ebullience makes me smile."

Hanging on the fridge, there'd been a third.

"As brilliant as you are, I'm pretty sure you could find the end of a circle."

The sweet affirmations reminded her of the letters her dad had written to her mom, and they made her weak in the freaking knees.

West was attracted to her. He'd made no secret about that. And he clearly liked her. But was it enough? He wouldn't tell her the reason for the two-month date-and-dump, and he wouldn't make an exception for her by trying for something longer-term.

They were doomed before they started.

"And what do we have here?" a voice asked, drawing her from her thoughts.

An older man in a suit and tie stepped in front of her, snagging her attention. His gaze remained glued to the tray in her hand. A woman around the age of three thousand stood beside him, her nose in the air. An old fart and a former debutante. Great. Monica's Christmas party slash douchefest had officially kicked off.

Jessie Kay lifted her tray higher, letting the gent get a whiff of the mystery ingredients masquerading as sausage balls and pasted a superbright smile on her face. "It's your lucky day. I have the best thing you'll ever put in your mouth."

The two sampled the food and walked away without another word.

"You're welcome," Jessie Kay muttered, deciding You've Got It Coming deserved a thousand dollar bonus on top of triple their usual fee. Because of the late notice, she and Brook Lynn had been unable to hire enough waitstaff, forcing them to don the uniform themselves: a white button-down, black slacks and tuxedo apron.

More and more buff young men and toned young women began to spill through the arched doorways. Trainers, no doubt about it. Monica's employees. Monica, who was as successful as Jessie Kay hoped to be—but never would be. The beauty not only starred in workout videos, but she owned a chain of gyms in Oklahoma City. Bodies by Monica.

The older crowd must be Monica's family. Or board members—if she had board members. Or maybe her finance team? Who knew.

Meanwhile, I'm struggling to make ends meet. I suck.

Jessie Kay wove through the grand ballroom, a room boasting luxuries a small-town girl like her had never dreamed possible. An arched ceiling with intricately carved rose vines reached toward a pair of dazzling chandeliers that dripped with thousands of teardrop crystals. Huge stained glass windows were draped in plum velvet and gold lace, the fabrics twisted into fancy knots on each side. Murals depicting English lords and ladies at a party of their own decorated the walls.

Ever the dedicated waitress—cough, because she loved her sister, cough—she stopped when she happened upon a group of the younger peeps. "I hope you brought your appetite. These babies are going to blow you away."

One of the girls reached toward the tray. Another

slapped her hand and whispered, "I think she's the one Monica warned us about."

The group turned away in a hurry.

Ouch. Well, screw them. *More for me.* Jessie Kay popped a ball into her mouth. Hey! Amazingly good, especially given the assigned ingredients Brook Lynn had to work with. A real testament to her skill.

A blond god of a man approached her. "I'd love one of whatever you're serving." He winked at her.

She took his measure in less than a second: another member of the royal one-and-done family. "A big boy like you should probably take two, don't ya think?"

He selected two, popped both into his mouth, chewed and swallowed. "Very good, but my appetite is far from satisfied. You offering anything else?"

"Just the food." She smiled at him, and he smiled back. He was a charmer. The kind of man she used to pursue, certain he was equally charmed by her. A pretense. Always a pretense. She lost her smile.

"I'm Evan, by the way."

"Well, you'll have to excuse me, Evan. This tray of goodies is the only thing keeping me from a *Lord of the Flies* situation. If you'll excuse me…"

Where the heck was West? With his precious schedule, he should have arrived right at 8:00 p.m. She checked her watch. Her gorgeous, glittery watch worth more than she could earn in ten years—8:12 p.m.

Maybe her thoughts conjured him. He walked through the front door a second later, Monica clinging to his side. Jessie Kay skidded to a stop, her ability to breathe suddenly gone. His muscular frame was perfectly complemented by a tailored pin-striped suit. His dark hair had somehow appeared both tamed and rebellious. But his eyes…his eyes haunted her. They were cold, amber icicles, no longer blistering with heat.

Frigid, unbreakable steel for Monica? Smoldering fire for Jessie Kay?

The sweetest flood of relief left her light-headed, almost giddy. Made her ache. Oh, how she'd ached.

Holding out for love. Lust is nothing special.

But it wasn't just lust. Not with West. They were friends, too.

And as his friend, she'd decided to do something special for him. Something she'd dubbed Operation Collage. *Won't let his stupidity—or my jealousy—stand in my way.*

She balanced her tray with one hand and withdrew her cell phone from the pocket in her apron with the other. Camera—on. She zoomed to West and snapped picture after picture, making sure to cut out Monica.

He'd once said no one cared enough about him to take pictures of him. Jessie Kay planned to prove him wrong.

When she finished, her gaze snagged on Monica, and crap, the girl looked incredible. Her red dress glittered with countless rhinestones, the deep vee in front dipping all the way to her navel, the bottom hem ending just below her pantyline.

The woman wasn't just smoking hot, she actually had her life together, her future figured out.

Envy rots the bones, Momma used to say.

Well, Jessie Kay's bones had just taken a major hit of decay. *I'm not even in the same league.*

Needing a sec to recover, she slinked into a shadowed corner.

Momma also used to say, someone else's good fortune couldn't hinder her own and she should rejoice that good things still happened in the world.

Right. That was right, and in a minute or two, she would compose herself and return to offering heaven on earth to people who'd forgotten how to say "please" and "thank you." Until then...

The gilded mirror in front of her offered an unobstructed view of the ballroom's occupants. Amid the sea of tuxedo-clad men and sequin-draped women, however, she lost sight of West and Monica. Was the girl still cuddled into his side?

"The indomitable Jessie Kay Dillon is *hiding*?"

Jessie Kay jolted in surprise, almost dropping her tray as she focused on a pale, shaky Harlow, who was dressed in the same uniform, holding a tray of bacon-wrapped shrimp with a sweet marshmallow cream sauce. The unhealthiest thing on the menu. Also the best.

She ate three of the things before she replied. "I'm on my smoke break." Frowning, she waved a marshmallow-smeared fingertip from the top of Harlow's head to the sole of her feet. "What about you? You look like you've been chewed up and spit out."

"You don't smoke. And I'm fine."

"First, how dare you! I won't be discriminated against. As a nonsmoker, I deserve as many breaks as my co-workers. Second, did I mention you look like ten miles of bad road?"

"You are *so* good to me," Harlow said drily.

"As Brook Lynn's second-in-command, I'm technically your boss, and I'm ordering you to take a smoke break and tell me what's wrong." Not too long ago, the girl was poisoned by a trio of creepers unable to forgive her former bullying ways—and for snagging Beck.

Mostly for snagging Beck. They'd only meant to cause embarrassing vomiting by putting eye drops in her drink, but they'd nearly killed her. She'd slipped into a coma for several gut-wrenching days. Jessie Kay still felt guilty for only visiting twice. Visits she'd managed only because she'd popped a few antianxiety meds.

In her defense, hospitals were death traps.

Despite the great waves of fatigue radiating off Harlow, a slow smile lit her entire face. "There's honestly nothing wrong with me. There's everything right. I'm actually... Well, I'm pregnant."

"What!" Jessie Kay shouted, only to cringe as her voice echoed.

"Oh, wow, that felt good to say."

More quietly, Jessie Kay asked, "Are you seriously heating a bun in your oven?"

"Yep. He or she will bake for another seven months, three weeks."

"You sneaky little hooker!" The feels were almost too much. "Why are you just now telling me? Who else knows?" In other words, who would feel the worst of her wrath for daring to hide the news?

"No one. You're the first."

Pleasure unfurled inside her. "*Of course* I am. Because I'm your best friend in the universe. Because you trust me to keep your secret as long as I possibly can while realizing *as long as I can* probably only equates to a day or two, but you love me so much you're willing to forgive me."

Harlow laughed. "I know you. You're a vault. Anyway, Beck and I decided to tell everyone together, after we'd gotten used to the idea ourselves, but you insulted my baby glow and I had to defend it."

"How long have you known?"

"Since the day of the wedding."

The wedding. Duh. "That's why you were worried about Beck not wanting to be with you anymore. Too big a change for the guy who despises change."

"Exactly. But he was *sooo* happy." Harlow rubbed the slight bump in her belly. "We both are."

"Well, *I'm* happy for you." Jessie Kay held her tray out of the way to lean into her friend for a hug. Tears burned the backs of her eyes, but she blinked them away, not wanting Harlow to see them and get the wrong idea. She was over-the-moon excited for the girl, but also a little sad for herself. The future she'd envisioned—Harlow and Brook Lynn leaving her behind to raise their families—had come sooner rather than later, and oh, crap, what kind of terrible person was she, concentrating on her loss rather than her friend's gain? "This marks the dawn of a new and perfect era. A new breed of human. Superhumans, they'll be called. And okay, okay. There's no need for you to ask. Yes, I will be your birthing coach, but only as long as you commit to a home delivery. Hospitals are the cesspools of our generation."

"Uh, wow, that's such a sweet offer. The best. But, uh, Beck is going to be my birthing coach. And I'm willing to risk the cesspool if it means I can be so drugged up I'll forget I'm pushing a watermelon through a pinhole."

"A soft no. Got it. You just need more time to think. Meanwhile, go home." Jessie Kay gave her a little push. "You shouldn't be on your feet."

"I'll be fine. Will you?" Harlow peeked around the corner, her concern melting away. She snickered. "Never mind. West might be here with another woman, but he's looking for someone else. Want to guess who it is?"

"No. Because it's not me. We're currently avoiding each other." When she'd woken up this morning, intending to sneak out, she'd discovered he'd already taken off. The jerk.

"He's getting mad, I think," Harlow said. "Oh! I'm no lip-reader, but I'm pretty sure he just told a guy to get the eff out of his way. Go over there and put him out of his misery. Just... I don't know, be gentle with him or something."

"What are you talking about? I'm always gentle."

Harlow snorted. "You once drove your boyfriend's truck into his living room. On purpose. You, Jessie Kay Dillon, are no delicate flower."

"The boyfriend in question cheated on me." Among other things.

"Oh. Well, good call."

As she peered from the shadows, dread and anticipation skittered along her nerve endings. West had moved into her line of sight. He stood in a circle of women. Monica still clung to his side, yes, and she was glaring at the interlopers, all *he's mine, bitches, back off,* but the bitches in question didn't seem to get the mental memo. As they spoke to him, they ran their nails down the sleeves of his jacket or playfully tweaked the end of his tie. To his credit, he remained stiff and distanced.

Finally, Monica got sick of the attention and shooed the women away. Of course, they were immediately replaced by a circle of businessmen who vied just as staunchly for his attention.

He scanned the room, searching for someone just as Harlow had claimed. Tremors nearly toppled Jessie Kay.

Please be me.

Please, please, don't be me.

When he reached her, he skipped right over her and her shoulders drooped with disappointment. But his gaze jerked back to her and stayed put.

As if she really was a treasure?

Trapped by his intensity, she could only stand there, staring back at him. The most delicious heat washed over her, flames licking and nipping at her. She felt like the only woman left in creation. The only woman West could see. The only woman he ever wanted to see.

The thick fan of his black lashes narrowed, and he tilted his chin to motion her over.

Harlow gave her butt a pat. "Go get him, tiger."

"Okay, but only because you're forcing me." Jessie Kay's tremors got worse as she moved forward. Men and women continually stepped in her path to snatch an appetizer, and by the sixth interruption, irritation got the better of her. She stuffed the last three faux sausage balls in her mouth, clearing her tray.

"All gone," she told the seventh couple, and okay, yeah, little bits of mystery meat might have fallen out the side of her mouth. Her mother would have been horrified.

Never let your mood dictate your manners. Feelings are fleeting. Impressions are forever.

"Jessie Kay." Amusement and desire fought for dominance in West's eyes. He leaned over to kiss her cheek and whispered, "You are completely adorable."

His compliment wrapped around her, a lover as dedicated to her pleasure as he was to her heart. A deception— right? "Mr. West. So good to see you again."

"What are you offering?" His gaze slid over her body rather than her tray.

To you? Everything.

No, no. Nothing. Not while he was on a date with another woman. "I *was* offering big, delicious balls, but I ran out."

The man at West's left choked on a laugh. He looked her up and down and grinned. "Why don't I escort you to the kitchen for a new tray? Along the way, we can get to know each other better."

"She doesn't need your help." West was stiff, stiffer than before, and a scowl pulled at the corners of his lips...lips that were full and pink, made for rapture...or slicing an enemy into pieces.

Monica nuzzled his shoulder and glared at Jessie Kay. "You're still on the clock, Miss Dillon. I suggest you stop fraternizing with my guests and actually do the job I'm paying you for. If that's too complicated, I can show you to the door."

Ouch. *Been put in my place.*

She could have lashed out; she wanted to. She was no stranger to catfights. But this wasn't the time or place to indulge in a down and dirty beat down. If she had to make nice with West's flavor of the next two months to preserve the good reputation of You've Got It Coming, she would. Anything for her sister. Besides, there was no way she'd lose the battle of tempers because of Monica Gentry. Especially since she'd *expected* Monica to act this way.

She cleared her throat. "You're right. Absolutely. I'll just mosey along to the kitchen—alone—and get those balls."

"I'd like to talk to you in private, Monica," West said with a decided lack of emotion.

Monica smirked at her before focusing on West. "Of course, darling."

Darling?

With her sensible flats, Jessie Kay hurried across the room. In the prep station connected to the ballroom, she exchanged her empty tray for one overflowing with goodness. Brook Lynn rushed around like zombies were headed their way, arranging new sets of appetizers to be served.

"Tell me everything is running smoothly out there," her sister demanded.

She pasted on a sunny smile. *Hide the hurt.* "Putting me in charge of the servers was the smartest thing you've ever done. I've only dropped, like, three trays, and thanks to the five-second rule, everyone loved the food anyway."

Brook Lynn stopped with a handful of garnish halfway to a plate and gaped at her. "You served food that had hit the floor? Jessie Kay! I'll claw off your face!"

"Are you throwing a temper tantrum?"

"What? Me? No!"

"Because I was kidding. I only dropped *two* trays."

This time, her sister rolled her eyes. "Your warped sense of humor—"

"Makes you want to throw something at me. Go ahead. I did you wrong, and I deserve to suffer for it."

"—is one of the things I love best about you."

Boo. Hiss. "Hey, just out of curiosity. If I were to spit in someone's food, would I lose our bet?"

Horror contorted her sister's features. "Yes! Oh, my gosh, yes!"

"Dude. You should see your face right now. There's a vein *pulsing* in your forehead." She swiped up a new tray, blew her sister a kiss and returned to the party, determined to avoid Monica and her insults…as well as West and the ache that came with him.

CHAPTER ELEVEN

"I WILL SAY this once and only once." West pinned Monica in place with a gaze usually reserved for businessmen trying to shortchange him for work he'd already completed. "If you talk to Jessie Kay like that again, you won't like what happens."

Now wasn't the time to push him. He'd been in a terrible mood since yesterday's lunch when Jessie Kay had looked at Daniel with adoration—and rightly so. The guy had stepped up in a big way, giving Jessie Kay the support and devotion she'd always wanted.

Maybe he'd guessed what West had. She feared not being good enough—which was why West had set out to prove she was one of the best people he knew. But Daniel, the bastard, had beaten him to the punch.

"West. Please." Monica grabbed hold of his lapels. "Don't be mad at me for chastising the girl. You can't see it, but she's trouble."

He'd dreaded this night. Because of Monica, who'd texted nonstop since he'd agreed to be her date, who'd even complained about Jessie Kay—*that blonde from the wedding better not mess everything up*. Because of Jessie Kay, whom he'd wanted to chain to his bed and keep safe from this very thing. Among other things. Because the last party he'd attended was the one he'd thrown in

Tessa's honor. He'd gotten drunk, and if he'd known a dealer in Strawberry Valley, he would have gotten high.

Jessie Kay hadn't judged him that night. She'd offered to leave the barn, where the party raged, and hole up in his bedroom to watch movies. In return he'd kissed one of her friends in front of her.

"Don't say another word to Jessie Kay," he said, "and we'll make it through the party without any more problems."

Fat tears welled in Monica's eyes.

He'd pulled her into the hallway right outside the ballroom—where he could still smell the champagne—not wanting to embarrass her in front of her employees. A courtesy she hadn't extended to Jessie Kay. One more insult, however, and he would unleash the kraken, uncaring who watched.

Already he battled an unholy rage. As Jessie Kay had raced off, hurt and humiliation had colored her cheeks. The girl with a heart as soft as marshmallows shouldn't be made to feel as if she were garbage.

"West—"

"I mean it, Monica. She's off-limits. In word and in deed."

The tears dried, an unholy rage of her own sparking to life. "You protect her? *Her?* Who is she to you?"

His roommate. His friend. His tormentor. His every fantasy made flesh. "You and I are not a couple, Monica." In fact, he wouldn't be seeing her again. In any capacity. "We never will be. I owe you no answers."

She whimpered…and then she erupted. "You bastard!" Steam practically curled from her nostrils as she stomped her foot.

Here comes the beast I read about online in three... two...

"I mean something to you," she hissed, "you just don't know it yet. You don't remember me, damn you. I never wanted you to remember, only wanted you to fall for the woman I am. Now I don't see any other way."

His brow furrowed with confusion. "You've lost me."

"Add a hundred and twenty pounds to me. Any clue yet?" She laughed bitterly. "Four years ago, you dated Patience Ludwick, my roommate."

Light bulb. Monica, the dark-haired girl who'd peered at him as if he were a god, who'd hung on his every word as if he were unveiling the secrets of the universe. She used to lament her lack of boyfriend, and he'd often complimented her to help build her self-esteem.

"For two months, you came to our apartment almost every evening. While Patience slept, you spent hours talking with me. You were always so nice to me." She tightened her grip on his jacket. "I knew you would fall in love with me if I lost weight. I knew it! But one day, out of the blue, you dumped her, said you didn't love her, that you would never love her. You took off and never came back, breaking her heart. Breaking mine!"

She'd just described every relationship he'd ever had since Tessa. "Patience knew how long the relationship would last before she ever agreed to be with me." He'd made sure of it. And there at the end, her heart hadn't been involved. He'd simply hurt her pride, because she'd thought—like so many others—that he would soften, change his mind. A critical mistake. He would never soften, and he would never change his mind. He'd set a schedule for reasons that hadn't changed, and he would stick to it. For better or worse.

But Monica still had stars in her eyes. "I knew deep down you just needed to see the woman I was inside, the skinny one, so I dieted and worked out and kept tabs on you, watching you date other women for two months, once every year, before you walked away. Whether you realized it or not, you were waiting for me, West. And don't try to deny it. When you saw the new me, you picked me. Me! The one you love inside and now, outside. We can be happy together. You just have to give me a chance to prove it."

He stepped away from her, severing contact. Shit. Shit! This wasn't his first boiling-bunny experience, but it *would* be his last. From now on, he would screen potentials more thoroughly. And yeah, okay, guilt welled up, spilling through him, hot enough to burn. He'd dated and dropped a lot of good women without any thought to their feelings, consoling himself with the knowledge that he'd been up-front and honest.

"West. Please." Monica reached for him, but again he stepped back. "Let's blow the party. We'll go to my place, drink wine, talk like we used to and finally make love. By morning we'll laugh about the blonde, I swear."

No, he would never laugh about his feelings for *the blonde*. "I'm sorry, Monica." He used his gentlest tone, not wanting to hurt her further but seeing no way around it. "I never should have asked you out. You and I never would have worked out. We want different things."

She shook her head. "I saved myself for you. I want my first time to be with you."

He'd been Tessa's first, and yes, it had been an honor, had made him feel as if he were king of the world. He'd experienced an extreme flood of triumph and had wanted to beat his chest like a gorilla—because of the girl, not her state.

Jessie Kay wasn't a virgin, and yet, if ever he got inside that woman, he'd still want to beat his chest like a gorilla.

He desired her more than he'd ever desired another.

Oh…shit. He did. The boy he'd been had desired Tessa, but the man he'd become desired Jessie Kay. There was no comparison.

"You and I would never work out," he repeated. "I'm interested in someone else."

Monica's eyes narrowed to tiny slits. "You're interested in *her*, aren't you? She's a whore!"

He took another step back, before he did something he would regret. "She's not a whore. And you and I…we won't be seeing each other again. Ever."

"No. No!" Desperation tinged her voice. "Don't do this. Please, West. Remember how good we were together, all those years ago, how we talked and laughed. We can have that again."

"I remember." She'd been sweet and shy and barely able to meet his gaze. "Now we want different things. I'm sorry," he repeated, and her desperation was instantly replaced by fury.

"Bastard! You're such a bastard!" She raised her hand to slap him, but he caught her wrist, stopping her. "I hate you."

"Hate me all you want. It's deserved, and I accept it as my due. But make sure you keep it directed at me."

With that, he released her and strode from the room.

Her tearful cry followed him. "I didn't mean it, West. I'm sorry. I'm so sorry. I don't hate you. I love you!"

He had to circle the room twice before he caught sight

of Jessie Kay—and of course, a swarm of drooling men surrounded her. He stalked forward, shoving his way to the center of the group.

"—tap my butt again, and I'll give you a high five. In the face. With my tray," Jessie Kay was saying, her smile sweet.

"I'm pretty sure it'd be worth it," the guy replied.

A punch of fury in West's chest, a kick of possessiveness in his gut. No one touched this girl. "You put your hands on her again, and you'll lose them."

The kid in question paled. The rest of the crowd backed up several steps.

"West." Jessie Kay stiffened, though her voice lacked any kind of heat. "How dare you. Threatening the guests is unprofessional."

"We're leaving." He did the smart thing—the only-way-to-survive-in-the-jungle thing—and kept the flaw in her admonition to himself as he confiscated her tray and handed it to the openmouthed kid. "Take this to the kitchen. Now."

"Yes, sir."

"Hey!" Jessie Kay placed her hands on her hips. "What are you doing?"

"I'm *trying* to abscond with you."

"Well, stop. You came with Monica. You can leave with Monica."

He thought he detected jealousy, what he'd once hoped she'd feel. But not here, not now. Not anymore. Jessie Kay put on a good game face, but he saw the insecure girl lurking underneath. She had no idea of her worth, and as long as they were friends—or whatever they were to each other—she would need reassurance.

High maintenance, some would say. But then, he was

higher maintenance. They were actually kind of perfect together.

"I want nothing to do with Monica." He tugged Jessie Kay away from the crowd, and this time she allowed it. Had he ever felt skin so soft? So warm?

"West," she said, breathless.

As he stopped to face her, he was hyperaware of her, locked in a world where only she existed. The sweetness of her natural perfume. The sudden hitch in her breath. The increasing velocity of her pulse. The way she leaned toward him, a subtle softening of her spine. The way her body readied itself for his possession, her breasts swelling and her nipples tightening.

With his free hand, he traced his thumb over the rise of her cheekbone. "What are you doing to me?"

She peered at him with eyes now heavy-lidded. "The same thing you're doing to me, I hope."

A clench of need low in his gut. "Let's get out of here."

"I want to, but I can't. Brook Lynn—"

"Will understand. The party is anathema to us both, kitten."

A smile pulled at the corners of her lips. "There you go, using fancy words again."

"Don't even think about protesting. I saved you from the clutches of a deadly spider, remember? You owe me."

"West!" Monica screeched, and the rest of the world came crashing back into focus. He looked over at her. Black mascara streaked down her tearstained face. With no thought to the scene she was creating, she barreled toward them. "West!"

"She looks… Wow." Jessie Kay's jaw dropped. "Did you murder her cat?"

"Don't know if she has a cat. I broke things off, not

that we were ever together." He tried to drag Jessie Kay away, but she dug in her heels.

"Slow your roll, sugar bear, and explain. I know you said you wanted nothing to do with her, but what do you mean by *broke things off*?"

"I told her I didn't want to see her again, and now she's out for blood. Yours, to be precise. Let's go." He pulled.

She resisted. "Why mine? What'd I do?"

"Isn't it obvious?" He rubbed the back of his neck. "You have the face I dream about and the smile I crave."

"I *what*?" she squeaked.

"You heard me. Now let's go."

Too late.

Monica reached them, hissing when she noticed their joined hands. "I was right. It's her. You have no idea what she's like. I asked around. She's trash! A slut! She'll sleep with anyone—and has."

West felt as if he'd been swallowed by a fury so deep, so all-encompassing, he'd never find his way free of it.

And she wasn't done. "I hope you enjoy the STDs she'll give you."

"You mean my *sexy table dances*? Oh, he will," Jessie Kay snapped. "Trust me."

West stepped between the two women, unsure what to do next, only knowing he could end up in jail if he handled things his way.

"Did tearing me down make you feel good, little girl?" Jessie Kay lifted her head with regal authority. "I hope so, because this next part is going to hurt you." She pulled back her elbow and let her fist fly.

Smack! Her knuckles went to war with Monica's nose, and the nose lost. Cartilage snapped. Blood spurted, and

Monica howled with pain, stumbling back, losing her footing and falling.

"Ow," Jessie Kay shouted, shaking her hand. "I didn't expect it to hurt me, too."

West wanted to smile. He wanted to curse.

"You'll pay for this," Monica rasped.

"For defending myself? Not likely." Jessie Kay spun, meeting the gaze of everyone around her. "She came at me. Everyone saw. You know the truth. And someone tell my sister I did *not* lose my temper. I remained calm the entire time."

West reclaimed Jessie Kay's hand—the uninjured one—as a tuxedo-clad Beck and Jase pushed their way through the crowd. Of course his friends had snuck in. Brook Lynn and Harlow were here.

"I know Brook Lynn probably feels her professional reputation is at stake," he said to Jase, "so it's up to her whether she stays or goes, but I'm taking Jessie Kay home."

"I know my girl," Jase said. "Her sister was insulted. She won't want to stay."

Both guys stalked off to find their women.

Outside the hotel, cars pulled up to the lamp-lit sidewalk, tainting the air with exhaust. Different valets rushed to climb inside different vehicles while guests meandered in and out, wearing everything from formal gowns to jeans and sweaters.

"I'm not leaving without talking to my sister," Jessie Kay said. "Or getting her money."

"I'll pay her." He showed his ID card to the valet, who'd just returned to the podium with keys.

The guy nodded, his gaze lingering on Jessie Kay just long enough to draw a growl from West.

"Today," West roared.

Footsteps suddenly rang out.

"First," Jessie Kay said, "I don't want your money, I want Monica's. Second, you weren't the one under attack. What's your rush? Let me go back and speak with—"

"You know your sister is packing up. As for the rush, I have many reasons. How many would you like to hear?"

She pursed her lips. "Start with three."

"One, an escalation of violence would have landed us both in serious trouble. Two, if Monica had hit you back, I would have lost it. I'm like the Hulk, and people don't want to see me when I'm angry. Especially when it comes to your protection. You have somehow become my favorite person, and I will do bad, bad things to keep you safe."

"That's only two reasons," she said on a wispy catch of breath.

"Three, I want to get your hand on ice. Your knuckles are already swelling."

Her features softened, the way he'd hoped. A second later, his car arrived, and he tipped the valet, who did his best to avoid glancing in Jessie Kay's direction. Only when West was on the road, the sprawling, five-star hotel nothing but a blur in his rearview mirror did he relax.

"I don't have an STD, you know," she said quietly, peering out at the night sky. "I haven't been with anyone in months, since…you know, and I've been tested."

"Good. I don't have one, either. And kitten," he said, his voice just as quiet, "I don't consider you a slut."

"You must."

"Because a double standard is mandatory to be considered a man?"

"Yes!"

"Hardly. I'm no one's judge. You know my history, right? Besides, if I were a girl, I would have bagged and tagged Jase and Beck, too. They're hot."

She smiled, but the amusement didn't last long. "You must hate that I've been with them."

"I hate the thought of you with anyone else and for a while, I thought I'd grow to resent the two for putting their hands on my woman. But now I realize it simply doesn't matter. They are the past, and I am the present."

"Your woman," she whispered, as if she couldn't believe he'd said the words. "The future." Gulping, she turned in her seat to fully face him. "How did Monica know you want to pretend I'm a human buffet?"

He gripped the steering wheel more tightly. "I told her."

A moment passed in silence. A moment he lacked any kind of heartbeat, the stupid organ waiting for a reason to beat.

"I want you, too," she admitted. "You know I do. But I won't do anything about it because I expect long-term and you insist on two months." A heavy pause. "Right?"

His body reacted to her words—*I want you, too*—growing hot and hungry, his heart now racing as an insatiable need for relief plagued him. "Right." He couldn't overlook his reasons for keeping this particular schedule. Not even for Jessie Kay. It would be an insult to Jase and Tessa, even Beck. It would be an insult to the pain they'd suffered on his behalf.

"Why?" she asked. "Why do you insist on two months? Tell me. Please."

"Not yet." He'd have to tell her sooner or later, he saw that now, but as for tonight, there'd been enough turmoil. "If we can't be together, you have to help me resist you.

Tell me all the horrible things you'd do if we were involved. Cling? Demand to know every detail about my rotten childhood?"

For a long, silent moment, she peered at him with yearning and hope, and it tore him up inside. He didn't think there could be anything worse—until both emotions were eclipsed by resolve.

"I would cling *so hard*," she finally said. "I would ask a million questions about not just your childhood but your day, every day, and if I thought, even for a second, you'd looked at another woman, I would punish you by refusing to sleep with you. For a week!"

"You mean you would punish *yourself*. But keep going. This is helping." Was it though? He wasn't disturbed by the thought of her questions and her punishment. He was intrigued.

"I would take horrible advantage of you," she said.

Again, he was intrigued. "Give me an example."

"Well, for starters, I would expect you to trade cars with me."

"Why?"

"Because any boyfriend of mine would *insist* I drive the safer vehicle."

Guess who would soon be getting a new—safer—car all her own?

But she wasn't done. "And I hope you like your girlfriends in baggy shirts and sweatpants. The moment I have you nailed down, I'll stop putting any effort into my appearance."

He gave a mock shudder.

"And despite your obvious aversion to gift-giving, I will expect a present for every anniversary. And, West? I believe every week together is a new anniversary."

The thought utterly terrified him.

The one gift he'd given his mother, she'd pawned. The first gift he'd given to a foster mother hadn't compared to the gifts she'd received from her own children. She'd proudly displayed theirs, and his—a drawing he'd slaved over—had ended up in the trash with the wrapping paper.

"Your turn to help me." Jessie Kay waved her hand at him. "Tell me the horrible things you'd do to me."

He brought her hand to his mouth, and licked between her knuckles. One taste. Just one… "I'd have a schedule drilled into your head by the end of the first day."

"Nothing new there."

"If you were a minute late to anything, I would pencil in a lecture and a spanking."

Her exaggerated gasp caused his lips to twitch at the corners. She placed her free hand over her throat, saying, "You're such a beast! Yes, I would deserve and welcome the spanking. But the lecture? Cruel and unusual. How long would it last?"

"Hours."

She tsk-tsked. "I hate to break it to you, sugar bear, but I wouldn't hear a word. I'd be too busy daydreaming about the joys of single life."

"Don't kid yourself, kitten. I'd deliver the lecture naked. You'd only want more of me, not less."

Goose bumps broke out over her skin. "What else?"

"I would demand to be the center of your world." He never had before, but with her, he was certain he'd make an exception. "Every minute of every day would belong to me. I would expect you in my bed every night and in my arms every morning. I would have you so often and

so hard you wouldn't be able to breathe without thinking of me."

Another moment passed in silence. Another moment
without a heartbeat.

He reached the house, parked in the driveway.

"Horrible," she finally said, her voice little more than
smoke—smoke that drugged him...lured him deeper
into her spell.

He shook as he got out of the car, walked around and
opened her door. "I need another reason. Now."

She stood before him, looking up at him with luminous eyes. "I would demand a hug at least ten times a
day."

He didn't have to fake a shudder this time. "I hate
hugs. I never know how long or tight to hold on."

"Well, I can fix that in a jiff." She stepped closer to
him, stepped *into* him, winding her arms around his
waist and pressing her cheek against his chest, where
his heart drummed a thousand beats a minute. "Hold
on until I say stop."

He obeyed without thought, wrapping his arms
around her and clinging.

"Tighter," she said. "Good. That's good." A tension-
laden pause. "Miserable yet?"

"Beyond," he whispered.

"Good. Now run your fingers through my hair."

It was a dangerous game, the most dangerous one
they'd ever played, and it utterly defeated the purpose
of what they were trying to do. Still he ran his fingers
through the silken strands of her hair, and she sighed
with contentment.

"Jessie Kay." A heated rasp.

She looked up, pressed a gentle kiss into his lips.

The contact, even as brief as it was, obliterated whatever armor he'd had around his mind…his heart? His every hidden desire was suddenly on display, like exposed nerve endings, raw and sensitive.

Suddenly he couldn't breathe. He lowered his head and pressed his lips against hers, stealing *her* breath when she opened for him.

Their tongues rolled together, soft and slow, and the incredible taste of her nearly unmanned him: the sugar that was a steady part of her diet laced with a hint of cinnamon. Two flavors he would forever associate with home…home…for the first time in his life, he felt as if he was home.

"Jessie Kay." As good as the kiss was, it had nothing to do with passion. Not in this stolen moment. Every stroke and thrust somehow deepened the *emotion* between them. She branded him. She took him to a place where the past no longer existed. There was only here and now, and they were the only two people alive.

"West," she gasped—then she pushed him away.

They stood at arm's length, both of them panting.

Goal: get her back in his arms. Without her, he had no anchor. He was set adrift, the past threatening to intrude.

He reached for her, but she sidestepped him. *Can't let her get away.*

He caged her against the car to prevent an escape, and as she trembled, he cursed. He wasn't this man. Needy and clingy—desperate.

"N-now that we got that out of our systems," she said, unable to look him in the eye, "the wanting should end."

"Yes," he croaked. "The wanting should end."

Please. Let it end.

CHAPTER TWELVE

DURING THE NEXT WEEK, Jessie Kay did her best to forget the earth-shattering kiss that had changed the very fabric of her being. A gentle kiss, the gentlest she'd ever experienced, more about emotion than physical desire. Though the desire had been there—was always there. No longer was she JKD. She was now JKD: Property of West. He *owned* her. Not that he knew it. Not that she would ever tell him.

We want different things.

But that didn't stop her from continuing to be his friend. Which meant Operation Collage was still a go. She managed to covertly take a million pictures of him and couldn't have been more pleased—unless he promised her the world, of course.

Why did he insist on the two-month expiration date? He'd never find happiness that way, and she wanted him happy. But...

She'd begun to suspect *he* didn't want to be happy.

When she suggested they relax and watch a movie, he turned her down because there was "cleaning" to do. Thing was, he didn't just clean the house, he *cleaned* the house within an inch of its miserable life. He scrubbed, polished, swept and vacuumed, and then he did it all over again.

A way to control his surroundings, maybe? Or did the reason go deeper?

Heck, maybe he just wanted to avoid her.

No, not that. He often called her just to check in. Though every conversation began with "Everything all right?" As if he expected something terrible to happen at any moment.

Didn't he know worry rotted your bones?

And so did OCD. Besides the cleaning thing, the different computer parts he continued to bring home were always lined up a certain way. Every so often she would find a bolt in the couch cushions, and she had to wonder if he put it there on purpose. He was too meticulous not to know.

A small rebellion against the order?

Once, she'd taped one of those spare bolts to the fridge next to a note that read, "YOU'RE TURNING THIS PLACE INTO A NERDATORY!"

The next day, she'd found her note replaced by another. "YOU'RE WELCOME."

She'd also noticed he checked and double-checked every window and door before going to bed. Oh, and he refused to leave Jase and Beck—even Jessie Kay herself—if he thought they were upset with him. He stuck around until everyone was smiling.

She thought she understood that part, at least. The last time he'd seen Tessa, the girl had been pissed at him, had made a poor decision and lost her life. He felt responsible. The way Jessie Kay felt responsible for both her parents.

She wanted so badly to help him. And she was! Maybe. Hopefully. Every morning, he presented her with a new schedule as well as a copy of his own. She continued to interrupt him throughout the day, asking for help with this, telling him a funny story about that. Not once did he dismiss her, and more and more, he came home from work smiling.

And maybe that was why he did his best to start her day with a smile. He would place a cup of coffee beside her schedule. When he was home, he would make quips like, *Here's some sugar with a dash of coffee.*

You do realize I'm your sugar daddy, right?

And, *No wonder you have such a sweet ass.*

Yeah. He'd gone there.

If he was gone before she crawled out of bed, he left her a note with a bad pun.

"Drink me. I don't want you depresso today."

"Time to get ready for the daily grind."

And her personal favorite, "You've had a latte on your mind lately. Just enjoy the moment."

In the evenings, he would teach her a new soccer drill. Not to pat herself on the back—she was totally going to pat herself on the back—she'd gotten pretty darn good at dribbling the ball. She'd even mastered that inside-hook thingie.

Dang it, why wouldn't he date her longer than two months?

The question was a poisoned seed inside her mind, growing poisoned branches and leaves until she almost couldn't see past the thick foliage.

Thankfully, she had a distraction. A few days ago, West, the beautiful bastard, had dumped responsibility for the WOH Christmas party on her, claiming, "We're best friends now. You can't say no."

"But Brook Lynn—"

"Is busy planning her wedding."

True, but Jessie Kay called her anyway. Usually her sister handled the menu, and Jessie Kay didn't want to take over something the girl enjoyed.

"You proved yourself with the Bodies by Monica party, even with that He-Man punch," her sister said. "Good form, by the way. You did exactly what I would have done, so I can't claim victory on our bet. Yet."

"It *was* a good punch, wasn't it? If ever the zombie apocalypse kicks off—"

"When."

"Right. *When* it kicks off, I want to borrow your sword. I'm one hundred percent positive that I'm sixty-three percent sure Monica will be one of the first infected, but I plan to take her head either way. It will be my trophy."

Brook Lynn laughed. "Your enthusiasm and determination prove you can handle the WOH party, no problem. Besides, I trust you. West trusts you. And you really would be doing me a huge favor."

That was all she'd needed to hear.

Since then, she'd spent the first half of every day making breakfast and lunch deliveries. After lunch, she would make calls and plans for the party. Yesterday Harlow had helped her. Today Daniel had helped her.

Both had asked about her relationship with West. Harlow, the sweetie, because she'd witnessed his alpha-tastic defense of her honor, and Daniel, the darling, because he was just plain nosy. Jessie Kay had given the two the same answer. "I don't know."

Her desire to be in West's bed…to be wrapped in his arms…

More and more, she forgot her reasons for denying him

a short-term affair—for denying them both. And, when she did remember, the reasons mattered less and less.

Sighing, she read over the list Brook Lynn had written at Two Farms—she'd taken a picture of it so that she wouldn't tear the paper by carting it everywhere—then fell against the pillows on her bed.

TO WIN JK FOREVER, WEST MUST:
—Watch a chick flick with you just to see you smile
—Cuddle you without sex because there's nothing he likes better than having you in his arms
—~~Hold you with one hand, and defend you with the other~~ (Monica's party)
—Know you're worth fighting for no matter how hard things get
—Compromise with you because your wants are just as important to him as his own
—Never hover because he trusts you
—Prove he'll be there for you no matter the situation
—~~Sometimes give you little gifts, just because you're always on his mind~~ (morning notes)
—Laugh with you, cry with you and dream about you
—See his future in your eyes
—Forget there are other women in the world
—Love you with all his heart

In stark black letters, she saw everything that had been missing from her life. Everything she'd never had and really wanted. How could she ever settle for less now?

She sent the photo of the list to Daniel, who'd left for

work a few hours ago. Maybe his opinion about West or even guys in general would put her on the right track. At this point, she was just desperate enough to ask *anyone*.

Be honest, Danny Boy. Impossible for me to expect???

She waited one minute…two…but he never responded. Fine. Whatever. Deep down, she already knew the answer anyway. Only the last was impossible. How could a man love her, when she didn't even like herself?

Oh…crap. She *didn't* like herself, did she? And West had known it from the very beginning.

You need to start liking yourself. Only a crazy person would dislike you.

For years she'd only ever focused on her faults, never really seeing her value. And she *did* have value! Her worth wasn't dependent on other people's opinions.

Only *her* opinion mattered.

And I'm a pretty cool chick. She had excellent taste in friends, and she would do anything for them. Absolutely anything! She could hold her own against someone of West's sexiness and intelligence. She could even talk circles around him. *Dude! Time is totally circular.* She enjoyed making other people happy and actively tried to help those in need.

I'm better than cool. I'm awesome!

Grinning, she jumped out of the bed and set the list on her dresser. She started a text to Brook Lynn to share her epiphany, only to hesitate. Her sister and Jase had driven into the city to shop for fabric so Jessie Kay could get started on the bridesmaid dresses. Why interrupt their time together?

But she had to talk to *someone* about this.

"West," she shouted and raced from the room. "West! Guess what?"

His bedroom door opened just as she skidded to a halt. He loomed in front of her, his hair sticking out in spikes. He wasn't naked—boo! He was still sexy and masculine in a plain white T-shirt and a pair of low-riding sweatpants. And oh, good gravy, he was more dangerous to her peace of mind than ever, stealing her breath.

He studied her with a strange expression on his face, one he'd never before projected at her, as if he didn't know whether to shake her or kiss her.

Guess which way she would vote?

Finally he said, "You've got a wild look in your eyes. Should I throw chocolate at you and run for cover?"

She ignored him, saying, "I like myself." Practically bubbling over with excitement, she twirled. "I'm amazingly amazing!"

He leaned his shoulder against the frame and crossed his arms. "Sorry to be the one to tell you, kitten, but this isn't exactly news."

"Well, it is to me." She gripped the collar of his shirt. "How can you just stand there? This is clearly a Disney moment."

His pupils flared. "You have me at a disadvantage. I have no idea what a Disney moment is."

"No problem. I'll break it down in a way even your testosterone-rotted brain can understand. I'm the princess, and you're my faithful cleaning mouse. We have to sing and dance to express our feelings about the importance of my self-discovery."

"First, I've heard you sing. I'll pay you not to do it again. Want to celebrate with a new car instead?"

"Yes!"

"Done. Second, why do I have to be the mouse? Why can't I be the prince?"

"Don't be ridiculous. I said this was a Disney moment, not a far-fetched fantasy."

He snorted. "Well, your moment is going to have to wait. Beck texted me. Harlow wants to go out tonight, with *all* of us, and arguments will not be heeded."

Ohhh. Maybe she planned to drop the baby bomb tonight.

"The limo will arrive at seven," West continued, "and we're to be ready or we'll suffer—and I quote—the pain of a thousand deaths."

Limo? "Sorry, but I have too much work to do. And what about your schedule?"

He hiked his shoulders in a shrug. "It's already shot. What's a little more damage?"

She examined him intently. He was irritated, but not stressed. Another reason to like herself—she had helped him.

"All right. We'll both go," she said, "and we'll have a blast."

"Are you going to ask me to dance?"

"I'm going to insist on it, sugar bear."

"Even if I take away your new car?"

"Especially if you take away my new car. What kind are you buying me, anyway? Since it's a bribe, it should have all the bells and whistles."

"It will." His gaze slid over her and heated. "Make sure you wear something I can get my hands under." As she reeled, he added, "Maybe we can watch a chick flick afterward. I do enjoy seeing you smile." *He* smiled before shutting his door.

Why would he say—

Oh, crap. Crap, crap, crap. She clutched at her now churning stomach. She hadn't sent the text to him...she couldn't have...

Leaping into motion, she raced to her room and swiped up her phone, quickly tapping in her password. She opened her texts and—

Crap! She *had* sent it to West. She'd been thinking about him and must have blindly typed in his name, her stupid phone auto-filling his number. Moaning, she banged her head against the dresser.

She'd just learned to like herself—but at the moment, she really kind of hated herself.

Jessie Kay waxed, oiled, dolled up her hair and makeup and picked a killer outfit. The end result pleased her. Her golden hair fell around her shoulders in glimmering waves. Her eyes were smoky and framed by spiky black lashes, her cheeks painted the perfect shade of rose, and her lips bloodred. And her dress...or rather, her *sure thing*. A fit-and-flare in dark blue fabric to match her irises, with cupcakes scattered about. Innocent and flirty, with a schoolgirl pin-up vibe.

The first time she'd worn it, men had practically mauled her.

As she swiped another coat of gloss over her lips, a text came in from Daniel.

Dinner 2nite?

Her: Sorry, I'm going clubbing w/ West! ☺

Daniel: Fine. I'll go on the date I had planned (yes, I was looking for a way out)

Her: Here's an idea. Don't ask out girls if you don't like them

Daniel: That's not an idea, that's a cruelty to all woman-kind

Ha! She grabbed a black clutch from her closet to fill with only the essentials: lipstick, breath mints, a small box cutter, a wine cork, a handful of business cards Brook Lynn had made for You've Got It Coming, a tiny tape measure, another shade of lipstick, a condom…no, no condom. It would only give her a reason to cave to temptation. She headed out.

In the living room, West stood in profile at the bay window, peering into the waning darkness, and oh, wow, he looked good. A black shirt hugged his biceps. He'd tucked a pair of roughed-up jeans into combat boots, the combination lethal to her resistance. A leather cuff circled one of his wrists, and two silver rings glinted on his fingers.

He was a bad boy in the flesh. A mountain she wanted so badly to climb. The desire only he was capable of summoning weakened her limbs. She trembled…over-heated.

"I've never seen you so street," she said. "I like."

"Street?" He turned his head toward her. No surprise in his eyes, as if he'd always been aware of her presence. He gave her one of those startling, stunning once-overs and growled a sound more animal than human. "You are gorgeous, kitten."

"I know, right?" She twirled, the hem of her skirt flirt-ing with her thighs. "I am what's known as a hot tamale."

His lips twitched at the corners. "Dinner and dessert, rolled into one."

She snorted. "You'd never guess I made the dress from a tablecloth, right. Right?"

A flash of surprise. "You made the dress that will forever haunt my dreams? I'm impressed."

Beaming at him, she said, "In high school, I tried to sell some of my designs to classmates, but no one showed any interest."

"Probably for the best. Had the girls bought your dresses, teenage pregnancies would have become epidemic."

Ha! "I wonder what would have happened if you and I had gone to high school together. What were you like?"

"Studious. Big fan of homework. Sometimes, when the teacher told us to take the weekend off, I would create my own assignments."

"You were beat up a lot, weren't you?"

"Maybe." He smiled. "What were you like?"

"Always a little rowdy. I considered homework a crime against humanity and even organized a few student protests. We probably would have been bitter enemies."

"Not if I did your homework for you."

"You would have broken the rules for me?"

"For a peek under that dress? I would have done *anything* for you."

The words were a molten stroke of sin against her flesh, honey in her veins, tendrils of silk against her bones. "West—" What? What did she want from him?

Everything on that stupid list.

Things he wouldn't give her.

"You are amazingly talented, kitten. If you decide to

try again, women all over the world will buy your designs. And on that note, why haven't you tried again?"

"Because…just because." For starters, the only girls who'd ever complimented her designs were Brook Lynn and Kenna, but they loved her so they had to, right? "You truly believe I can be a success?"

"I do. And I'm always right." He rocked back on his heels. "If it's something you're interested in pursuing, I can help. Creating killer websites is in my wheelhouse."

"I… Thank you. I'll think about it." Later. With the holiday, holiday party and Brook Lynn's wedding on the horizon, her sister needed more help than ever. There was no way Jessie Kay would let her sister down again.

West glanced at his wristwatch, a habit she still hoped to break—*going to teach him to enjoy the moment.*

"West." She closed the distance and smoothed her hands over the width of his shoulders. As their gazes locked, the air between them sizzled. "I know we're not a couple, but we *have* admitted to a major case of the hots for each other and we've kissed. We should probably create a few ground rules for tonight."

"Like?"

"Like no flirting with other women."

He arched a brow. "You were planning to flirt with other women?"

"Ha-ha. Seriously. You do it, and I'll probably go nuclear."

His pupils expanded, black spilling over gold. "The same applies to you and other men."

Good. That was good. "And…well, I guess that's it. I can't think of anything else." As his heat and scent enveloped her, she could barely think at all.

"I can." He brushed the tip of his nose against hers.

"If you begin to ache for a man…for a kiss, a touch, fingers…anything…you come to me. You tell me. You get it from me. No one else."

CHAPTER THIRTEEN

THE MUSIC BEAT in tune to West's heart: hard, too fast and with an undertone of desperate need. He'd once thought there could be no greater torture than cocaine withdrawals. The chills, the aches, the tremors and the bone-deep physical pain. Days…weeks of it. Wondering if he'd survive, some nights praying he wouldn't. And when every symptom faded, the gut-wrenching cravings for the high he'd once loved.

But this…worrying about Jessie Kay, hungering for her and yet trying to keep her at a distance, was far worse. And it was *killing* him.

He didn't mean to worry, but how could he not wonder if he would lose her the way he'd lost Tessa? She'd be here one day and gone the next.

At least they were together in the madness. She hungered for him, too.

But to have her, he'd have to do a lot more than offer long term.

He'd read her list. See his future in her eyes? Done. Cuddle her just because? Pretty please with a cherry on top of her. Fight for her? With pleasure. To him, there *weren't* other women in the world.

And yes, he could fall in love with this girl.

An addiction? So what. No longer a problem. He would willingly deal with the consequences.

What he *couldn't* do? Stop hovering. His past still pulled his strings. He also couldn't offer forever. Not yet. And if he couldn't offer forever, he couldn't "always be there for her."

For the next five years, he could only offer two months out of every twelve. After that, when the clock zeroed out, the game would change and he could be with anyone he wanted for however long he desired.

His hand tightened on his glass of water, causing the ice cubes to clink together. He just had to get through the next five years.

Would she wait for him?

Could he ask her to?

"A thousand dollars for your thoughts," Beck said.

West snapped out of his head and into the present. He was at Black Cherry, a nightclub in the heart of Oklahoma City. He and his friends sat at the most coveted table in the upstairs VIP lounge, where music wasn't as loud and they could actually hear each other speak. Even better, they had an unobstructed view of the dance floor below, where Jessie Kay, Brook Lynn and Harlow danced with abandon.

"Most people would only pay a penny." And they still wouldn't get their money's worth.

"Inflation," Beck said with a shrug. "Plus, I'm like the devilishly handsome, filthy rich alpha tycoon in Harlow's favorite romance novel. I can afford it."

"You're humble, too." Jase drained his soda and frowned at West. "I can't believe I have to say this—again—but I don't like seeing you this way."

"You mean unmanned?" Obsessed and possessed.

"So determined to cling to your misery."

Not miserable. Not anymore. I'm tormented. His gaze

sought Jessie Kay. She lifted her arms above her head, her wrists crossing as she gyrated her hips. A highly sexual move, something she would do in bed with him. Sweat beaded on his forehead as blistering heat swept through him.

"You're still punishing yourself," Jase said. "Why?"

"*Why* is the wrong question. You assume I'm like you, that I seek absolution and crave a pardon. I don't. I never have."

"I assume nothing. And no, *why* is not the wrong question." Jase leaned forward, anchoring his elbows on the table. "I didn't ask your objective, only your reason."

A muscle clenched in his jaw. "You know why. We've been over this."

"You're right. We have. Unfortunately, I've never gotten through to you. What will it take to make you understand I've never blamed you and Beck for staying quiet while I was in prison? It's what I asked for. I've never blamed you for the things that happened to me behind bars. Never blamed you for losing your scholarship to MIT. You were screwed in the head. We all were. And if I don't blame you, why should you blame yourself?"

West ground his teeth. "I inflicted the most damage to Pax." Tessa's rapist. An entitled prick with better looks than sense. "*I* picked you up and drove you to the scene. *I* threw the first punch. *I* threw the last. You fought him, yes, and you were punished. I deserve to be punished, too." And so, that's exactly what he'd done: punished himself.

"What about me?" Beck asked. "Do I deserve to be punished? I was there. I hit Pax so many times I broke eleven bones in my hands."

He shook his head. "Another crime to lay at my door. I should have gone to him alone. I should have—"

"We loved Tessa," Jase interjected. "We had a right to avenge her."

Beck, who rarely touched alcohol in front of West, traced the rim of his ginger ale. "Let's get to the heart of the matter, shall we? You want Jessie Kay, and she wants you, but you insist on being together for only two months, and she insists on a try for forever. Yeah. We know. You may not give us all the details, but the women do. You won't let yourself be happy. As Jase said, you actively seek misery."

West drew in a sharp breath, slowly released it. "How would you feel if your actions led to Harlow's death? How would you feel, Jase, if your actions led to Brook Lynn's? Would you think you deserved a happy life? The life your woman will be forever denied?"

Both men paled.

Yeah. That's what he'd thought.

"I missed the last few months of Tessa's life," Jase said, "but I remember the kindhearted girl she was. She would hate what you've done to yourself, would hate what you're *doing*. She would tell you to move on, to find and embrace happiness."

The words were supposed to comfort him, but they failed. In that moment, more than any other, he missed the euphoria that came with a single hit of coke, when he wouldn't care about *anything*.

A horrifying image suddenly filled his mind. He was lying on a dirty bathroom floor, bits of vomit dried around his mouth and caked on his stained, wrinkled shirt. Jessie Kay straddled him, frantically trying to restart his savaged heart.

He physically recoiled, shaking his head. No. He would rather die.

Jase leaned over and patted his shoulder. "You need to talk to someone about your problems. Doesn't have to be a professional. You can give Jessie Kay a shot. Tell her everything, even my shit. It'll make a difference."

Yes, but for better...or for worse?

"When I told Brook Lynn about my past," Jase continued, "everything changed for me.

"Not for the best, not right away." Brook Lynn had run from him, afraid of him.

"But look at me now. Look at *us*. We share an unbreakable bond."

"Tessa would want you happy," Beck said.

"It doesn't matter what Tessa would want. She's not here."

"Are you sure about that?" Jessie Kay slid into the booth beside West and fanned her sweat-dampened cheeks. "If I died, I'd expect my guy to mourn me forever, and if he tried to hook up with someone else, I'd haunt him till he ended up in a crazy house. Then I'd haunt the girl."

West leaned into her, experiencing instant peace and instant turmoil. Somehow, she'd become the eye of every storm.

Jase glared at her. "You're not helping."

"Help shmelp. The truth is the truth," she said and slitted her eyes. "You guys need to take a step back before I start pushing. This is supposed to be a night of fun, remember? And guess what? I consider myself the guardian of West's good time. Deal with it."

Beck looked ready to slap a hand over her mouth.

"Be afraid," West told the guys. "Be very afraid."

"I think I liked it better when you two were always fighting," Beck grumbled.

Jase nodded his agreement.

"Also," she said with a sunny smile, "y'all need to lighten up. You look like the harbingers of doom." She winked at West. "Did you hear that? I used a fancy word."

His gaze lowered to her chest. "Unfortunately, you don't seem to have the same reaction—I spoke too soon." Her nipples pressed against her dress…and his erection pressed against his zipper.

As a waitress walked by, Jessie Kay snagged her pen with a gleeful "Thank you!" Grinning, she rolled up one of West's shirtsleeves. "You need help relaxing, and I know just the thing." She began to write on him.

The tip of the pen glided over his skin. The warmth of her breath wafted against him. The pecans-and-cinnamon scent so familiar yet so unique to her intoxicated him. He closed his eyes to hide the dark, dangerous desire that flooded him, uncontrollable as it warred and conquered more ground…until nothing else remained of him. She'd broken him down to the studs, remade him into sensation rather than flesh.

I am Desire.

"What do you think?" she asked, a tremor in her voice.

He opened his eyes to find her straight white teeth nibbling on her plump bottom lip. Looking away required Herculean effort, but he managed it. As he read what she'd written, something long dead inside him came to vibrant life.

10:30—slap Jase
10:31—slap Beck

10:32—take victory pic w/ JK
10:33—dance the night away!

A schedule. A schedule she'd given him.

She got him. Despite her own hang-ups—or maybe because of them—she understood him in a way even his friends did not, and West…he reeled. He laughed inside, a little manic.

And then the walls came tumbling down.

He had to have her. Resisting had been futile.

He would talk to her. He would explain the reasons for his dating schedule. She would understand. She had to understand. She would agree to the terms he set. She had to agree. She would be his for the next two months… and two months every year for the next five.

After that, their relationship could be whatever she wanted it to be.

Jessie Kay leaned over and whispered in his ear. "Check the time."

He had to kiss her, craved it more than anything, but he glanced at his wristwatch as requested. 10:30. He reached across the table and gave Jase a solid pop on the jaw.

"Hey! What was that for?" Jase demanded, rubbing the pink spot.

Jessie Kay laughed and clapped. "Take it like a girl, Jaslyn—FYI girls take it better than boys. You deserved it, and you know it."

Beck chuckled—until 10:31 rolled around and West popped *him* on the jaw.

Fist-pumping the ceiling, Jessie Kay called, "Yeah! That's what I'm talking about!"

"Thank you." West dug into her pocket and pulled out

her phone. He knew the code, had watched her plug it in countless times. 1, 2, 3, 4. He'd tried to talk her into changing it, but of course, she'd refused.

So simple, no one will ever think to try it, she'd said. *But more important, I won't forget it.*

He smashed his cheek against hers, snapped a string of photos while making different faces, and returned the phone to its rightful place.

"One last item on your schedule, kitten." He clasped her hand, stood and helped her to her feet, unwilling to release her as they headed downstairs.

He glanced back at her and smiled. Jase had wanted him happy—*I'm happy.*

She blew West a kiss, and as his blood quickened, inspiration hit him. He hadn't designed his own video game in quite some time. Instead, he'd designed for others who'd lacked the technical skill. Suddenly a new game began to take shape. One man, two versions of him—good versus evil—one heart up for grabs. The prize? A tall, seductive blonde.

"What a great day." Jessie Kay rested her head on his shoulder. "I learned my every wish is your command, even if I tell you to betray your closest friends, as long as I put those commands in a schedule."

"This is true. But kitten? There's a slight problem with your timeline."

"No way." The ends of her pale hair brushed over his arm, a sensual caress. "I meticulously planned every detail."

"Another fancy word," he said, squeezing her hand in approval—pausing to watch as her nipples beaded for him. "But you're wrong. You did mess up." He led her past the dance floor, into the hallway leading to the bathrooms, then tugged her in front of him, only to back her into a shadowed corner.

Her eyes widened as he cupped her cheeks. "Wait. What's happening right now? What are you doing?"

"To thank you properly, I'll need at least an hour." He lowered his head slowly, slow enough she could stop him with a single word while he prayed she wouldn't. "All you have to do is say yes."

A second. An endless second.

"Say yes. I'm here with you," he said. "No one else. You're my date. You're the one I want."

"Yes," she whispered.

He fell into her, pressing his mouth into hers, drinking in his second taste of Jessica Kay Dillon. And this time, there was no hint of gentleness. He devoured, two words screaming inside his mind. *Take. Now.*

Yes. Yes. She was paradise. Nirvana. Elysium. Every dream. Every wish. Every fantasy he'd ever had. He kissed her with abandon and learned her with determination, every second more than pleasure—every second bliss. He was utterly overcome.

He took and he took and he took, then he gave—how could he deny this woman anything? He poured into her all the passion she'd stirred within him.

She breathed his name as if it were a prayer, melting against him, meeting his tongue thrust for wanton thrust. Nerve endings thrummed with new life as electric pulses rode the waves rushing through his veins. Need devolved into endless desperation, a white-hot burn from which he would never recover, would never want to recover, pushing him to the razor's edge of pleasure…and the most exquisite agony.

He ran her plump bottom lip between his teeth, combed

his fingers through her hair to angle her head and take her ever deeper. A sound more animal than human, part war cry, part victory shout—one only she could elicit—rose from deep within him, heralding a change he couldn't stop…didn't want to stop.

"You're mine, kitten." *All mine.* If she denied him…

"Yes, yes. Yours."

He melted against her, his tongue meeting hers in a new kiss, brutal and savage, his world careening out of control, revolving only around this woman. *Will make her scream, gasp and beg.*

Beyond them, the tempo of the music slowed. A love song. A languid melody, seductive and sultry, but West didn't slow the kiss. He couldn't, his need far too great. He devoured his woman with teeth and tongue, taking more, giving more. Demanding everything.

She gripped his shirt, pulling him as close as she could get him. "West." She whispered his name, a benediction so sweet he knew there was no obstacle he wouldn't destroy just to hear her say it one more time. "Wanted you so long…more…give me more."

More. Yes. Now. As rainbow-colored lights rained from the strobes above, flashing over them, he kissed her harder, nipped and licked his way to her jawline…to the pulse hammering at the base of her neck. The silk of her skin…the heat she radiated…the perfume that had fused with her every cell…

He cupped and kneaded her breasts, brushing his thumb over the points of her nipples…the softness of her curves, a delicious contrast to the hardness of his…the way her breath hitched every time his fingers moved… he couldn't get enough, wasn't sure he would ever get enough.

"West...don't...please, don't stop," she gasped out.

"Never." A crazed madness had overtaken him. He'd been stripped down to the studs yet again, was nothing but hunger and thirst and reckless need, burning from the inside out. "I want my hands all over you—and before we leave this club, I want them in your panties."

"Anyone could see," she whispered.

It wasn't dread he heard in her tone but scandalized excitement. "It's dark, and you're the only one I see." He nudged the neckline of her dress with his chin, baring her breasts, taking her nipple in his mouth and sucking. "Are you wet for me, kitten?"

"Soaked," she said on a moan.

He continued to suck, and he wasn't gentle about it. When she quivered, when she began to gasp incoherently, he gripped her under her thighs and lifted her off her feet, pinning her to the wall with his weight. She wound her long legs around him, clinging to him, creating an irresistible cradle. Irresistible...so why even try to restrain himself?

He grunted as her nails sank into his back; she might have even sliced through his shirt, but he loved it. How easy it would be to bunch her dress at her waist, rip through her panties, tear open his fly and sink inside paradise...nirvana...elysium. Not just touch, but own.

"I have to taste you. Let me."

"West—"

He ground his shaft into the sweetest part of her, the action as instinctual and as necessary as breathing. "Please." He'd beg. For her, only ever her, he'd beg.

He'd take her here. An appetizer. He'd take her in the limo and then again at home. The meal. He'd have her on the bed in the dark hours of the night...he'd have her on the floor in the bright light of the morning. He'd have her in the shower, on the kitchen counter.

"You've ruined me for everyone else. I should punish you for it, but I only want to pleasure you. I'll make you feel—" Something—someone—bumped into his side, and he nearly lost his footing. West snarled with the kind of white-hot rage he had not experienced since his days with Tessa.

"Sorry, man. Sorry," a slurred, unfamiliar voice announced. A guy tripped past them, muttering about needing a bathroom before he puked all over his shoes.

West would *not* take this precious woman next to a puddle of vomit.

His heart raced toward an invisible finish line as he set Jessie Kay's feet on the floor and stepped away from her. He was trembling, panting. She had somehow burrowed under his skin and become an itch, and from this moment on, he knew there was no point during any given day that he wouldn't be aware of her, or of his desire for her. Her taste had changed the chemical makeup of his brain. He was no longer West; he was Jessie Kay's man.

Her tremors matched his own as she smoothed her tangled hair into place. She could do nothing about the red, swollen lips just begging for another kiss.

"Well." She cleared her throat. "That was certainly… interesting."

He shoved his hands in his pockets before he reached for her again. "Interesting isn't the word I'd use." Spectacular. Sublime. *Necessary.* "Do you want to do it again?"

CHAPTER FOURTEEN

THE KISS HAD utterly *wrecked* Jessie Kay. Even more than the last one! West had owned her mouth. Heck, he'd owned her body. Whatever he'd wanted, she would have given him. Whatever he'd demanded, she would have done. For him or to him or with him. Time and place had ceased to matter. Consequences had seemed insignificant. An audience? So what. Enjoy the show.

Only two things had held any importance to her. *More.* And *now.*

She'd been a live wire of sensation—was *still* a live wire of sensation. She ached. She tingled. She burned. And despite their separation, things were only getting worse. She was shaking, fighting for breath and light-headed, desperate for any kind of relief.

He'd asked a question. *Do you want to do it again?*

It. The kiss. Yes, yes, pleeease yes, and thank you. But nothing had been settled between them. And really, now that she'd proven the first kiss hadn't been a fluke, that passion really did burn white-hot between them, she was scared out of her ever-loving mind.

Don't just want long term...want forever.

"Right now," she said on a wispy catch of breath, "I think we should put a pin in the conversation and dance."

"If I put my arms around you, we'll be arrested for lewd acts in public. Let's go back to the table." He tugged

234 THE HARDER YOU FALL

her out of the shadows, putting an end to the moment, the stolen minutes when his kiss had created a wall between past and present, when what she'd done once upon a time had no bearing on what she did here and now.

"Just so you know, if we end up in jail, Brook Lynn will bail us out. She knows the routine."

"Been arrested before, have you?" He had to speak louder to be heard over the music.

"Only four times."

He arched a brow, all *wow, only four?* "Your crimes?" There was a thread of amusement in his voice.

"Thrice for public intoxication, once for reckless driving."

"Naughty girl. I've never kissed a criminal."

If she'd lived in any other town with any other sheriff, the reckless driving charge would have come with time behind bars. As Harlow once reminded her, she'd driven her rust bucket into her boyfriend's house. But then, the bastard had secretly recorded them having sex. She'd found out only because he'd shown his friends and they couldn't resist taunting her.

Where'd you learn to ride like that?

I thought you'd be a screamer.

Horrified and humiliated, she snuck into the guy's house, found and confiscated the video, then destroyed his freaking house with her car. It was only later, after she'd watched the recording so that she'd know what, exactly, the others had seen that she discovered the boyfriend had cheated on her with citiots. Bimbos living in the city, eager to slum it with a small-town prick.

She should have wised up afterward, should have been more careful about the men she picked, but nooo.

Her choices had only declined from there. Until now. Until West.

"Was it different?" she asked, unable to hide her uncertainty. "Kissing a criminal, I mean."

He flicked her a glance loaded with heat and sizzle. "Different in the best ways. I'm dying to do it again."

Shivers cascaded through her, decadent and heady. "Me, too," she admitted at last.

He stopped to stare at her. Was he going to kiss her again, right here and now? Maybe, if Brook Lynn and Harlow hadn't joined them.

"Hurry! I'm thirsty," Brook Lynn said.

Resignation in his eyes.

When they reached the table, the girls cuddled their men as if a twenty-minute separation had been *harrowing*. Soon, the foursome was talking and laughing while West and Jessie Kay sat across from each other, silent, brooding—still staring hungrily.

He knew her taste, the shape of her breasts, the feel of her nipples as they puckered for him and the cradle of her body as she rubbed against him. And oh, crap, the aches were back, breathing a little more difficult.

He licked his lips. Low and quiet, he asked, "What are you thinking about?"

Why lie? Matching his tone, she whispered, "The things you did to me." *Everything I want you to do again...*

The tension between them thickened exponentially.

"Share with the rest of the class." Beck wiggled his brows at her. "What'd he do to you?"

"Yes," Brook Lynn said, clearly trying not to laugh. "Do tell."

Jessie Kay looked to West for help, but he merely repeated Brook Lynn's words. "Yes. Do tell."

Warmth bloomed in Jessie Kay's cheeks.

"Wait. Are you *blushing*?" Harlow demanded, incredulous.

"West must have a magic…touch," Brook Lynn said with a snicker

"I think you girls are forgetting I'm privy to your secrets." Jessie Kay smirked. "Shall I share with the rest of the class?"

Harlow shrank back, her hand flying to her belly. A little more rounded now.

"Go for it. I don't have any secrets." Total confidence, Brook Lynn flipped her hair over her shoulder.

The action delighted Jessie Kay. At one time, the girl had been so self-conscious about the devices in her ears that she'd constantly reached up to make sure they were hidden.

Smiling evilly, Jessie Kay focused on Jase. "The night Brook Lynn gave up her V-card, I heard her tell the guy to let her know when she had an orgasm—"

"Oh, my gosh! Shut up!" Brook Lynn blurted out. "And everyone leave my sister alone, stop tormenting her."

Jase pulled at his earlobe. "You weren't sure…what, angel? That you'd be able to figure it out?"

"Happy place, happy place," Brook Lynn said, her own cheeks glowing.

"Speaking of happy places…" Beck kissed Harlow's temple. "I think it's time to head home. My boo bear gets cranky when she doesn't get her beauty Zs."

"Agreed." Jessie Kay faked a yawn. "Beauty Zs are important."

"*Very* important," West said.

Soon we'll be alone...

"I'm not saying a word about your obvious urgency," Brook Lynn said to her.

"What? I'm tired."

"Yes. Tired of wearing your dress."

Chuckles abounded as the group walked to the back of the lot, where the limo waited. The night was thick and dark, perfect for lovers, the moon a golden hook in the sky.

Soon...

Jessie Kay peered out the window the entire drive home, her mind racing. Would West want to pick up where they'd left off? Would he prefer to talk about what had happened? Or would he do what she feared most and ask, again, for a two-month affair?

Finally the limo stopped. West climbed out, extended a hand to help her stand, then held her steady when her knees wobbled. Her mind began another race. How did *she* want the night to proceed? Sex? But what then? And how would she feel in the morning?

"You guys are sooo going to get it on." Brook Lynn laughed, clearly determined to have her revenge. "West, be sure to give her a very strong paddling first."

"Don't worry. I'd already penciled a paddling into my schedule." He shut the car door and with his arm draped around Jessie Kay's waist, led her forward. Only when they were sealed inside did he release her, and only to move in front of her and press her against the door.

"I want you more than I've ever wanted anything. I want to strip you down and fill you up. I want my mouth and hands on you, and I want your mouth and hands on me."

Tingles. Heat.

Surrender…

But he wasn't done. "I can only offer you two months out of a year for the next five years."

This again. Disappointment threatened to crush her even as hope sparked. He hadn't offered a chance at forever, but he had offered more than the standard arrangement.

"Tell me why there's a limit," she said gently.

A muscle ticked beneath his eye. "When Jase received a ten-year sentence, *I* received a ten-year sentence."

"By whom?"

"I am my judge, jury and executioner, and I decided on ten years of misery. Then, when Tessa died, I tacked on another five years."

Everything finally clicked into place. "You punish yourself."

"Someone has to."

"What about time off for good behavior?"

"No."

"But…you got clean. Surely that counts for something."

"I never should have gotten high in the first place. My mom was an addict and I'd seen firsthand the price she paid. I knew better. And what's worse, I didn't get clean in time."

"In time for what?"

He pushed out a ragged breath. "So many things. I was high the day Tessa died. Later I overdosed and missed a visit with Jase. Beck returned, pale and shaky, told me Jase had been… I'm sure you can guess."

Yes. Her stomach churned with acid. "Tell me anyway. Purge."

A stiff nod. "Beck told me another inmate—a big guy, older—was in the visiting room and he winked at Jase multiple times, blew him kisses. On the guy's way out, he even thanked Jase for the happy ending."

The sickness spread through the rest of her. "Rape."

"Yes. I wasn't there for Jase, just like I wasn't there for Tessa, and that day, that minute, that very second, I decided to get clean. But you know what? I didn't succeed the first attempt, or even the fourth."

And the failures had agonized him. Clearly. Even after all these years, he hadn't forgiven himself. Didn't *want* to forgive himself. He preferred to wallow—probably thought all he deserved was despair.

You can't help the ones who won't help themselves, Momma used to say.

"If you seek misery," she said, proceeding gently, "why date at all?"

"Even the condemned are allowed conjugal visits." He cupped her cheeks. "Every year, for the two months we're together, I will devote myself to you. You have my word."

"What happens the rest of the year?"

"We remain friends."

Impossible. "What if I date other men while we're just friends? Because, according to your reasoning, I would be punishing myself if I remained single."

The muscle *really* ticked, but he offered no response. What could he say, though, without sounding like a total dick? He didn't want her to see other people—how selfish of him. He expected her to remain devoted to him while he punished himself—how wrong of him.

No doubt about it, he hoped to have his prison cake and eat it, too.

In the past, she would have tried to talk him around, and failing that, she would have tried to work him around, would have placed her hope in her ability to succeed, to make him see things her way: if she gave it her all, she could overcome anything, right? She would have dreamed of the battle he would wage against his feelings—the battle she would convince herself he would lose, slowly ceding his heart to her. But she was wiser now, and she knew she could give her all to no avail. Just like she knew a relationship couldn't last if she was the only one making an effort.

"I want to be with you, West, but not like that. I won't help you hurt yourself. I won't help you hurt your friends…me."

"Jessie Kay—"

"No. I'm worth more. And so are you."

Torment ravaged his features.

"Just think about what I said. Okay?" she asked softly.

A crackling pause. A clipped nod.

She did her best to lighten the mood. "You should be thrilled I'm giving you a pass right now. Valentine's Day is closing in quick, and I would insist on taking thousands of pictures together. Then I would cut those photos into heart shapes and make a poster board detailing our grand romance."

Disappointment, remorse, longing, acceptance and amusement—each flashed through his eyes. "You would demand I hang the poster on my wall, wouldn't you?"

She fluttered her lashes at him, all *bless your dear heart*. "Only after I'd forced you to show it to every single one of your friends."

"Evil." He relaxed a little. "I'd most likely forget the holiday."

"Most likely? Ha! You would. You're a guy. You're missing half your brain cells."

"I would scramble to find you a gift at the last minute, finally deciding lingerie is the perfect choice."

"Such a pig," she said, nodding her approval. "I would insist that what is mine is mine and what is yours is mine."

"So…if I had thirty dollars and you had ten…"

"I'd have forty."

"Good girl. I'm properly horrified."

"Good boy. I am, too."

He stared at her, what little amusement he'd gained quickly fading, and she stared right back, her will wavering. He wanted her. He'd said so. They could have ten months together, parsed out over the next five years. It was something. More than they currently had, more than he'd given another. What could it hurt?

Danger! Danger! She cleared her throat. "Well. I guess this is good night." She walked away, then, and the sad thing, the part of the evening that sucked the biggest donkey balls? He didn't try to stop her.

If she gave him what he thought he wanted, she really would be participating in his punishment. So, yeah. Saying yes would hurt them both. Badly.

She barricaded herself in her bedroom, showered off the night—the imprint West had left on her skin—and crawled into bed. Since meeting him, tossing and turning had become the norm, and by morning her eyes were dry and gritty, her body a mess of aches. Her resolve was stronger, at least.

Until he pardoned himself, they were stymied.

She brushed her teeth and hair, dressed in a red

sweater and black leggings, and was just tying her boots when a knock sounded at the door.

"Today's schedule is hot off the press," West called. He sounded as grumpy as she felt. "First up, exercise."

"Yes, please." She wrenched open the door—and had to swallow a whimper. He looked good enough to eat. Dark hair shagged around his model-perfect face. He hadn't shaved, a shadow beard dusting his jaw. He wore a pair of sweatpants and a long-sleeved T-shirt that hugged his chest and biceps with loving splendor.

His golden eyes swept over her, and he traced his tongue over his lips as if she'd just offered to be today's breakfast buffet. "Get changed."

"Why?"

"To exercise, remember? Ex-er-cise."

"Are you kidding me? I thought you said *extra fries*. There's no way I'm exercising."

"No take backs." He handed her a piece of paper with the words "5:30 a.m. RUN" in bold letters up top.

"I'm a girl. I can take back *anything*."

"I'm afraid I have to insist, kitten. There *is* such a thing as stranger danger. I can't go out on my own."

"Stranger danger…you mean the single moms who might attack you?"

"Exactly. So. You need to change. You need to change *now*." He shut the door in her face and called, "I don't hear you changing."

"I *do* hear you being annoying." She changed into a sweatshirt that read "I'll Always Be Miss Strawberry Valley. Bow." A gift from Brook Lynn soon after Jessie Kay's reign ended. She kept the leggings on, and after exchanging her boots for tennies, decided to forgo a coat and suffer the cold so that West could have a front row seat to her bouncing breasts.

She opened the door. He hadn't moved out of the hall.

He glanced at her, the heat returning to his eyes, then glanced at his watch and nodded with satisfaction. "Only took you two minutes. I'm impressed."

"Then life if worth living again." She placed her hands on her hips. "Hey, maybe you should bring an extinguisher. The friction from my thighs might set my panties on fire."

He rolled his eyes and unceremoniously pushed her outside—where she immediately cursed her stupidity. The cold! Five minutes, and she'd be eaten up with frost-bite, guaranteed.

"Don't worry," he said. "You'll warm up by the third mile."

"What!" A whimper escaped. He expected her to make it three whole miles?

He barked out a laugh, tweaked her nose and took off. Groaning, she followed after him. Bitter wind slapped at her, and it wasn't long before her cheeks and fingers morphed into blocks of ice.

"How are plans for the Christmas party coming along?" he asked as casually as if they were seated in-side an office, a desk between them.

Air burned going in *and* coming out. How was that fair? "Very well." The words were barely audible. *Stamina? I has none.* "Heart…beating so fast… I'm going to die of…myocardial infarction."

"Do you dabble in hypochondria in your spare time? You're fine, kitten. I would never let anything bad hap-pen to you." He bumped her shoulder. "Now, tell me more about the party."

He was half prince charming, half evil overlord, and she foolishly liked both sides of him. "Well," she said, sucking it up and doing her best to sound unaffected, "I finally nailed down the mechanical bull, and Edna at Rhinestone Cowgirl agreed to make all the party favors. Strawberry shaped belly rings."

He tripped over his own foot but righted himself before doing a face-plant, and she laughed.

"Tell me you're kidding, Jessie Kay."

"Well, do you want me to lie?"

"Jessie Kay. The party is only a few days away."

"Fine. Fine. I'm kidding. Everything will be top-notch, first-class, blah, blah, boring. Just the way you like it."

He breathed a sigh of relief. "Thank you."

She shrugged. "I'd plan your funeral if the price was right."

He ran a circle around her and gave her nose another tweak.

"Have you noticed we're the only two people dumb enough to be outside?" She waved her arm to indicate the barren roads. "Even drivers stayed indoors today."

"*They* are the dumb ones. Look around."

Yeah, yeah, he had a point. The soft pink-and-amber glow of the sun was dazzling, the blue sky dripping into a wealth of towering trees, blackbirds flying from limb to limb.

"Why are we doing this anyway?"

"Why do you think?" His tone was flat, even. What would it take to exhaust him? "I'm primed. You're primed. This will help."

"So...we're friends helping each other out by running off our physical desires?"

"Unless you'll agree to my terms."

"West—"

"It's more than I've ever offered another, Jessie Kay."

"That's true in a sense. You didn't offer Tessa more, but you did give her more."

"Not really. She died soon after Jase went to prison."

So…Jessie Kay really was the first.

As she panted, she said, "I'm not saying no, but I'm not saying yes. Like I told you, I have no desire to help you punish yourself. I *do* have a desire to make things better for you."

He stopped. Oh, praise the Lord! She hunched over, cold yet hot, sweating and shivering at the same time, still wheezing, her nose running and her stomach threatening to erupt.

"Being without you *is* a punishment." His ravaged gaze pinned her in place. He threaded his fingers together and pressed them to the back of his nape, his head falling back as he peered up at the sky. His T-shirt rode up, revealing a delicious strip of bronzed skin, and her shivers intensified, the heat she'd worked up intensifying. "The way I ache for you…it's unbearable."

"West…"

"No, it's okay. You need time to think, and I understand. I didn't mean to pressure you. Let's go back to the house."

More running? "I can't. I need a stretcher and an IV, stat."

"How about a ride?" He thrust his shoulder into her stomach and hefted her off her feet so that she draped over him. Of course, a car finally appeared, the driver slowing to hang her head out the window.

"Dirty girl," Sunny Day called. "No wonder you've turned me down lately."

Jessie Kay spread her arms, all *I can't be blamed*.

Sunny grinned and shook a fist at them before speeding off.

West showed no signs of fatigue as he carried Jessie Kay home. Only when they were inside did he set her on the couch. Silent, he strode off…soon returning with a blanket he wrapped around her, taking such good care of her she could almost convince herself this was enough, that nothing else mattered. Almost.

"Jessie Kay," he rasped, toying with the ends of her hair.

If he kissed her, she'd be lost. "You told me I needed to like myself, West, and now I'm saying the same to you. You're an awesome guy. Smart, driven, witty, fun and your mouth should be classified as the eighth wonder of the world. Or a lethal weapon, slaying panties everywhere. But you're allowing the past to dictate the terms of your future, even though you aren't the man you used to be."

He opened his mouth to reply, but she shook her head.

"No," she said, giving him a little push. "My heart is still racing from the run, and I'm pretty sure I'm on my death bed. No more heavy talk. Fix me a cup of sugar with a dash of coffee."

He stared at her a long while before standing. "All right. For you…anything."

If only that were true.

CHAPTER FIFTEEN

TWO DAYS PASSED. Jessie Kay slaved over final details for the WOH Christmas party, attended a dress fitting with Brook Lynn and began sewing the bridesmaid dresses.

For the most part, West kept his distance. He still called often to check on her—*Everything okay? You good?*—and he still marched through the house every night to check the doors and windows. Since their jog, however, they'd had only two conversations.

The first?

"You'll be my date to the party," he'd said, "not a server."

"Sorry, sugar bear, but that's not possible. Brook Lynn is going with Jase, and Harlow is going with Beck. Someone has to man the fort."

"Kenna can do it."

"Kenna is going with Dane, and Dane is one of your best clients. I'm the only option."

"Jessie Kay."

"West."

He'd crossed his arms over his chest. "What happens if I take someone else?"

"I make a huge scene and embarrass you in front of your peers."

He'd growled. "I want you by my side, whether we're together or not."

Her heart had skipped a beat, but she'd said, "Too bad. I have a work ethic now."

He'd glared at her before storming away.

Later that day, he'd handed her a key. "Your new car," he'd said.

"What! I thought you were kidding about that."

"It has all the bells and whistles."

"I'm sure. But I wasn't hinting—"

"Your beater isn't safe."

"I know—"

"It's not a gift," he'd added. "It's therapy—for me. Now I can stop worrying you'll die in a crash."

He *did* worry...

"Would you let me finish?" Most girls would probably refuse to accept such an extravagant non-gift. They would claim to feel like a hooker. Bought and paid for. That simply wasn't her style. "I wasn't hinting, but I'm super grateful. Thank you."

She'd hugged him, and he'd hugged her back. They'd held on for minutes...possibly hours, neither willing to let go.

"You're getting better at hugging," she'd told him.

"I had a good teacher."

The words had been whispered, and their bodies had begun to...rub. They'd finally sprung apart.

Now, alone in her room, she mulled over the only thing capable of distracting her: his suggestion to run her own business. A website selling her clothes. Day dresses, formal gowns and even wedding dresses. For the first time in her life, she was excited by the thought of a job. Making upscale clothing for women on a budget.

She had to go for it, didn't she?

After the holidays, she'd have a sit-down with Brook

Lynn to discuss the future. If her sister cried about losing her, well, she'd nix the website and remain at You've Got It Coming. Scratch that—if Brook Lynn revealed even a speck of disappointment, she'd nix the website. Over the years, the girl had given up so much for her. How could she do any less now?

And really, all too soon helping her sister would be the only quality time they spent together. Brook Lynn would have her new family.

And I'll be alone.

One day, she'd even lose West. His new house would be built, and he would move out of this one. Would he go back to avoiding her? Her business might be her only source of comfort.

Ugh. Decisions, decisions. *Between rocklike biceps and a very hard head.*

She glanced at the clock West had mounted over her bed. Three-sixteen in the afternoon. In four minutes flat he would knock on her door. The day of the party had finally arrived, and he was determined to drive her.

If I can't be your date, he'd said earlier this morning, *I'll be your ride, and I'll hear no protests on the matter.*

She grabbed her phone to send updates to her peeps. First up, Brook Lynn:

About to leave to set up at inn. DON'T WORRY. I probably won't destroy everything you've built in a single night

Second, Daniel:

You coming to the party or not??? I sent you an e-vite but you never RSVP'd—jackass

West had wanted to throw the party in a fancy hotel in the city, the same place he'd used every year before, but she'd overruled him. He no longer lived in the city. He lived in Strawberry Valley, and in her completely unbiased opinion he needed to pour his money into the community…as well as invite said community to the festivities. Like…everyone within the city limits. Which she'd done. Surprise!

Third up to bat, Harlow:

Why haven't you told people there's a bun in your oven?? I'm ready to start talking names. Jessica Lynn? Brook Kay?

Last up, Jase and Beck:

You better make sure West enjoys himself or I'll convince your women to wear chastity belts for a month!

Replies came in fast.

Daniel: Like you could really keep me away. Get ready to meet my date—she's as mean as a rattler. I think I might marry her

Harlow: The secret will be shouted from rooftops tomorrow! (Beck has been having too much fun keeping quiet) The names you suggested might need a little…tweak

Brook Lynn: Happy place!

Jase: I don't think his good time will have anything to do

w/ us, but your threat has had the desired effect and if I have to, I'll Magic Mike just to make him smile

Beck: Hint: if you flirt w/ him & pretend other guys are invisible, he'll have an awesome time—but I too will Magic Mike if necessary (you're welcome, world!)

Aaand right on time, a knock sounded at her door. Her heart morphed into a jackhammer.

"One sec." A full-length mirror hung on the inside of her closet door, and she gave herself a once-over. Ponytail—check. Mascara, blush and lip gloss—check. Ugly clothes—whimper. She wore the same white button-down, black slacks and black flats she'd worn to Monica's shindig, with a few minor holiday touch-ups. The crisp white shirt now boasted a glittery red bow tie and a spray of mistletoe rested over her breast.

If anyone dared ask to kiss her boobs, she'd go nuclear. Bet with her sister or not.

But oh, what she wouldn't give to be a guest rather than a server, wearing one of her own creations. A sexy white gown with streams of red lace. She would dazzle West's business associates—of course—and he would smile at her with pride and adoration.

Hey, it could totally happen...in five years.

"Jessie Kay." Her name was followed by three hard raps. "Check your watch. We need to leave."

Her watch! She fastened the beauty around her wrist and replied, "Dude. I've got another minute to spare."

"Yes, but I can't go another second without seeing you."

Heart beating even faster, stomach flip-flopping—was this how her mother had felt when she'd read

Daddy's letters?—Jessie Kay rushed to the door. As always, West stole her breath with only a glance. He was gorgeous in a pin-striped suit, glossy red tie and ridiculously expensive Italian loafers. He'd tamed his hair, brushing it back, but he hadn't shaved; the clash of sophistication and bad boy made her shiver.

Who was he tonight? The in-control computer genius or the passionate rule breaker?

He looked her up and down, his body vibrating. "You are the most beautiful woman I've ever seen, but the mistletoe is coming off." He didn't wait for her reply but removed the foliage from her shirt and tossed it on the floor, stomping on it for good measure.

"Hey! Brook Lynn asked me to wear that."

"Brook Lynn experienced a moment of insanity. Besides, I'm paying her for her services, which means I'm her boss—and yours. No mistletoe."

"Do you really think someone will crouch under my cleavage and demand a kiss?" she asked, pretending she hadn't entertained the same fear.

"I don't think someone will do it, I know they will." His tone was flat, leaving no room for argument. "That happens, and there will be bloodshed, the party ruined."

"Such a caveman."

He banged on his chest. "Me, man. You, my woman."

As she laughed, he twined his fingers with hers. Their watches clinked together. He pulled her forward only to press her against the wall. "Have you thought about my offer?"

Her mouth went dry as his heat and scent enveloped her. "I've thought about our last kiss," she admitted. "How much I would love another one."

Minty breath fanned over her, the hardness of his

body forcing the softness of hers to conform. "The next time I kiss you," he said softly, fiercely, "I won't stop kissing you until I have you naked and on your back. And then I'll only stop because my mouth will be busy doing other things."

If shivers were currency, she would have reached millionaire status just then.

"If you want that," he said, "I'll happily blow off the party. All you have to do is say yes. You'll be mine."

He would rearrange his precious schedule just to be with her? It was such an intoxicating thought... "Lovers for two months, friends for ten, then lovers again for another two. And so on and so forth."

His nod was stiff.

Did he not understand what torture those ten months apart would be? Or was he counting on it?

"What if I asked you to pardon yourself?" she asked softly. "To give me everything?"

"I can't. You know I can't."

No, he *wouldn't*. There was a difference. "If you were mine," she whispered, "I would worship you with my mouth, hands and body." She flattened her palms on his chest, felt his heart slamming against his ribs. "I'd let you do anything you desired to me, let you take me in ways no one else ever has."

Fire in his eyes, his pupils expanding in a starburst. His body was taut as he cupped her jaw.

"But you're not, so we need to leave," she managed to squeeze out past the barbed lump in her throat.

He didn't immediately step back. He continued to gaze down at her, projecting longing, need, desperation...utter devastation. "I'll be good to you, kitten. I swear I will."

"You've said that before, and I believe you." She really did. That was part of what made her decision so tough. He would be good to her, and she would crumble when they returned to being "just friends."

"Are you telling me no, flat out?" he asked, gravel in his voice.

"I'm telling you I need more time to think." But how long would he wait? When would he decide enough was enough and make the decision for her—by withdrawing his offer?

He surprised her by saying, "All right. Take all the time you need," before leading her to the car.

THE STRAWBERRY INN had been transformed into a winter wonderland. West gazed about in amazement. In the center of the spacious dining room were three Christmas trees that formed a triangle. Actual presents spilled between them, and every kid under the age of eighteen would get to pick one. Lush, green holly twined with the lights that had been wrapped around the strawberry-shaped chandeliers Jessie Kay begged West to buy Carol Mathis, the inn's owner. A thank-you for allowing him to rent the place on such short notice. Faux frost covered the walls and red lace draped the tables and chairs set up in the far corner of the room.

Jessie Kay had far surpassed every party WOH had ever thrown…but it would have been even better if he'd allowed her to rent a mechanical bull.

Next year.

"Great party, son, but you should have brought more whiskey." Mr. Porter of Swat Team 8—*We assassinate fleas, ticks, silverfish, cockroaches, bees, ants, mice and rats*—thumped him on the shoulder as he walked past. "Just thought you should know."

"There's more. I'll have a glass—"

"Bottle."

"Bottle," he corrected with a smile, "brought to you."

The entire town had flocked to the inn. Edna, an eccentric grandmother figure, looked like she was having a seizure on the makeshift dance floor. Anthony Rodriguez, the only "stylist" in a twenty-mile radius—though word on the street claimed Trisha Shay-Rivers was using her garage to give perms to the over-fifty crowd—did the electric slide and robot. At the same time.

Laughter abounded among the town's citizens. WOH customers—gamer geeks and serious businessmen—didn't yet know what to make of them.

West spotted one of the servers Jessie Kay hired—a waitress from Two Farms—and closed the distance. "I'd like you to personally ensure Mr. Porter's glass never goes dry. Stay by his side with a bottle of our best whiskey."

The girl stared up at him as if he was the answer to her prayers.

"Now," he said.

"Right." She raced off.

He glanced at the door in back, where the waitstaff came in and out with trays. No sign of Jessie Kay. He'd had to watch different men eye her up and down as if she were an appetizer to be sampled, and he'd had to fight a killing rage. *Mine!*

But she wasn't his. Not yet.

So far he'd had to eject seven pricks from the party. All had been Strawberry Valley residents who'd insulted her.

You giving lap dances with those shrimp, Jessie Kay?

You look good in your uniform, but I'd rather see you out of it—again.

Bastards. They'd accidentally run into his fist on their way out.

"Oh, West. You've got it bad." The delighted female voice came from his left. "Worse than I'd realized."

He tore his attention from the door—Jessie Kay'd had six minutes to restock her tray, plenty of time. Where was she?

"I'm not complaining, mind you," Brook Lynn added with a smile. "You're one of the rare few good enough for my big sis."

He lifted a brow in haughty derision. "A *rare few* implies there are others you wouldn't mind seeing her with."

"You've met Daniel, right?"

He rolled his eyes. Daniel was here with his date. A six-foot, stick-thin ice queen.

Dotty Mathis, Carol's daughter, hadn't stopped watching the pair since they'd arrived.

West had noticed because he, too, had been watching Daniel. Anytime Jessie Kay neared him, the two made funny faces at each other. Their relationship reminded West of the friendship Jase and Beck had had with Tessa. Teasing, taunting, but with an underlay of mutual respect.

"Daniel is like Jessie Kay's brother," he said.

Brook Lynn snorted. "Dane Michaelson is Kenna's stepbrother, but they still hooked up."

He looked to Jase, who stood at Brook Lynn's side, and lifted a brow. "Do me a solid and control your woman."

Jase spread his arms, the world's most helpless male. "Don't you think I've tried?"

"He has." Brook Lynn smoothed her hands over the waist of her dress. A dress Jessie Kay had sewn. She'd been holing up in her bedroom more and more lately to practice creating the most amazing designs anyone has ever seen, ever.

West moved his gaze across the room, spotted Beck and Harlow. Harlow was currently an unflattering shade of green. She clutched her stomach as if someone had pulled the eject cord and she only had moments to prepare herself for an evacuation. Beck draped his arm around her waist and led her forward, pushing his way through the crowd.

"Something's wrong," West told the others.

As soon as Beck reached them, he announced, "Surprise! Harlow is pregnant. Now we're going home. She's not feeling well."

"What!" Brook Lynn exploded.

Jase shook his head as if he'd misheard.

West reeled. A baby? A little Beck? *I'm going to be an uncle.* A smile stretched full and wide and fast...only to fall even faster. Tessa had loved children. She'd once told him she wanted to start trying for a kid as soon as they married, that she wanted two boys and two girls so their kids would always have a friend. She would have loved being an aunt.

Tessa couldn't live her dreams; during his self-imposed sentence, he shouldn't live his.

He rubbed at his heart, at the new ache deep, deep inside it. Did Jessie Kay want marriage? A family of her own?

Five years. Just five gut-wrenching years, and he could give her everything she wanted...could take everything *he* wanted. Her...all of her. Desire for her was a fire in his blood. He'd already realized he craved her more than any other woman…but he realized now he craved her more than he'd ever craved coke.

Her presence alone filled him with a sense of peace. Her smile distracted and delighted him. Her laugh enchanted him. Her wit charmed him.

Where was she? When would she make her decision?

As Jase and Brook Lynn talked excitedly about Baby Becklow—Hark?—West stalked toward the door in back. Along the way, he ran into Dane and Kenna, the two just coming off the dance floor, glowing with love, light and happiness.

"Uh-oh," Kenna said. "Jessie Kay must be in trouble."

West frowned. "What makes you think so?"

"You only wear that particular scowl when you're thinking about her."

That couldn't be true. "She's not in trouble." Yet. "Have you seen her?"

Dane kissed Kenna's temple, his lips lingering over her skin. "Last time I saw your firecracker, she was dealing with a situation. Looked like she had everything under control," he added when West went still.

A situation? "Excuse me." He picked up the pace. Three other couples got in his way, but he barreled onward, eye on the prize. A server hurried past the door, her features drawn and pale, and West slipped inside the room.

"—ruin this party," Jessie Kay was saying.

The kitchen had white walls papered with strawberries, a long pink-and-white marble countertop and top-of-the-line appliances. Apparently business had picked up substantially for the few months Harlow had worked here, allowing Carol to make long-needed updates.

Between the stove and fridge he found Jessie Kay—alive and well—and he was finally able to breathe. Then he spotted the woman tied to a chair in front of her.

Monica Gentry.

"Binding me is a crime." Monica wore a two-piece red dress, her midriff bared. She'd lightened her hair, the once chocolate strands now a yellowish blond.

Trying to look more like Jessie Kay?

Seriously. Was a bunny boiling on the stove right this very second?

"Trespassing is also a crime," Jessie Kay stated flatly. "And I made a citizen's arrest, so I was totally within my rights to bind you."

"We're on public property. I did nothing wrong," Monica insisted.

"Please. The party is invitation only—meaning private—but I'm done arguing with you. I have work to do."

"What's the matter?" Monica lifted her nose in the air. "Can't stand a little competition?"

"Oh, honey. We're not even in the same league."

"You're right. You're nothing but a gold-digging whore."

Red winked over West's vision, and he took a step forward, unsure about what he was about to do but knowing the end result would be ugly.

"Wait. West is rich?" Jessie Kay gave a mock gasp, and West stopped to watch the antics. "Dang. I should have taken him up on his romantic proposal of marriage and a house full of rug rats. How could I have been so foolish, thinking I should hold out for love? Noooo!" Jessie Kay ran a fingertip down her cheek, mimicking tears. "Such a wasted opportunity."

The red faded, and West actually found himself fighting a grin.

"You lie! He would *never* propose to the likes of you." Monica struggled to free herself. "He won't want you when I put a bullet in your heart. Let me go. Now!"

Aaand there was the red again.

Jessie Kay smirked at her, not the least bit intimidated. "In the talent competition of the Miss Strawberry Valley pageant, I hog-tied a calf. You ain't getting free, princess."

New fantasy: Jessie Kay in her tiara and sash.

"I've hog-tied a calf or twenty myself. I've also bagged and tagged deer and wild hogs. My dad still has their heads hanging in his study. Exactly where yours will hang when I'm done with you."

All right. Enough. "Let her go, kitten."

Both women jerked in his direction. Jessie Kay glowered at him, even stomped her foot. "No! Never!"

Monica brightened, casting him a bright smile. "West! This crazy bitch tied me up."

"Hey! I may be a bitch, but I'm a reasonable one."

"Untie her," he said. "Please."

Hurt danced over Jessie Kay's features, and he wished he could close the distance, pull her into his arms and hold her close. Give her a little of that comforting she liked, but there was no way in hell he would add fuel to Monica's fire.

"Fine." Huffing and puffing, Jessie Kay obeyed. "I hope you enjoy your psycho. She's all yours."

Monica raced to him with every intention of throwing her arms around his neck. He caught her wrists to stop her. "Come on. I'll show you out." Looking at Jessie Kay, he said, "Stay here."

West exited the door that led into the hallway rather than the ballroom, Monica protesting the entire way. In the lobby, he texted Jase.

Find Sheriff Lintz & bring him to the lobby

Jase: On it

"What's going on?" Monica demanded.

He didn't say another word until Jase and the sheriff strode around the corner. "This is Monica Gentry," he informed Lintz. "She's not only trespassing, she threatened Jessie Kay with bodily harm."

Monica gasped. "I did no such thing. I would never—"

"She threatened to put a bullet in Jessie Kay's heart."

"Well, now." Lintz pushed back the brim of his hat. "We can handle this one of two ways, Miss Gentry. I arrest you and you spend the rest of the weekend in my jail while we wait for the judge to recover from tonight's hangover—or I walk you to your car and you don't return to this town. Choice is yours."

"This isn't... This can't be..." She pressed her lips together as all three men continued to stare at her, unfazed. "Fine." She raised her chin, squared her shoulders. "Take me to my car."

West released her, placing her in the sheriff's care. "Stay away from Jessie Kay, Monica. You and I aren't going to happen. Not now. Not ever. Understand?"

Her anger faded, tears filling her eyes. "But I love—"

"You need help."

Her sobs followed him into the ballroom.

Several people tried to stop and chat with him, but he kept moving, returning to the back room. Where there was no sign of Jessie Kay.

One of the servers, a college-aged kid with stars in his eyes, tapped him on the shoulder and pointed. "She's out there, sir. And if I may be so bold, your video game—"

Don't have time for this. "Thank you. Call the WOH offices and I'll make sure you get a booklet detailing all the Easter eggs."

"Thank you. Thank you so much."

West took off and sure enough, he found Jessie Kay carting a tray of champagne glasses. He closed the distance, reaching her as she smiled up at an older gentleman, her sexiness nearly giving the guy a heart attack.

With only a glare, he sent the other guy packing.

Jessie Kay tried to step around him, but he stepped with her, remaining in her way. "Out of my way. I'm giving you the silent treatment."

He ignored the flaw in her statement. "Why are you upset?"

Not one to hold back, she spat, "You picked her over me. Then you dared—dared!—to come to my rescue."

"I never picked her over you. I got rid of her. And I don't see the problem, my coming to your rescue."

"You didn't trust me to get the job done on my own. Something you're paying me to do. Now, if you'll excuse me." She stepped to the side.

Again, he stepped with her. He took the tray from her kung fu grip, flagged down a waitress and handed it over. Then he took Jessie Kay's hand, holding tighter when she tried to wrench free.

"What are you doing?" she demanded.

"The only thing I've wanted to do since the party started, so just settle your fine ass down. This is happening whether you want it to or not."

CHAPTER SIXTEEN

MY FINE ASS?

My video gamer is a poet at heart.

As West led her onto the dance floor—her, a lowly server rather than an honored guest—the businesswomen stared at Jessie Kay quizzically while the females of Strawberry Valley either cheered for her or pouted that she'd (so obviously) won the affections of the most eligible bachelor in town.

When he reached the center of the dance floor, he drew her against the hard strength of his body. Shock held her immobile. This was happening. This was really happening.

From the corner of her eye, she spotted Brook Lynn, who was giving her an exuberant thumbs-up. Jase, who mouthed, "No Magic Mike?" Dane, who was nodding his head in approval. Kenna, who was grabbing a handful of jalapeño-stuffed mushrooms from a passing tray. The girl had called last night and begged Jessie Kay to add them to the menu—*I have a craving and I'll owe you forever and ever and I'll make sure Dane writes a big fat check to the Christmas charity of your choice, pleeease*—making Jessie Kay wonder if she suffered from the same condition as Harlow.

"You're embarrassing yourself, you know," she muttered, and oh, what the heck. She melted against him. Being in his embrace…nothing had ever felt so right.

"It's my company. I can do what I want."

"Wow. That's *such* a mature response."

"How about this?" Deadpan, he said, "I will not exhibit servile compliance or be beleaguered by pompous expectations."

As thrums of heat wafted through her, she scraped her teeth over the lobe of his ear. "You know I hate when you talk all fancy like that."

"And you know I hate the way you hate it."

Darling man. And bad Jessie Kay. Bad! Molesting him in public. "You do realize your business associates think you're slumming it, right? The computer mogul with the poor—but gorgeous—waitress."

"I'm not slumming it. If anything, I'm stepping way out of my league."

She smiled at him. "I'm loudmouthed, irreverent and just a little crude." Also the girl with the bad rep. She'd been propositioned about a dozen times tonight. One guy asked her to sneak away to play seven minutes in heaven. Another patted her ass and told her how much he'd been missing it. Old insecurities had rolled in with a vengeance, and she'd realized liking herself wasn't just a one-time deal. She'd have to actively work at it for the rest of her life. "How are you, the perfect gentleman, not out of *my* league?"

He bent a little, coming down to her level, tucking his head into the hollow of her neck and she thought maybe…maybe he was giving her a hug. The kind he'd once claimed not to like. The kind he suddenly seemed to need more than air to breathe. "You are the sun, and I'm one of the lucky planets allowed in your orbit. Nothing and no one else exists for me."

Oh, sweet heaven. Another item to check off the forever list. One she'd thought impossible.

Forget there are other women in the world.

"What am I going to do with you?" she asked on a sigh.

"I know what I'd like you to do." He kissed her where her shirt gaped at the collar, his hot tongue stroking her pulse. "Say you'll go deeper into the rabbit hole with me."

Her heart, the traitor, skipped a beat. "I require clarification. Is 'rabbit hole' a euphemism for sex or nerdspeak for the relationship you offered?"

"Nerd speak, but not just for the relationship." His head lifted, his eyes hot with longing. "I want more data. I want to know everything about you."

"You know the worst stuff already."

"And the best, but I still want more." He curved his hands around her waist, the heels of his palms resting on her hips, squeezing just hard enough to hold her in place. Lest she decide to bolt? "I want to know everything in between. The details are my drug of choice. Feed my addiction."

Could he *be* any more romantic right now? "I— Well, I'm not sure where to start." Tremors swept through her as she met his fire-ravaged gaze. This man…this beautiful man…wanted to be with her. He wouldn't use her for sex, disappearing in the bright light of the morning. He would stay in her bed, holding her close—enjoying her. But at the end of their two-month affair, he would still let her go.

"Start anywhere. I'll be riveted."

"Well, *my* drug of choice is Taylor Swift and Carrie Underwood. Eargasm! When I finally get a pet, I'm choosing a feral cat that will love me and only me and try to claw the eyes out of everyone else. I'll name him Admiral Snuggles. Oh, and I hate hospitals as much as I hate spiders. They are palaces of pain, I don't care what anyone else says."

"Guess what music will be playing in my room 24/7 from now on? And Admiral Snuggles is a name I can respect. I often refer to myself as Colonel Cuddles."

Too adorable for words.

"Why do you hate hospitals?" he asked.

Easy. "As a kid, Brook Lynn underwent surgery after surgery for her ears. I would walk the halls as I waited for an update and I witnessed one person after another writhing in pain, spewing blood and other things, soiling themselves... I heard one person after another scream for help...and I even watched someone die." She whispered the last part.

His arms tightened around her. "When Harlow was sick you went to see her. Twice."

"Yes, but only because Brook Lynn was by my side... and I'd popped a few Xanax."

"You should have come to me." His hands slid up, up to cup her jawline. "I would have distracted you."

Hardly. "You hated me back then."

"Wrong. I hated my reaction to you. I wanted you, but I thought I couldn't allow myself to have you."

"And now?" The question croaked from her.

"Now I'll do *anything* to have you."

Not true. He wouldn't pardon himself.

He must have sensed the direction of her thoughts

because he changed the subject, asking, "What's your favorite food?"

"Dessert."

"Favorite *specific* food?" he amended.

"Sugar. No, chocolate. No, sugar."

His lips quirked at the corners. "Do you prefer mornings or evenings?"

"Afternoons. Obviously. Not too early and not too late."

"Fitting." Chuckling, he leaned down to rub his cheek against hers, tickling her skin with the most delicious warmth. "If you had only one day left to live, what would you do?"

Besides make love to him, over and over again? "Brook Lynn and I actually talked about this one night. And because my sister is who she is, a zombie-believing list maker, I already have a game plan."

"Do tell."

"I'm going to withdraw every cent I have and give it to the local animal shelter. Then I'm going to update my Facebook status to 'dead soon.' I'll take bets about how many likes I'll receive. Then I'm going to write postcards to all my friends and tell Brook Lynn to mail them a month after I'm gone so everyone thinks I'm writing from the great beyond. Oh, and my personal favorite, I'm going to find a Khal Drogo look-alike and get myself a very happy ending."

West eased her closer, taking over her personal space, consuming her. "I could give you a happy ending tonight."

Lightning bolts of need shot through her. *Stay strong.* "Sugar bear, let's be honest. You can't really handle me."

"I just need practice."

She gave him a *keep dreaming, buddy* look. "Tell me what you'd do if you were going to die in a day."

"After I spent twenty-three hours in bed with you, giving you multiple happy endings?"

"Obviously."

"I'd write up detailed instructions about where I want my surviving loved ones to spread my ashes…and every location will exist only in my video games."

As she snickered, delighted with him, the song came to an end. Nooo! But she pulled from his embrace, despite her desire to remain in his arms, and cleared her throat. "Well. Thank you for the break, but I need to get back to work. Everything has probably gone to hell without me."

"Jessie Kay—"

She hurried off before he convinced her to blow off the rest of her duties. As it turned out, everything had *not* gone to hell—boo, hiss—but had continued to run smoothly.

As she resumed her duties, her gaze constantly returned to West. Her prince and her tormentor. She lost her breath every time he looked her way, tension arcing between them.

He spoke with a group of young businessmen then moved off and winked at her. As she waved, a beautiful woman sidled up to his side. Jessie Kay slammed into one of the guests, spilling champagne over his jacket.

"Crap! I'm so sorry," she burst out.

"Don't worry about it. It'll dry," he replied with an easy smile. "You're the one who danced with Lincoln West."

"Yeah. That would be me."

"Are you two dating?"

"Wow. Get personal right at minute one, why don't you."

"Sorry. Habit." He held out his hand to shake. "I'm Dan Escada with *Other Worlds Daily*, a digital subscription for gamers. I'm doing a story on Mr. West and would love to speak with—"

"No comment." She strode away and ended up handing her tray to another server. Who was the woman with her man? And he *was* her man, whether they were officially dating or not.

"Hey. Who's the witch with West?" Carol Mathis stepped in front of Jessie Kay. "Doesn't she know he belongs to you?"

Edna Mills, who stood at Carol's side, nodded emphatically. "I might trip her the next time she passes me. Accidents happen all the time."

"You know I love your team spirit, but I'm not actually dating West," Jessie Kay said.

"Pfft." Carol waved her hand through the air. "Anyone with eyes can tell you're both crazy about each other. And he's a Strawberry Valley boy now. He needs a Strawberry Valley girl. No one else is good enough."

She wasn't wrong.

Jessie Kay watched as the hooker in question walked her fingers up West's tie. *Look away, look away. Don't you dare fly across the room and fight Dillon-style.* Also known as DDAK. Down-and-dirty ass-kicking.

Except, she had no right to throw a punch. West wasn't her boyfriend, she reminded herself. They'd made no promises to each other. And they wouldn't—unless she agreed to his terms. But dang it, agreeing to his terms would feel too much like surrender. Giving up. Saying goodbye to a chance for more. For better. But *not* agreeing to his terms would also feel like surrender. Zero chance for more.

"Oh, no, she did *not* molest his tie. Hold my shoes, Edna." Carol removed a pump. "I don't want to slip when I boot that girl into the middle of next week."

"I love you both but do not, I repeat, *do not* do anything to the brunette—not out in the open anyway." Her gaze landed on Daniel, who waved her over. "I'm being summoned. Gotta go."

She pushed her way through the crowd. Daniel greeted her with a hug before motioning to West with a tilt of his chin. "Do I need to feed that boy his own testicles?"

"Sweet of you to offer, but no."

His date—a beautiful blonde—looked Jessie Kay up and down and offered a very fake smile. "Hello."

"Kiki, this is Jessie Kay," he said. "Jessie Kay, this is Kiki. You may not remember, but she used to live in Strawberry Valley."

"I was in sixth grade and you were in eighth," Kiki said, "but we had the same math class. Oh, and you slept with my boyfriend the summer of my junior year."

I like myself. I do.

Daniel stiffened.

"Bobby Turner, right?" Jessie Kay shuddered with legit revulsion. "He told everyone he'd dumped you. He also secretly recorded the girls he banged so you should probably thank me. Anyway, you two enjoy the party."

When she turned, Daniel grabbed her hand. "Stay. Kiki owes you an apology and—"

"No, she doesn't. And I can't stay. I have to tend to the guests." She spotted her sister and Kenna in a far corner and closed the distance. In lieu of a greeting, she said, "When I get home, I'm soaking in the tub and burning West's tie."

"Why?" Brook Lynn nudged her shoulder. "Did it say something to offend you?"

Kenna fought a smile. "I wouldn't worry. I've never seen a tie look more uncomfortable."

Really? She glanced over, and yeah, okay, West—and his tie—radiated all kinds of tension. His posture was rigid, his legs braced for flight.

Brook Lynn wound her arm around Jessie Kay's waist. "Guess what I just found out? Tomorrow our girl-power group will be getting facials, massages, scrubs, painted and polished nails, and as a bonus our hair and makeup will be professionally styled."

"There are only three days till Christmas, which means only two shopping days," Jessie Kay pointed out. "Currently I've bought zero presents."

"I know you. Tomorrow you'll wake up, tell yourself you've got one more day and end up doing nothing." Brook Lynn gave her a squeeze, released her. "It's what you do every year."

That was…kind of true. "Fine. I'm on board."

"Why did you change the subject?" Kenna nudged Brook Lynn's shoulder. "Tie Whore needs a beating. Encourage your sister to give it to her."

Jessie Kay wagged a finger in the redhead's face. "You want me to lose my temper so Brook Lynn wins the bet. Why? Has she offered to let you pick one of my outfits or something?"

"She has." Kenna rubbed her hands together. "I'm trying to decide between a tie-dyed unitard and a hot-dog costume."

"You guys suck," she muttered.

Both girls giggled as she flounced off. She stopped here and there to pick up fallen napkins and look over at West. He drew her gaze in a way no other man ever had, as if he were somehow connected to her.

Tie Whore was still at his side, but he'd clearly stopped listening to her. His eyes were hot on Jessie Kay, reminding her of a predator about to strike.

She shivered, liquid heat pouring through her.

He'd demand an answer, she thought, and he'd demand it soon.

JESSIE KAY CURSED. It was the butt-crack of dawn, the day after the party, and Brook Lynn was already blowing up her phone, here to collect her for their spa day. She'd stayed up way too late watching a movie with West. Well, pretending to watch a movie while her nerve endings wept for contact they never received.

Watch a chick flick with you just to see you smile.

Meanwhile, West, Jase and Beck would be playing— winning—a soccer game and enjoying time as best bros.

With a sigh, Jessie Kay rolled out of bed and grabbed her go-bag. A backpack stuffed with everything she might need in an emergency situation. A change of clothes, a box of baby wipes, a toothbrush, tube of toothpaste, an empty water bottle as well as a full water bottle, an Xbox 360 controller—just in case West offered to play a video game with her—a squeezable container of mustard, yellow dish gloves, a box of tampons, a six-pack of beer, one packet of instant coffee and a box of raw sugar packets. Plus the dress her sister demanded she bring.

On the drive to the spa, she brushed her teeth with the toothpaste and toothbrush and spit the suds in the empty water bottle. She cleaned her face and armpits with the

baby wipes—a whore's bath, according to Momma—
then changed out of her pajamas and into a wrinkled
T-shirt that read "Zombies Only Love You for Your
Brains" and a pair of sweatpants.

"So." Kenna occupied the front passenger seat of
Brook Lynn's brand-new SUV—a gift from Jase. She
twisted to face Jessie Kay, who sat in the back next to
Harlow, who held a jar of pickled okra. The breakfast of
pregnant champions. "We've already talked to Harlow,
asked her how she's doing—better, in case you hadn't
guessed. Now we want to talk with you. Anything happen between you and West?"

"No. I stayed at the inn to clean up. He stayed and
helped me, because he was my ride, then we went home
and vegged out. We didn't really say anything to each
other."

What more was there to say, really? Other than "yes"
or "no."

"Did your bodies do the talking for you?" Brook Lynn
wiggled her brows in the rearview mirror.

"I wish." Her body hungered for that man in a bad,
bad way.

The rest of the drive passed quickly, the slow pace of
Strawberry Valley giving way to the hustle and bustle of
the city. Brook Lynn parked in the spa's lot, and Jessie
Kay glanced at her wristwatch. Right on time.

They made their way toward a metal warehouse.

"You sure we're in the right place?" Harlow asked.

"We'll find out." Brook Lynn opened the front door,
and Jessie Kay soared inside.

And oh, wow. Yeah. They were definitely in the right
place. Perched in the middle of a luxurious lobby was a
large waterfall fountain, a marble mermaid resting on

the top tier and colorful seashells on all the others. Soft red carpet pillowed her feet, and the plush black chairs pushed against the walls beckoned the weary to relax.

A well-dressed twentysomething greeted them with a bright smile before showing them to a locker room, where they stripped, showered and donned white robes. Afterward, they were ushered into a smallish room in back.

"This is where you'll prepare for the magnificence to come." With that, the receptionist—hostess?—was gone.

The only place to sit was the floor, where pillows and cushions were scattered around a blazing fire pit. A light mist that smelled of honey and sunflowers drifted from an array of vents above, the droplets heated by the fire as they fell. Soft music played in the background.

"So... I've been holding out on y'all." Jessie Kay held her hands toward the fire. "West asked me to be his next two-month date-and-dump for the next *five* years. And don't ask me why there's a time limit. I won't say." Betraying his confidence wasn't something she would ever willingly do, even for advice. "Anyway. I don't know what to tell him."

"First off, we need more deets. Are we offended or happy on your behalf?" Kenna asked.

"Neither. Both. Oh, I don't know. Needless to say, he's offered me more than he's ever offered another."

What would Mom say?

Do you want the whole enchilada or only a nibble?

Did she really need to think about the answer? "But if I do it," she added with a sigh, "heck, even if I don't, I'll want more from him. I *do* want more. I want everything."

Harlow reached over and patted her hand. "Trust me. I understand your dilemma. I've read more romance novels than you can possibly imagine. They've featured rakes and rogues and alpha douche bags. And let's not forget my real-life application. I bagged Beck, the one-night-stand king, after he offered me only twelve hours in his bed."

But look at her now, the epicenter of Beck's world. Could Jessie Kay, the girl no guy had ever kept for more than a handful of weeks, pull off that kind of miracle? Could she win the guy no other woman could tame? Well, no other living woman.

If she were being honest with herself, she would admit…she wanted to try. Desire for West lived in her bones, and it wasn't going away, was only growing stronger. But oh, the fear of failure was entrenched in her *soul*.

See! Fear shackled.

"So far I haven't heard any advice," Jessie Kay said. "Go ahead. Amaze me."

"You'd actually trust my advice?" Brook Lynn asked. "You never have before."

"You've always been like a grandmother to me. Of course I'd trust your advice."

Brook Lynn rolled her eyes. "I don't think you need advice. I think you need…drumroll please…a pros and cons list."

"What! No! Absolutely not." Jessie Kay shook her head, adamant. "Your last list—"

"Was excellent," Harlow said.

"Was something every woman should expect from her forever man," Kenna agreed.

"Read by West," Jessie Kay finished.

"Good." Brook Lynn brushed her hands together, clearly considering the job well done. "Men do better when they have a user's guide."

Yeah, but did the list ask too much from him? Or did it not ask for enough?

"I owe West an answer," she said, "and I've already gone over a pros and cons list in my head. Like, a thousand times. What if I make the wrong decision? What if I ruin everything? What if he breaks my heart? Oh, my gosh, what if—"

Crack.

Brook Lynn's palm connected with Jessie Kay's cheek. The slap, though gentle, stung a little, and she glared at her sister. "What was that for? And did I just win our bet?"

"No way. I was calm and helpful." Brook Lynn settled back against her pillow. "You were starting to panic and I had to act fast. You're welcome."

Ugh. Those stupid panic attacks.

"I remember the good ole days when you two would throw each other on the ground and box it out," Kenna said wishfully.

"Have I mentioned you guys suck?" Jessie Kay muttered.

"Look," Brook Lynn said. "We saw the way he held you yesterday. You mean something to him. You mean *a lot* to him. But that doesn't matter if you don't mean *enough*."

Good point. Depressing point.

Her shoulders slumped in. This wasn't the kind of advice she'd expected the girls to give her. Where were the old classics? *If anyone can win him, Jessie Kay, it's you. Just give him a little more time.*

Kenna reached over and patted her hand. "If you're living in limbo while you wait for the guy you want to give you everything else you want, you're doing nothing but eroding your self-esteem. I love West. I do. But I also love you, and I want the best for you. You have to make a decision. Do you settle? Or do you walk away?"

CHAPTER SEVENTEEN

WEST WAITED IN the lobby of the spa...*impatient*. Jase, Beck and Dane flanked him, and their big bodies ate up every bit of space, making him think the four of them were taller and wider than the people who normally visited the place, because damn. Sardine, anyone?

Wouldn't have been so bad if the receptionist hadn't stared at West as if he was a circus bear in a tutu.

"You're Lincoln West," she finally said. "I *just* saw your picture in this morning's edition of *Other Worlds Daily*."

Ah. About an hour ago, a reporter—Dan something— had emailed him a link to a story on the website.

Title: Game On.

First line:

Lincoln West, creator of some of our most beloved video games, is a man of wealth and renown, and like the characters he brings to life, he has his choice of lovely ladies—it looks like he's finally chosen.

There'd been pictures of him at the party, several of him mingling with his friends. More of him with Jessie Kay, his arms wrapped tightly around her, his attention so intently focused on her it was obvious the rest of the world had ceased to exist for him. Seeing his desire for her so blatantly displayed had left him reeling. Would have scared the shit out of him…if he hadn't seen *her* desire for *him* just as clearly.

He'd printed the photos and planned to frame them.

There'd even been a few pictures of him with the brunette who'd cornered him and put a death grip on his tie. She'd asked multiple questions about his current workload, almost panicking every time he tried to walk away. Which now made sense. She, too, was a reporter, at the party only for a story.

"Can I have your autograph?" the receptionist asked.

"Sure." He signed a blank piece of paper.

"How much longer?" Beck shifted from one foot to the other, unable to hide his impatience.

"Just a few more minutes." She smiled at West. "They're dressing."

While Jase had arranged for the girls to be pampered, West had insisted on paying Jessie Kay's part of the bill. He loved Jase, would die for him and even kill for him, but there was no way in hell his friend's money would finance anything having to do with Jessie Kay. West's sense of possession simply wouldn't allow it. *She's mine.*

Whether they were together or not.

And, really, he liked the thought of money he'd earned paying for things that would make her happy. He'd had a freaking hard-on when he'd given her the key to her new car.

"I should have selected a spa in Strawberry Valley," Jase muttered. "At the very least, Mr. Rodriguez could have given the girls a trim, and we could have collected them an hour later."

"Rodriguez specializes in buzz cuts," West reminded him.

"Your point?"

"Hate to break it to you, but you're both amateurs." Beck gave them both a pitying frown. "You don't hand your girl to someone else. You draw her a bubble bath, light some candles, paint her toenails, and suddenly you're the best thing to ever happen to her—and you never had to leave your bedroom."

I wish. But the day of pampering had been necessary, and wouldn't end here at the spa. The guys—West included—had used the time apart to plan romantic dates for the girls.

Jase would be taking Brook Lynn on a hot-air-balloon ride. Beck would be taking Harlow to a book signing for some bestselling romance author, and Dane would be flying Kenna to LA to pick a new sword for her collection—like Brook Lynn, she believed the zombie apocalypse would kick off any day. West would be taking Jessie Kay to a candle-lit dinner. Their first date.

They had unfinished business.

Minutes ticked by, his anticipation only growing. Finally the girls filed into the lobby, squealing as they spotted their men. Jessie Kay gazed about excitedly, though warily, stopping when she found him. At the moment of connection, awareness jolted him.

With her, awareness *always* jolted him.

Golden waves tumbled to her elbows. Her makeup had been lightly applied, but her eyes were now smoky and heavy-lidded. Her skin glowed the most delicious shades of bronze and pink...an erotic flush he would kill to taste. Her dress was angelic white, flowing and loose, wickedly short. *Teasing me...*

A backpack was slung over her shoulder, completely at odds with the elegance of the dress. So Jessie Kay.

Smiling, he offered his hand to her. She hesitated a

moment—a hesitation he understood…this thing between them was too strong, too powerful—nibbling on her bottom lip. Finally she closed the distance and twined her fingers with his.

He kissed her knuckles. "You, kitten, are exquisite."

Goose bumps broke out over her skin. "And you, sugar bear, are a dream come true." Her navy blues swept over his suit and tie and heated. She straightened the tie, saying, "I wasn't going to ask, but I've decided what the heck. Who was the girl last night?"

"A reporter. Congrats. We made the front page of a digital paper."

"Seriously?"

"Seriously." He withdrew his phone and keyed the article.

A little laugh escaped her as she read, a sensual stroke along his senses. "Dang, I rocked that uniform, didn't I. No wonder you wanted to bang me."

He bent down to run her earlobe through his teeth. "Want. Present tense."

Her breath hitched. "I met the guy who wrote this. Well, I spilled drinks on him. He asked if we were dating."

"What did you tell him?"

"No comment."

"You can tell me," he insisted. "I won't be mad." As long as she'd told the guy they were, in fact, *something* to each other.

"I just did, dummy. I told him I had no comment for him."

"Ah." Well, it was better than the alternative. "You ready to go?"

"You're absconding with me?"

"Definitely. Guys," he announced. "We're heading out."

Beck patted his shoulder. "Don't do anything I wouldn't do."

"You do know you just told him it's okay to do every dirty, freaky fantasy he's ever had, right?" Jessie Kay winked at her sister and waved goodbye to the group. As West led her outside, she muttered, "Oh, crap! The cold!"

He draped his jacket over her shoulders, then opened the car door for her.

"I've been meaning to ask," she said as he settled in his seat. "Have you heard from Monica lately?"

"No. Why?" He turned the heater to high and turned the vents in her direction. "Has she contacted you?"

"No. Maybe. I don't know. During my massage, I received eighteen calls from an unknown number. I answered the first few—and I don't need a lecture about forgetting phones to achieve proper relaxation, the masseuse already gave me a good one—but no one ever said anything, and I began to wonder if crazypants was the culprit."

His hands tightened on the wheel. "I'll find out." He had ways. "You don't need to worry about her showing up at our place." *Our place.* He liked those words. "I have someone monitoring her 24/7 now."

Her eyes went wide. "First, I wasn't worried. Second, you are paying someone to *follow* her around?"

"I don't take your safety lightly, Jessie Kay." A fact she'd have to accept. In this, he wouldn't back down. "If ever she calls and says anything, let me know immediately. Or maybe we should change your phone number." Maybe he should add an app that allowed him to track incoming calls, private number or not.

"But why? I mean, not the part about changing my number." Her voice was small, filled with uncertainty. "Why am I so special to you? Were you like this with any of your other girlfriends?"

"Only with Tessa." He knew Jessie Kay and he knew her insecurities—her personal demons—were coming out to play right now. Through experience, he knew some days were better than others, some battles easier than others. "Kitten, you are special to me because you *are* special. It's as simple as that."

Features growing soft, luminous, she asked, "Do I remind you of her or something?"

"No. Not in the slightest."

She shifted, the hem of her dress riding up, revealing more of her succulent thighs, making his blood heat—and his shaft press against his zipper. "Tell me about her."

A command he would have refused if it had come from anyone else. But this was Jessie Kay, his greatest peace and his sweetest torment; they'd already shared so much with each other. Why not everything else? "I met Tessa not long after I met Beck and Jase. The three of us were assigned to the same foster home, and she lived down the street. We were young, not even teenagers. She was outside playing with her friends, and when a beam of sunlight hit her, I swore she was an angel come to save me."

"Love at first sight."

"Yeah, but I didn't know it at the time. I didn't exactly feel romantic toward girls yet. They had cooties. But she was fun and I liked her. When I moved to my next home, I stayed in contact with her, wrote her letters. Then, when I was sixteen, Beck, Jase and I pooled our resources to buy a car and I went to see her. We were together from that day on."

"That kind of devotion is so rare," she said, a wistful edge to her tone. "It's precious. A real treasure."

He would be just as devoted to her. If she asked for the moon and stars, he would do everything in his power to procure both. But the time constraint he'd placed on their relationship... He'd never before resented his need to contain his happiness to short bursts, living in misery the rest of the year, but he hated it now.

"Tessa was incredibly smart—" he continued.

"Hey! I'm smart!" A pause. "Sometimes."

"You're smart *all the time*. When I said you two were nothing alike, I meant in looks and temperament, nothing else."

She nodded, satisfied. "Just so you know, you saved yourself from a beating."

He fought a smile. "Her family placed little importance on education and she ended up dropping out her senior year of high school." Amusement gone in a blink, his next words contained an edge. "She was never diagnosed, but I think she was bipolar. She had days of manic happiness, and days—weeks—of severe depression. Her emotions were a roller coaster."

"Um, don't take this the wrong way, but she sounds a little difficult. What made you stay with her? Love isn't always enough."

"The days she was happy, she glowed. She would laugh and dance and play. She could make *me* laugh, and for a little while I'd actually feel like the kid I was supposed to be, something no one else had ever done for me." And maybe *he'd* suffered from white-knight syndrome. If he could save her, the way he'd failed to save his mom, he would be worthy of happiness.

Another pause, this one thick with tension. "How do *I* make you feel?"

"Crazy." When she stiffened, he reached over, took her hand. "Impossibly hard. Wild. Unsure. Young again. Impossibly hard. Hungry. Calm. *Impossibly hard.* In other words…crazy."

She tightened her grip on him. They remained silent—and connected—the rest of the drive. He wondered what thoughts rolled through her mind but knew guessing would do him no good. She was a complex woman who possessed a logic he was only just coming to understand. She was a wealth of contradictions—independent but starved for affection, as tough as stone and yet as soft as marshmallows. Both things he lo—

Liked about her. Only liked.

The restaurant he'd chosen happened to be located in the middle of a historic hotel. The black-and-white marble floor mesmerized. Towering columns at every doorway enchanted, and a tin ceiling awed, reflecting light from two massive chandeliers.

"A hotel? A little presumptuous." Jessie Kay gave his shoulder a teasing bump. "But not exactly unwelcome."

"I'm a lot *hopeful*. But we're not here for a room. When I finally get you into bed, it'll be my own." And they wouldn't leave for days. Maybe weeks.

Her breath caught, a sensual reaction, one that fueled his own, making him harden painfully—pretty much a constant state now.

"This is our first real date," he said. "It could be the start of something great, and I hope our surroundings reflect that."

"West," she said softly, reaching out to trace her fingertips over the shell of his ear. "I hereby dub you Most Romantic Man Ever."

He nuzzled her cheek. "Only with you."

"You aren't crazy—you're crazy for *me*."

A hostess interrupted them, almost earning a snarl from him when Jessie Kay dropped her arm to her side. The girl led them through a spacious room lit by hundreds of candles. The dark walls and carpet only added to the dim, dreamlike feel. As he'd requested when he called to make the reservation, their table was in a corner in back, as far away from other guests as possible.

He ordered the oldest red for Jessie Kay, despite her protests.

"Jase and Beck will drink in front of me, but only occasionally, and they're always uncomfortable about it. I don't want my hang-ups to deprive you of something you enjoy."

"All right, but no wine. Gross. This girl likes whiskey, scotch and bourbon."

He changed the order and as she sipped her whiskey, he sipped his water, leaning back in his chair to study the woman he was so determined to have. The soft, luminous candlelight looked good on her. But then, everything did.

"Have you ever been in love?" he asked.

"I've been in love with the idea of love."

"No special man?"

"No. Though I should probably admit I once told Brook Lynn I wanted to marry Jase."

"No." He gave a violent shake of his head as every cell in his body screamed in protest. "You shouldn't admit that. Not ever again."

She shrugged, all *it is what it is*. "I craved security,

that was all. An easy way to save Brook Lynn from the mess I'd made of our lives."

"You didn't make her life a mess. You didn't make her decisions for her."

"No, but I didn't make those decisions easy for her, either. Honestly, I was like a noose around her neck."

"Now you're one of the lights of her life."

The waiter arrived to take their order and West didn't appreciate the way the guy's gaze lingered on Jessie Kay. Anger hit, but he breathed through it—with the unwitting aid of Jessie Kay.

"I want to make it clear he's paying," she told the guy, and pointed to West. "Right?"

"Of course," West replied.

She brightened. "I'd like the double-lobster dinner, please, with extra butter. But nix the side of vegetables and add a side of lobster. Oh, and crab legs. And a skewer of shrimp."

The waiter laughed as if she'd just told a joke, but she continued to stare at him expectantly, and he frowned. "Would you, uh, like a salad before your meal?"

"Rabbits eat lettuce. I am not a rabbit." She actually shuddered. "I'll have the lobster bisque. With a side of lobster."

Now the waiter appeared confused. "You'd like one of your lobsters brought out with your soup?"

"Don't talk crazy. I want an *additional* lobster. No one ever puts enough meat in the soup."

West covered a laugh behind his hand. He ordered "the same" because why not? "I want to point out I remembered your desire for lobsters the day at the diner."

"Patting yourself on the back to woo me?" In a stage whisper she said, "It's working."

"Have to admit, I'm a little jealous of seafood right now."

"You should be." She took another sip of her whiskey. "If I could, I'd marry a Maine lobster and have little lobster babies. If the right Alaskan king crab came along, I could be convinced to have a torrid affair."

He chuckled. "You're the first woman I've ever dated who isn't afraid to eat in front of me."

"Well, I know what it's like to go hungry. As teenagers, Brook Lynn and I often survived on canned goods given to us by the church. Sometimes there were other families in worse shape, so we'd opt not to take anything. I'm *never* afraid to eat when given the opportunity."

Though he ached for the kid she'd been and the trials she'd faced, he welcomed the peek into her past. It only strengthened his admiration for her. "Have you made a decision about us, Jessie Kay?"

She twirled a lock of hair around her finger, the pale strands a lovely contrast to the bronze of her skin, and shook her head in negation. "You want the full truth?"

"Please."

"Both choices seem right, but at the same time, both choices seem wrong. Either way, I know I'm going to get hurt. Just in different ways."

Hurting her was exactly what he didn't want to do. He scrubbed a hand down his face.

The fix was simple. Pardon himself. Try for something real. Solid. Lasting.

Something more.

But could he? He would become responsible for Jessie Kay's happiness, yet he wasn't sure he could identify happiness if it bit him on the ass.

He asked, "Are you looking for a guarantee we'll last forever?"

"No, but I'd like a *chance* at forever." She opened her mouth to say more, snapped it closed. Open, closed.

He regarded her from across the table, drinking in the flicker of candlelight across her skin. Gold twined with shadows, both licking at her. Since the moment he'd met her, his desire for her had only grown stronger day by day, hour by hour, minute by minute. And, really, no matter how he crunched the numbers, relief didn't wait in his future—unless he gave her what she wanted.

What part of him wanted, too.

"Let's not talk about the future right now, okay?" she said. "Let's just enjoy each other."

"All right." Knowing her—and he was beginning to—she hoped to take the pressure off him, something he understood. He didn't want her feeling pressured, either.

"So…did you win your game today?"

"We did. Three to one."

"I'm only surprised you didn't score a dozen more. The ball belongs to you."

He winked at her. "My mind was on other things. The ball wasn't what I wanted."

"Ha! I have no illusions. If you had to pick between a soccer ball and me, I'd have my ass handed to me in a hurry."

He traced his finger over the rim of his water glass, imagining the fingertip trailing over different parts of her. "Kitten, the only hand on your ass will be mine. After I kick the ball out the door."

She blushed the sweetest shade of rose and glanced away from him, suddenly—enchantingly—shy. "You have a talent. Making kind things sound dirty."

He winked at her. "We should resume your soccer lessons."

She arched a brow at him. "Will you actually work with me or Mr. Miyagi me?"

The grumble in her voice made him smile. "I'll be hands-on from this point forward. You have my word."

"When I'm good enough, I want to play on your team."

"No." He could have sidestepped the issue, but he wanted no confusion between them.

"No?" She snapped her fingers. "Just like that?"

"No." His hard, flat tone left no room for argument. "Just like that."

"Dang, that's so harsh."

"I don't want you playing coed. You could be harmed."

"How did I not realize you were a chauvinist?" She glared daggers at him. "I'm not some delicate Southern belle, you know. You've heard of my temper, right? It's infamous in twelve counties!"

"I've heard stories about your temper, yes," he said, "but I've never actually seen an example."

"Of course you haven't. You're still alive."

He leveled her with a hard stare. "If your temper is bad, mine is worse. I'm not some tame house cat who will stand idly by while you're injured. If some guy shoves you, I will go for his throat. If some guy steals the ball from you, I will still go for his throat."

Any other woman would have shrunk back in fear, might have even thrown down her napkin and walked away, afraid of such intense aggression. But not Jessie Kay.

She leaned back in her chair, eyeing him with something akin to awe. "You'd get in trouble."

"I wouldn't care."

The awe only magnified. "That's mighty possessive of you, sugar bear."

"I protect what's mine." He had to. As a kid, he'd had very little, allowed to take only what he could fit inside a single suitcase whenever he switched foster homes. A small suitcase, at that. He'd had to make a choice. Clothes or toys. Clothes had won, every time. Need before want. And if he'd wanted to keep the things that he'd needed, he'd had to defend them against other boys. "I want you to be mine."

She nibbled on her bottom lip, a nervous habit. Her teeth were adorable, the two in front set slightly ahead of the others.

The appetizers arrived. When the waiter wandered off, neither of them dug in. They continued to stare at each other, tension thick between them, making it difficult to breathe in a way he'd grown used to, even craved.

You know what you have to do...

Could he do it? He didn't have to like it. He just had to live with it.

Would he grow to resent her for forcing him to deny Jase and Tessa their due?

It didn't matter, he supposed, because he absolutely could not live without her.

"I'm going to be difficult to manage," he told her. "I'll be obsessed with your whereabouts and safety. I'll hover."

She went still, not even seeming to breathe. "You already are, and you already do."

"You think I've been bad? Kitten, you've only had a taste. I've limited myself to a handful of calls and texts a day." If they were together, he would stop counting and contact her whenever the urge struck. Just to make sure she was safe, that she wasn't upset with him or anyone else. "I'll insist you stick to a schedule, and I'll be pissed if ever you're late. Can you deal?"

"Again, I'm already dealing. But in the interest of full disclosure, I should probably confess I purposely screwed with your schedule."

He frowned. "Explain."

"Well, I've called and texted when I knew you had phone conferences."

"And you did this…why?"

"To show you the joys of spontaneity."

Had she said anything else, he might have gotten angry. But his marshmallow girl wanted everyone around her happy. How could he fault her?

"Just…don't do it again," he said.

"I won't. Maybe. Okay, I probably will."

Never try to change perfection. "Either way, I accept your terms."

Her brow wrinkled with confusion…and hope. "I don't understand."

"We'll be together," he said. He would give her what she wanted—and fight any resentment—but in return, she would have to give him what *he* wanted. "You and me, Jessie Kay. Indefinitely. No time limit. I'm yours. And you…you are mine."

CHAPTER EIGHTEEN

JESSIE KAY THRUMMED with excitement. West had just...
he'd just agreed...

They were going to be together? No limits?

"West," she said, staggered to the depths of her soul.
"I don't know what to say."

*Compromise with you because your wants are just as
important to him as his.*

See his future in your eyes.

Check and check.

"Say yes, kitten."

"Yes." He'd done the unexpected. He'd compromised.
He'd set himself free of his self-imposed prison sentence—
for her. To have a future with her. He'd placed value on
her. A value he'd never placed on any of the others. "Yes,
yes, a thousand times yes."

Satisfaction flared in the dark eyes she saw every
night in her dreams...then he picked up his spoon and
began to eat his soup.

Her stomach curled into knots, and she only managed
a few bites of the creamy indulgence before giving up.
She had experience in the bedroom, and she shouldn't be
nervous about what was to come but, yeah, she was nervous. She'd never been with a man like West. So devoted
to time management. So OCD about his workspace. So...

possessive and aggressive with her alone, and maybe even just a little twisted in the most delicious ways.

"Not hungry?" he asked.

Not even a little, not anymore. Not for the food in front of her. "I guess I expected you to carry me home and ravish me." When she realized she'd grumbled the words, she blushed. "I didn't think we'd continue as if nothing had changed."

"Who says I'm not ravishing you right this very second?"

The silk of his tone… She shivered. Heck, maybe he *was* ravishing her.

The waiter arrived with the rest of their meal, and as she picked at her food, West cleaned his plate, meticulous with every bite. She wondered…was he this meticulous in bed?

Great! Another shiver, this one strong enough to rattle the legs of her chair.

He motioned for the waiter and ordered dessert. Just to torture her, she was sure.

"If you try to feed me by hand," she said, "I'll shove my fork in your eye. I swear I will."

"Mmm. There's the temper I've been looking forward to seeing."

"You don't sound afraid." She regarded him over the rim of her whiskey glass. "I'll have to change that."

"I'm only afraid of naked women," he said, deadpan. "Terrified of them."

Good try, funny man. "Are you trying to tell me you don't know what to do with them?"

His smile was slow, but oh, so wicked. "Will you teach me?"

He was going to be the death of her, wasn't he?

She kicked off her shoe and ran her toes up…up…toward the holy grail. But he clasped onto her foot, stopping her, and began to massage the arch, using her tricks against her. She tried not to moan.

His dessert arrived an eternity later—a rich chocolate soufflé—but he paid it no heed, choosing instead to maintain his hold on her.

"Problem?" she asked.

"Yes. You're too sexy for your own good. The world would be a safer place if I locked you in my bedroom."

She flattened her hand over her heart. "Not that. Anything but that."

"Yes, that." He released her and threw money on the table. "Starting now."

He stood and helped her to her feet after she'd righted her shoe. His arm wrapped around her waist to hold her steady, his fingers curved over her hipbone. A protective, possessive clasp.

He led her outside, the cold air kissing her fever-hot skin. After he opened the car door for her, he walked to the other side.

Breathless, she withdrew her phone to fire off a quick text to him.

Guess what? I'm not wearing any panties.

Amusement glimmered in his eyes as he paused to pluck his phone from his pocket…but as he read the screen, his back went ramrod straight. His gaze flipped up to meet hers, narrowed and hot, and she slowly traced a fingertip along the seam of her lips—sucked that fingertip deep into her mouth.

He nearly wrenched his own door from its hinges.

Seated, the engine purring, he said, "If we wreck, you're to blame."

Reaching out, she traced the seam of *his* lips with her now-moist fingertip. A kiss by proxy. "If we survive the drive, what's going to happen when we get home?" She needed to know, to prepare. Would they go to her room or to his? Would they jump right into bed or spend time talking?

As the questions reverberated in her mind, her nerves kicked back up and she kind of wanted to puke.

Wouldn't *that* be a whole lot of sexy?

He probably expected her to be the best lay in town. But if she rocked the mattress mambo, wouldn't someone have already locked her down?

What if she was the *worst* lay in town?

"I'm going to be on you, all over you," he said in warning. "We're going to rid ourselves of months of frustration, no matter how long it takes us. That's what we're going to do."

Unless, of course, she failed him.

"West." Was it hot in here? When had the car become a sauna? She pulled at the bust line of her dress, saying, "I've got to tell you something you're not going to like hearing.

He stiffened, only to relax a second later. "It doesn't matter, whatever it is."

"It does. What if I'm all talk? What if I suck at sex?"

He looked as if he was fighting a smile. "We'll practice. We'll practice *a lot*."

Unless her fumbling caused a deflation.

Oh, crap!

When he reached the house, the tires squealed as he

parked. He was eager to be with her. The poor guy was going to be hugely disappointed, wasn't he.

He ran around the car to open her door and help her out—only to shove his shoulder into her stomach and heft her up. "You aren't moving fast enough, kitten."

She squealed, then laughed as amusement overshadowed nervousness, and she beat at his back. "Let me go, you beast! I'm a lady. I should be treated all proper and crap."

"Beg for mercy."

"No!"

He smacked her bottom. "Beg."

"Never!"

One of her neighbors—Mrs. Brashear—rushed onto her porch to bellow "I heard shoutin'. Should I call Sheriff Lintz, Jessie Kay?"

"No, no," she called. "I'm not gonna harm West, I swear!"

West snickered as he made his way inside the house. He kicked the door shut, saying, "You and I, we're different. Our relationship is different. So, we're going to proceed differently. I'm not using you, and I'm not rushing to the finish line. We'll take this a step at a time. Okay?"

"I—" She couldn't quite catch her breath. "Yes. Okay."

"Good. Step one is making out in the living room." He threw her onto the cushions. As she bounced, he loosened and removed his tie. "Tonight your only job is to feel good."

She was one step ahead of him already, warm and wet, desire like a drug. "Are you planning to bind me with that tie?"

"No. I've never understood the appeal of bondage. I want your hands all over me." He placed a knee on the couch, right beside her thigh and his other knee *between* her thighs.

She gasped a needy sound of encouragement.

He lifted the hem of her dress, cool air once again kissing her flushed skin as he peeked at what lay underneath.

"Panties," he said. "Tiny, white and sexy. *Nice.* But someone told a fib."

"Maybe the future Jessie Kay was the one who texted you, Mr. Smarty Pants. Ever think of that?"

"Impossible. Future Jessie Kay is too sated to move, which means present Jessie Kay has to be punished." With a single tug, he ripped the sides of the panties. "Lesson learned?"

"No." As she shivered, he grinned and tossed the ruined garment to the floor. "I still have the urge to do bad, naughty things."

"I'll have to be hard on you, then. Very hard."

She almost laughed. For her, sex had always been just that. Sex. The coming together of two bodies to sate a physical need. But West had already taken the experience to a whole new level—before he'd even gotten inside her! He teased and delighted her, meeting an emotional need she'd never known she had, affecting not just her body but her mind.

"Present Jessie Kay is confused. You're unwilling to bind me, but you're more than happy to punish me?" She rubbed her knee against his hip. "Contradictory? Maybe." Sublime? Definitely.

"With your criminal history, kitten, someone has to keep you in line."

"Isn't this a case of the bad leading the bad?"

His gaze glimmered with heat and need as he

smoothed her dress back into place. "It is. But I'm your man, and I have a job to do, so I'll do it."

Her man...quivers in her belly. "The destruction of my underwear was my punishment?"

"No. That was a reward. For myself. To teach you a lesson, I won't be buying you a new pair."

"Oh, the horror!"

He unfastened one, two, three of the buttons on his shirt, giving her the barest glimpse at his chest, all bronzed skin and delicious muscle. "Here is what's going to happen. I'm going to kiss and touch you, and you're going to do whatever you want to me, whatever you want to yourself, while focusing only on sensation. You clear on your instructions?"

"Sir, yes, sir."

He flashed a grin, leaned forward until he loomed over her. He caged her against the couch, his big body surrounding her, and...he kissed her with such devastating passion she knew she'd never again be the same, his tongue sweeping in to roll against hers, to duel, to conquer, to give and to take. The sensations only he seemed able to ignite overwhelmed her, and with a moan, she melted into the cushions.

Needing him closer, as close as she could get him, she wrapped her arms around him and tugged until he just sort of fell on her. She felt deliciously pinned, reverent yet uncivilized, wild yet serene, desperate yet confident.

He cupped her breasts, kneaded them, and her nipples rose to greet him, seeking his attention.

"You're so responsive, kitten."

"It's you," she said on another moan. "Only you." He drowned her in pleasure and agonized her with her own vulnerability.

"You doing your job?"

"Yes, yes." Right? Enough! No thinking. No wondering. He wanted her to focus only on sensation; she would focus only on sensation.

Do whatever she wanted…

Instinct led her to hook her feet behind his knees and bow her back, pressing the softest part of her against the hardest part of him. She gasped. Bliss…rapture… Little infernos igniting in different parts of her, a greedy throb aching between her legs. Heady desire intoxicated her. As she arched up to rub against him a second time…a third, fourth…she lost what remained of her breath. Lost her sanity, too.

"Not sure I'll ever be able to get enough of you." West placed kisses along her neck…between her breasts. He suckled at each of her nipples before continuing down the plane of her stomach, his tongue wetting the fabric of her dress.

Would he taste the hottest part of her? "West." A rasp. A plea.

He went still…and then the rat bastard kissed his way back up, saying, "Uh-oh. You've distracted me. Made me lose track of what I was doing. Now I have to start over."

"West." A curse.

"You complaining, kitten?" He kissed her neck, between her breasts and once again suckled at her nipples, licking and nipping until she writhed against him. Then, oh, then, he began to kiss his way down her stomach again…yes, yes…he trailed his fingers lower, lower still, stopping at the hem of her dress. "You ready for me?"

"So ready. Don't stop. Please, don't stop."

His laugh was nothing but evil and smoke. "Uh-oh. You've distracted me again."

"I just answered *your* question!"

He showed no mercy. "Definitely distracted. I have to start over again."

She whimpered.

Two could play this game. As he kissed and laved her neck, she slid her hands under his shirt, putting them skin to heated skin. She traced her fingertips along his spine and thrust up her hips, not just rubbing but grinding herself against his erection.

"I want to come, sugar bear. I *need* to come."

"All in good time." The words were strained, his tone no longer quite so teasing.

"Now." She bit him on the chin. "Gimme."

"Naughty, naughty kitten. You've earned another punishment. Sorry—not sorry—but you don't get to keep your dress." He sat up just enough to pull the material over her head, leaving her completely exposed.

Covering herself wasn't even a thought. His gaze utterly *devoured* her, and she reveled it.

"You're even better than I imagined." He cupped her breasts, ghosted his thumbs over her nipples. "I imagined you like this *a lot*."

The tingles she'd experienced before? Nothing compared to the tempest beating through her now. The time for teasing was over. "West. Please. I've wanted you so long."

He must have understood. His desperation—his absolute starvation—must have rivaled hers. He dove down and fed her a kiss that scorched, his tongue hard and hot, demanding its due...but all too soon he slowed the pace to languidly consume her.

"No," he said. "No. I told you I'm not rushing this. You feel good, so good, so damn perfect, but I want our

first make-out session to be a marathon, not a sprint."
One of his thumbs brushed over her distended nipple again and again, sending ripples of bliss speeding
through her, while his other thumb drew circles on her
inner thigh, tickling her skin. Soon the playful caresses
became an addictive torment.

"There's nothing wrong with a good sprint." She
worked a hand between them and, with a hard yank,
popped the buttons of his shirt the rest of the way. The
material gaped open, exposing the sexiest chest on the
planet—and the name of his only love. Jealousy flared,
followed by sadness, but she tamped them down. He
was with her. Here and now, he was with her, and that
was all that mattered.

Emboldened, she lifted her head to flick her tongue
over his nipples.

The tone of the kiss changed, once again rocketing
into a wild frenzy of tongues and teeth and hard aggression. She writhed against him, dragged her nails down,
down his spine before dabbling at the indentations in his
lower back and cupping the tight globes of his ass. His
pants stopped her from doing anything more.

Criminals break and enter. It's expected.

She tunneled her hands beneath the waist of the
pants...under his boxer briefs. *Keep me out?* Not in this
lifetime.

"Jessie Kay." He gripped her behind the knee, lifted,
forcing her leg to bend...until his hip pinned it to the
side of the couch, leaving her open, more vulnerable
than ever...ready. He released her, only to cup her between her legs. A second later, his finger speared deep
into her hot, wet core.

She cried out, back arching, head falling back. "Yes. Yes!"

"You...are...incredible." He gritted the words as he lapped at the pulse hammering in her neck, his finger moving in and out of her...in and out...fast, faster, driving her pleasure high, higher, and oh...oh! He wedged another finger inside, stretching and burning her despite the wealth of her wetness, but it was good, so very good, because it was *his* fingers, *his* body poised over hers. This man who wanted more than one night with her—more than two months with her. This man who didn't think of her as disposable but as someone to covet.

"Almost there...please." She bit into his collarbone, clawed at his back and might have shredded his skin. "Sorry, sorry." Need held her in a tight clasp, stealing her breath.

"You're so luscious, kitten. I thought I could give everything tonight and take nothing for myself. Foolish." He drew the lobe of her ear between his teeth before he sat up and anchored his pants and underwear under his sac. "You're too great a temptation, and I can't resist. Lick your hand and put it on my length."

Lick, lick, lick, she coated her palm and each of her fingers. Trembling, she gripped his long, thick shaft.

"Yeah, kitten, like that. Now move with me."

As his fingers surged deep, deep inside her, she stroked down his erection. As his fingers pulled out of her, she stroked up. He gave another of those animal growls, fueling her excitement, and she quickened her pace, forcing him to do the same.

Their heated breaths intermingled, ensuring she inhaled his air and he inhaled hers. An intimacy as beautiful as it was necessary. She stroked him again, and again, and he continued to reward her. Pleas poured from her mouth, but they were incoherent, emerging as ragged gasps. Her head thrashed over the cushions, her hair tangling around her shoulders. Sweat slicked her skin, slicked his as well, and as they writhed together, their chests rubbed, rubbed so perfectly, her nipples gliding over the hard planes of his chest, the friction pouring fuel on the flames of her already blazing desire. She burned from the inside out. Sizzled. Liquefied.

"Come, kitten. Give me your pleasure." As he spoke, he pressed the heel of his palm where she ached most.

Like that, she soared over the edge of satisfaction. Muscles clenched and unclenched. A scream exploded from her lips. Her nails cut into his back, drawing blood as she arched into him, clinging to him. And she must have squeezed his length harder, must have set off a chain reaction inside him, because a second later, his roar echoed off the walls and his climax jetted onto her stomach.

CHAPTER NINETEEN

WEST COULDN'T QUITE compute what had just happened. He was a grown-ass man who'd been with his fair share of beautiful women. As a rule, he wasn't governed by his body or his passions. But today, with Jessie Kay, he'd lost control. He'd come, he'd come fast, and he'd come fast because of a hand job.

Any other time, he would have been embarrassed. Now? He was just too sated to care.

He shrugged out of his ruined shirt—where had all the buttons gone?—and used it to clean Jessie Kay's belly before tossing the material in the direction of the kitchen to be disposed of later. As he rolled to his side, keeping his sweet little kitty in the strength and warmth of his embrace, his heartbeat began to slow at last. Contentment settled over him, a strange thing he almost didn't recognize. How many years had passed since he'd experienced it? Had he *ever*?

"If you need proof of life," she muttered, "I'm afraid I can't give it to you."

"Good." He reached back, opening a drawer on the side table, and nimbly plucked one of the caramels he'd hidden inside. As he unwrapped it, he said, "If you're dead, you can't steal my candy."

"*Such* a rookie mistake." She snatched the treat from his hand and popped it into her mouth. "You should

have checked for a pulse. You'd have known I was simply lying in wait, ready to attack."

"A fact you should know about me?" He rolled on
top of her and anchored her arms above her head...then
kissed her until she melted into the cushions, the sweetness of the candy only making the chemistry that burned
between them better—or worse.

How was this possible? He was hard as a rock again,
the idea of taking things slow suddenly abhorrent. *Want.
Now.*

He lifted his head before he lost all sense. "I believe
in tit for tat," he finished and returned to her side.

Goose bumps broke out over her flesh, and she licked
her lips, the action pure, wanton seduction. "Sugar bear,
if the best things come in small packages, you're the
worst thing that's ever happened to me."

As he barked out a laugh, she leaned over him to reach
for her clothes. He snatched the fabric from her hand and
tossed it beside his shirt.

"You lost all rights to the garments. Your punishment, remember?" As she sputtered in indignation, he
anchored her to his chest with a gentle headlock. "This
is the part where you say, 'Thank you, West. I appreciate your taking the time to teach me manners.'"

"Never! This is the part where you say, 'Thank you,
Jessie Kay. Thank you for allowing my testicles to remain attached to my body.'"

He shuddered and placed a hand protectively over
his junk.

She laughed. "I'll let you keep your testicles if you
tell me you penciled in pillow talk."

"I did."

"Really? Seriously?"

"You sound surprised."

"I am. I'm not used to anyone sticking around after the main event."

He almost asked the unthinkable—*Not even with Jase and Beck?* But he swallowed the question because, now more than ever, he hated the thought of his friends with her. *Mine. I won't share.*

"You stiffened," she said, worry dripping from her tone. "What's wrong?"

"Nothing's wrong." He kissed her temple. "It's fine."

"We're gonna lie when the truth is hard? That's how this relationship is going to work? All righty, then."

One of the pitfalls of being with a perceptive, stubborn woman: she knew your bullshit and wasn't afraid to call you on it. "I thought of you with Jase and Beck," he admitted. "I didn't like it."

Her nails dug into his chest hard enough to leave a mark. "I can't change my past, West."

"I know." Things were new between them, tentative, and he had to tread carefully. But he was new to this—*how* did he tread carefully?

For the first time since Tessa, there was time to figure it out. He actually had months…years to work through any issues that came up.

"I don't want to change your past, kitten. I like who it's made you. But I know the truth now. Once a man has touched these—" he cupped her breasts, and rolled her nipples between his fingers "—and this—" he slid a finger into the white-hot wetness between her legs, the new center of his world "—he will never be the same. He can never forget. I don't know how my boys can look at you and not jump you."

"For starters, we already know they're wackadoodle because they let me go."

"This is true. You're catnip."

"You mean man-nip." She rubbed her knee up and down his leg, a contented little kitty. "I'm probably the best in the world."

He hid a grin. She'd tried to sound unaffected and confident just then, but there'd been too much pleasure in her voice, revealing a vulnerability that squeezed at his chest.

"Probably," he agreed.

A mock gasp of outrage. "How dare you!" Her claws returned to his chest. "I think you want to rephrase that."

"Definitely. But we both know you need my goods and services more than I do, so be kind to them." He pried her fingers loose and nipped her knuckles. "To answer your earlier question, yes, I really did pencil in pillow talk. Having no idea what you'd decide at dinner, I made a schedule for every possible outcome."

"Even one where we're a couple indefinitely?"

"All right, not *every* possible outcome."

"Well, color me intrigued." Pale hair spilled over his chest as she ran his nipple between her teeth, and he marveled at her beauty, at the flawless, sun-kissed skin now touched with a strawberries-and-cream glow of satisfaction—satisfaction he'd given her. "What's the longest amount of pillow talk in your vast array of choices?"

"Twelve hours."

"The shortest?"

"Eleven hours, fifty-nine minutes."

She grinned at him. "Why the minute-long discrepancy?"

"If you rode me into a satisfied coma, I figured I'd need time to recover."

She giggled—a sound that enchanted him—before kissing him just over his inked heart—an action that threatened to destroy him. "Do you remember when I told you I'd ask a million questions if ever we got together? Well, good news. The inquisition starts today. When did you get the tattoo? And why did you pick such a gruesome image?"

Sharing with her was instinctual, something he did without thought. "I'd been clean about a year, and I decided to honor Tessa with an outward expression, not just talk a big game inside my head. When I told the artist I wanted a heart, he showed me these neat and tidy designs, but to me, love wasn't—isn't—neat and tidy. It can be ugly and messy, so that's what I asked for."

"Well. It's official." She sat up, her hip pressed against his, and hooked a lock of hair behind her ear. "That tattoo is now my favorite thing about you."

He blew her a kiss, and as she pretended to catch it, the truth of their situation hit him—and hit hard. He wasn't just engaged in a passionate relationship with her, one without a time limit, he was actually having fun. Enjoying life. Enjoying her and looking forward to tomorrow.

No thought for making things up to Jase and Beck. No thought for making things up to Tessa.

Until now.

Guilt climbed into the boxing ring inside his head and beat the shit out of him.

What right did he have to enjoy anything? How could Jessie Kay want him to?

She studied him for a long, silent moment, then traced

a fingertip along his breastbone. "Do you need some time alone? It's okay if you do."

Attuned to his mood already?

"I just need you." He took her hand, wrapped her fingers around his shaft—once again growing thicker, longer and harder. "*This* is your favorite thing about me, and I'll prove it."

"WE HAVE A major problem, sugar bear." After make-out round two, Jessie Kay wedged her body between her boyfriend—her boyfriend!—and the couch, and proceeded to kick said boyfriend to the floor.

He—her boyfriend!—landed with a hard thud.

Won't ever get tired of those words.

"I picked at my dinner and now I'm hungry. Starved! As my boyfriend slash gentleman lover, it's now your job to feed me." She pointed to the kitchen. "Hop to, man slave."

He stood and fastened his pants. "How many jobs am I going to have, exactly?"

"Thousands, but all revolve around one thing— whatever I want, I get."

"Well, then. I better make you a sandwich." He strode away, disappearing into the kitchen.

Jessie Kay released a pent-up breath as worry she'd tried to fight at last bombarded her. There for a bit, West had been tense and, if she had to guess, angry. His eyes had been narrowed, his lips pulling tight over his teeth in a scowl.

Did he already regret being with her? Wish he'd stuck to his guns and insisted on only a two-month affair?

Maybe she shouldn't have pushed for more. What if two months passed and he grew to resent her?

Had she done herself a disservice, insisting they do things her way?

When had her way ever been the right way?

Dang it! She liked him. She really, really liked him. More than she'd ever liked another man. A lot freaking more. And even though they hadn't yet had sex, she felt closer to him than she'd ever felt with another, had shared more with him than any other, and the idea of losing him already devastated her.

Well, screw "what if." Fear shackled.

She was enjoying the time they had together, and that was that.

She spread a blanket on the living room floor, and when West returned with a sandwich, patted the spot beside her.

"Another picnic?" He sat willingly.

"A naked picnic. You're overdressed."

He stripped in a hurry.

To her surprise and delight, he snatched the BLT from her hands once…twice to steal a bite.

When the sandwich—and crumbs—had been devoured, he kissed her shoulder and said, "Time for my dessert?"

"Yep. Bon appétit."

He paused to tilt his head to the side. He frowned. "I think we have visitors."

"What!" She raced to the front window just in time to watch Jase, Brook Lynn, Beck and Harlow exit an SUV. With a screech, she burned rubber all the way to her bedroom to dress.

How would West act around the others? How did she *want* him to act?

Easy: totally devoted to her.

When she emerged, she pasted a sunny smile on her face. She had to take this relationship one step—one day—at a time and not expect everything to be perfect now, now, now.

Jase and Brook were already snuggled on one side of the couch, and Harlow sat in Beck's lap on the other. West, who'd pulled on a T-shirt and a pair of jeans, had claimed the center, right where they'd made out.

The memory alone heated her blood.

Jessie Kay waved at the lot of them. "Hi, guys. I'd like to say I'm glad to see you, and if I can find a way to sound convincing, I will. What's going on?"

"Well." Brook Lynn grinned. "Jase and I had just experienced the most romantic hot-air-balloon ride ever when everyone in town decided to call me to ask if you were okay. Seems your roommate decided to get physical with you. Not only did he carry you over his shoulder, he made you beg for mercy."

For goodness sake. Mrs. Brashear! "I never begged for mercy."

"The way I remember it, *I* was the one who begged," West said and everyone laughed. He cocked a finger at her. The moment she was within reach, he grabbed her by the wrist and tugged her onto his lap.

She curled close, loving his heat and scent—now fused with hers—and his unabashed affection for her in front of the gang.

Perfection!

"We decided to check on you, make sure you hadn't been killed—by pleasure," Harlow said with a toothy grin of her own.

"You two certainly seem more relaxed than usual."

Jase rubbed his jaw. "A day at the spa must have been just what the doctor ordered, huh, Jessie Kay?"

"You know who's going to die tonight?" She waved her fist at him. "You guys."

"Please. You need me alive." Brook Lynn rested her head against Jase's shoulder. "Tomorrow is Christmas Eve."

"Oh, crap. My last day to shop."

West stiffened against her. "Are you staying in Strawberry Valley or going into the city?"

"City."

"I'll go with you. I—"

"Oh, no, no, no. You're staying here. I'm picking up your gift."

He *really* stiffened. "We're exchanging gifts?"

Did he think it was too soon for that?

"Yes. We are *all* exchanging gifts." Beck wrapped a lock of Harlow's dark hair around his finger. "I've already been informed. And found not-so-discreet hints about what to give."

Harlow shrugged, unabashed. "I figured you could use the help."

West scrubbed a hand down his face before standing, forcing Jessie Kay to stand with him. "You guys have officially overstayed your welcome. Get out." He pointed to the door.

She slapped his hand. "*So* rude."

"I know," he said. "They're still just sitting there."

The guys laughed while Brook Lynn and Harlow snickered, but they *did* leave.

Brook Lynn gave her a hug and whispered, "I'm so happy for you," before following Jase out the door.

"Lincoln West." Jessie Kay stomped her foot. "What's wrong with you?"

"I'm tired." He led her into his bedroom, stripped her, then himself, and moved the covers for her to slide underneath. He settled beside her.

He held her all night long without making a move on her—another item to scratch off the list her sister made for her.

Jessie Kay tossed and turned. She remembered what he'd said when he'd given her the watch. Not a gift, but a necessity. What he'd said when he'd given her the car. Not a gift, but an insurance policy. And yet, they *had* been gifts. He just hadn't liked the label. Why?

As the sun rose, she finally said, "If you don't want to exchange gifts—"

"It's fine. It'll be fine."

Fine. "You sound like a girl."

"Isn't that better than sounding like a man?"

Smart ass. "Talk to me, West. Tell me what's bothering you."

He sat up, balanced his legs over the side of the bed and rubbed his face. Ignoring her plea, he said, "Be careful today. Text me often." Then he rose and padded into the kitchen. Soon pots and pans rattled.

Stomach twisting, she returned to her own bedroom to shower, brush her teeth and dry her hair. She dressed in a tacky holiday sweater and leggings, trying to decide whether she should push West for answers or let him come to terms with whatever was bothering him on his own.

She'd seen Jase and Beck push him before, and *she* had pushed him before. Look where it had gotten her.

Unsure, questioning every decision. Well, this time, she would wait him out and see what happened.

As she left her room, he rounded the corner at the end of the hallway. He was more handsome than ever, his hair damp and darker, a T-shirt hugging his chest, and a pair of sweatpants hanging low on his waist. Clearly he'd just come back from a run.

His stride never slowed; he just kept coming toward her. Without a word, he yanked her against him, swooped down and smashed their lips together. His tongue invaded her mouth and demanded a response. A response she willingly, happily gave, melting against him.

He teased her, tempted her and thrilled her to her soul. His hands cupped her breasts, his thumbs ghosting over her nipples. Her knees went weak, threatening to buckle.

He revved her up—and then he pulled away.

She gripped the collar of his shirt to remain steady on her feet. "Good morning to you, too," she said, her voice breathless.

His eyes glittered down at her. "You better miss me while you're gone."

"Every minute." The rasped words were revealing, far too revealing, but she didn't take them back. Truth was truth.

He withdrew a pen from his pocket, lifted her arm and began to write. "Here's your schedule. Follow it, and I'll make you glad you did." Then he walked away, shutting himself inside his own room.

She glanced at her arm—and burst out laughing. NOW O'CLOCK: TEXT WEST

She might not ever understand him, but she would always enjoy him. Smiling, she anchored her purse over her shoulder and poured herself a cup of coffee. What the—

Her fridge and cupboards were fully stocked with food and juice. All her favorites, meaning almost everything was high in sugar and/or her drug of choice, high-fructose corn syrup. The things that weren't, West had taped little messages to the boxes.

"You should try this. Your body will like it."

"This has vitamins. No, vitamins aren't a myth."

"Eat me. I will increase your life expectancy."

Her eyes burned with tears, her hands coming up to form a steeple over her mouth. West had done this. Sweet, beautiful West, making sure she never went hungry again.

I'm so going to screw his brains out.

Before she gave into the temptation to jump him now, now, now—*can't give my sister a macaroni necklace I made by hand...not again*—she headed to the farmhouse. In her brand new car. The sleek black Mercedes practically floated over the roads.

When she arrived, Brook Lynn bounded outside. She settled into the passenger seat, looking gorgeous in a white sweater and worn boot-cut jeans. "Please tell me you made a list of everything you want to buy this time. And wow, West has good taste. This baby is *tricked.*"

"Only the best for his woman." Her heart swelled with pleasure. "As for presents, I know what I'm getting West, but everyone else...well, let's just say I'll know it when I see it."

Her sister groaned as if she'd just been stabbed in the gut. "That's what you said last year and we ended up running around the department stores looking like chickens with our heads cut off—and not buying a single thing."

"Why are you complaining? You got a beautiful macaroni choker, a JK original, that you can wear with anything."

Snort.

Snow-covered trees blurred as they soared down the highway. Not many drivers were out and about this early in the morning. Well, not in the stretch of flatlands between Strawberry Valley and Oklahoma City, but traffic picked up when they hit the shopping district. Slackers like her always came out in droves the day before Christmas, desperate to find those last-minute gifts.

"You look so happy," Brook Lynn said. "West is good for you."

"He really is." She opened her mouth to tell her sister his suggestion that she sell her dresses online. But… but…Brook Lynn might be saddened or even panicked at the thought of losing her. Why bring it up now, potentially ruining the holidays? What would another few days hurt?

She released a breath she hadn't known she'd been holding.

Forced to park a mile from the mall, she and her sister were blocks of ice by the time they made it inside. They moved to the side, away from the crowd, to gain their bearings and devise a game plan.

"Do you know what you want to get Jase?" she asked.

Brook Lynn shook her head. "I shouldn't admit this, considering I just gave you a hard time, but…I have no idea. He has buckets of money, and he buys whatever he wants whenever he wants it. What do I get a man like that?"

"Duh. A nude portrait of yourself." The scandalized look on her little sister's face made her laugh. "What? I bet Harlow could whip one up, no problem."

"And where would Jase hang it? Over the fireplace?"

"You guys are having a house built, and you'll need *some* kind of art on the walls."

Brook Lynn wrinkled her brow, shook her head. "Not just no, but heck no."

Jessie Kay hiked her shoulders in a shrug. "Well, I tried. But now that I've presented you with such an amazing idea, everything else is going to suck donkey balls in comparison. Be prepared."

Brook Lynn covered her face with her hands and moaned. "She's wrong," she said to herself. "She has to be wrong."

Can't laugh.

Brook Lynn straightened, saying, "So, what are you getting *Lincoln*? Is that what you call him? Now that you guys are begging for mercy with each other, I mean."

"I call him Mr. Hot Buttered Buns. And you'll have to wait and see what I got him. But it's awesome. Probably the greatest gift anyone has ever gotten anyone in the history of the universe. Even a nude portrait fails to compare."

"Tell me!"

"Never."

"Oh, my gosh. You are such a witch."

"Name calling?" Jessie Kay stuck out her tongue. "I'll pray for your eternal soul."

Brook Lynn snorted then linked their arms together. "Did you ever think our lives would turn out so perfectly? I mean, I'm going to marry Jase, and you're going to marry West, and we're going to be sisters-in-law."

"Uh, I hate to break it to you, but we're already blood sisters. And cool your jets. I'm only dating the guy. We've had one dinner and a few raunchy make-out sessions. We're not picking out china yet." But…was marriage something West would ever be interested in? Or was it out of the question entirely?

Crap! She should have asked him before pushing for a commitment. What if they expected different things? And what about love? Would he ever love her the way he loved Tessa?

She was well on her way to falling head over heels for him and—crap again! She was, wasn't she? Falling down, falling hard…soon to go splat.

"Uh-oh. I know that look." Brook Lynn led her toward the first shop. "I wore it every day while navigating choppy dating waters with Jase. You have nothing to worry about. I've seen the way West watches you, the reverent way he touches you. He's in it for the long haul."

He was, yes, but not necessarily of his own free will.

Her phone rang, saving her from a reply. She dug the device from her purse, West's number peering up at her. "Get started without me," she told her sister. "I need a minute."

Brook Lynn wiggled her brows and said, "I think you'll need more than a minute."

"Ha!" As her sister wandered off, Jessie Kay answered the call. "Hey, you."

"Everything okay?"

The worry in his voice caused her heart to clench. "Everything's fine, sugar bear. We just got here."

"You're being careful?"

"I am. I'm even considering heading into the packing store for Bubble Wrap. That way, if I'm stampeded, I'll have a better chance of survival."

"That's not funny."

"It kind of is."

He sighed. "I told you I'd be difficult, Jessie Kay. I didn't take good care of Tessa. I'm not going to make the same mistake with you."

"Sweet and wackadoodle at the same time, but I can forgive you because I'm awesome and you're so good with your hands. Speaking of, I haven't seen your schedule, so I don't know what you're planning to do with me later."

Static crackled over the line before he rasped, "You'll just have to wait and find out."

WEST TURNED OFF the blowtorch and removed the welder's mask. He studied the bracelet he'd created with old computer parts and frowned. Would Jessie Kay like it? Or hate it?

Yeah, she'd probably hate the piece of shit.

Sweat beaded on his brow as he tossed his gloves on a workbench scattered with different tools. Forget the gift he'd given his mom, the one he'd paid for with change he'd picked up off the streets—the one she'd pawned. Forget the picture he'd drawn for his foster mom, the one that had been thrown away. He'd never given a girlfriend a gift, not even Tessa. Every year for her birthday, he'd taken her to dinner.

So badly he wanted to hand Cora a credit card and tell her to pick something nice for Jessie Kay. But he knew, deep down, that was the coward's way. So he'd give Jessie Kay the piece-of-shit bracelet and deal with the consequences—seeing disappointment cloud her face.

He cursed. He would hedge his bet, he decided, and give her a few other things he had in the works. He just...

With every fiber of his being, he didn't want to mess this up. He owed her. She'd set him free, overwhelmed him with pleasure, excitement…joy. So much so, he was already addicted to each. So much so, guilt, remorse and resentment had lost their foothold inside him.

Can't ruin her holiday.

Christmas had always been his least favorite time of year. While other kids had enjoyed being spoiled, he'd been mostly ignored. Back then, he usually *preferred* to be ignored.

Come over here and sit on Uncle Sam's lap, boy. I've got something for you.

The memory breeched the surface of his mind and with a roar, he punched the wall. Metal crinkled and caved. He so rarely thought about the years spent with his mother and the men she'd allowed into their apartment. Sam in particular. Some things were better off locked in a box and hidden in a shadowed corner.

West dunked the bracelet in a bucket of ice water, dried it off and stuffed it in his pocket. He stalked to the farmhouse, the frigid temperatures outside cooling the fire in his blood as he breathed in, out. The land distracted him. Countless trees, their branches naked and gnarled. Bramble patches to be cleaned, piles of firewood to be stacked.

In three weeks, construction for his house would begin. Jase's, too, though they'd be on opposite sides of the property. When everything was completed, West expected Jessie Kay to move in with him.

Would she agree? They already lived together. Why not live together in a bigger, newer house?

His phone beeped, and some of the tension drained

from him. Jessie Kay had been sending him proof-of-life texts every hour, and they'd become the highlight of his day. In them, she'd posed with mannequins and danced on counters as cashiers looked on with horror.

This time, the image she'd sent made him laugh out loud. She'd burrowed inside a rack of clothes to press her face between the metal bars. A "here's Johnny" moment. Her text read: This criminal is practically begging for another punishment...

He. Liked. This. Girl.

Tension eased from him as he entered the farmhouse through the back door. Jase sat at the kitchen table, wrapping a gift to Brook Lynn. He sucked ass at the task. The paper was torn and wrinkled, completely misshapen.

Frowning, he glanced up. "How do women make this look so easy?"

"I think they practice in secret so they can taunt and torment us in public. I can't believe I ever dreamed of being part of holiday festivities." West combed a hand through his hair. "The pressure is killing me."

Jase went still. "Want a drink?"

A sobriety test. Long overdue, and irritating. "I have something to live for. You don't have to worry about me anymore."

His friend kicked out a chair. "Are you telling me you've finally forgiven yourself?"

He plopped down. Opting for honestly, he said, "No. I'm saying I've stopped actively seeking misery."

"That's a start, I guess. By the way, Brook Lynn texted me." Jase motioned to his phone. "You'll want to read the message."

West glanced at the screen.

It's awesome that West & my sister are dating but you need to know something—if he hurts her, I'll kill him & you'll bury the body

Exactly what he'd once expected to happen. Now, though, he wasn't afraid. "If I hurt her, you won't have to bury me. I'll bury myself."

"I figured." Jase pushed the hideous gift aside. "Look, you're a problem solver. You can figure out what to get your girl. Think back to all the conversations the two of you have had and make a list of everything she said she liked. Or wanted. Or needed."

"A list? You're becoming your girlfriend."

"I'll take that as a compliment, considering she has the best taste and she only ever has good ideas. Now shut up and do what I told you."

Well, he could think of one item right away. His body. The girl had a jones for his scones.

He smiled.

"See?" Jase said, standing. "It's working already."

CHAPTER TWENTY

CHRISTMAS MORNING DIDN'T kick off the way West had planned: waking up with Jessie Kay in his arms, bringing her to orgasm with his hands, then showering with her and bringing her to orgasm with his mouth. They'd spent the night at the farmhouse with Jase and Brook Lynn, Beck and Harlow, but they hadn't slept in the same room. They should have, but she'd never come to bed.

She'd holed up in the shed out back, claiming she had to wrap the presents she'd purchased. Then she'd just never come inside.

He'd spent the evening watching the back door and fielding questions and teasing from his friends.

"Looking pretty tense tonight, bro," Beck had said. "The little woman put you in the doghouse already?"

"Bad news is, you can't walk out of a doghouse." Jase had laughed. "You have to crawl."

"I'm not in any kind of doghouse." He'd gone to the shed multiple times to knock on the locked door, thinking she might have fallen asleep, but every time she'd frantically told him to stay out.

Now West showered, dressed and made his way to the shed—finally finding Jessie Kay in the kitchen, the beautiful blonde vortex standing next to Brook Lynn, the two cooking breakfast and chatting.

"—how you guys usually celebrate?" Harlow was saying as she washed dishes at the sink.

"Well, we bought each other the cheapest gifts possible—all we could afford—ate the creamy sausage and biscuit casserole you'll soon enjoy, and gorged while watching old zombie movies," Brook Lynn said. "How about you?"

"The past few years, my mom and I spent Christmas Eve baking cookies. We'd eat them in the morning and give each other compliments, my favorite present," Harlow admitted. Tears welled in her eyes. "I miss her. This is my first Christmas without her."

Jessie Kay looked to Brook Lynn. "I'm sorry Mom's not here for you." There was a tremor in her voice. "I'm sorry you missed so many Christmases with her. I'm sorry—" She dropped her knife, and as the metal clanged on the floor, she gripped the counter as if dizziness threatened to knock her down. She breathed deeply. In. Out. In. Out.

West took a step forward as Brook Lynn let go of the biscuit she'd been pulling apart and combed her flour-dusted hands through her sister's hair. "Enough. You know I've never blamed you."

He stopped.

"I'm so sorry," Harlow said, suddenly pale with concern. "I shouldn't have mentioned…"

"You didn't do anything wrong," Brook Lynn told her. Then she refocused on Jessie Kay. "Want to know what Jase said to me the other day? He said there are five ways to tell a woman's mad at you. One, she yells at you. Two, she goes silent. Three, she acts the same. Four, she acts completely different. Five, she murders you in cold blood."

Jessie Kay's breathing finally slowed. A good sign, but not good enough. West closed the distance and as gently as possible moved Brook Lynn out of the way. He framed Jessie Kay's face with his hands, forcing her gaze to remain on him. Her pupils were blown, and what remained of her irises was wild.

"Kitten, this is unacceptable," he said. "We didn't schedule a panic attack today."

Her accelerated breathing slowed a little bit more.

"If it keeps up," he added, putting a little heat in his tone, "I'll be forced to punish you."

"Hey!" Brook Lynn anchored her fists on her hips. "You can't punish my sister. She didn't do anything wrong. And even if she did, you have no right!"

"You better run," Harlow told him, her ocean blues narrowing. "I'm pregnant, my hormones are completely out of whack, and I can't be blamed for my actions. I can rip your tongue out of your mouth and no one will convict me of a crime."

He ignored both women, keeping his focus solely on Jessie Kay. She'd calmed considerably, the wild glaze gone, her pupils returning to normal. "Looks like someone might just *want* to be punished," he said softly.

Jessie Kay's lips twitched at the corners. "Am I going to have to open my Christmas presents in the buff?"

Her dry tone made him smile. "One more infraction like this, and I'll seriously consider thinking about it."

A new gleam entered her eyes—wanton, seductive. A gleam he would kill to see every day for the rest of—

He ground his molars. There might not be a time limit on their relationship, but he had to be careful about his expectations. She might not be willing to put up with him forever.

"Let me check my watch," she said, pulling back the sleeve of her shirt. "Yep. It's time for your butt-kicking."

"So we're okay with West threatening to punish you?" Harlow asked, confused.

"That depends," Beck said as he strolled into the kitchen to steal a pinch of steaming sausage patty. He kissed Harlow's lips and nuzzled her nose. "What's the punishment?"

"Nakedness," Jessie Kay said.

"What about it?" Jase headed straight to his fiancée, wrapping his arms around her to draw her against him and kiss her neck. "Merry Christmas, angel."

A pang cut through West's chest. The two couples were so happy, so at ease with each other, no hint of worry for the gift exchange to come.

The gift exchange. Shit.

Soft fingers brushed over his cheeks, so warm and familiar he leaned into the touch. "You okay?" Jessie Kay asked quietly.

"Come here." West took her hand and led her into their bedroom. He shut and locked the door.

Her eyes went wide. "Are we going to mess around?"

"Yes. No." He helped her sit on the edge of the bed and paced in front of her. "You need to know something. For the past nine years, Beck and I worked on Christmas. While other businesses were closed, there was no one to call and disturb us, no one to come knocking at our door, so we'd get caught up on all our projects and eat Chinese food while pretending it was just another day."

"Oh, dang. That's so sad," she said, her hand fluttering over her heart.

So necessary. "This is my first Christmas with Jase in almost a decade." Jase's first Christmas outside of prison, which was a true reason to celebrate. "This is my first Christmas with you."

Her head tilted to the side as she studied him. "And you're...nervous?"

"I'm happy. Of course I'm happy."

"Well, then, someone should inform your face. My sugar bear looks ready to barf."

His hands fisted at his sides. "I have presents for you. Let's get the exchange over with, okay?"

"First, your enthusiasm is humbling. But I get it now, the reason for your man-fits every time I use the word *gift*. You *are* nervous." She stood up, stepped in front of him. "Second, everyone plans to open their gifts in the living room at the same time. That's the way Brook Lynn and I have always done it, and the way we'd like to continue."

He felt the heat drain from his face.

"You have nothing to worry about. If you got me an actual gift rather than a homemade coupon book for sex, you're already miles ahead of every other guy I've ever known."

"I could have given you a coupon book for sex?" he asked, trying to make light of his thunderous emotions.

She laughed, sweet and feminine, joyous, her entire face glowing. Just like that, she made him feel welcome, as if she'd invited him to a secret club: life and happiness with Jessica Kay Dillon.

"Just because I got you the best present anyone has given anyone is no reason for you to feel bad about the second-rate gift you got for me." She kissed his cheek. "I'll forgive you, and we'll move on."

Would they? "Gifts," he corrected. "I have three for you."

Expression growing serious, she said softly, "They're from you. I'm going to love them."

He went still, wasn't even sure he was breathing. This woman…oh, this woman. The pang returned to his chest. With her, he was rarely without it. His body hardened painfully. He wanted inside her, wanted to lay siege, lay claim, brand her with his hands and his mouth. Wanted to hear her shout his name at the height of passion, then whisper it in complete satisfaction.

"And you'll love my gift just as much…right?" she asked.

He heard the uncertainty in her tone and had a startling realization. He wasn't the only one nervous about the exchange. "Absolutely right." No question.

She rewarded him with a breathtaking smile. "Suddenly I'm feeling like a slacker, though. Since you got me three gifts, I should probably step up my game." Eyes growing heavy-lidded, she slowly sank to her knees before him. "And since we're back here…alone…"

Every muscle below his zipper clenched. "What are you doing?" The words didn't sound as if they'd come from him. They were too rough, too fierce.

"What do you think? I'm giving you my first gift." She popped the button on his pants, slid down the zipper and anchored his underwear under his sac, freeing his swollen shaft. "Besides, you dragged me out of the kitchen, deprived me of a meal. Now you have to feed me." More and more she sounded drugged, and he loved it.

Fire in his blood. Savage desperation in his gut. She closed her luscious little mouth over his tip…then slid all the way down, taking him to the back of her throat. Sharp pleasure lanced through him, and he hissed.

"Jessie Kay." A croak of need.

She rode his length up, down again, then back up, sucking on him all the while. Weakness invaded his knees, but he locked them, digging his heels into the floor.

"Harder, kitten. Faster."

Obeying him, she practically inhaled him, picking up speed, her cheeks hollowing. Up. Down. Again and again. Then she paused...but only long enough to unfasten her jeans and slide her fingers underneath her panties. *Sexy little piece.* The image would be forever branded in his brain. Jessie Kay on her knees, lips red and swollen, eyes glazed, her determination to get them both off a palpable thing.

He threaded his fingers through her hair, guiding her motions, helping her take him deeper, deeper, and oh, shit, it was good, so good. "I'm close, kitten. If you don't want—"

She sucked even harder, worked her mouth even faster, and he hurled over the edge, jetting into her throat.

When he finished, she pressed her temple into his abdomen. A hug without being a hug. Comforting and carnal at the same time. Then she smiled up at him seductively, a woman who thrilled in her power over him. "I like you better than the caramel candies."

He traced his fingers through her silken hair before helping her stand. He took the fingers she'd had between her legs and licked away the sweetness.

Breath caught in her throat.

"Lie on the bed, kitten."

Her heavy-lidded eyes started another fire in his veins. "Is that your way of saying you liked what I did?" She sounded drugged.

"I loved it, but I'm going to love what happens next even more." He pushed her jeans and panties to the floor, lifted her out of them and threw her on the bed. "You weren't fast enough."

He didn't give her time to respond. He dove on her, lick, lick, *liiicking* at the very heart of her, getting drunk on the heady taste of her. Crying his name, she fell back on the pillows, leaving herself completely open to him.

He took full advantage, sucking on her, even spearing her with his tongue. She writhed against his face, her hips undulating, creating a beautifully carnal rhythm. He added a finger, thrusting it deep…then added a second finger, stretching her, pumping it inside her hard and fast, loving the feel of her, so hot and wet.

"I'm close…so close. There!" Her knees clamped his temple as her back bowed. She pulled at his hair, her body trembling. "Lincoln!"

He loved hearing his name on her lips. Loved her reaction to pleasure. Loved the taste of her climax.

He licked her until she went lax against the mattress. Almost dizzy with rapture, he lifted his head.

Passion-glazed eyes peered at him. "That was…"

He kissed the inside of her thigh. "Something I want to do morning, afternoon and evening."

"Well, consider this your eternal permission."

As she dressed, he righted his clothing. He led her into the living room and sat on the couch. When she attempted to sit beside him, he dragged her into his lap.

"Want you close." He nipped her ear…cupped her breast. "As close as I can get you."

"Okay, y'all. Food is in the oven," Brook Lynn said as she walked into the living room. "Oh! My eyes! Hurry, someone come bleach my corneas."

Jessie Kay snorted, and West reluctantly removed his hand.

Jase trailed behind the blonde, and Beck and Harlow behind him.

"Your inner drama queen is showing," West said. Jessie Kay stayed right where he wanted her. "Don't make me break my oath about never ever ever talking about the time I found you and Jase naked on the kitchen counter."

Harlow snickered behind her hand.

"You are such a—" Brook Lynn began.

"Temper, temper," Jessie Kay said with a grin.

"Sweetie pie. You are such a sweetie pie. And now it's time for the main event. Presents!" Cheeks bright red, Brook Lynn began dispensing the gifts to their rightful recipients. Then she frowned at Jase. "Did you guys not get each other gifts?"

"No," Jase said.

"But—"

"We never do," Beck added.

Jessie Kay twisted, facing West. "Seriously? I know you said you guys didn't celebrate, but I didn't think you meant you never exchanged goodies with your buds."

He nipped at her lips. "I think we need to return to the bedroom. I'm getting worked up again."

"Later." She nipped back. "I just drafted a new schedule and the first order of business is facing your fears."

"I can't believe you guys never got each other presents," Harlow said, tearing up. "Everyone should get a gift from everyone else."

Dude. Pregnancy hormones were a bitch.

Beck drew her close for a hug. "We will from now on, baby. Promise. Right guys?"

"Right?" he and Jase said in unison.

Jessie Kay clapped, no longer nervous. "Open this!" She shoved a gift under his nose. "Now, now, *nooow*!"

He smiled, but the way he was trembling like a puss overshadowed any kind of enjoyment. "You first. Open your gifts from the others, then mine." That way, if his gifts sucked as bad as he thought, he could toss them out before she saw them and IOU like an SOB.

The others had begun opening their presents. Brook Lynn squealed over the retractable zombie-killing sword Jase gave her, and Harlow erupted into sobs of joy over the pregnancy-safe paint set from Beck, plus a bag of M&M's with his face etched in the center of each candy.

Jessie Kay tore through her gifts. Brook Lynn had made her a T-shirt that read "I Go South on West." Harlow had taken a set of wineglasses and painted her picture on each one. Jase bought her a pink tool set, and Beck wrote her a "B. Ockley first edition" called *Driving West For the Super Ignoramus.*

"You guys," she said, tears welling in her eyes. "I love. Love!"

My turn. His weren't nearly as good, but they were workable. West handed her the first of three boxes, his trembling only growing worse. Like a kid at, well, Christmas, Jessie Kay ripped into the paper at lightning speed, revealing a small, thin box.

A grin stretched from ear to ear. "It's another watch, isn't it? I knew you'd get me another watch." When she popped the top, the bracelet gleaming in the light, she gasped.

Sweat popped out on his brow. "I made it. It's imperfect," he said. As if she couldn't tell. "If you never wear it—"

"Never wear it? Are you kidding me? West, it's amazing. It's better than amazing, and the fact that you made it…it's the most beautiful piece of jewelry I've ever owned, and I've owned some amazing pieces because, duh, you bought me that watch, and Brook Lynn made me necklaces and earrings when she worked at Rhinestone Cowgirl, and those were pretty cool, but they're crap compared to this…no offense, sis."

"None taken," Brook Lynn said with a laugh.

"West, I love it and I'll never take it off ever." Jessie Kay clutched it close to her chest, tears actually streaming down her cheeks now. "Thank you. I will cherish it always."

The pang in his chest sharpened, cut at him, made his soul bleed, and he wasn't sure if the bleeding purged the poison inside him, or created a new wound. "I'm glad. Open the next one."

After she reverently anchored the bracelet around her wrist, next to the watch, she tore into the second box, revealing the Drogo costume he'd bought—in his size. A laugh burst from her.

"It's lingerie, but it's not for you," he said and wiggled his brows. Every second, a little more of his nervousness drained away. "I'll wear it, and you'll cross off one of the items on your bucket list."

"It's absolutely perfect. I love it!"

He loved her delight.

"Last but not least." Shreds of paper flew in every direction as she unwrapped the final gift. When she opened the box, she frowned with confusion. "It's wonderful and I adore it, but…what is it?"

"A flash drive. I've been working on a new game, and you, Jessie Kay Dillon, are the star of it."

She gaped at him. "Wait. Did you just say I'm the *star* of a new game? Oh, my gosh. West! Tell me everything. Every detail!"

"A war between demons and humans. You, of course, are the angel of mercy." He explained the ins and outs, and she listened raptly.

"An angel. Me." Her trembling hand flattened over her heart. "Lincoln. I don't know what to say."

She'd used his first name again and he knew, deep down, it meant something. Something significant. He just didn't know what.

"These are the *best* gifts I've ever received, but now I don't want you to open yours. It doesn't compare." She tried to snatch the box away from him. "I'll get you something else."

"No way," he said, holding it out of reach. "I want this one."

"Gimme!"

"This is happening. Get used to the idea fast."

"But…but…"

Keeping her at bay with one hand, he peeled back the red-and-green paper with the other. He popped open the lid of a large white box…and found a blanket folded inside. She settled as he shook out the material—

And stopped breathing.

"I spent all night sewing the panels together," she said quietly. "That's what I was doing in the shed."

The entire cloth was covered in pictures of him. Jessie Kay smiled from many of them, doing her best to photobomb while also sneakily taking the pictures. There were images of him at work, images of him at home. The ones he'd taken at the club, when their faces had been mushed together—their victory photos. There were a few of him sleeping, two of him playing soccer.

"You once told me no one cared enough about you to take photos," she said. "I wanted you to know I do... I care."

CHAPTER TWENTY-ONE

IN THE ENSUING DAYS, Jessie Kay decided dating West was like playing chess. Not that she knew how to play chess. But honestly? Her lack of knowledge only made the analogy more accurate.

She doubted any amount of experience—with chess or guys—would have prepared her for West. He was in a class by himself.

After the gift exchange, after he'd hugged her and kissed her and thanked her with tears in his beautiful eyes, an uneasy tension had grown between them. They'd ended up having an impersonal breakfast with the others. They'd watched movies, played her new video game—it rocked!—spent time with Daphne and Hope when the two arrived, and sat next to each other at dinner. But they hadn't held hands or even flirted.

The next evening—*every* evening after that, in fact—he gave her another soccer lesson. The physical interaction always stimulated them both. They'd take a shower together, and they would pleasure each other with their hands and mouths, but they wouldn't have sex.

The lack was beginning to hurt her deep, deep inside.

Cuddle you without sex because there's nothing he likes better than having you in his arms.

She wanted to push, but couldn't bring herself to actually do it. The thoughtfulness of his gifts had ripped through whatever shell had still been erected around her heart, leaving her vulnerable in the worst—best— possible way. In that moment, while she'd held the hand- made bracelet, *Game of Thrones* costume and flash drive, she'd absolutely, utterly fallen for him. Like, jump from a skyscraper, fall at warp speed, land with a splat just as she'd feared—fallen.

She loved him. Loved him with her whole heart. Noth- ing held back. He was it for her. The one, the only. The man of her dreams. The man she had always craved.

Her forever man.

And the knowledge only solidified when she received a call from the local animal shelter. A thank you for the massive holiday donation made in her name. She hadn't had to ask who'd actually forked over the cash. West, the sweetheart, had listened to her deathbed plan and turned it into a life plan.

Losing him wouldn't just hurt her. Losing him would destroy her. She would never recover, never be the same. And oh, that scared her more than anything!

She wondered—hoped—he'd experienced a similar reaction to *her* gift. That he loved her and was now reel- ing.

As another new morning dawned and sunlight streamed into her bedroom, she was surprised to find he wasn't beside her. No lesson, then. She texted Daniel to ask if he wanted to meet for coffee—his YES came only a second later—before showering on her own. She dressed and fastened both the bracelet and watch around her wrist. The thick silver links of the first glittered just as brightly as the diamonds on the second, mesmeriz- ing her with its beauty. The man was *beyond* talented with his hands.

Dang it, she wanted her friend back. The one she teased. The one who teased her in return.

With a sigh, she dragged her feet to the kitchen. A note waited on the kitchen table.

Kitten,
Out on a run. I have a very important meeting from 7:00-8:00. No spontaneous calls or texts unless there's an emergency, all right? Think about me today. I'll definitely be thinking of you.
West

She left *him* a note she thought he would appreciate.

JK's Schedule for the Day
6:00ish—meet Daniel for coffee and remember the last time West kissed me...wonder when it's going to happen again
7:00ish—picture West naked
8:00ish—make my deliveries and wonder if West is imagining ME naked
10:00ish—track West down and find out

Whistling a jaunty tune, she grabbed her car keys and strode out of the house.

She met Daniel as planned and asked his advice—*how do I break through West's walls and convince him to ravish me?*—and sighed over his simple answer.

"Pretend you don't want it. He'll be foaming-at-the-mouth eager to change your mind."

She rolled her eyes. "I'm not playing games with him."

He shrugged. "You're making my point for me. You're obviously not banging him, either."

"Someday, some woman is gonna turn your life up-side down."

"No way. I prefer to be right side up while having sex."

Afterward, she drove to the farmhouse to help her sister make breakfast sandwiches. With Christmas over, it was back to regularly scheduled programming. Sparkles, the mangy mutt, rested at Brook Lynn's feet, sleeping peacefully. Though he did open one eye to glare at Jessie Kay, a warning to behave around his mistress or else.

"My cat, when he picks me, will totally kick your ass," she muttered at him.

Brook Lynn smiled at her.

"Look what I brought." Jessie Kay held up the first bridesmaid dress she'd completed. A spaghetti-strapped sheath with pleats that began at the bustline. The fabric floated down to just above the knees, making the entire thing whimsical and yet classic.

"Oh, Jessie Kay! It's wonderful."

"I know." And, crap! It was time to come clean, wasn't it? If she waited for the perfect opportunity to state her case, she'd end up waiting forever.

Nut up or shut up.

She draped the dress over a chair. "So…I've been thinking." She heard the extreme volume of her voice—almost a scream—and cringed. Taking a moment to calm, she grabbed a bowl and fork to beat some eggs.

"Okay, well, thinking is always a good sign," Brook Lynn said.

Funny girl. "What if I took some time off?"

"Sure. No big deal. I can get Kenna or Harlow to help me while you're gone." Brook Lynn winked at her.

"Why? You going to whisk West away for a naughty New Year's?"

Her first New Year's with West. Her boyfriend. Would they be on better terms? Kiss passionately at midnight?

"I just… I was thinking about designing dresses again. I've rediscovered my love of sewing. I mean, you remember when I made our dresses out of Dad's old suits, right? I'd like to sell my creations through a website, and West said he'd help me. Though it's probably not a good idea to mix business and pleasure, I really, really, *really* want to let him do it. Because *I* want to do it."

"Oh, sis!" Brook Lynn threw her arms around Jessie Kay and hugged her tight. "Yes! Yes, of course. Do it."

"Seriously?" That easily?

"I never wanted you to live my dream. I've always wanted you to live your own. So, again—yes, yes, of course. Oh, and I'll consider this your two weeks notice."

Tears of gratitude filled her eyes, spilling onto her cheeks. The crybaby thing had been happening a lot lately. In the shower when she was alone. While doing her makeup. While picking out her clothes for the day. She'd gotten good at sobbing silently so that West wouldn't hear her. And she wasn't pregnant. She was on the pill and besides that, she and West hadn't yet had sex. Her stupid emotions were in turmoil and getting the best of her, that was all. Once the tension between them eased, she'd go back to her normal self.

"You're too good to me," she told her sister. "I mean it. You should rail at me for leaving you and swear you'll never forgive me. Something! Anything!"

Brook Lynn rolled her eyes. "What is there to forgive? I'm beyond happy for you."

"Yeah, but I'll be leaving you in the lurch. There's no one in the world who will be a better employee than me."

"I'll find a way to persevere," Brook Lynn replied drily.

Jessie Kay bumped her hip. "At least you'll finally get to live your dream of interviewing people and asking outlandish questions."

"Yes, and the first will be, 'If you were a bowl of cereal, what would you be and why?'"

"Cheerios. Obviously. I'm classic and traditional."

Brook Lynn fought a grin, failed. "You are Froot Loops, no doubt about it."

"Well, this Froot Loop is going to miss spending so much time with you."

"We'll make sure to have a slumber party at least one night a week."

"I would *love* a slumber party."

They hugged again then worked alongside each other for several minutes, silent but in sync. Happy! Movement caught her eye—a flash of black—but as she gazed out the window that looked into the backyard, she saw only the sway of tree limbs.

"Are things still strained between you and West?" Brook Lynn asked.

She'd noticed. That obvious, huh? "Yeah. I think we hit a new emotional level, and it scared us both."

"The same thing happened with Jase and me. As soon as we stopped fighting it…" Her sister shivered. "My mind is still being blown by a serious case of the feels."

She made it sound so easy. Just, snap and *I'm over it, let's do this*. "I happen to carry a little more baggage than you."

"That's your problem. You carry your baggage rather than leaving it behind."

"I would love to leave it behind, but how—"

An alarm screeched to sudden life, sending jolts of shock through her. She spun in a circle, her mind trying to make sense of what was happening…until a pungent waft of smoke hit her nostrils and she figured it out in a hurry. Something was on fire.

Grimacing in pain, Brook Lynn turned the devices in her ears to silent. "Jase!"

Jessie Kay grabbed the girl and forced her to the floor. Jase was here—crap. Where was he? The thickening smoke drifted from the back end of the house, where the bedrooms were located, and she coughed. She pulled her sister forward, toward the front door. She'd get Brook Lynn outside, away from the danger, then go back in for Jase.

"Jase!" Brook Lynn wasn't keen on waiting. "Jase!"

Expression as hard as steel, he came barreling toward them. "You okay, angel?"

"I'm fine. We're fine."

He hefted Brook Lynn into his arms. "Stay directly behind me, Jessie Kay." He had to shout to be heard over the alarm.

"Okay."

"What about Beck and Harlow?" Brook Lynn demanded.

"They're already on their way out."

The moment they cleared the front door, she breathed deeply of the cold, clean air. Jase lowered Brook Lynn beside Harlow, who sat at the end of the driveway, peering at the farmhouse with horror while tears poured down her cheeks. Beck cradled her close with one arm and held a phone to his ear with the other. Probably 911.

He hung up, looked at Jessie Kay with the same steel as Jase. "Do *not* let her back inside."

"I won't. Promise."

Then, as Harlow protested, he raced into the backyard with Jase. Intending to fight the fire?

Harlow, who wore a tank top and a pair of boxer shorts, choked on a sob. This was her childhood home, where she'd made memories with the mom she'd lost earlier in the year...where she planned to raise her child. And she had to be freezing her butt off.

"Stay here. I mean it." Jessie Kay raced to her car to grab the coat she'd left inside it. Back with the girls, she wrapped the material around Harlow's shoulders. "We can't see the flames." Only the smoke. "There might not be that much damage."

"But...but...how did this happen?" she asked through her sobs.

"I don't know. Faulty wiring?" But hadn't Jase torn down walls, replaced the wires and pipes and put everything back together? He wasn't one to half-ass a job.

"Whatever damage *is* done," Brook Lynn said, "Jase can fix it. He can fix anything. It'll be okay."

Sirens sounded in the distance, claiming her attention. Jase and Beck returned to the front lawn, soot streaking their faces, their T-shirts soaked with water.

"It's out, baby," Beck said, crouching in front of Harlow. "It was a small fire, contained to West's bathroom."

"Won't take longer than a day or two to fix," Jase added. "Especially if I hire out."

"Really?" Relieved, Harlow collapsed into Beck's chest.

Jessie Kay flattened her hands over her stomach. West's bathroom. Thank the good Lord he'd moved in with her. If he'd been here, perhaps in the shower, distracted... She shuddered with horror. Even the *thought* of him in danger sickened her.

"Did a wire short out or something?" she asked.

"It's possible," Beck said. But the boys shared a hard look, making her think it wasn't likely.

"We'll let the firemen tell us what happened," Jase said.

What the heck was going on?

The Strawberry Valley firefighters studied the damage and took notes. With the danger officially over, Jessie Kay's rush of adrenaline crashed, leaving her weak and shaky. She wanted West's arms wrapped around her. He would make her forget that something bad had happened. But when she dialed his number, she went straight to voice mail.

Why— The meeting, she remembered. Right. But... he wouldn't *not* answer, right? He was too much of a worrier, and he'd told her to call only if there was an emergency. Well, this was definitely an emergency.

She dialed his number again...went straight to voice mail.

He's...ignoring me? Has to be.

Either he doesn't trust me or I'm not as important to him as I thought.

"I need to call my customers," Brook Lynn said, "and tell them orders are canceled today."

"Okay," she said, barraged by waves of hurt and anger. "I—" *What? Can't stay here.* "I'm going into the city to buy fabric for my first line of dresses." A distraction. Perfect.

"No, no. Don't go. Not until we know what happened."

"I *need* to leave." Before she broke down. Before Jase and Beck came out and tried to stop her.

Her sister must have realized something more was going on. She gave a reluctant nod. "Call me later."

"I will." She typed a text to West.

Hope you're enjoying the meeting. There was a small fire at the farmhouse. Want to know how I am? Well, too bad!

Send.

She hugged her sister, said, "I'll see you later, okay?" and climbed into her car.

Roughly five minutes later, her cell phone rang. West's number appeared on the screen. A screen she turned off, letting him go to voice mail.

He called again…aaand she let him go to voice mail again.

When she reached her destination, curiosity got the better of her and she checked the messages. In the first, he sounded concerned: "I'm so sorry, kitten. I thought you were playing games. I should have known better. Where are you? I need to hear your voice."

In the second, he sounded ticked. "I told you what I'd be like. Don't shut me out." *Click.*

Her anger redoubled. Don't shut him out? Jerk! *He'd* already shut *her* out.

Almost rebelliously she toured the first fabric store… which was too expensive for her, but extremely inspiring. The patterns were amazing. She took pictures on her phone and emailed herself ideas, losing herself in the possibilities. That one would make a gorgeous day dress.

Capped sleeves. Straight bustline. Belted waist. Horizontal ruffles, three rows. Hem just above the knees. Very flirty. Pair it with the right necklace and shoes, and bam, the lucky buyer would be ready for a night on the town.

Feminine murmurs rose throughout the store, some scandalized, some titillated. She glanced up from her typing and frowned. What was—? Then she saw him. Lincoln West, his narrowed gaze pinned to her as he stalked forward, ignoring everyone else. He was tall, strong, more beautiful than ever, dressed in a partially buttoned collared shirt and wrinkled black slacks. No tie, no jacket. His dark hair stuck out in spikes, as if he'd toweled off excess moisture and let the strands dry naturally.

Her heart thundered in her chest. Nothing about his expression said "civilized" or even "reasonable." The man coming for her had no polished veneer—it had been ripped away, leaving the animal beneath.

She lifted her chin, held her ground. "What are you doing here? How did you find me?"

"I talked to Brook Lynn." The words were thrown at her like daggers. "There are only so many fabric stores in the area. Finding you wasn't difficult."

"Well, you should have stayed in Strawberry Valley. I needed time away from you."

"Don't worry. You'll get it, but not here and not now. Monica set the fire. Until she's found, you need an escort."

What! "How do you know she—"

"If you'd bothered to answer my call—" he began.

"If *you'd* bothered to answer *my* call."

His eyes narrowed. "Get in your car. I'll follow you home. Jase and Brook Lynn will be moving in with you and I... I'll be moved out by the end of the day."

CHAPTER TWENTY-TWO

ONLY ONCE BEFORE had West experienced a fury as all-consuming as this, and the outcome of it had ended in bloodshed and death. A stain on his soul that could never be cleansed. His schedule had ceased to matter. Time had become inconsequential. Consequences hadn't mattered.

As promised, he followed Jessie Kay home, reeling with every mile gained. He could have lost her today. She could have died. There one moment, gone the next. No time to say goodbye. No way to help her. And just like with Tessa, he would have to live with his guilt, loneliness and never-ending despair.

He might have to anyway. He should have answered Jessie Kay's call, never should have assumed she was messing with his schedule again. He knew her. He knew better. And now, she had every right to her own anger.

He punched the steering wheel. He didn't have to wonder who had set fire to the farmhouse. On his way to the city, the guy he'd hired to watch Monica had called to say he'd lost track of her bright and early, had tried to find her with zero luck.

She must have driven straight to the farmhouse. Only one question remained: Why go with fire?

West had done his homework the day after Monica crashed the Christmas party and learned she'd told the truth about her hunting experience. She'd grown up on a

ranch several counties over, and had a competent knowledge of guns, rifles, knives and bows. Why not use one
of those?

"Call Jase," he told his car, and the number began to
ring a few seconds later.

"Did you find Jessie Kay?" Jase asked in lieu of a
hello. "Brook Lynn is frantic and pissed as hell that I
wouldn't let her call her sister."

West hadn't wanted Jessie Kay distracted and panicked while driving to the store. "She's fine. I'm following her home…and then I'm moving into the office."

A crackling pause. "Are you sure you want to do
that?"

No. Yes. If he was Monica's target, Jessie Kay would
be safer without him around. If Jessie Kay was the target, Jase would protect her. As another layer of security,
West had already hired Daniel Porter and his new firm.
They were working on security at the farmhouse right
now. Jessie Kay's house would be next.

"It's for the best. See you in a bit." Before Jase could
say anything more, West ended the call.

At the house, he parked directly behind Jessie Kay's
car then stormed up the porch, past the door. She waited
in the living room, wringing her hands together. He
passed her without a word and entered his bedroom.
He grabbed his bag from the closest and began stuffing
clothes inside.

"West." She stood in the doorway, glaring at him.
"You aren't moving out. I won't let you."

"You can't really stop me."

"You're mad at me, and I'm mad at you, but we
shouldn't let it destroy everything we've—"

"I'm not destroying anything." Was it already destroyed? He stuffed another shirt into the bag. "I don't want to end things, not right now, but I do think we could use a little time apart."

She closed her eyes for a moment. "Don't do this, West."

"Until Monica is apprehended, you'll stay here with Jase and your sister, and I'll stay at the office. We'll use the time apart to think. We're both so damaged, I'm not sure we can—"

"No. Don't you dare say it. We *can* make this work." She wrapped her arms around her middle. "Damaged or not, we're better together."

He zipped his bag with a hard yank and wound his fingers around the handles. "Certainly doesn't feel like we're better together right now."

She stared at him for a long while. "You're going to leave no matter what I say, aren't you?"

Like he'd told Jase… "It's for the best."

"An excuse!" With a hiss, she closed what little distance there was between them, ripped the bag out of his hand and threw it across the room. "You've been looking for a way out this whole time, haven't you? That's why you've been so tense lately." Her temper had been unleashed, her eyes glittering wildly. Her skin darkened with a fever-flush as she beat her fists against his shoulders, his chest, anything she could reach. "Well, I'm not going to beg you to stay. Go if you want. Go!"

"I'm trying to protect you," he snarled, his own temper pulling at its reins.

"Bastard! You're trying to protect *yourself*. You're falling for me and you're scared. You can't control me, what I do, where I go, what happens to me, and you're scared. Scared—"

"Enough."

"Scared, scared, scared."

One second he stood before her, struggling to breathe, the next he was on her, smashing his lips into hers. Her accusations were *killing* him. He had to shut her up. Had to—

She offered no resistance and threw her arms around him, her tongue a wild thing, her sweet taste driving his need for her higher and higher. His control…utterly… snapped. He gathered the length of her hair in his fist, a tight fist, pulling at the strands. She whimpered with a combination of lust and discomfort, but he didn't loosen his grip. He angled her head, taking her mouth deeper, harder. Heat washed over him, drowned him, but it wasn't enough. Kissing wasn't enough, no matter how much he demanded or how much he gave.

She rubbed against him and he groaned, swept up in the agony of wanting her, *needing* her. In insatiable desperation. He rubbed back, grinding his erection against her, earning another whimper. A prize, the sound of it going straight to his head, drugging him.

Somehow he found the strength to let her go, severing contact. She reached for him, but he stepped back, shook his head.

"Take off your clothes, Jessie Kay, and get on the bed."

JESSIE KAY ACHED and trembled with longing she could no longer deny, with joy and triumph. Her anger had pumped her full of adrenaline, and West's first kiss had been a jolt to her system. But then the need had hit. The need to have him, at long last. The need to hold on to him and never

let go. The need to make amends, to receive amends...
the need to consume, to brand.

He's mine, and I'll prove it.

He wanted her naked, so he'd get her naked. She toed
off her shoes and socks, then tugged her shirt over her
head and dropped the garment to the floor. Her bra soon
followed. She unfastened and unzipped her pants, shim-
mied out of them. Hooking her fingers through the elas-
tic band of her panties, she pushed the tiny scrap of fabric
to the floor and stepped free. Then, she straightened,
giving him a full-on frontal view.

As she stood before the object of her fascination, she
was panting and shaking. This situation, this moment...
it felt different than any other. Far more significant.

What they'd had before had died. This was the start
of something new.

West, the savage, utterly devoured her with his gaze.

"I'm on the pill," she said. "I want you, nothing between us. I've never done that with anyone."

He swung her around, turning with her, and prowled
forward, backing her into the bed. "You are every fantasy I've ever had."

Limbs trembling with more intensity, she sat at the
edge, leaned back and parted her legs. Cool air stroked
her feminine core, a lick of chill against white-hot heat.
A delicious sensation, but also a torment, the ache almost unbearable now. *Need him so bad.*

As he looked her over, the air thickened and crackled with a tension so strong she feared she would be
wrenched in two.

"What are you doing to me?" she rasped.

He moved between her legs, ran his fingers between

her legs, making her shiver. "The same thing you're doing to me, I hope."

The exchange struck her as familiar, and she recalled they'd had it once before, only they'd switched roles, proving they'd come full circle.

They were two parts of a whole.

Slowly, so slowly, he unfastened the buttons on his shirt. His gaze remained on hers as he shrugged out of the material, baring his chest, that beautiful chest with row after row of muscle, the bronzed skin that made her mouth water and the etching of Tessa's name that now made her heart sigh dreamily...and with longing.

Love me the way you loved her.

He yanked at the button on his pants, lowered the zipper. Jessie Kay sucked in a breath. *Mine, all mine.* His shaft was so long and thick the head stretched past the waist of his underwear. Underwear he discarded before gripping his length.

"You want this?"

"I do." No reason to play coy. Desire had to be glistening between her legs. "Give it to me."

He leaned over her, bracing his hands at her sides while sucking her nipple into his mouth, hard enough to draw a gasp from her and leave her hovering on the fine edge of ecstasy and agony.

Then he kissed his way down...down and sucked on something else.

Too much...not enough.

As she trembled, he surged up to flick his tongue over each of her nipples. Then he went back down... up...down again...trying to consume all of her at once.

"Lincoln." She wrapped her legs around his waist, hooked her ankles just over his ass and arched up. Finally. Male to female contact, and it was like plugging into a power outlet. She felt singed from the inside out. "I need you."

"You're going to kill me, kitten." His weight pinned her to the mattress as he lifted his head to feed her the kind of kiss every woman longed to experience but so few ever did. A kiss that swept her up and dropped her straight into the middle of a storm, where lightning flashed and need thundered. Deep, all-consuming and naughty—she could taste herself on his lips.

Every stroke of his tongue was a promise of body and soul. And for the first time in her life, no part of her felt like the slacker sister, or the disappointment, or the one unworthy of any kind of affection. The one responsible for every bit of trouble. She was desired by a man who'd managed to resist the temptation of so many others. She was cherished by him, his touch as hungry as it was reverent.

"You want me bare?" He anchored one of his hands behind her knee and bent her leg, opening her wider.

"Yes. Please."

"Then that's how you'll get me." The kiss continued, not pausing as he positioned himself at her entrance— and thrust inside her.

In an instant he filled her up, stretched her, and a scream bubbled up, an orgasm slamming through her with the force of an avalanche. Just like that. The pleasure…oh, the pleasure! Exquisite, earth-shattering. Taking her over, reducing her to nothing but tremors and gasps.

He breathed her name, a prayer or a curse, she wasn't sure, and began to hammer inside her. He hammered hard, and he hammered fast, rocking the entire bed. A dam must have burst inside him because his control—if he'd had any—was now gone, his finesse destroyed. He was total animal aggression, a piston, and she loved every second of it.

They were slicked with sweat, his flesh sliding against hers, creating the most delicious friction...which caused her nerve endings to gear up for *another* climax.

He tilted her hips up, forcing her to take him even deeper, deeper, and she clung to him, scratched at his back, bit at his tongue and lips, her desires chained to his, her need for relief insatiable.

"Don't stop," she gasped. "Don't ever stop."

"Would rather die." The headboard slammed against the wall. "It's good. Not supposed to be this good." Another thrust, another and another.

As his tongue mimicked the motions of his shaft—in, out, in, out—her heart galloped, racing the pleasure that whooshed through her veins. The two worked in tandem, clouding her mind, narrowing her focus to West, only West, and this moment—this orgasm. Screaming as satisfaction hit, she dissolved around him.

He cursed, buried his face in the hollow of her neck, and surged into her one last time. He held her tight as he came...and came, shuddering against her.

When he stilled, he stayed inside her, keeping her pinned. His breath fanned over her face, a droplet of sweat sliding from his temple and landing on her shoulder.

He lifted his head and peered into her eyes. He looked...resigned.

Her stomach sank, and she prepared herself for the worst.

CHAPTER TWENTY-THREE

ONE MINUTE STRETCHED into another, and all Jessie Kay could do was brace herself for rejection. For West to look away and tell her, *This was a mistake.* Then he would pull out, dress and leave her. But he continued to hold her gaze, seeking…something.

What?

"Did I hurt you?" he finally asked. His voice was gruff, the emotion behind it hidden.

Okay. Not a bad start. "No. If you couldn't tell, I enjoyed the rougher side of you."

He peered at her a few moments longer before pulling out of her at last and…rolling to his side. He wasn't going to leave her?

"I'm sorry I yelled at you, sorry I threatened to leave you," he said. "I *should* leave you. Just until Monica is found."

"No," she said. "I want you with me. And I'm so, so sorry I worried you. I get your fear, I really do. The thought of Monica hurting you…"

"You'll be safer with Jase."

"He'll be busy protecting Brook Lynn, and rightly so. You and I, we can protect each other."

He thought for a moment, sighed. "I'll call Daniel, maybe there's more he can do. Like set up cameras to alert us if anyone so much as looks at the property."

"Thank you," she said softly, her chest clenching. He wasn't taking a break from her. Instead, he was crossing another item off the list.

Know you're worth fighting for, no matter how hard things get.

Beautiful man.

"I know I'm a lot to take on," he said. "I know I worry too much and go to extremes. I just... I don't want to lose you."

"I don't want to lose you, either." She kissed him, sweet and slow, a cocoon of warmth enveloping her, his scent—now mixed with hers—intoxicating as she breathed him in.

"If something happens to you, or even around you," he said, "you have to tell me right away. You can't leave me to worry. And I swear to you here and now, I will never purposely ignore your calls and texts."

"I won't purposely worry you," she vowed. "Not ever again."

"The day Tessa crashed..." He stiffened, but continued. "I'd promised to throw her a party for passing her GED exam. She came over expecting guests and gifts and games, but it was just Beck and me, and I was already high as a kite. She broke down, yelled at me for being the world's worst boyfriend and drove off. I was in no condition to follow and ended up snorting a few more rows. A few hours later, I got a call. Tessa had crashed into a tree and flown through the windshield. She died on the way to the hospital."

"Oh, West. I'm so sorry."

"Her face was so mangled, I had to identify a birthmark on her lower back."

Tears cascaded down Jessie Kay's cheeks. No wonder he always expected the worst.

And she… Well, she'd let her own fears make her decisions for her, and as a consequence, she'd made this powerful man worry about her well-being.

He traced a fingertip along the links of her watch, then her bracelet. "I don't think I'll ever be rational when it comes to your safety."

"We'll work on it. We'll work on my knee-jerk reaction to lash out when I get hurt. We'll finally go all in."

"I'm already all in, kitten."

"Don't kid yourself. We've both done our best to keep this relationship in a box. Want each other, but not too much. Be with each other while also maintaining distance. Be intimate, but not too intimate. We've been trying to protect ourselves, not realizing we're stronger together."

He offered no reply.

She forged ahead anyway. "I will do whatever it takes to keep you, Lincoln West." Almost losing him had been a shower of ice water on her soul. If she wanted this man, she had to fight for him daily. A constant battle, just as liking herself was. A war worth fighting.

Today, she enlisted.

A moment passed in silence, and still he offered no reply. Though it bothered her, even hurt her feelings, she sucked it up. The Monica thing had dredged up guilt about Tessa, and really, West might not have fully given up the deep-seated need to punish himself. Jessie Kay could be patient. She'd have to be.

To lighten the mood, she said, "Now that we're finally official—"

"Finally?"

"—we should probably sync our schedules."

"Agreed. In fact," he said, "your schedule will include a guard every time you leave the house."

"Is that your way of saying you want to tag along on all my daily errands?"

"Yes. I'll do whatever proves necessary to keep you safe."

It was something her dad would have said to her mom, and it completely undid her, pleasure drifting through her, a soothing balm she hadn't known she needed.

"Next time Monica strikes—" she said, and West stiffened. Oops. "I mean, if she strikes, which she probably won't, because you'll have caught her and scared the crap out of her. But if she does—which she probably won't—" Jessie Kay repeated, "I'll be ready for her."

He brought her hand to his mouth, kissed her knuckles. "You are my favorite thing in the world. I *can't* lose you."

Reeling—*I'm his favorite thing!*—she grazed his nipple with her teeth. "I'm proud of you for admitting such an embarrassing truth, but you still have to ace my interview before I can give you the exalted position of my boyfriend." Brook Lynn wasn't the only one with an interview fantasy.

"Before?" he asked with an arched brow. "Even though we're naked and in bed together?"

"Even though," she said as sternly as possible, considering she wanted to giggle.

"Fine. Let's get the interview over with."

How enthusiastic he sounded. "Describe your life with the title of a movie. And you have to answer honestly. If you lie, I'll know it, and then I'll have to blue-ball you."

"Oh, I'll be honest. If you don't admit you're mine, the answer will be *American Psycho*."

Ha! Funny man. "I guess that means my answer is *Sleeping with the Enemy*."

He gave her a light tap on the butt, and her giggle finally escaped.

"What is your spirit animal?" she asked as soon as she sobered. She did her best to sound businesslike and professional, an almost impossible task as she rubbed her knee up and down his leg.

"I'd have to go with…Pikachu."

Peek-a-what now? "You can't make up animals, Westlina."

"You, kitten, need to learn nerd speak. In fact, I'm insisting on it—if you want to keep the exalted position of my girlfriend. I assure you, the Pikachu is very real."

"Then why did you pick him?" she asked, exasperated.

"Because I, too, would refuse to enter a Poké Ball."

"What does that even mean? You know what? Never mind. Describe yourself in three non-nerd words."

"Done. With. Interview." He rolled over, pinning her to the mattress. Her legs spread automatically, making a cradle for him. A cradle he took full advantage of, his erection prodding at her entrance. "Now, tell me I'm yours. Otherwise I'm tying you to the bed. You'll be my prisoner."

Teasing him was fun, but there was a hard, desperate gleam in his eyes, a bit tortured and a lot anguished. Reassuring him would be a lot *more* fun. She wound her arms around his neck, molding her body around his. "Lucky, lucky man. I'm yours. Now. Whatever are you going to do with me?"

A slow, wicked smile bloomed. "I'm going to cherish every minute I have with you," he said and slid inside her.

WEST KEPT JESSIE KAY in bed for the rest of the day and night. He allowed her to leave the safety of his arms only twice. The first time because Daniel and his Army buddies arrived to take care of security, the second to make a sandwich, and only because they were both dying of hunger.

If they weren't making love, they were working on her new website. He'd gotten to delve deeper into her past for the bio page and what he'd learned had only made him like her more.

Her grandmother on her father's side had taught her to sew. Then she'd taught her mom how to sew. The two had picked out patterns together and had often gone on "fabric dates."

When she made a dress, she said, she didn't think about the past, or her mistakes, just the smile Brook Lynn would bestow upon her when she finished. And that, West thought, was what set this job apart from all her others. Because it *wasn't* a job. It was a passion with rewards.

By the time a new morning dawned, bringing cracks of thunder and a torrent of rain, a sense of contentment surrounded him.

He loved that contentment, but he wasn't used to it, and wasn't sure how long it would last—he wanted it to last. He was so used to everything going to hell.

Worry drove him from the bed, though he was careful not to wake Jessie Kay.

What would happen if ever he lost her?

He dressed in a pair of low-hung sweatpants and made

his way to the kitchen. Rather than digging through the fridge to begin cooking breakfast, he stopped at the sink, curling his fingers around the ledge and peering out the window. Hail hammered the backyard.

Just then, he kind of felt like the ground. Like he was taking a beating.

He'd lived with misery for so long—and by choice—that he had no idea how to deal with this kind of happiness. But he needed to figure it out, and fast. Jessie Kay had nailed the issue.

We've both done our best to keep this relationship in a box. Want each other, but not too much. Be with each other while maintaining distance. Be intimate, but not too intimate.

He'd thought he was all in. He hadn't been.

Until now.

He'd tried to give this but not that. Enjoy this but not that. And it hadn't mattered. He'd almost lost her. Despite trying to keep a part of himself separate, despite trying to protect his heart, he would have felt the same: devastated.

He lowered his head, his chin pressing into his sternum. He'd once told himself he wouldn't fall in love, wouldn't marry, wouldn't have a family because Tessa couldn't have those things, and for ten years he'd stayed true to that vow. He'd chosen women he wanted but didn't like, and he'd parted with them easily.

Until Jessie Kay.

On paper, she was wrong for him in every way. A past as checkered as his own. She'd been with both his friends. She operated by Jessie Kay Standard Time, sometimes ignoring West Central. But despite all of that, she complemented his life. She made him laugh. She constantly surprised him with the things she said and did. She had a sensitive heart, a caring heart. A giving heart.

They could build something real.

All he had to do was let go of what remained of his guilt and grab on to her. A true early release. Not just with words, but with action. With emotion.

At the thought, razors slashed at his chest and sweat beaded on his brow.

Arms wrapped around him from behind. Through the fabric of a T-shirt, soft breasts pressed against his back, Jessie Kay's heart beating against his ribs. She rested her head against his shoulder, the softness of her skin reminding him of silk. The fragrance of pecans and cinnamon enveloped him, delighted him.

"I missed you," she said softly. "Wanted to wake up in your arms."

Let go of the guilt...grab on to her...

"I once asked you to forgive me for the way I treated you," he said, "but what right did I have to ask you to do something I've never been willing to do myself? I think it's time to forgive myself for the past. All of it."

Guilt was an anchor. Bitterness was poison. If one didn't kill you, the other would. They caused happiness, joy and contentment to dry up and wither away, leaving nothing but emptiness behind. An emptiness he'd once struggled to fill with drugs and misery. An emptiness *Jessie Kay* could now fill with laughter and light.

I'm sorry I let you down, Tessa. I'm sorry I put something toxic above my feelings for you. I've hated myself so long and fought so hard to hang on to what could have been, but I'm letting go now.

I'm sorry for what I did to Jase, for staying quiet,

for letting my friend rot behind bars while I rotted behind guilt.

West had learned from his mistakes. He'd grown up.

"I'm so proud of you," Jessie Kay said, giving him a squeeze.

He stared into the storm raging outside and for the first time in years, the storm inside *him* calmed. The razors in his chest dulled. The sweat on his brow evaporated. He pried his fingers from the counter, one at a time, the action symbolic. He did it—he let go. Let the guilt drift off into the ether like a discarded balloon.

A heavy weight lifted from his shoulders. A massive pressure eased from his chest, one he hadn't known he'd borne.

He turned to face Jessie Kay, banding his arms around her, holding on tight to the new center of his world. "You missed me, huh? Good. My master plan is working."

"Mmm. Do tell."

"Step one, draw you into the kitchen..." He swung her around and placed her on the counter. "Step two, have you for breakfast."

CHAPTER TWENTY-FOUR

WEST, HER PASSIONATE, deliciously filthy lover, turned out to be a dirty, dirty traitor!

After a night of worshipping her body, he'd picked up the phone and dialed Brook Lynn, saying, "Jessie Kay lost her temper yesterday. She was mad at me and threw my bag across the room. She even beat on me a little bit, and I have the bruises to prove it. Congrats! You won the bet. Make sure you collect your prize."

Now Jessie Kay had to wear outfits of her sister's choosing for an entire week. The horror! She would discover the atrocities to be visited upon her in two hours, when she headed over to help with lunch deliveries. You've Got It Coming was back on track, the fire already an afterthought…to everyone but West.

He was still hovering, but he was different in other ways. Forgiving himself had changed him for the better, and she wasn't yet sure how to handle him. The way he looked at her now…soft and sweet, as if she were a treasure he was seeing for the first time. The way he touched her now…as if he'd never felt anything so luxurious—or wanted anything more.

"Building up your stamina on the field may turn out to be the death of me in the bedroom," he said during their morning soccer practice. He'd erected a shelter of sorts in her backyard, a goalpost on the left side and a goalpost on the right, a tent stretching high overhead between the two, protecting her from the wind and rain. He'd even warmed the area with industrial-sized heaters, allowing her to go without a coat in the dead of winter. Two strategically placed halogen lights illuminated the area, chasing away the storm's thickest shadows.

"You're welcome," she replied. "What a way to go, huh?"

He tweaked her nose. "You are too precious for words."

He kept doing that, kept complimenting her. It was disconcerting! If he'd been charming before, he was now irresistible, the difference both stunning and amazing her, leaving her careening. She didn't just love this man…she would die for him. Kill for him. Do *anything* for him.

He checked his watch, the action drawing her back into the present. "All right, kitten. Time for us to shower or you'll be late to the farmhouse."

"Time for *me* to shower, you mean, or I'll definitely be late."

"Time is circular, remember?" He followed her to the bathroom. "According to Jessie Kay Standard, no matter what time you get there, you won't be late."

"Yes, well, I'm dating Mr. Obsessive now. I've had to adjust my thinking." She gave him a smile—then she gave him the finger—and shut the door in his face.

That should teach him not to tattle!

He burst out laughing, surprising her, filling her heart with joy. "You've earned yourself a punishment, kitten. You've lost the privilege of wearing a bra for the next twenty-four hours. And yes, there will be an inspection."

She lost more than her bra. She lost her breath, because dang it, he was sexy as hell.

She showered and dressed…and she did *not* wear a bra. But then, she didn't need one. The day dress she selected—one of her older creations—had a halter top that hugged her breasts, holding them in place. She draped a sweater over her shoulders and warmed her legs with thick black tights.

West did indeed inspect her, standing behind her and sliding his hands underneath her top. His warm breath tickled her as he nibbled on her earlobe. "I'm glad you take your punishments seriously."

"As the moral compass for this relationship, I have to learn better manners."

"That's right. You do. That's why you're going to stand in front of Mr. West's class tonight and do a little show-and-tell. I'll want to hear all about the impact of this particular lesson." He kneaded her and pinched her nipples before he released her. "Let's get you to your sister before our schedule is completely blown."

Our schedule, he'd said. Not his. Not hers. Theirs. She smiled.

"I'll drive you to the farmhouse," he said. He wore a T-shirt and jeans, which meant he had no meetings today and would be working on a game.

She knew better than to argue and tell him she wanted to drive herself. He'd told her how things would be, and she'd told him she understood—which she did. Stupid Monica!

Jessie Kay dared the girl to show her face today. The bitch would pay. Playing nice? Not anymore! Why bother, anyway? She'd already lost the bet with her sister, so there was no longer any reason to remain calm.

When they reached their destination, West walked her to the door. He looked a little panicky, his eyes wild, his grip on her tightening. However, he surprised her by saying, "Text me and keep me updated. Think about me today. I doubt I'll be doing anything but remembering you."

Had sweeter words ever been spoken? "I'll be *aching* for you," she whispered.

White-hot desire flashed over his features. In a snap, he drew her in for a sizzling kiss, his tongue thrusting against hers in a mimic of the down-and-dirty sex they'd had before soccer practice. This one didn't last long, just enough time to rev her motor.

When he straightened, he breathed, "You might just be the best thing that's ever happened to me," straight into her ear and then…just…left.

Her knees threatened to give out. Sweet fancy. She had to fan her overheating cheeks as she made her way into the kitchen. West was, without a doubt, the most perfect man in the world. He not only said the nicest things, he'd decided to trust her to take care of—

Nope. He hadn't decided to trust her to take care of herself. Jase stood watch at the back door, a tower of muscle and determination.

Should have known.

"Why aren't you refurbishing the bathroom?" she asked. The faint scent of smoke still permeated the air, a sobering reminder that life could change in a blink.

Blink. Almost lost West. *Blink.* Won him back.

"I paid someone to work all night so I could spend time with you and Brook Lynn today," he replied.

Yeah. That was why.

"Ignoring me won't make me go away," Brook Lynn said as she chopped vegetables.

Crap! "I know you've got my first outfit stashed some-where. Let's see it."

Her sister jumped up and down, clapping with excite-ment. "West made a special request. Said it was only fair since he compromised his principles and ratted out his girlfriend." An anticipatory pause, Brook Lynn's smile growing wider. "Jase. Please do the honors."

Jase stepped to the side, revealing the clothing hang-ing from the upper lip of the door. One of the Kevlar vests Brook Lynn kept stashed in the zombie shed, paired with fire-retardant pants firefighters wore. Well. It could have been worse. Not by much, but okay. Whatever.

"We are about to embark on a week of fun, amuse-ment and all-around amazingness," Brook Lynn said. "For me."

"And all the rest of us," Jase said.

Brook Lynn smirked at Jessie Kay. "New Year's is only three days away and I'm throwing a party for my closest friends. Which means you have to come. Which means you have to wear what I say."

This. This was worse. "You're going to remember you love me and ensure the rest of the outfits flatter me, right?"

"Yeah. Keep dreaming."

Jessie Kay made deliveries with Jase at her side, the guy tense and alert and probably armed. She saved West's sandwich for last because yes, he'd called and put in an order. Either he'd wanted to check on her, or he'd hoped to have a quickie in his office. Maybe both.

Fingers crossed!

As she and Jase trekked the sidewalks through the town square, the storm continued to rage. At least the hail had stopped. They were able to stay semidry under the gargantuan umbrella he held.

"Since I can't ditch you, I've decided to use you for information about West. And don't try to pull any bro-code crap and tell me you can't talk about him. I'll be forced to remind you of our past connection and the fact that I never tried to stop you from pursuing my sister. And yes, I will use this to guilt you into doing whatever I want for the rest of our lives. Deal with it."

One corner of his mouth kicked up. "I hope you're like this with West."

"Because I'm awesome and he deserves the best?"

"That's as good an explanation as any, I suppose."

She gave his arm a playful punch.

There was no one more private than Jase, and she knew from experience just how difficult it was to get him to open up. A task she'd failed to do. Brook Lynn, however, had pried him open as if he were a clam.

"What was West like as a kid?" Even though Jessie Kay had poured on the guilt trip, she expected failure.

When the next clap of thunder quieted, however, Jase surprised her by saying, "By the time we met, we'd both been through a lot and were leery of letting anyone in. A childless couple hoped to help the most troubled boys in the system, so Beck was there, too, along with three others. Believe it or not, I was the scrawny one of the bunch. Just skin and bones. The other three boys, I don't even remember their names, they took one look at me and decided I'd make the perfect whipping boy."

Hanging on his every word, she cursed when another clap of thunder rang out. "What happened?"

"When the couple went to bed that first night, the boys snuck into the room I shared with West and Beck and yanked me out of the top bunk I'd been assigned. They stuffed a gag in my mouth so I wouldn't wake the fosters, but West and Beck were right there and heard the commotion. They jumped out of their beds and beat the shit out of my tormentors. Two against three, and they won by a landslide. We've had each other's backs ever since."

Her heart ached for the boys they'd been. Abandoned, mistreated, abused.

West was a wounded warrior. As a kid, he'd faced down bullies of every age. As an adult, he'd relived his fears simply to share with her.

"What's that you're wearing, Jessie Kay?" Mr. Porter— Daniel's dad—suddenly called. As always, he sat in front of Style Me Tender with Mr. Rodriguez, playing checkers under the calm of an awning. The two were more reliable than the local mailman.

"I lost a bet with Brook Lynn," she called back. "She gets to pick my wardrobe for a week."

The two males nodded as if they'd never heard anything more reasonable.

"She up for suggestions?" Mr. Rodriguez asked.

"Definitely," Jase replied. "Just give her a call."

Jessie Kay gave him another punch in the arm. They turned a corner, the two men falling out of view…and WOH appearing on the horizon. Her stomach began to churn for a different reason. West! So close!

"You're good for him," Jase said. "He's different with you. More like the West I knew when we were kids. Lighter—not that we were ever light—if that makes any sense."

"It does," she said, pleasure blooming. *She* was lighter with *him*.

They reached the office building, a bell tinkling over

the door as they stepped inside, the sound like musical chimes. Cora sat at her desk and waved in greeting. Jessie Kay stopped short when she spotted West in his office. The walls were glass, offering a clear view. He could have pressed a button and caused an opaque film to cover every inch, but he hadn't. He stood in front of his desk...a young woman standing before him.

The problem? The bitch had her hands on his shoulders.

"Someone is going to die today," Jessie Kay muttered.

Jase followed the line of her gaze and cursed. "You've got to be kidding me." He looked to Cora. "Do you know the woman's name? Patience...something?"

Cora checked the notes in front of her and nodded. "That's right. Patience Ludwick."

"Who is Patience Ludwick?" Jessie Kay demanded, her fingers squeezing the sandwich she held, smashing the bread.

"He used to date her," Jase admitted reluctantly. "I never met her, but he kept me up-to-date on his life, visiting me in prison and showing me pictures."

Jessie Kay took a step forward, only to draw short again. When West took Patience by the wrists and forced her hands off his shoulders, she breathed a sigh of relief. He backed the woman into a chair, and when her knees hit the edge, she just sort of tumbled onto the cushion. He immediately took a step away from her, widening the distance between them. There was a hard gleam in his eyes, and tension pulled his lips into a thin line. Not the sort of sensual tension he usually projected at Jessie Kay, but something steeped in anger.

His gaze moved...drifted over Jessie Kay...came right back to her. She smiled with genuine happiness and blew him a kiss. Relief poured over his features. Patience turned to find out what had claimed his attention, and when her eyes landed on Jessie Kay, she frowned. Her mouth began to move. She was saying something to West, but he didn't seem to care. He stalked out of the office, closing in on Jessie Kay as if he were a heat-seeking missile and she was on fire.

The moment he reached her, he wound his arms around her. "Anything out of the ordinary happen today?"

"No. I'm fine." She kept a firm grip on the ruined sandwich and returned her man's hug. "Jase was a good little bodyguard, just like I told you in my thousand texts." Every five minutes, she'd sent him a new one.

Doing great, but missing you…and my bra.

Doing even better, but uh oh, now I'm missing my panties, too.

All in one piece—but aching for you.

"Good. That's good. There's been no sign of Monica. The woman in my office is Patience Ludwick, her former roommate and once my…"

"Girlfriend. Yeah, I know. You can say the word. I promise not to claw off your face."

He tweaked the end of her nose, and she realized it was a new habit he'd developed. "I called her, questioned her about Monica, but she hadn't seen or heard from the girl, either. Then, to my surprise, she showed up about ten minutes ago."

From the look of things, she was hoping to rekindle

the spark. "We'll find Monica," Jessie Kay said. "Even hobbits have to leave their caves every once in a while."

He grinned down at her. "Kitten, that actually made sense. Hobbits live in luxurious underground holes in the Shire."

"I know! I'm learning nerd speak just like you told me. Because I'm a better girlfriend than you are a boyfriend."

"Don't kid yourself. You're good, but I'm far superior." He slung his arm around her shoulders, confiscated the sandwich and looked over the broken remains. He shook his head at her. "You, Miss Dillon, owe me another sandwich. I'll collect payment tonight at home, after your show-and-tell. And I'll require interest."

He'd just referred to her house as his home. Could life get any sweeter?

"Come on." He led her toward the office. "I'll make introductions."

"Yeah. Hi," Jase called. "Good to see you, too, man."

West waved at his friend without turning around.

Patience stood as they entered the office. She wasn't as tall as Jessie Kay, but she was slender and well put together in a dark green dress suit. She'd pulled her dark hair into a bun, dusted her pale-as-snow skin with shimmering rose color, and painted her lips bloodred. The scent of her perfume—soft and floral—teased the air. Something meant to entice, no doubt about it.

"Jessie Kay, this is Patience," West said. "Patience, this is my girlfriend, Jessie Kay."

Disappointment flashed in eyes the prettiest shade of hazel, more green than brown, and as Patience took in the drape of his arm over Jessie Kay's shoulders, she did so longingly. "You're a lucky girl, Jessie Kay."

"Actually, I'm a lucky man," he said before Jessie Kay could respond.

She beamed. "He's also an honest man. And a smart one."

"Well, I should be going." Patience picked up the purse she'd left in the chair. "I'll call you if I hear from Monica."

"Thank you."

A few seconds later, Jessie Kay was alone with her man. He leaned over the desk to press a button. The opaque film began to dust the glass walls at last.

Were things about to get naughty?

He waved a sheet of paper in front of her, then snatched it away when she tried to grab it. "This is your schedule. You distracted me this morning at practice with your bouncing breasts and short shorts, and I forgot to give it to you."

The wicked gleam in his eyes...

She shivered. "I'm sorry, Mr. West. It won't happen again."

"Oh, I'm sure it will. That's why I'm going to punish you right here, right now." He wadded up the paper, tossed it into the trash can and lifted a black marker from the desk. "You're going to wear my schedule on your skin."

CHAPTER TWENTY-FIVE

WEST CONSIDERED SKIPPING Brook Lynn's New Year's bash. He'd rather stand in a field bare-ass naked as a tornado approached at warp speed. If his balls ended up wrapped around a cow and two trees, it would pain him less than waiting for Monica to strike. No one had seen or heard from her since the fire, and it was driving him to the brink of sanity. Every day his fear grew worse.

He jumped at every noise. He basically went ninja on every shadow. Not because he cared what the woman would try to do to him. Bring it. But because of what she might try to do to Jessie Kay. The smart-mouthed blonde had come to mean more to him than… Shit, he didn't know how far she'd burrowed under his skin. He only knew he would burn the world to ash if ever she were harmed.

He'd talked to Sheriff Lintz, but there was no proof Monica had started the fire, so there was nothing the lawman could do but keep a lookout for her.

West had a conceal and carry license but until now he'd rarely ever put it to use. Now he kept a .44 holstered at the back of his waist. Just in case.

Jessie Kay wanted to attend the party, and with a few strategically placed kisses, she'd convinced him to take her. One, the number of guests would be limited. Jase and Brook Lynn, Beck and Harlow, Dane and Kenna.

Two, the risk would be minimal; Daniel and his boys would be patrolling the acreage all night long.

"I'm fixing to start a shower." Jessie Kay walked into his room without knocking. Not that he cared. What was his was hers.

"Fixing to start?"

"You gonna join me or what?"

He'd been in the process of cleaning his gun. He put the pieces back together, placed the weapon on his nightstand and stood. "You already know the answer to that, kitten."

"That's right, I do. I also know you suck!" She swiped a dirty shirt from his hamper and threw it at him. "You've reverted to your jerkish behavior—jerk!"

The garment hit his chest before falling to the floor. For the past three days—ever since he'd written on her skin and made love to her in the office—he'd kept his hands to himself. When she got naked, he got stupid. He lost track of his surroundings. He cared only about climax—his as well as hers. Monica could have snuck in the office, and all he could have shot her with was a load of baby batter.

Yeah. No, thanks.

Until she was caught, he had to remain alert.

"I have needs, you know." Jessie Kay stomped her foot.

"You'll have to meet those needs in the shower. Alone." His erection begged to differ as it pushed against his zipper.

"I'm not talking about the need to come, you moron. I'm talking about the need to be with *you*."

Killing me. "I need you, too, kitten." Sweat beaded

on the back of his neck as a fire raged through his veins. "But your safety—"

"Is important. Yes, I know. You've told me. But Monica hasn't tried anything since the fire."

She hadn't returned home to the city, either.

"She's probably long gone," Jessie Kay added. "Running scared. Afraid of my pimp hand."

"The *world* is afraid of your pimp hand, but I still can't risk it."

"You're letting her ruin your life—*our* life—and it's hurting my heart."

The words nearly unmanned him. "I'm being proactive. She knows how to shoot a gun, Jessie Kay."

"So do I. So do all my friends. So does everyone in the state."

"You're important to me. I can't lose you."

"You're important to me, too. And so is your happiness. So is mine!" She toyed with the hem of her T-shirt. It read "Swat Team 8. We assassinate fleas, ticks, silverfish, cockroaches, bees, ants, mice and rats." A suggestion courtesy of Mr. Porter. Brook Lynn had decided a beret and camo pants completed the outfit.

Yesterday, Brook Lynn had made her wear a dress that looked like it'd come straight off the set of *Little House on the Prairie*. The day before that, Jessie Kay was forced to wear a T-shirt that read "Wild Hogs" that had nearly gotten her mobbed when she'd made her breakfast deliveries. Apparently the Wild Hogs were the greatest rivals of the Strawberry Valley Stallions.

"We're not happy this way," she said.

"It's just for a little while."

"Is it? What happens if she's never found? What happens when the next threat comes?"

A muscle ticked below his eye. "Are you trying to tell me I'm smothering you?"

"I'm trying to discuss a real issue with you. I'm trying to tell you I need *something* from you before I decide to go after Monica myself."

He scrubbed a hand down his face. Caught between the instinct to protect and the instinct to make his woman happy.

"If you won't have sex with me, fine," she said. "How about you tell me another one of your secrets? You can talk and protect me at the same time. Right? And I love learning about you. Makes me feel close to you."

Love…

Did she love *him*?

Did he want her to love him?

Longing ripped through him—yeah, he wanted her to love him. Because he already loved the hell out of her.

How could he deny it when their relationship was reflected back at him from every nook and cranny of the home they shared? Her fabrics were strewn all over the couch and had been for days, but he'd never felt the urge to fold them or put them away. The blanket she'd made him was spread over the floor where they'd recently had another picnic. Their notes and plans for her website were scattered over the coffee table, along with his flash drives and tools. Things that turned a house into a home. Their home.

He loved this woman. He loved her with all his heart, soul and body. She'd broken his shackles and freed him from a prison of his own making. She'd become the lighthouse in the storm, the reason he woke every morning and the reason he smiled every night.

She was everything he'd ever needed. His happiness rather than the misery he'd once sought.

"Come here," he said. She wanted his secrets; she would get them. The worst of them. He would share the rest of his burden and trust her to handle it.

She glided over and eased onto his lap, her arms automatically wrapping around his neck.

"What I'm about to tell you, I've never told anyone else. Not Jase and Beck. Not Tessa."

Her eyes widened. "Really?"

He nodded. "You know my mother was a drug addict. She sometimes had to sell herself to afford her drugs. Sometimes she'd leave me in the apartment alone and hit the streets. I preferred those times. Other times, she let guys come over."

Jessie Kay must have suspected where he was going with his story because she tightened her hold.

"She'd get high, do whatever the guys demanded and pass out. Most times the guys would leave. Sometimes they stayed. A few of them noticed the handful of toys I had scattered about and looked for me. There were so few places to hide…"

Tremors shook her.

Shook him, too. He had to force the rest out. "The first time, I screamed and fought and woke up my mom. She attacked him. He hit her and left. I don't know whether or not she forgot he was the one who'd punched her or if she was so desperate for cash and drugs she stopped caring, but she let him come back. When he found me that time, I stayed quiet…let him do whatever he wanted. I didn't want her hurt again. After that…"

"How old were you?"

He closed his eyes for a moment. "It started when I was four. I was six when it ended."

"I want to kill the guy. But first I want to rip out his eyes and stomp on them. I want to cut out his tongue and put it in a blender. I want to peel his skin, douse him in salt and—"

West chuckled at a time when he would have sworn amusement was impossible, and for that, he would be forever grateful to this precious woman. "He died a long time ago, kitten. I checked."

She drew in a deep breath, slowly released it. "I'm ripped up inside for you." She placed the sweetest kiss against the pulse at the base of his neck. "I ache for the boy you were, and I crave the man you are. I need you, and right now, you need me, too. Forget about Monica and what she might do. She's ruined enough. Let me comfort you—and myself."

She was right, wasn't she. He *did* need her, more now than ever, and he *had* allowed Monica to ruin enough.

Jessie Kay deserved better.

And he would give it to her. He wasn't going to let fear drive him anymore, and he wasn't going to stand passively while his fear of tragedy tried to steal his new-found happiness. He was going to fight the good fight.

An idea took root, and he almost smiled. He said, "How about a bath?" careful to moderate his tone.

"A bath...with you or by myself?"

"With me."

"Really? Yes!" she shouted before he could respond. "Yes, yes, a thousand times yes. No take backs!"

Smiling, he stood, pulling her up with him. "I want to see you first. I've missed you."

Her eyes flared with instant desire. Her every motion

a study of femininity, she tossed aside the hat and removed her shirt, and he sucked in a breath. His schedule
was still visible on her skin.

The words *1:00—Knead Breasts* were faded but
scrolled across her collarbone, and they made his hands
itch for contact.

She popped the center clasp of her bra. Red lace. Nice.
1:05—Pinch Nipples.

"You like so far?" she said, her voice low and husky.
Her fingers went to the button on her pants.

"Love."

She shivered. Down went her zipper. Down went the
camo. "What are you going to do to me?"

1:10—Touch Here. The words stretched from one hip
bone to another. In the center, an arrow pointed down.

"Finish stripping, and I'll tell you."

Another shiver. She watched him, intent, as she removed her panties, making his blood *boil*.

With a grin, now confident in her power over him,
she kicked the garment at him. He caught the scrap of
barely there lace and brought it to his face, rubbing it
over his cheek.

"Naughty boy," she said.

"This naughty boy is going to make you the happiest little kitty in the world." He nodded toward the hall.
"Draw the water, and I'll join you in a bit. Gotta do a
few things first."

"But—"

"Nonnegotiable."

"Fine. The longer you make me wait, the more of my
good time you're going to miss." Lips turned down in
the most adorable pout, she strolled down the hall, the
motion of her hips making him moan.

Though he wanted to rush to get to her, he carefully gathered the supplies he needed and placed them inside a black bag. By the time he joined Jessie Kay in the bathroom, she lounged in the tub, surrounded by bubbles.

"How's the water?" He breathed in the vanilla scent that saturated the air. His girl always chose edible fragrances. "Warm enough?"

"Almost perfect." She dazzled him with a slow, seductive smile. "All it needs is you. As you can see, you made it just in time. I haven't yet gotten started."

He kneeled beside the tub and set the bag at his side. "Did you know we've passed the two-month mark of our relationship?" She stiffened and he added, "I might not have admitted it before, but I've been yours since the day we met."

Slowly she relaxed and licked her lips. "Well, you're a guy. You don't always understand things right away."

"This is true. I don't always do the right thing at first, either, but I can rectify that. Starting with your list." He smiled innocently. "The one with all the things I need to do before I can keep you forever."

She sat up straight, water sloshing over the rim of the tub. "West, you don't have to—"

"According to my calculations," he interjected, "I only have two items to complete: stop hovering, and always be there for you."

"Three items," she rasped. "Love me."

"We'll talk about that one later. Right now, I'm about to tackle the two I mentioned."

Her brow furrowed in confusion. "How?"

"I'm sorry, kitten, but there really is no other way." He withdrew a glass jar from the bag and held it up—a glass jar containing two large, hairy spiders. He'd found them this morning, intending to show them off and brag about saving her life and demand rights to her soul.

"West," she gasped out. "What are you doing? Get those things out of here!"

"One day you'll thank me for this." He twisted the lid. "I'm sure of it."

Screaming, she jumped to her feet, bubbles and rivers of water rushing down her naked curves. She held out her arm to ward him off. "Don't come near me. Don't you dare."

"I've realized I can make you happy or I can return to my misery. I can't do both. Congrats! I pick you. I will *always* pick you. So. I'm going to free the little beasts," he said, merciless, giving the lid another twist. "You'll be in horrible danger. The worst danger you've ever faced, but I'm not going to help you. I'm not going to hover. I'm going to trust you to overcome this terror all on your own. Then, after you've defeated these monstrous creatures, I'm going to be there for you, holding you close, comforting you. We will discuss my new schedule."

"No. No!" She backed up as far as she could go, the cold tile making her gasp all over again. "Please, no."

But he did it. He lifted the lid and dumped the spiders on the edge of the tub.

JESSIE KAY RELEASED another earsplitting scream as two sets of beady eyes locked on her. She knew they locked on her. She could almost hear their forked tongues scraping over their razor-sharp fangs. They craved human blood…*her* blood…and they were crawling forward… crawling toward her!

Panting, she leaped out of the water and raced to West.

She tried to use him as a human shield, but the bastard pulled from her clasp.

"You can do it," he said. "I believe in you."

"West, you idiot! Don't believe in me. I can't do it. I just can't."

"You can."

"No, no, I really can't."

"Yes, yes, you really can."

Her stomach dropped to her feet. He wasn't going to help her, was he?

I demanded he face his fears. Now I have to do the same.

"Wretched man," she muttered. Though she trembled, she returned to the bathroom and picked up the jar...almost dropped it when she looked at the little demons, but managed to catch it before it shattered into a million pieces. She leaned toward the first spider, screamed for no reason, and hopped backward. The devil's minion ran across the tub, disappearing in a crack in the tile.

Okay, okay. Good. Only one left.

"You can do it," West called. "They are more afraid of you than you are of them."

"Liar!" But she took a tentative step toward the second minion.

It *wasn't* afraid of her. It raced toward her.

Playing chicken? He won! With a screech, she sprinted into the corner. The murderous creature veered at the last second, disappearing under the sink.

She threw the jar at West, then threw herself into his arms.

He wrapped those arms around her, holding her tight. "There, there, kitten. You survived all on your own. You're going to be okay, and I'm here to offer comfort."

"You are such a jackass! We'll both be dead by morning. You want to know why? Because you set them loose, and now they're hiding, waiting for the perfect time to strike. While we're sleeping!"

He chuckled. "You are so precious to me, kitten. You are the best part of my life, and for the first time, I'm grateful for my past. It brought me to you. It prepared me for you, shaped me into the man you needed me to be. I love you."

She gasped up at him, the spiders momentarily forgotten. "You—what?"

"I love you."

This couldn't be happening. But the truth shined from him in so many ways. The way he held her. The way he touched her. The way he spoke to her. The way he looked at her. The way he took care of her. The way he refused to give up on her.

"I love you more than any man has ever loved a woman."

This *was* happening.

"I love you, too," she whispered. The emotion swelled inside her, a beautiful deluge. "I love you and I like you, and I thank God you came along and showed me the pure, undiluted joy of being with a man who sees a future with me rather than a moment." A man who respected her and delighted in her. A man who held each of their encounters close to his heart.

He went still, even seemed to stop breathing. "You love me?"

"With all my heart. But the more amazing fact is that I still like you after you unleashed a horde of spiders."

"There were only two."

"Like a said, a horde."

"We'll hunt them together."

"No. You'll do it alone."

He squeezed her tight and, with a whoop, spun her around. A laugh escaped him. A genuine, no-hint-of-misery laugh and oh, it was a lovely thing. "I like you, too. So much. I'm addicted to you. You are my drug of choice, kitten, and you have made me the happiest man in existence."

Could life get any better? "What's your new schedule?"

"To always do everything in my power to make you happy."

"This, you diabolical fiend, is the perfect start."

"And…" He dropped to one knee in front of her and held out a silver bolt that matched the bracelet he'd made her. "I want to marry you. I want to give you my last name and spend the rest of my days being happy *with* you."

Her hands formed a steeple in front of her mouth. "Lincoln."

"Say yes."

She didn't need to think about it. "Yes. Yes, yes, a thousand times yes. I'm going to marry you and one day, I'll even have your babies."

"I'm thinking four."

"I'm thinking two."

"Three."

"Two. And I'm going to love and like you all the days of your life—but just not inside this house. Forget the spider hunt. We're burning this place to the ground!"

CHAPTER TWENTY-SIX

BEST. NIGHT. EVER.

Jessie Kay glanced at her ring for the millionth time. She hadn't stopped smiling since West slid the one of a kind beauty on her finger.

To his chagrin, she'd opted to call her sister rather than jump into bed with him after he'd found and released the spiders into the wild. A girl had to prioritize.

Brook Lynn had screamed louder than Jessie Kay had when the spiders rushed her. Then her sister had proceeded to invite everyone in town to the farmhouse for a New Year's slash engagement celebration.

West, true to his vow to lighten up, had taken things in stride. He'd called Daniel, who would be patrolling the property with his crew all night, and let him know the change of plan. Now the spacious farmhouse overflowed with guests.

Brook Lynn, Harlow and Kenna beamed at her from across the living room.

Sunny Day gave her a shoulder bump. "Congrats, hooker. You suck for leaving me in the dust."

Mr. Porter and Mr. Rodriquez gave her a thumbsup. They even took a moment to pat West on the back.

Mr. Porter said, "You got lucky, boy. Hope you know that."

"I do, sir."

"And if he ever forgets," Jessie Kay said, "I'll make sure to remind him."

Pearl from the flower shop gave her a hug. "I knew that man was crazy about you the moment he put together your bouquet. Not many guys do that, you know."

Edna and Carol approached Jessie Kay and West with huge smiles.

"I'm happy for you, but truth be told, I'm mostly happy for myself," Carol said, her cheeks flushed. She held a bottle of expensive champagne. That she guzzled. "I've had to fend off six advances tonight."

"*We've* had to fend off six advances." Edna claimed the bottle and took a swig. The two women were adorably round but pushing the softer side of sixty.

"Virgil is looking this way," Carol said, giggling behind her hand. "Do you think he'll pinch my bottom again and make it an even seven?"

"Let's walk by him and find out!"

And then the two were off.

"When can we kick everyone out?" Jessie Kay asked West. Only two hours till midnight. She wanted her fiancé—her fiancé!—in bed and naked so they could ring in the New Year with more than a kiss.

Start the way you want to end, Momma used to say.

"How about we ditch and make out in my old room?" West nipped her ear and whispered, "I've got a private celebration penciled in our schedule."

Shivers danced through her as he led her down the hall, unlocked his bedroom door—had to keep unwanted guests out *somehow*—and dragged her inside the room. Rather than throwing her onto the bed, he took her into the bathroom. The odor of smoke was gone, the walls brand-new, the black-and-white floor tiles gleaming.

"I want you," she said.

"You want, I procure. Always."

"Well, it's no wonder I love you and like you so much."

He turned on the shower—to mask the sounds they would make, she suspected—and picked her up to place her beside the sink. He parted her legs, pushed between them and had her jaw in his hands a moment later, his grip firm but gentle.

"You were right before, you know. I let Monica come between us. I let fear destroy the good thing we had going, and I'm sorry."

She combed her fingers through his hair. "I understood your caution. And I know I need a monster slayer at my side if there's a monster out to get me, but I also need my man."

"I'm your man," he said, and smiled slowly.

"You better be. I'm wearing your ring."

He grinned at her. "Tomorrow I'll be wearing your name."

"Seriously? You're going to get my name etched into your flesh?"

"Why not? It's already etched into my heart." Then his lips were on hers, pressing firmly, demanding fiercely, his tongue thrusting into her mouth, taking up the reins of control.

She moaned with satisfaction, with pleasure and need, his masculine taste teasing her, revving her desire for him higher. It wasn't long before the tether to her own control snapped. In seconds, she was flooded by all-consuming arousal and heat, desperate to have this man, this precious man, deep inside her. It didn't matter that a party raged just beyond the doors or that her sister or Harlow could be looking for her, or Jase and Beck could be looking for West. Or that, when they couldn't be found, everyone would know where they were and what they were doing.

"Naked," she rasped out, pulling at the hem of his shirt. When the material cleared his head, she tossed it aside. "Now."

He gave her shirt the same treatment, then unhooked her bra's center clasp, her breasts spilling free of the restraint. Cool air kissed her nipples, making them pucker. The reaction drew his attention, and he swirled his thumbs over each distended tip, sending sharp lances of pleasure hurling through her.

He yanked off her shoes. He tugged at her pants and when the button and zipper finally gave, he slid the material from her legs, along with her panties, leaving her totally bare while he still wore his jeans. There was something so very naughty about that.

"Just how badly do you want me inside you, kitten?"

"Enough to forgive you for the spiders," she confessed, breathless with longing.

He smiled as he pushed open her legs, making him the picture of masculine aggression.

"Look how pretty you are." He reached out, slid a finger deep, deep inside her. "How hot and tight. How wet. How mine."

A cry split her lips as her back arched. "I need you. It's been too long. Days…"

He continued to torment her, those naughty fingers working her, driving her into a mindless state where only pleasure mattered. She writhed. She tugged at his hair and bit at his lips, but whatever she did, it wasn't enough. More. She had to have more.

"Yes, yes." No! Her orgasm was closing in way too fast. "I want to come with you. Please."

"That word on your lips is priceless." He pulled back, tugged her from the counter until her feet hit the floor. He grabbed her by the hips and spun her around, forcing her to face the mirror. Her wild, wanton expression stared back at her. Pale hair in complete disarray, tangled around her shoulders. Her skin was flushed with the fever of passion and scraped by the shadow of his beard. Her pupils overshadowed her irises, glazed with the greatest hunger she'd ever known.

He drew her gaze, held it captive. "Look at us. See how good we are together."

Her breath caught. He was so beautiful behind her, his hair as tangled as hers, his skin just as flushed. Tension branched around his mouth, pulling his lips taut. His shoulders were so wide, so strong, he practically engulfed her. He slid his hands around to cup her breasts, and what a contrast they made. The warrior protecting the damsel. His strength a shield for her vulnerability.

"I see."

"You are so beautiful it almost hurts to look at you," he said as he kneaded her breasts.

Her nipples peeked out from between his fingers, like little pink rosebuds. "It's you. You make me that way."

He ran her lobe between his teeth, and the muscles in her lower abdomen quivered. "I don't care how many came before me, Jessie Kay. I care that no one will come after. You are mine, now and forever. Do you understand? You are mine."

His words affected her as potently as his touch, and she whimpered.

Down, down his fingers traveled. He tormented her

between her legs, rubbing, circling, spreading her moisture…thrusting in deep. Her head fell back, resting on his shoulder, exposing the length of her neck. He took advantage, kissing his way to the pulse that pounded at the base, then he sucked, hard, leaving a mark behind. His mark. Sensation rocked her.

"I want to brand you in every way possible," he rasped.

Reaching over her head, she scraped her nails along his scalp. "You have. You already have."

A low growl rumbled from him as he kicked her legs apart. He kicked off his shoes, tore at the waist of his pants. He eased those pants to the ground rather than chucking them aside, and she heard a *thunk*. She frowned…until he flattened his palm on the back of her head, and with a slight pressure, eased her forward. Her belly rested against cold marble and she shivered with anticipation.

"Going to take you hard, kitten." It was the only warning he gave her before he positioned himself and slammed in, filling her, stretching her the way she loved, making her scream at the rightness, the pleasure, the absolute perfection of the moment.

True to his word, he rode her hard, a jackhammer moving in and out of her. All the while her gaze remained fixed on the mirror…on the beauty of him. He had her pinned, spread and vulnerable. Damp strands of hair were plastered to his forehead. His eyes were on her reflection as if transfixed. His lips were pulled back, his teeth bared as if he longed to bite her. He was raw sex and pure masculine instinct and—

Oh! Oh! He angled his hips, hitting her deeper and she cried out as she was propelled over the edge, satisfaction utterly consuming her in seconds, setting her entire body ablaze. His lids flipped up, his gaze meeting hers. She saw animal aggression and wicked savagery. Whatever he saw in her must have pushed *him* over the edge, because he roared, shoving into her one…two… three more times before pouring into her.

She wasn't sure how much time passed before her heart rate slowed and the fever cooled from her skin. Finally, though, he pulled out of her and cleaned both their bodies. He was trembling, and the sight of it delighted her in a way she couldn't articulate. She dressed, watched as he dressed—and realized the *thunk* she'd heard came from the gun he had sheathed at the back of his waist.

Dude. Why was that so sexy?

She threw her arms around him, saying, "That blew my circuits. Thank you."

A corner of his mouth twitched. "When did you become a computer?"

"When you rebuilt and rewired me."

He squeezed her tight, placed a soft kiss on her lips. "Do we have to go back to the party?"

"Heck no. You're my property, and I'm keeping you to myself."

He smiled at her. "Your words are poetry, kitten."

She gave his chest a little push and stood on shaky legs. "Just one of my many tal—"

The sound of shattering glass registered. A mighty wind slammed into her, knocking her forward. She would have landed on her face, but West caught her, keeping her on her feet. Only he didn't release her. He eased her to the floor, laying her on her side rather than her back. His features were pale and agonized, even horrified.

Was he hurt?

She tried to ask, but even though she moved her lips, no sound escaped. Then sharp pains exploded in her left shoulder and spread through the rest of her. Wave after wave of warmth—blood?—poured out of her, leaving her cold and trembling.

West's gaze was wild as it met hers. "It's okay, kitten. It's going to be okay. Just don't look down. All right? Don't look down and stay still." He reached out with a shaky hand to grab a towel. As he pressed the material against her chest, sending even more sharp pains exploding through her, he withdrew his phone and dialed three numbers.

911?

And what did he mean, don't look down? She looked down—of course she looked down.

The shaft of an arrow protruded from her chest.

Oh...crap. "I've been... I have a... There's a..." Darkness swallowed her whole, and she knew nothing more.

CHAPTER TWENTY-SEVEN

WHEN JESSIE KAY'S eyes closed, West almost lost it. He trembled as he felt for a pulse. *Thumpthump...thumpthump...* Pause...*thumpthump.* Too fast, even skipping a beat, but there. Thank God!

His own heart thudding against his ribs, he stayed close to the ground as he gathered her into his arms and crawled out of the bathroom, not wanting Monica able to fire off another shot, not wanting to push the arrow in deeper or pull it out farther.

Once he cleared the bathroom, he kicked the door shut, blocking any view from outside, but still he remained as low as possible as he barreled into the hallway. He wanted to shut down, to let his mind go somewhere else, and if not that, to hurl accusations at him—*my fault, never should have relaxed my guard, not for a minute, not for a second*—but he refused to give in to old fears and forced himself to carry on. Jessie Kay needed him to keep his shit together, so he would keep his shit together.

"Jase! Beck!" People spotted him with the unconscious, bloody Jessie Kay and gasped, some scrambling to get away, some trying to get closer. He scanned the farmhouse to ensure he avoided the windows. When he was certain Monica couldn't spot Jessie Kay through curtains or glass, he stopped and shouted, "An ambulance and the police are on the way, but she needs a doctor *now*."

"I'm Dr. Chastain." A man who looked to be in his late thirties, early forties pushed through the crowd. West had never met him, but he was suddenly glad the party had expanded to include the entire town. This might have happened regardless of the crowd—probably would have.

Jase and Beck were right behind the guy, Brook Lynn and Harlow right behind them. Brook Lynn took one look at her sister and screamed.

She rushed forward, gasping out, "Jessie Kay, Jessie Kay, I'm here. I'm here. Stay with me, okay?"

"Lay her across the coffee table," Dr. Chastain said. "Make sure the arrow doesn't touch it or the floor."

West obeyed, even though setting Jessie Kay down violated every instinct he possessed. Hold on. Keep her. Protect her.

"She's bleeding so much," someone muttered.

"How did this happen?"

"Our poor Jessie Kay."

Making everything worse.

West met Jase's gaze. "Get everyone out. Now."

The man immediately began herding the guests out the door. Mr. Porter and Mr. Rodriguez proved stubborn, planting themselves at the far wall, refusing to budge.

"My son is out there." Mr. Porter rested his hand on the hilt of the gun peeking from the waist of his pants. "I'm staying."

Daniel must have warned him about the danger.

"Scissors," Dr. Chastain demanded and a frantic Harlow rushed off. She returned what seemed an eternity later, and the doctor cut away Jessie Kay's blood-soaked shirt. Crimson smeared her skin, saturated her bra.

West's stomach twisted at the sight of the arrow protruding from her chest. "Tell me she's going to be okay." People had survived worse.

"Please," Brook Lynn said, her voice trembling. "Tell him."

"I don't know," the doctor admitted, his features strained. "If the arrow nicked her heart…"

West shook his head in denial. "No. It didn't. It *didn't*."

Brook Lynn's knees buckled. Jase raced to her side and gathered her close. A sob left her as she buried her face in the hollow of his shoulder.

"There has to be something you can do." West pointed at the doctor. "So you do it. You hear me? You do it."

The front door flew open, and Daniel came stomping inside, a crossbow in one hand and a protesting Monica in the other. He tossed the weapon on the couch, out of reaching distance, spotted Jessie Kay and cursed. A curse West echoed at the bitch who'd just tried to kill the love of his life. She'd slathered on mud to camouflage her presence.

"I'm so sorry," Daniel rasped. "Is Jessie Kay going to be… I can't believe… We didn't spot this bitch until the window shattered."

Monica beat at his chest. When she realized the man couldn't be budged, she swung around to face West, anger glowing in her eyes. "She's wrong for you. You can't see it now, but you will. You'll see, and you'll want me again. I'll forgive you, and we'll be together."

A roar scraped his throat—and if Beck hadn't held him back, he wasn't sure what he would have done to the girl.

The commotion woke Jessie Kay. She moaned, her eyelids fluttering open. "West?"

She asks for me. Not her sister. Me. He took her hand. "I'm here, kitten. I'm here."

Pain glimmered in her eyes. "Monica?"

"She shot you with a crossbow, but Daniel caught her. She'll never hurt you again, I swear it. Now, I want you to save your strength. Dr. Chastain is here, and an ambulance is on the way. All you have to do is get better." She had to get better.

"Slut," Monica snarled, fighting against Daniel once more. "You don't deserve him. You'll never deserve him."

"Shut her up," West snapped. "Now."

Jessie Kay began shaking. "West?"

"Keep her still." Dr. Chastain cut strips from the towel West had used and wrapped them around the wound to hold the arrow in place and prevent unintentional movement of the shaft. "Splinters will cause even more damage."

"Shh, kitten." West forced Jessie Kay's head against his shoulder, holding her immobile with the crook of his elbow. "Shh. I know you're terrified of hospitals, but I'll be with you every step of the way. We're facing our fears together, all right?"

Sirens sounded in the distance, and Monica realized she was out of time. She let her knees buckle, the full brunt of her weight ripping her from Daniel's arms. When she hit the floor, she pulled a knife from a sheath at his ankle—then stabbed him in the thigh before he had time to react.

Howling, he stumbled back, and she flew toward Jessie Kay.

What happened next happened in a split second.

In unison, West, Mr. Porter and Mr. Rodriguez pulled

their guns and aimed. Three ear-piercing shots rang out, the scent of gunpowder filling the air. Each shot was meant only to wound, but combined they did major damage. Monica flew backward, slamming into the wall, falling to her ass and leaving a river of crimson behind. She sat there for a moment, stunned as she gasped for breath.

"You…shot me." Her gaze lifted, found West's and pleaded with him to help her. "Help me. Please."

Mr. Porter rushed to his son as fast as his arthritic body would allow, then did his best to bind the wound. Mr. Rodriguez kicked the blade out of Monica's hand and applied pressure to the cache of bullet holes in her chest.

West held Jessie Kay tighter.

"West… West…you okay?" She struggled to sit up, to aid him, only doing more damage to herself.

"Keep her still," the doctor demanded.

"I'm fine, kitten, but you have to remain immobile, all right. For me. Do it for me."

Her teeth began to chatter. "Y-yes. Okay."

A few seconds later—an eternity—two paramedics rushed through the door at last, big black bags in hand.

"Did someone call—" The one in front took in the scene. "Yeah. We're in the right place."

The two men branched off, one going for Jessie Kay, the other for Monica, Daniel's injury the least concerning at the moment.

"What happened?" the second guy asked.

Jase explained the situation as the men pulled medicine and bandages from their bags and got to work.

Dr. Chastain introduced himself and told the men what he knew about Jessie Kay's injuries.

"We need to get her to St. Anthony's while she's stable," the paramedic said. "Which means as soon as possible."

"Y-you'll come with me, right?" Jessie Kay stuttered. "Please, West."

He clasped her hand, kissed her knuckles. "I'll be with you. There's no place else I'd rather be."

"You the husband?" the paramedic asked him as he rushed over to Daniel, exchanging his gloves for another pair.

"Yes," West replied, suspecting they'd try to keep him away from her otherwise.

"We'll need you to ride with us and sit behind her on the gurney, hold her up. I'll be driving, and Patrick over there will be monitoring the vitals of both women. Things aren't looking good for the other one, I'm afraid." The paramedic finished bandaging Daniel and said, "There isn't room for you to go with us. Can someone drive you and follow us?"

"I will," his father said. "I'll drive him."

West sat behind Jessie Kay on the gurney as instructed, holding her upright as they were wheeled to the ambulance.

"I love you, kitten." He said it over and over again, doing his best to distract her while the paramedic performed CPR on Monica. The girl's heart had stopped and wouldn't start again.

She was pronounced dead the moment of arrival, and Jessie Kay was wheeled off to the ER for emergency surgery, a six-hour process during which West paced inside a private waiting room, Jase holding a crying Brook Lynn and Beck holding a crying Harlow.

Sheriff Lintz stopped by to question everyone separately. West answered honestly and was finally told he,

Mr. Porter and Mr. Rodriguez would not be charged with a crime. They'd acted in self-defense.

As West waited for answers from the team of doctors working on Jessie Kay, he had a thought that history was repeating itself and time really was circular—*what is present will become what is past and what is past will become what is future*. But in the past, when Tessa had gotten hurt, he'd buckled. He'd gotten high. Now there had never been a better time to sink back into old habits, to once again lose himself to the euphoria of coke, but he had absolutely no desire to do so.

He only wanted Jessie Kay.

When finally he learned the arrow had been successfully removed and she would make a full recovery, that he would get to see her as soon as she woke, he collapsed into a chair, his eyes burning with tears of his own.

Jase patted him on one shoulder, and Beck patted the other. He took them by the wrists and held on. The three of them, they'd been through a lot together. And at one time, they'd only had each other. Now they had these amazing women—women who'd made them step up and be better.

I'm better. I'm so much better.

Like his friends, he was finally getting a happily-ever-after. The kind he'd never dared to hope for. Until Jessie Kay. Until her light chased away his darkness.

Life, he thought, was a precious gift. And he wasn't going to waste his ever again.

CHAPTER TWENTY-EIGHT

DURING THE NEXT three weeks, everyone in town stopped by the house to visit with Jessie Kay, and no one came empty-handed. She was given casseroles, homemade desserts, balloons and even a strawberry-shaped pillow. Never had she been so pampered, and she decided taking an arrow to the chest should become an annual event.

When she told West, he threatened to spank her.

West—sweet, protective West—who made sure no one overstayed their welcome or tired her out.

He really had gotten a tattoo of her name. When he'd shown it to her, he'd said, "You are the center of my world. You are the glue that holds me together, and now your name proves it."

Her name stretched from his sternum to his navel— *Jessie Kay*—the letters forming a perfect line down the center of his chest.

Darling man! He'd finished up the website for her business—Jessie Kay's Closet. Since she'd been confined to bed, she'd already designed the first line of dresses she would sell.

He took care of her in every way. In fact, he made sure she ate three meals a day. He drew her a bath every morning, and even washed, dried and styled her hair. Though his attempt at a ponytail had been laughable, he'd been unbelievably adorable, so how could she correct him? He'd even gifted her with a cat from the local shelter. Their first pet together, he'd said.

She freaking loved that cat! The black-and-white fur baby wasn't feral enough for a military title, so Jessie Kay had named her Miss America—America for short. The little beauty queen always strutted through the halls like she owned them. Because she did.

West also taught Jessie Kay the secrets to winning the video game he'd given her at Christmas. Even how to beat him! Which she hadn't. Yet. Boo, hiss. But on the plus side, the heroine really did look like her. Tall, blonde and model gorgeous.

Hey, it wasn't bragging if it was true.

By the time the city doc cleared her to return to regularly scheduled activities, she was a cauldron of lust and basically attacked West, ripping off his clothes. Afterward, as they lay naked and sated, they talked about getting married in a small, quick ceremony like Beck and Harlow, but in the end, decided they wanted to invite the entire town so everyone would know they were officially and legally off-limits.

Was it any wonder she loved him so dang much?

Miss America would, of course, be the flower girl.

Jessie Kay floated on clouds of bliss until the day of Brook Lynn's wedding. A bright, happy day with only one storm cloud. Their parents wouldn't be there to see their youngest daughter walk down the aisle.

There's a rainbow after every storm, Momma used to say. *Never look back, just keep marching forward and you'll see it.*

I will, Momma. From now on, I'll only march forward.

"I love you. So much." Jessie Kay gave Brook Lynn a hug. "You know that, right?"

"I know it, and I love you, too."

Her sister had woven pink flowers through her pale hair. And her dress…well, it was a masterpiece. She'd ditched the store-bought gown and asked Jessie Kay to make her one. Which Jessie Kay had. Grecian in design, with a halter top and cinched waist, silk overlaid with antique Brussels rose-point lace, pleats falling in different lengths, each one covered in hand-sewn pearls.

"You are a vision. An angel."

"Really?" Brook Lynn asked nervously. "You think so?"

"Really. And my opinion is the only one that matters." She smiled when her sister laughed. "If Jase rips the dress when he takes it off you, I will remove his heart with a rusty spoon."

Brook Lynn's laugh turned into a snort just as the music started up beyond the double doors in front of them.

The time had come.

"All right, sister dear." Jessie Kay straightened her shoulders, linked arms with her sister. "Let's make an honest woman out of you."

Together, they sailed past the doors leading into the sanctuary of the Strawberry Valley Community Church. As Jessie Kay walked her younger sister down the aisle, a white carpet at their feet, Jase stared at his bride-to-be and dang if tears didn't gleam in his eyes.

Jessie Kay shifted her gaze to West—she just couldn't help herself—who stood at Jase's side. His co–best man. *My man*. Mouthwateringly gorgeous in a tux, and oh, heck. He was focused wholly on Jessie Kay, the heat in his eyes scorching. He was so beautiful, so strong and completely devoted to her. He still liked to plan every second of every day, but he never minded when Jessie Kay crumpled up the paper and demanded he make love to her *now*.

There was nothing he wouldn't do for her, and nothing she wouldn't do for him. They spent every day talking and laughing, and spent every night cocooned in each other's arms. He was happy, so gloriously happy, and he never tried to fight it—which was one of the things that made her happiest.

Not that he'd changed drastically or anything like that. He was still possessive and protective. He still kept others at a distance. In fact, a few nights ago, she'd attended a business dinner with him. As his fiancée rather than a server, thank you very much. The restaurant had been rented out for some company West had agreed to work with—blah, blah, blah—and while he'd smiled and charmed some of the ladies in attendance, Jessie Kay hadn't experienced a single twinge of jealousy. He was different with her. Everyone else got a polite version of him. She got the real deal. The wicked seducer and ruthless caveman.

"Who gives this woman away?" Pastor Washington asked, his voice echoing through the sanctuary.

"I'm not giving her away," Jessie Kay said. Several people in the crowd gasped. "What? I'm sharing her." Once she'd feared losing her sister to Jase and the family the two created. How silly. She was *part* of their family, now and always.

Jase winked at her and wrapped an arm around Brook Lynn's waist.

Jessie Kay took her place between her sister and a noticeably pregnant Harlow, riveted by the sight of the church, which had been transformed into a dreamland.

A sea of pink and white roses spilled from the ceiling, adorned every pew and dripped from the arch the bride and groom now stood under. Twinkling lights had been strung overhead, like stars, and woven through the cords were more flowers.

Nearly everyone in town had come to witness the blessed union of two staples of the community.

Jessie Kay's wedding would take place next month. Why wait any longer? Fear had stomped on her dreams long enough and now she was going to live every moment to the fullest.

Tears filled her eyes as Jase and Brook Lynn promised to love each other forever. And when he kissed his bride, the entire congregation went wild, cheering and throwing random things in the air. What looked like a fly swatter. A beach ball—where had that come from? Even a roll of toilet paper.

Jase and Brook Lynn glowed as they floated down the aisle together, hand in hand, now man and wife.

West offered Jessie Kay his arm, and they followed after the bride and groom.

"Shame on you, Miss Dillon. The maid of honor isn't supposed to eclipse the bride, but you sure did."

She rested her head on his shoulder. "You only think so because you love me."

"I know so because I have eyes."

How could she *not* love this man?

They exited the sanctuary and traversed the halls, finally stepping outside where a large tent and tables were set up for the reception. The warmth of spring had arrived at last, bringing the wild strawberry patches that grew throughout the entire town to vibrant life, sweetening every inhalation. A live band already played in the corner, a soft ballad meant for lovers drifting on the air.

West pulled her onto the dance floor. "I couldn't go another moment without having you in my arms."

"Good, because I couldn't breathe another second without being in yours."

He chuckled against her ear, his breath warm and minty. "Are you trying to out-romance me?"

"Trying?" She gave him a pitying look and patted his cheek. "I believe I just succeeded, sugar bear."

"Well, I'm not worried. I have a lifetime to redeem myself."

"YOU CAN DO IT, sis!" Brook Lynn shouted from the bleachers. "I'm so proud of you!"

Jessie Kay took her place, ready to begin the second half of her first indoor soccer game. She'd trained with the best, and was finally showing off her new skills. She was a striker—a goal maker, baby! The money shots! Not that she'd made any today. Boo! Hiss!

West had started a new coed team just for her. A wedding gift, he'd said, because really, he could deny her nothing.

From across the field, he winked at her. She winked back, her heart so full she thought it might burst. He'd given her the world. A family of her own. A business that had already become a major success, thanks in part to his advertising. And contentment like she'd never known.

"Kill them!" Harlow called, and Jessie Kay gave her a thumbs-up. "Kill them dead!"

Harlow had had her baby. Babies, actually. Twins! The most beautiful humans ever, as suspected. Two little girls. Kresley Cast and Roxanne Monroe, after four of Harlow's favorite romance authors.

Speaking of babies, Brook Lynn was pregnant with her first child.

A buzzer sounded, and players burst into action and… it wasn't long before West had possession of the ball! And, oh, crap—*I mean, yay*—he was headed her way. He kicked it in her direction.

She dodged the guard at her side and stopped the roll of the ball with a slide of her foot, then turned, taking the ball with her to avoid the slashing foot of another player who'd come in hot.

What do you know? I'm kind of awesome.

She dribbled her way down the field without wheezing, while West knocked anyone who approached her into the wall. The goalie was waiting for her, shifting from side to side. Her heart rate increased as a serious case of nerves overtook her. The score was 0 to 0, and the thought of tying her first game kind of sucked. She would prefer to annihilate the other team, but she'd settle for a one-up victory.

She kicked the ball with all her might, held her breath—watched as it went flying back onto the field, blocked by the goalie. The goalie who smirked at her.

She gave him the finger.

West patted her butt. "You're amazing, kitten. Keep it up."

"Amazing? I missed."

"Even I have missed. Once." He smiled at her and gave her a push toward the ball now being dribbled toward Jase, their goalie. "Be ready. I'll win our ball and you'll try again." Off he went.

He did indeed steal the ball for her and oh, was he glorious while he did it. He passed it to her, and she again tried to score a goal—only to fail.

Dang it! Frustration jabbed at her temper but she refused to react. She kept playing, even throwing herself into big, beefy bodies whenever necessary.

Finally, only two minutes remained. They were down to the wire, the score still 0 to 0. West had the ball. Part of her wanted to shout at him to take the shot himself, but she went ahead and bodychecked him, stealing it from him before he had the opportunity to pass it her way, if that had been his plan. Saved time. Maybe. Probably. Okay, not really. Whatever.

Just like before, the goalie shifted from side to side, waiting. Jessie Kay breathed deeply as she headed toward him. What would West do in a situation like this?

Kick ass.

She faked left, spun and kicked with her right leg, sending the ball flying. This was it, the moment of truth—

Score!

The ball collided with net. The goalie dropped to his knees, despondent as the buzzer sounded.

Joy spiraled through her and a second later, she found herself being twirled around.

"You did it," West said. "You won the game."

She clung to him, wrapping her legs around him, smiling and laughing, crazy in love.

"We'll go all the way to the championship," he said.

"Uh, hold on there, sugar bear. I played and won a game. I'm good now. I quit."

He set her on her feet. "You're done? All that work and you're done? Just like that?"

"Yeah. I'm going out on top." She fist-pumped the sky.

"Because I rock! Now I want to stop exercising and concentrate on my sugar intake—and making our babies."

"Way to bury the lead," he said and barked out a laugh. "You are one of a kind, Jessie Kay. One of a kind. And I would be honored to make those babies with you. Want to start in the locker room or wait till we get home?"

They still lived at her house for now, but as soon as his place—their place—near the farmhouse was done, they'd be moving in there. In fact, he'd let her look over the plans and make as many changes as she'd wanted.

"Home," she said, "but only because I want to hear you shout my name."

"You're going to insist I call you by your full name again, aren't you? Jessica Kay West."

"Well, it's an *awesome* name."

He grinned at her. "Have I told you how happy you make me?"

"You have. You've also told me I'm the best thing that's ever happened to you."

"You are. Which is why I love you and I like you. And kitten, I want you and I need you. Also, I'm going to have to punish you for knocking me down."

"I'm looking forward to it."

* * * * *

BROOK LYNN'S BACON AND
MARSHMALLOW SANDWICH SUPREME

4 strips of thick cut bacon
½ banana cut into slices
2 pieces of favorite sandwich bread
To spread:
Butter
Marshmallow cream
Strawberry Jam

Fry the bacon until thoroughly cooked and crispy.

Butter each piece of sandwich bread on one side and toast.

Spread marshmallow cream on one slice of bread (untoasted side).

Spread strawberry jam on other slice of bread (untoasted side).

Place the bacon across a slice.

Cover with banana slice.

Press sandwich together and enjoy!

The Closer You Come

JASON—JASE—HOLLISTER carted the petite bundle of fury into the backyard. She fought him every step of the way, the little wildcat, but he held on as if she were a well-deserved war prize. The party guests watched with wide grins, enjoying the show. A few even followed him, no doubt curious to see how the scene would play out.

He resented their presence, actually hated that they were here. Truth be told, he liked to keep his two friends close and everyone else at a distance. His head wasn't screwed on right on the best of days, and today wasn't the best of days. He hadn't had a best day in a long time.

Behind him, the firecracker he'd just slept with shouted, "Put my sister down this instant, you overgrown Neanderthal!"

If he hadn't already regretted sleeping with Jessie Kay before Wildcat had stormed into his bedroom—she was also known as Brook Lynn, apparently—he would have regretted it now. Before moving to Strawberry Valley a few weeks ago, he'd decided to end his sexual bender. A five-month carnal odyssey, Beck had called it, not quite realizing how right he was. It *was* an odyssey. Straight into hell. Jase had expected pleasure, maybe a little fun, but he'd had trouble relaxing around the women, and it had made for bad sex, great guilt, and even worse memories.

Tonight had been more of the same, another regret to add to his ever-growing list. He'd had trouble focusing, constantly on alert for a sneak attack.

The nine-year habit would be hard to shake.

Besides, the move here was supposed to be his fresh start in a place that represented everything he'd never had but had always craved. Roots, permanence. Peace. Wide-open spaces and community support. A clean canvas he'd hoped to keep clean, not mar by creating a perfect storm of drama, pitting two sisters against each other.

Too late.

Though he'd had no desire to shit where he ate, so to speak, and mess everything up with a scorned lover, he'd had a few beers too many tonight, and Jessie Kay had crawled into his lap, asked if she could welcome him to town properly, and that had been that.

At least he'd had the presence of mind to make it clear there would be no repeat performances, no blooming relationship. He'd earned his freedom the hard way—and he would do anything to keep it.

Women never stuck around for the long haul, anyway. His mother sure hadn't. Countless foster moms hadn't. Hell, even the love of his life hadn't. Daphne had taken off without ever looking back.

Light from the porch lamps cast a golden glow over the swimming pool, illuminating the couple who'd decided to skinny-dip. They, like everyone else within a ten-mile radius, heard the commotion; they scrambled into a shadowed corner.

"Pay attention, honey," Jase said to Brook Lynn. "This isn't a lesson you'll want to learn twice. You throw a tantrum in my room, you get wet." Jase tossed the little wildcat into the deep end, hoping to calm her down.

Jessie Kay beat at his arm, screeching, "Idiot! Her implants aren't supposed to be waterlogged. She's supposed to cover them with a special adhesive."

Please. "Implants are always better wet." He should know. He'd handled his fair share.

"They aren't in her boobs, you moron. They're in her ears!"

Well, hell. *I'm on silent*, she'd said, the words suddenly making sense. "Way to bury the lead," he muttered.

Brook Lynn came up sputtering. She swam to the edge of the pool and climbed out with her sister's help, then arranged her hair over her ears before glaring up at him, reminding him of an avenging angel.

He'd hoped the impromptu dunk would lessen her appeal.

He'd hoped in vain.

Water droplets trickled down flawless skin the color of melted honey. The plain white button-up and black slacks she wore clung to her body, revealing a breathtakingly erotic frame, legs that were somehow a mile long, breasts that were a perfect handful...and nipples that were hard.

Those traits, in themselves, would have been dangerous for any man's peace of mind. But when you paired that miracle body with that angel face—huge baby blues and heart-shaped lips no emissary from heaven should ever be allowed to have—it was almost overkill.

Damn, I picked the wrong sister.

Well, what was done was done. Another piece of broken glass in his conscience. Another memory to leave a sticky film on his soul, like a spider determined to catch flies.

"I'm sorry about your hearing aids, or whatever they are," he said, "but catfights aren't allowed in my room. You should save all disputes for the next Jell-O Fight Night."

She watched his lips. Her eyes narrowed, an indication she'd understood him.

Without looking away from him, she said, "Jessie Kay, get in the car. If I have to start counting again, you'll regret it."

For the first time that evening, her sister heeded her command and took off as though her feet were on fire.

West and Beck arrived a second later and scoped out the scene: a gorgeous woman who was soaking wet, probably chilled, stood as still as a statue, her hands fisted at her sides, while Jase couldn't seem to look away from her.

"What the hell happened?" Beck demanded, running a hand through his hair.

"This is between him and me." Brook Lynn pointed to Jase. "You guys go inside."

"Your hand is bleeding." West frowned and reached for her.

"I'm not your concern." She stepped away, avoiding contact, and would have toppled back into the pool if Jase hadn't caught her arm.

With her sex-kitten curves, he was surprised by the slenderness of her bones. Even more shocked by the soft silk of her skin, the warmer-than-melted-honey temperature. She wasn't chilled, after all, and the longer he held on, the more electric the contact proved to be, somehow cracking through the armor he'd spent years erecting around his emotions, until he practically vibrated with the desire to touch *all* of her…to hold her…

To devour.

What the hell?

He released her with a jolt and widened the distance between them. His inner armor wasn't something he maintained just for grins and giggles. It was for survival. As a boy abandoned by his parents and sometimes mistreated by fosters, he'd learned emotions were a weakness that could be used against him. To feel something for a person or object meant he'd placed value on it—whether for good or ill.

Feel nothing. Want nothing. Need nothing. For the most part, the motto had served him well. There had been times the armor vanished, the darkest of emotions consuming him…pushing him to do things he shouldn't. Trouble had always followed.

Brook Lynn peered down at her wrist, as if she'd felt something she couldn't explain, before focusing on him, her eyes narrowing once again.

To Beck and West, who'd remained after her command to leave, Jase said, "Get everyone inside. I'll handle her."

Looking for a holiday story that sizzles?
Check out this excerpt of New York Times
bestselling author Vicki Lewis Thompson's
A COWBOY UNDER THE MISTLETOE,
where sexy cowboy-turned-lawyer
Ty Slater can't seem to keep his hands off
Whitney Jones as they get ready for the holidays...

A Cowboy Under the Mistletoe

"This would have been tougher working alone." Whitney handed the lights to Ty. "Come to think of it, when I trimmed my apartment tree in Cheyenne, I always roped somebody into helping me." She laughed. "So I'm continuing my pattern. Consider yourself roped in."

"Glad to do it."

He admired the ripple of her golden hair as she leaned over to pull out a second strand. He imagined running his fingers through it and gazing into her eyes. He wanted to taste those full lips. He closed his eyes briefly as he imagined how amazing that would feel.

"Ty?"

"Sorry." *Caught.* He took the lights from her. "Got distracted." Joining the first set to the second, he thought of the terminology for the connecting ends—male and female plugs. He and his foster brothers used to joke about that when they were raunchy teenagers who thought about sex constantly.

"You must have been thinking of something nice."

"I was."

She didn't pursue it, which probably meant she knew the sort of thing he'd been thinking about.

They traded the bunched cord back and forth, winding the lights around the branches until Ty looped the end at the top. Then they both stepped back and squinted at the lit tree to check placement.

"It's almost perfect," she said. "But there's a blank space in the middle."

"I see it." He stepped forward and adjusted one strand lower. Then he backed up. "I think that does it."

"I think so, too."

He heard something in her voice, something soft and yielding that made his heart beat faster. He glanced over at her. She was staring right back at him, her eyes dark and her breathing shallow. If any woman had ever looked more ready to be kissed, he'd eat his hat.

And damned if he could resist her. His gaze locked with hers and his body tightened as he stepped closer. Slowly he combed his fingers through hair that felt as silky as he'd imagined. "We haven't finished with the tree."

"I know." Her voice was husky. "And there's the dancing afterward…"

"We were never going to do that." He pressed his fingertips into her scalp and tilted her head back. "But I think we were always going to do this." And he lowered his head.

She awaited him with lips parted. After the first gentle pressure against her velvet mouth, he sank deeper with a groan of pleasure. So sweet, so damned perfect. She tasted like wine, better than wine, better than anything he could name.

The slide of her arms around his waist sent heat shooting through his veins. As she nestled against him, he took full command of the kiss, swallowing her moan as he thrust his tongue into her mouth.

She welcomed him, slackening her jaw and inviting

him to explore. He caught fire, shifting his angle and making love to her mouth until they were both breathing hard and molded together. As he'd known, they fit exactly.

He registered the swell of her breasts, the curve of her hips and the press of her thighs. The red haze of lust threatened to wipe out his good intentions, but he caught himself before he slid his hands under her sweater. Gulping for air, he released her and stepped back.

Looking into eyes filled with the same need pounding through him nearly had him reaching for her again. He fisted his hands at his sides. "Let's... Maybe we should... back off for a bit."

She swallowed. "Okay. Care to say why?"

"I had a really valid reason a second ago."

She laughed. "It's a good thing you're so damned cute. I'll give you a minute to collect your thoughts."

"Thanks." He rubbed the back of his neck and struggled for clarity. Then he remembered why they needed to put the brakes on. Boy, she'd really fried his circuits. But the tree trimming had stirred up neediness in both of them. She might not be overly affected by it, but he was.

Saying all that out loud, though, would mean bringing up a touchy subject, one he wasn't prepared to discuss. Maybe a distraction was in order. "What's your schedule tomorrow?"

"My schedule? Why?"

"Humor me."

"Working pretty much all day and for a couple of hours in the evening, too."

"Any breaks?"

"Yeah, for an hour between one and two and again from six to seven."

"Let me take you to lunch at one and dinner at six."

She blinked in obvious bewilderment. "You're kidding."

"No. We'll go to that little diner. It's close."

"For both meals?"

"You don't like the food?"

"I like it fine, but I'm confused. What's going on?"

"I...want to spend more time with you before we're in a kissing situation again."

A slow smile curved her kiss-reddened mouth. "Speaking of that, I'll leave the coffee shop at nine tomorrow night. Is there a chance you might want to drop by then?"

"If you'll have me."

"Now, there's a loaded statement. How should I answer that?"

He groaned. "Don't try. You'll get us both in trouble. I'll be at the shop at one." He walked toward the kitchen and got his coat.

"You're leaving?"

He grabbed his hat from the counter before turning to face her. "If I stay, I guarantee things will get out of hand."

"Not necessarily."

He gazed at her without speaking.

"Okay, you're right."

He dropped a quick kiss on her cheek and headed for the door. "See you at one."

"You don't have to take me out for two meals. That seems silly."

He turned back and smiled at her. "Just go with it, okay? I want chaperones to make sure we sit and talk."

"Does that mean we won't be talking tomorrow

night?" She stood in the glow of the colored lights, her skin flushed and her breathing shallow. He'd never seen a sexier woman in his life.

He gripped the door handle to remind himself that he was leaving, by God. "Probably not much." And he walked out before he changed his mind.

Don't miss a single story in New York Times *bestselling author Vicki Lewis Thompson's*
THUNDER MOUNTAIN BROTHERHOOD *series:*
MIDNIGHT THUNDER
THUNDERSTRUCK
ROLLING LIKE THUNDER
A COWBOY UNDER THE MISTLETOE

REQUEST YOUR FREE BOOKS!

2 FREE NOVELS
FROM THE ROMANCE COLLECTION
PLUS 2 FREE GIFTS!

YES! Please send me 2 FREE novels from the Romance Collection and my 2 FREE gifts (gifts are worth about $10). After receiving them, if I don't wish to receive any more books, I can return the shipping statement marked "cancel." If I don't cancel, I will receive 4 brand-new novels every month and be billed just $6.49 per book in the U.S. or $6.99 per book in Canada. That's a savings of at least 19% off the cover price. It's quite a bargain! Shipping and handling is just 50¢ per book in the U.S. and 75¢ per book in Canada.* I understand that accepting the 2 free books and gifts places me under no obligation to buy anything. I can always return a shipment and cancel at any time. Even if I never buy another book, the two free books and gifts are mine to keep forever.

194/394 MDN GH4D

Name _____ (PLEASE PRINT) _____

Address _____ Apt. # _____

City _____ State/Prov. _____ Zip/Postal Code _____

Signature (if under 18, a parent or guardian must sign) _____

Mail to the **Reader Service:**
IN U.S.A.: P.O. Box 1867, Buffalo, NY 14240-1867
IN CANADA: P.O. Box 609, Fort Erie, Ontario L2A 5X3

Want to try two free books from another line?
Call 1-800-873-8635 or visit www.ReaderService.com.

* Terms and prices subject to change without notice. Prices do not include applicable taxes. Sales tax applicable in N.Y. Canadian residents will be charged applicable taxes. Offer not valid in Quebec. This offer is limited to one order per household. Not valid for current subscribers to the Romance Collection or the Romance/Suspense Collection. All orders subject to credit approval. Credit or debit balances in a customer's account(s) may be offset by any other outstanding balance owed by or to the customer. Please allow 4 to 6 weeks for delivery. Offer available while quantities last.

Your Privacy—The Reader Service is committed to protecting your privacy. Our Privacy Policy is available online at www.ReaderService.com or upon request from the Reader Service.

We make a portion of our mailing list available to reputable third parties that offer products we believe may interest you. If you prefer that we not exchange your name with third parties, or if you wish to clarify or modify your communication preferences, please visit us at www.ReaderService.com/consumerschoice or write to us at Reader Service Preference Service, P.O. Box 9062, Buffalo, NY 14240-9062. Include your complete name and address.

Blaze

Red-Hot Reads

Save $1.00

on the purchase of

A COWBOY UNDER THE MISTLETOE

by Vicki Lewis Thompson, available November 17, 2015, or on any other Harlequin® Blaze® book.

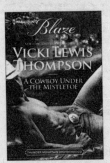

Available wherever books are sold, including most bookstores, supermarkets, drugstores and discount stores.

- ✂

Save $1.00

on the purchase of any Harlequin Blaze book.

Coupon valid until February 29, 2016.
Redeemable at participating outlets in the U.S. and Canada only.
Not redeemable at Barnes & Noble stores. Limit one coupon per customer.

52613223

0 65373 00076 7   (8100)0 12115

Turn your love of reading into rewards you'll love with
Harlequin My Rewards

**Join for FREE today at
www.HarlequinMyRewards.com**

Earn **FREE BOOKS** of your choice.

Experience **EXCLUSIVE OFFERS** and contests.

Enjoy **BOOK RECOMMENDATIONS**
selected just for you.

PLUS! Sign up now
and get **500** points
right away!

Earn
FREE
REWARDS
Join
Today!
HarlequinMyRewards.com

MYR16R

GENA SHOWALTER

77991	THE DARKEST PASSION	___ $7.99 U.S.	___ $8.99 CAN.
77969	THE HOTTER YOU BURN	___ $7.99 U.S.	___ $8.99 CAN.
77962	THE CLOSER YOU COME	___ $7.99 U.S.	___ $8.99 CAN.
77743	BEAUTY AWAKENED	___ $7.99 U.S.	___ $9.99 CAN.
77581	THE DARKEST SURRENDER	___ $7.99 U.S.	___ $9.99 CAN.
77549	THE DARKEST SECRET	___ $7.99 U.S.	___ $9.99 CAN.

(limited quantities available)

TOTAL AMOUNT	$ _____
POSTAGE & HANDLING	$ _____
($1.00 FOR 1 BOOK, 50¢ for each additional)	
APPLICABLE TAXES*	$ _____
TOTAL PAYABLE	$ _____

(check or money order—please do not send cash)

To order, complete this form and send it, along with a check or money order for the total above, payable to HQN Books, to: **In the U.S.:** 3010 Walden Avenue, P.O. Box 9077, Buffalo, NY 14269-9077; **In Canada:** P.O. Box 636, Fort Erie, Ontario, L2A 5X3.

Name: _____

Address: _____ City: _____

State/Prov.: _____ Zip/Postal Code: _____

Account Number (if applicable): _____

075 CSAS

*New York residents remit applicable sales taxes.
*Canadian residents remit applicable GST and provincial taxes.

HQN™

www.HQNBooks.com

PHGS1215BL